An Empty Death

AN EMPTY
DEATH

Laura Wilson

FELONY & MAYHEM PRESS • NEW YORK

All the characters and events portrayed in this work are fictitious.

AN EMPTY DEATH

A Felony & Mayhem mystery

PRINTING HISTORY
First U.K. edition (Orion): 2009
First U.S. edition (St. Martin's): 2011
Felony & Mayhem edition: 2012

ISBN: 978-1-937384-37-1

Manufactured in the United States of America

Printed on 100% recycled paper

Library of Congress Cataloging-in-Publication Data

Wilson, Laura, 1964-
 An empty death / Laura Wilson.
  p. cm. -- (A Felony & Mayhem mystery)
A reprint of the first U.S. edition, "A Thomas Dunne book," published
by Minotaur Books (2011).
ISBN 978-1-937384-37-1
1. Police--England--London--Fiction. 2. Serial murderers--Fiction. 3. World
War, 1939-1945--England--London--Fiction. 4. London (England)--Social
conditions--20th century--Fiction. I. Title.
PR6073.I4716E47 2012
823'.914--dc23
                                    2012038278

To Freeway
basset hound and beloved friend,
1998–2008

ACKNOWLEDGEMENTS

I am very grateful to Jane Burch, Jade Chandler, Tim Donnelly, Stephanie Glencross, Jane Gregory, George Harding, Liz Hatherell, Jane Havell, Elizabeth Hillman, Maya Jacobs, Fenella Mallallieu, Jemma McDonagh, Claire Morris, Sebastian Sandys, Gillian Sheath, June and William Wilson, Jon Wood, Daphne Wright and Gaby Young for their enthusiasm, advice and support.

Other "Historical" titles from

FELONY&MAYHEM

ANNAMARIA ALFIERI
City of Silver

DAVID STUART DAVIES
Forests of the Night

KEITH HELLER
Man's Illegal Life

PETER LOVESEY
Bertie and the Seven Bodies
Bertie and the Crime of Passion

FIDELIS MORGAN
Unnatural Fire
The Rival Queens

KATE ROSS
Cut to the Quick
A Broken Vessel
Whom the Gods Love

CATHERINE SHAW
The Library Paradox
The Riddle of the River

LAURA WILSON
The Lover
The Innocent Spy

DAVID WISHART
Ovid
Germanicus

An Empty Death

'A man's alter ego is nothing more than his favourite image of himself.'

Frank W. Abagnale, *Catch Me If You Can*

'The version of ourselves we present to the world bears no resemblance to the truth. There isn't one of us who could afford to be caught. That's all life is. Trying not to be found out.'

Willie Donaldson's Diary

Part I

CHAPTER 1

June 1944, Fitzrovia: the night was bright—a bombers' moon—but the planes were far away. The other side of London, the man thought. He glanced round the rubble-strewn site. Five or six houses must have been knocked out, because all around him were crumbling interior walls with tattered wallpaper, torn-out fireplaces with weeds sprouting in hearths now for ever cold, and window frames, some with the grey remnants of slashed curtains, the harshness of their destruction softened by the pale light. The edges of ill-secured tarpaulins flapped in the light breeze, and nettles pushed their way through mounds of plaster, glass and broken wood-work. The man could even make out the looming bulk of the Middlesex Hospital across the way.

It was time to die again. That was how he thought of it—dying and being reborn, at the same time. He always felt a sense of loss at such times, although he couldn't have said what it was that he was losing. He'd been relieved—delighted—to walk away from his first life, to cease being the useless, despised failure who got everything wrong. The selves that came after, personas of his choosing, had been more successful, but it was never enough. This one would be different. He'd wanted to be a doctor ever since he was a child, and now he had a name—a life—ready and waiting for just this opportunity. This was simply the penultimate step in his plan. He hadn't expected it to happen quite like this, but that did not matter.

He stared at the corpse at his feet. The blood on the face had congealed. The body had, simply and with silent finality, stopped working. He'd seen hundreds of cadavers since he'd started his job in the hospital mortuary, but as most of them had been dug up from the ruins and carted in, they hadn't been fresh. Good job he'd made the most of the chance to study anatomy at first hand, even if a lot of the specimens were pretty mangled—crushed, or with missing limbs, or even, in some cases, decapitated. He'd pieced his knowledge of anatomy together with each human jigsaw, and, once acquired, such information was never wasted. He was already well prepared, but there was a great deal of work still to be done. He'd start tonight.

Best not hang about. If anyone saw him, his new life would be over before it had even begun, and this one, he knew, was going to be the best yet. 'Goodbye,' he murmured to the body. It was no longer a man in the sense of being a person; it was merely a vacuum, a space that he would fill. The original owner had no use for it, or—more importantly—for his job any more, so what he was about to do wasn't stealing; it was simply retrieving something that had been discarded. True, the discarding hadn't been voluntary, but it was too late to worry about that now. After all, he couldn't bring the bloke back to life, could he? Nevertheless... 'Thank you, Reynolds,' he muttered with a moment's awkward reverence. 'Much appreciated, old chap.'

Then he turned away, entirely indifferent to everything but the inward surge of excitement and certainty that told him he was, once more—as he had planned all along—the sole controller of his fate. Buoyed with a new sense of purpose, he walked, as quickly as he dared, across the rubble and down the moonlit street. In the distance—somewhere north-east, he thought—bombs were falling.

CHAPTER 2

Tottenham: the siren woke them at nearly two. Stratton, startled from sleep, sat up too quickly and whacked his head on the low ceiling of the cage-like Morrison shelter that sat in the middle of their front room. 'Bloody—'

'Sssh...' said Jenny, his wife.

'Sorry, love, I didn't mean to—'

'No, really, *sssh*...Lie down. Listen.'

It was the tell-tale chugging noise—two-stroke engine gone wrong—of one of the new flying bombs. 'It's coming here,' whispered his wife, grabbing his hand and squeezing it. 'It's right on top of us,' he heard her mutter. 'Keep going, don't stop, don't stop...'

Stratton held his breath. *Chug-chug-chug*—And then it cut out. There was a second's silence, into which he heard Jenny murmur, 'Oh, God.' Stratton held her hand as tight as he could and turned towards her, shielding her rigid body with his—the thought *for all the good it will do* flashed through his mind but if they were going to go then at least—

The enormous bang rattled the doors and windows as the house seemed to shiver, rock, then settle back once more. There was a crash from the kitchen—plates, perhaps—and Stratton saw a white haze, like November fog, overtake the blackness in the room as plaster drifted down from the ceiling.

Stratton and Jenny remained where they were, silent, for a couple more minutes. 'Lucky,' said Stratton, disengaging himself from his wife and stroking her cheek with the back of his hand. 'Looks like we're still here.'

'That means somebody else probably isn't,' said Jenny, grimly. Then, turning to him, she clutched his shoulder. 'What about Doris? It could have been over there.'

'Wait.' Doris was Jenny's favourite sister. 'I'll see if I can see anything.'

Stratton slid out of the Morrison and fumbled in the dark for his torch, which he took to the front door. It was a clear night and, a couple of streets away, he could see a column of smoke rising through the dark blue sky. 'Looks like Larkin Avenue.'

'That's close. We'd better go and see. Come on.' Jenny got up and started banging about trying to find her slacks and jumper. 'Put some trousers on, at least. You can wear them over your pyjamas. And take your coat...'

There was a tense silence while they pulled on their clothes, and then they were through the front door and into the street. They could hear people arriving at the incident, vehicles and running feet, the distant clang of bells. The air was full of the raw, brutal stink of destruction—a mixture of high explosive, coal gas, brick dust and burnt earth.

Stratton held Jenny by the hand and they walked as fast as they could, following the torch beam, to the end of their road. Rounding the corner, they passed the end of another street, then another, and then—

'You were right,' said Jenny.

The two houses at the end of Larkin Avenue had disappeared. In their place was a mountain of debris and a crater some thirty feet across that stretched into the road itself, where there was a scattering of lumps of clay mixed with macadam surface, and, here and there, a piece of kerbstone. The third house down now consisted only of a front door and half a passageway, a gaunt, bare chimney-breast, and ugly, tileless rafters jabbing skywards. An Anderson shelter, which must have been in one of the gardens, had been uprooted at one side, and its curved, corrugated iron roof was split open so that the ragged ends made it look like a huge sardine tin peeled open by a giant key. In front of it, a broken gas main flared, sending little rivulets of fire along the ground. 'Watch where you're treading,' Stratton said, as they went over to join the band of onlookers who were being held back by several wardens.

The clanging noise grew louder and then stopped abruptly as a fire engine pulled up and AFS men jumped off and began scrambling over the rubble, shouting to each other as they tried to locate the source of the gas leak.

'Ted!' Jenny's sister, Doris, and her husband Donald appeared, looking dishevelled.

'You two all right?'

'Fine. That was a near one. We thought it might be you.'

'We thought the same,' said Stratton. 'Who got it?'

'I don't know who lives at One or Five,' said Doris, 'but it's the Lightollers in the middle. You know her, Jen. Big woman. Works in the bakery.'

'Yes. And they've got a son. He was—'

'Quiet, please!' All chattering ceased as the rescue party appeared and began scrambling and tapping their way up the mound of debris, pausing in their ascent to listen for the voices of survivors under the rubble. One of them had a searcher dog, who was scrabbling about, zigzagging through the muddle, pulling its trainer unsteadily behind it as it sniffed for bodies. Recognising a local bobby, Stratton presented himself and asked if he could help. 'Best wait till the dog's done its stuff, sir,' said the constable. 'Let's hope it's quick,' he added, grimly.

Stratton, who had seen more than his share of mangled, broken and suffocated bodies, nodded. 'Do you know how many people are under that lot?'

'Four. That house,' he pointed to the ruin, 'was empty. We're checking the rest of the street.' He pointed further down to where a couple of wardens, identifiable by the glint of moonlight on their white tin hats, could be dimly seen knocking on doors and chalking walls if the occupants were present and unharmed. Stratton wondered about the efficacy of this—most of the street appeared to be gathered around the crater—but said nothing. Donald appeared at his elbow.

'A Mrs Ingram at the end, apparently. Neighbour said she's not been there long. Can we do anything?'

'Wait for the dog, they said.'

Just then, there was a single, sharp bark.

'Down here!'

'They've found someone. They'll have to dig a shaft,' said the constable, 'and bloody quick, too.'

The dog was removed, and the rescue squad retreated from the rubble to fetch baskets before forming a chain. Some of them, on the opposite side to the crowd, didn't bother with the baskets, but simply threw the bits of debris back between their legs, as rabbits do. There was a tense silence, broken only by the thud of bricks hitting the earth and the panting breath and curses of the men as they worked.

Stratton went to find Jenny, who was standing with Doris. 'Do you know a Mrs Ingram, love?'

Jenny shook her head. 'The people down there,' she whispered. 'They'll die, won't they? They'll be crushed.'

'Don't, Jen...' Doris laid a hand on her sister's arm. 'They will save them, won't they, Ted?'

'If they're quick,' said Stratton. Not wanting to pursue the subject, he said, 'Do you know Mrs Ingram, Doris?'

His sister-in-law shook her head. 'Someone must, though.'

A stout, elderly woman standing behind them, wearing a shawl and, bizarrely, a straw hat, said, 'She's only been here a couple of months. Husband's in the army. Very quiet—not seen much of her.'

'He's away now, is he?' asked Stratton.

'I think so. Tell you the truth, I've never seen him. She was on her own when she came here.'

Donald weaved his way through the crowd and clapped Stratton on the shoulder. 'Come and give a hand. They need to widen the hole at the top of the shaft,' he explained, as they went to collect picks from the rescue squad truck, 'so the weight doesn't cave it in.'

Stratton got stuck in, chipping steadily at the strange mixture of brick and plaster rubble, shattered joists and beams, pieces of broken furniture and crockery, rugs and curtains, all pressed together, until it was loose enough to be shovelled away. It was easy at first, and they made good progress, but then they began to hit London clay—the subsoil, thrown up by the blast, was mixed in with the rest of the mound, making it harder to shift. Picturing what was below all too clearly—crushing weight caving in fragile human ribcages so that they punctured the lungs beneath—he redoubled his efforts. His back and arms soon began to ache as if they were on fire, and he was glad of the brief break every time the man at the bottom of the shaft yelled for quiet.

Eventually, he heard, 'That's enough! I've got something down here. Hold that bloody torch still—I can't see bugger all.' The crowd, who had been talking amongst themselves, were quiet. 'Right,' said the man. 'This one's had it, but I can hear someone else further on. Faint, but it's there.' Stratton put down his pick and went to look down the shaft. It had been dug to about eight feet, and he saw, by the light of a torch, that it would have been impossible to use a pick or shovel down there—there wasn't enough room, and joists and other woodwork criss-crossed the narrow space. The man who had wormed his way down there was kneeling, pointing to what appeared to be the end of a stair post.

The foreman beside Stratton asked, 'You sure?'

'Course I'm bloody sure!' Then Stratton saw that what he thought was a knob was actually a plaster-coated fist and an arm, bare to the elbow, protruding from the side of the rubble.

'Right, start tunnelling.' The foreman turned to Stratton and looked him up and down. 'You got a long reach—get down there and help Smithie clear the stuff out.' He appeared not to have noticed—or, if he had, not to care—that Stratton wasn't a rescue worker.

As Stratton took the proffered hard hat he heard shouts behind him and turned to see Jenny scrambling up the mound, her eyes wide with panic. 'Ted! Please…'

'It's all right, love.'

'But what if it all falls on top of you? You could be buried, you could—' She was silenced by a bellow from the bottom of the hole as an avalanche of earth and bricks, loosened by their feet, plummeted downwards.

'It won't,' said Stratton. 'It's under control. I'll be fine.'

Jenny shook her head rapidly, blinking, and Stratton could see that she was trying not to cry. 'It's all right,' he repeated. 'I'll be back in no time. There's people down there, love.'

Jenny shook her head again. Then, standing on tiptoe, she gripped him fiercely round the neck and, kissing his cheek, whispered, 'Be careful. Please…just be careful.' Letting go abruptly, she picked her way back down to Doris and Donald on the pavement, her nightdress flapping beneath the hem of her coat.

Stratton watched her for a second, then clambered down the shaft, lit by torches from above, and a basket was handed in after him. The two men scrabbled with their hands, trying to free the debris from around the body, grunting as lumps of earth crashed down on their heads and shoulders. Stratton piled the stuff into the lowered baskets and raised them to the workers at the surface, trying to dodge the constant showers of muck that made his eyes smart. Slowly, from the hole they'd made, a head, and then shoulders, began to emerge. 'It's a boy,' said the man, in what seemed to Stratton a horrible parody of a doctor attending a birth.

'A boy,' he shouted up to the foreman. 'Fifteen or thereabouts.'

'There's something pinning the legs down,' said Smithie. 'I can't move it. Get them to give you a torch.'

When Stratton shone the light into the narrow crevice that they'd dug out round the corpse he saw, lying on top of the boy's legs, the back of a dog. It appeared to be curled up, as if asleep in a basket. He touched it and discovered, under the coating of plaster, long black fur. Running his hands in both directions, he located a tail and a head with a long nose. 'We should be able to pull it out—it's not that big.'

Smithie shouted instructions and a length of rope was lowered. They managed to secure the rope around the dog's midriff, chest and bottom, as though the animal were a parcel, and pull it away from the boy. It was a black spaniel, its rib cage and front legs crushed. 'Poor beast,' said Smithie. 'I hope it went quick.'

Stratton held the free end of the rope up to the men on the surface, and they hauled the dog up and took it away. After that, freeing the boy's body proved not too difficult, and, by the time they'd done that, they'd made enough space—horizontally, at least—so that another man could join them, forming a chain. As he slid, clumsily, to the bottom of the hole, he brought down what seemed like a ton of earth, so that Stratton was completely blinded. There were yells and curses above, and he could hear gasps from the women watching. 'Fucking hell!' shouted Smithie in fury as they pawed at their faces. 'Watch it!'

'Not my fault,' said the man, plaintively.

'Never mind whose fault it was,' yelled Smithie, 'dig, can't you? We need this lot out of here now, or no-one else stands a chance.'

Wiping the dust from his eyes, Stratton found himself waist deep in rubble, scarcely able to move. Coughing and spluttering, the three men began digging once more, piling the stuff into baskets until they had more freedom, Smithie urging them on with curses. 'Bleeding hurry up, you fuckers—we're running out of time.'

Stratton could see, every time he looked up, the face of the foreman peering down at them, strained beneath its coating of dust and plaster. 'Can you hear anything?' he called.

'Give us a chance, mate.'

'Ted!' Jenny's voice, loud and frightened, from the pavement. 'Are you all right?'

'Yes, love,' he bawled back. 'Don't worry!'

Eventually, they cleared enough space to start crawling forward again. Smithie kept stopping the digging to listen; at first, Stratton thought he must be imagining things when he said he could hear something—all *he* could hear was the ominous, steady trickle of falling earth—but when, after a few times, he moved to the head of the chain he heard a wailing noise, very faint, like a small animal—a cat, perhaps—in pain. He turned back to Smithie and nodded.

'Told you. Get on with it, then. I'll shine the torch in behind you.'

Stratton, crawling forward in virtual darkness because his body was blocking the meagre light from the torch behind him, was suddenly aware that his hand was on something that wasn't rubble. It was soft, giving, yet somehow more solid than the debris. 'Bloody hell!'

'You trod on one?'

Stratton turned, with difficulty. 'Don't look like that,' said Smithie. 'It can't be helped. Come on, let's have a shufti.'

'Do you think,' asked Stratton, trying to move his knees enough for Smithie to crawl past, 'that our one is behind this one?'

'*These* ones,' said Smithie. 'There's two of 'em. Hold up.' They listened again, and heard the faint wailing. 'Must be,' said Smithie. 'Can't dig another shaft, though—too risky. Have to carry on here.' Peering over his shoulder Stratton could see two bodies, covered in dust, their arms and legs entwined, discoloured pyjamas blending with the rubble as if they were just another part of the debris.

'A man and a woman,' said Smithie.

To Stratton, they just looked like human-shaped lumps of clay. Earth to earth, he thought. 'How can you tell?'

Smithie shrugged. 'You get used to it, mate. Besides,' he gave Stratton a wink, 'that's what they said. A boy, a man, and two women. Come on.' He took hold of the nearest limb—an arm— and tugged at it with difficulty. 'Going stiff,' he said. 'Must have died before the boy did. We can't separate 'em, so we'll have to get 'em out before they're rigid, or we're in real trouble. Get some more rope—tell 'em we need lots of it.'

Stratton passed the message back, and was duly given a coil of rope. He handed it to Smithie and watched, amazed, as—despite the confined space and with minimal help from Stratton—he proceeded to make a hoist, passing it under the buttocks of the corpses and knotting it into a harness, so that, when finally aloft in the shaft, the two bodies seemed locked in reluctant intercourse. The man—handling them had made the sexes obvious—was missing a foot, and as the woman's head lolled backwards Stratton could see, beneath the plaster that coated her face like a thick layer of ill-applied cosmetic, that she had bled from the mouth. As the bodies emerged at the top of the shaft, he heard the gasps and groans of the crowd and a single scream, followed by low, agitated murmuring.

'Those must have been the Lightollers,' said Smithie, shifting more rubble, 'so now we're looking for Mrs Ingram.' He paused again to listen, and shook his head. 'You all right in there?' he called. 'Not long now.'

Again, the faint wailing sound.

'She got a husband or anyone who can come down and talk to her?' asked Smithie. 'Sometimes that helps.'

'Away,' said Stratton. 'I don't think there is anyone else, unless the vicar—'

'Sod that. Still...' He handed Stratton a full basket. 'Get cracking, will you?'

'Right.'

After twenty minutes' further rubble-clearing, the ends of Stratton's fingers were raw and his knuckles bleeding profusely. His arms and shoulders felt as though they were on fire, and his lower back ached from bending over, but, just as he thought he couldn't carry on for even another minute, Smithie said, 'Right, I can see her. Pass it back.'

Stratton did as instructed and then, inching towards Smithie, said, 'Where?'

'Down here. Watch out, you're on top of her—get back a bit.' Stratton jerked backwards, appalled, smacked his head against a clump of bricks, and swore.

'I don't think it's her head,' said Smithie. 'She must be laying the other way. Can you talk, love? Can you hear us?'

Silence. 'Stop shifting about,' said Smithie, 'I can't hear.' Stratton, a crick in his neck and his thighs protesting as he squatted in the confined space, kept as still as he could. Without warning, Smithie bent forward and began scrabbling energetically, like a dog after a buried bone. 'I think she's still with us,' he panted. 'Come on, give us a hand.'

A further ten minutes' work, accompanied by increasingly loud creaking noises from above which Stratton tried to ignore, revealed the slight body of what looked like a young girl. She lay with one hand bent behind her head and her legs pulled up so that she formed a gentle S curve. She was entirely grey—like a plaster relief, Stratton thought. Peaceful, like something one might see on a gravestone.

Smithie took up her unresisting hand and felt the wrist for a pulse. 'Still there,' he said, 'but only just. No room for a doctor in here. Have to get her to the bottom of the shaft before the bloody lot caves in. Get hold of the feet—I'll manage this end.'

Stratton looked at him doubtfully. 'Come on,' said Smithie, irritated, 'get on with it—don't want the whole fucking lot down on your head, do you? Just be thankful she won't be much of a weight.'

Crawling backwards on knees and elbows in the pitch dark, tugging on the woman's ankles, while Smithie pushed, the short distance to the base of the shaft seemed to last an eternity. Mrs Ingram moaned slightly, but didn't regain consciousness, despite the bumps.

Finally, Stratton heard, 'All right, you're there. Get clear,' and, with huge relief, straightened his back, blinking in the light from several torches being shone down into the shaft. 'Get out of the bloody way,' yelled Smithie from behind. 'We need a doctor.'

Stratton stood upright with an effort and flattened himself against the side of the shaft as the doctor was lowered down, looking incongruous with his dark coat over his pyjamas, his tin hat and black bag. It wasn't, Stratton saw, Dr Makepeace, but the retired senior partner, elderly and shakily uncertain in his movements. He knelt unsteadily to feel the woman's pulse and ran his fingers over the limbs and the hair, which was matted with dust and blood into a pink paste. He grimaced, shook his head, then, moving with surprising deftness, jammed a hypodermic into the grey, encrusted flesh of her arm. 'That's the best I can do,' he said. 'Nothing broken, as far as I can see. Get her out.'

Stratton could now see that the woman's nightdress was ripped off at the thigh, so that the legs were exposed. The doctor called for blankets, and they managed to wrap her and get the ropes around her, so that, like the others, she could be borne upwards and stretchered away to the ambulance.

Smithie got himself upright, using Stratton as support, and they scrambled up the rickety ladder that had been lowered. Stratton could feel Smithie behind him, shoving him roughly upwards, all the while intoning, 'Come on, move your arse.' They'd just made it to the top when there was a crash behind them and several tons of rubble, dislodged from the other side of the shaft, roared downwards, obscuring it entirely.

'Christ!' shouted Smithie, from somewhere around Stratton's knees. 'Too fucking close for comfort, if you ask me.'

'You all right?' Stratton pulled him to his feet. Smithie only came up to the middle of his chest.

'Blimey,' he said, looking up. 'Surprised you didn't get stuck and all. You're too big for this work, mate. Who sent you down?'

'The man in charge.'

'Bit irregular, that. Still, never mind.'

The doctor peered at them through dusty glasses and said, 'Inspector Stratton, isn't it?'

'That's right.'

Smithie's face was a picture—the eyes flew open in consternation. 'You a policeman?' he asked. 'Sorry I was ordering you about like that, but—'

'No need to apologise,' said Stratton. 'You knew what you were doing, I didn't.'

'Glad there's no hard feelings,' said Smithie. 'We got the job done, at any rate, didn't we? Better climb off this lot before anything else happens.'

Back on the pavement, Stratton, who felt as if he'd swallowed most of a rotten blanket, was glad to be given a milk bottle full of water to rinse his mouth. As he spat out the last of it, he saw Jenny pushing her way through the crowd. Fiercely and wordlessly she embraced him, holding him so tightly that, when she finally let go, he saw that she, too, was coated with plaster. 'It's all right,' he said. 'I'm here. Let's go home, shall we?'

She nodded, clutching his arm. They said goodnight to the rescue squad, and to Doris and Donald, and went home in the feeble dawn light in silence. As they walked, Stratton felt a strange feeling of elation come over him. It was the events of the night, he knew, but somehow it felt like being drunk—the early stages, at least. A light, reckless feeling, an exultation such as he hadn't experienced in a long time. When they reached their garden gate he stopped and pulled Jenny round to face him. He could see, from the way her eyes sparkled, that she was experiencing something similar.

'We're alive,' he said, drawing her towards him.

'Yes.' Jenny put her hands on his arms. 'I was so worried. We could see all this earth going into the hole, and people kept saying it was going to collapse on top of you…Doris kept telling me you'd be OK, but I don't think she believed it, and we really thought… You were only just in time, Ted, getting out. Was it horrible down there? It looked pretty grim, what they brought up.'

'Mmm.' Stratton tried to embrace her.

Jenny pushed him away. 'Not in the street. People might be looking.'

'Who cares?' said Stratton, and took her into his arms.

'I think,' said Jenny, when they'd shut the front door behind them, 'that I'd better run you a bath.' She sounded serious, but her face was full of mischief. 'We heard "Raiders passed" while you were down the hole, so it'll be safe to go upstairs.'

'And I think,' said Stratton, taking her hand, 'that you'd better join me. You don't look any too clean yourself.'

Jenny stared at him, scandalised, for about ten seconds, then laughed. 'I don't think we'll both fit.'

'We can have a damn good try,' said Stratton. 'Go on.' He gave her bottom a slap. 'Run the bath.'

When Stratton came upstairs, Jenny was standing by the bath, monitoring the water to make sure it didn't go over the five-inch-high black line marked on the porcelain. When he came up behind her and put his arms round her, she gasped.

'Sorry, love, I didn't mean to give you a shock.'

'No, it's not that—your poor hands! They look like pieces of meat.'

'Moving all that stuff. You can put something on them later. And leave that tap on, for God's sake—we'll need a bloody sight more hot water than that to shift this lot. And,' Stratton nuzzled the back of her neck, 'you'll have to wash me. I can't do it myself.'

'I suppose,' said Jenny, sounding severe, 'you need me to undress you, too.'

'Sounds like a good idea.'

Jenny laughed and wriggled round to face him. 'All right,' she said. 'Keep still.'

Jenny got into the bath behind Stratton—it was a tight squeeze, but they managed it—washed his hair, and soaped his back. Despite the bathroom's chilliness, her breasts felt warm against his skin...'What about the front?' he asked.

'Don't be impatient,' said Jenny. 'I'm going from the top down.'

'I should point out,' said Stratton, 'that some things are nearer the top than they were five minutes ago.'

Jenny giggled.

The water was like black soup by the time they got out. By then they were too engrossed to go back downstairs to the Morrison shelter. Stratton simply picked Jenny up, ignoring her protests, carried her across the landing, and laid her down on their double bed.

Stratton was exhausted, and it was only seven in the morning. Hardly surprising since he'd been up most of the night, and his raw knuckles ached like buggery, but dragging himself to the bathroom had seemed to take the same amount of effort as climbing a mountain.

Yet another wet morning, and the bathroom was cold, as usual. You'd never know it was summer, thought Stratton. Standing shirtless before the basin, he screwed up one side of his face and scraped at it, ineffectually, with the blunt blade. He gave up, dropped the razor into the grey water and eyed himself in the mirror: with bags under his blue eyes and a much-mended vest, it wasn't a pretty sight. Not that he'd ever been a matinée idol, even as a younger man—his looks were always too rugged for that, and the nose, broken early, had put paid to any chance of refined handsomeness. At six foot three he was taller than most, broad shouldered and, thanks to nature and a lot of hard work on the allotment, muscular, but all the same...Thirty-nine, he thought, and I'm starting to look like an old man. At least—the thought made him grin—Jenny doesn't seem to mind. He ran a hand through his hair—still thick and still, mostly, black, which was something to be grateful for, anyway—then bent down to pull out the plug and clean the basin before padding back to the bedroom to put on his shirt.

Come to think of it, he couldn't remember the last time, unless you counted about twenty minutes in the small hours of this morning—Stratton grinned again—when he *hadn't* felt tired. The fatigue was partly physical but mainly, he thought, the mental weariness engendered by a world of constant discomfort, dirt and scarcity: clothing that was darned and frayed; battered, rickety furniture; houses—those still standing—falling to pieces from neglect, buses and tube trains crammed with heavy-eyed, putty-faced people...Even the girls looked shabby, hair done up in scarves, dressed in slacks or with bare legs, which, in cold weather, were marbled pink and white like potted meat. And the trees, too, despite their green leaves, looked dusty and tired.

Except the ones in Larkin Avenue, of course. He hadn't been able to see last night, but he was fairly sure they wouldn't have any leaves left. Flying bombs seemed to have that effect. They also, judging by the results he'd seen so far in daylight, had a nasty habit of replacing the missing leaves with shreds of human flesh. So many horrors...In the last four and a half years he'd seen more than his share: houses burst open, filthy, scarred and exposed raw to the sky, buses hurled into the sides of buildings, severed arms, legs and heads coated with a new skin of plaster-dust, and as for last night...

Feeling nauseous, he went down to breakfast. He didn't really fancy it—besides the sick feeling, he wasn't awake enough to be hungry—but Jenny would be worried if he didn't eat anything. At least the hens that he'd persuaded her to keep in the garden were laying well, although they did, as she often complained, attract flies. Not that he blamed her for grumbling—she was tired, too, what with working at the Rest Centre till all hours, and the drudgery of queuing and juggling the ration books as well as the housework. Besides which, she was missing the children even more than he was: after a year at home, Monica (now thirteen) and Pete (now eleven) had been re-evacuated to Suffolk when the flying bombs started.

He sat down at the kitchen table and accepted a cup of tea. Jenny, in her dressing gown, slid an egg into a pan of boiling water and sat down opposite him. He loved the way she looked in the morning, with her chestnut hair rumpled and her pretty face, washed but not yet powdered, glowing and fresh, even after practically no sleep. Not that he'd ever say so, of course—it would be taken for flannel and not believed. 'Won't be long, dear,' she said. 'How are your hands this morning?'

'A lot better, thanks.' Stratton winked at her.

'Ooh, I forgot to tell you—Doris says Mr Bolster said yesterday that he might be getting some toilet paper in.'

'That's good.' Mr Bolster, and what he might or might not have in his shop, figured largely in their conversation nowadays, as, Stratton suspected, it did in that of every other house in the road. Knowing that his sister-in-law was a pretty reliable source of this type of information, he added, 'She didn't say anything about razor blades, did she?'

''Fraid not. I'll find out, though.'

Stratton, who was expecting a further bulletin—this part of the chat usually took up at least five minutes—was momentarily surprised when Jenny fell silent and started fiddling with her cutlery. Then, realising what she was thinking about, and not wanting to engage with it, he wondered—the triumph of hope over experience, this—if he might be able to avoid the subject by ignoring her change of mood, and spent a minute or so staring into his teacup, trying to gather some energy. Finally, he said, 'What's up?'

'Nothing, just…' Jenny repositioned her knife for a further thirty seconds, then said, 'I was thinking about that poor woman, last night…'

'I know, love. But at least she's alive, and she'll be well looked after. And…' Stratton reached across the table and squeezed Jenny's hand, 'last night wasn't *all* bad, was it?'

'Well…' His wife inclined her head to one side and pretended to consider this. 'It had a few moments.'

'A bit more than just a *few* moments, thank you.'

Jenny grinned and wrinkled her nose at him, but then she frowned, and, after a brief hesitation, said, '*Do* you think it'll be over soon, Ted?'

Stratton sighed. She'd been asking this, with the hopeful persistence of a child, ever since the invasion of France had begun two weeks before. Privately, he didn't agree with the people who said that the war would be over in a month, but he wasn't going to tell Jenny that. The odd thing was, though, he'd had the impression that she was going to say something entirely different—he didn't know what, but not that. Perhaps he'd imagined it. In any case, he was too tired to pursue it.

'I honestly don't know,' he said, 'but whatever happens, we'll manage. We're a lot better off than some—like that poor woman last night. And when it's over, we'll have the kids back. That's something to look forward to, isn't it?'

'Oh, yes.' Jenny's face lit up briefly, and then she frowned. 'But they might think it's even more of a let-down this time, coming back here after...'

Stratton, who knew what was coming next, cursed himself for leading the conversation into a potentially difficult area. Although Mrs Chetwynd, on whom Pete and Monica had been billeted, was very kind and couldn't do enough for them, she was also upper-class and wealthy, and, when the children came back after the end of the Blitz, it had taken some time for them to settle back into their old life. Now, back in Suffolk since the flying bombs started, they were, of course, a bit older, and he thought—although he didn't voice it—that the adjustment to home life would be as hard, if not harder, than it had been before. Jenny, who'd seen the children more recently than Stratton, fretted constantly about it.

'They even *sound* like her now,' she said. 'It's as if they don't belong to us any more. They're used to that big house, and all the space, and...oh,' Jenny gave him a despairing look, '...everything.'

'They're still ours,' said Stratton. 'Especially Monica—she's just like you. Anyone can see that.'

'That's just how she looks,' said Jenny. 'She doesn't think like us any more. Neither does Pete.'

'They'll come round,' said Stratton. 'They're good kids. They'll grow up and be a credit to us, and give us lots of grandchildren, and we'll have more time for doing things together.' Realising that she was looking at him oddly, he added, 'If you can stand the thought, that is. Come on, love, buck up. It's not like you to be gloomy.' More to divert her attention than from any desire for food, he added, 'How's that egg doing?'

'Sorry, dear.' Jenny jumped up and, grabbing a tea towel, went over to the cooker. 'My saucepan! It would be the last straw if it boiled dry—it's the only aluminium one we've got left. Doris heard they had some in at Tooley's but they'd gone by the time I got there.'

After breakfast, Stratton kissed Jenny and strode, head down, through the now driving rain to the bus stop, reflecting as he did so that her frequent absences at the Rest Centre—which was where she was going today—made him appreciate her a great deal more. Not, he told himself, that he'd ever taken her for granted—at least, he hoped she didn't think he had. There was nothing actually wrong with the meals she left, but somehow the house didn't feel right without her in it and he hated eating alone.

By the time he got off the bus at Piccadilly, the rain had abated, although—Stratton squinted up at the sky—that was obviously going to be temporary. He sniffed the now familiar smell of smoke mingled with dust. Must have got it somewhere round here last night, too. Stratton hoped it wasn't the station again. When West End Central had been destroyed in the Blitz of 1940, it had taken months to get back to anything approaching normality. Stratton made his way down the rain-slicked pavement of Regent Street, past the taped shop windows with their pitifully small displays of goods.

He turned down Vigo Street, round the corner of Savile Row, and into the lobby at West End Central to find three beefy-looking women involved in a catfight, with Cudlipp, the desk sergeant, shouting 'Ladies! Ladies!' and thrusting out his arms like a boxing referee in a vain attempt to keep order.

'What was all that about?' he asked Sergeant Ballard, who was waiting for him in his office, perched on a corner of his desk.

'Sorry, sir.' Ballard, who was tall, dark, neatly handsome and unconsciously elegant in a way that Stratton secretly envied but could not resent because he was a decent bloke and not flashy, slid off the desk and stood to attention.

'As you were.' Stratton waved a hand at him and sat down.

'Yes, sir. They're all married to the same man. They've only just found out.'

'Likes the fuller figure, then,' Stratton murmured.

'Yes, sir. He's a soldier. Got the three of them drawing allowances for him. They're not happy about it.'

'So I gathered. What else?'

'Chap forging petrol coupons—caught him trying to flush five hundred of them down the toilet, apparently...More information on that NAAFI robbery, from Brighton...Someone with a basement full of army tyres...More hooch—this time it's a club in Coventry Street. Five people paralysed, one gone blind. Came from a still in Dagenham...Trouble with the GIs at Rainbow Corner—*again*—they broke a window this time, bunging a bloke through it. Oh, and there's some new information on those two robberies from last week...It's all here, sir.' Ballard placed a stack of papers on Stratton's desk and withdrew.

Stratton began reading the details of the forged petrol coupons. It was unusual to trace forgeries back to their source because they were so well protected by the gangs. A good source, too—inspecting the sample, Stratton knew that he wouldn't have been able to tell the difference. God, he was tired. What he needed was a nice uneventful day so he could recover. Fat chance.

Sure enough, ten minutes later Ballard stuck his head round the door. 'Message, sir. Body on a bomb-site. End of Berners Street, near the Middlesex. The warden thinks it might be suspicious.'

'Balls!'

'Sir?'

'Sorry, Ballard, not you. We had an incident a couple of streets away last night—flying bomb. Didn't get a lot of sleep.'

'Sorry, sir. I noticed your hands. The fresh air might perk you up a bit.'

Stratton regarded Ballard for a moment, reflecting that it wasn't only his looks but his optimism and instinctive kindness which made him so popular with the girls. 'I doubt it,' he said, reaching for his hat and coat. 'I feel as if I might fall asleep on my feet, like a horse. Or Arliss.' Arliss, one of the old, steam-driven brigade, was the station's most incompetent policeman.

Ballard grinned. 'I always could prop you up, sir.'

'You might have to,' said Stratton grimly. 'Come on. After all,' he added, waving a hand at the paper-covered desk, 'it's not as if we've got anything else to do, is it?'

CHAPTER 4

They hadn't taken any precautions. Seated in front of her dressing table mirror, Jenny Stratton put her head in her hands. How could she have been so *stupid?* She hadn't even realised until Ted made that remark about grandchildren at breakfast. With all the business last night, she just hadn't thought of it. And he hadn't asked—well, why should he? It was her responsibility, not his, always had been. If only she'd remembered, warned him to be careful...

She *couldn't* have another baby. They'd always said they'd have two, then stop, and they'd got one of each, which was perfect, exactly as they'd planned. She couldn't face going through it all again, especially not *now.* Surely, as it had only happened the once, it would be all right? Of course, once was all it took, but just the same...It would be so unfair. If there were any justice in the world—which, frankly, there didn't seem to be, at least at the moment—she wouldn't be pregnant.

Her period was last week, so she wouldn't know for ages... There was no point worrying—if she was, she was, and there wasn't a damn thing she could do about it. The alternative was illegal, and, in any case, she didn't think she could face it. Perhaps she wouldn't have to...Now she thought about it, she was glad she hadn't said anything to Ted. No point worrying him over nothing. Let's hope—Jenny crossed her fingers—she wouldn't have to at all.

It had been nice, though, messing about in the bath and everything. Really, she was lucky—even after fifteen years of marriage, Ted was still keen on her *like that*, and she on him. A virgin when she married, Jenny hadn't been entirely sure, despite euphemistical explanations from her mother, what to expect, and she'd been gratified to find that—after the first time, at least—it was not only comforting, but nice as well. But imagine being eight or nine months pregnant and having to sleep in the Morrison shelter, and what if a raid started just when— *Stop it*, she told herself. Be positive.

She stuck two of her precious remaining hair-pins between her teeth and, lifting up her hair, commenced winding it round a sanitary pad to make a victory roll. Although her chestnut hair was thick and naturally wavy (thank goodness) it was now lank and hard to manage—hardly surprising when there was no shampoo, and after last night the dish in the bathroom contained only an almost transparent sliver of soap which had to last them both for at least four more days.

Jenny opened the drawer that contained her small reserve of powder and lipstick. She felt guilty about buying cosmetics on the black market—Ted would be furious if he knew she was breaking the law—but it wasn't fair to expect her to do without them altogether. Even if no-one else cared about her nose being shiny, *she* minded. And, she reasoned, whatever he might say, Ted wouldn't want her to neglect her appearance. She looked quite tired enough as it was…She'd look a jolly sight worse if she were pregnant, though. All that standing in queues really would be tiring, especially later on…

'Don't,' she said to herself. 'It's going to be fine.' She applied the barest minimum of the precious powder and gave her hair a final pat before picking up the photograph of Pete and Monica and giving it a wipe with her sleeve before kissing it. 'Have a nice day,' she murmured. 'I'll see you later.'

Still, present worries very much aside, as Ted had said at breakfast, they *were* fortunate. Their house—unlike poor Mrs

Ingram's—was still standing and the children were safe, and, even if Pete's handwriting did seem to be getting worse with each letter, at least he was too young for the call-up.

She donned her coat and headscarf and left the house. Walking briskly through the forlorn streets to the Rest Centre, she passed boarded-up windows, cracked panes and houses piebald with flaking plaster. Crossing the top of Larkin Avenue, she inspected the huge, ragged crater where the flying bomb had plummeted to earth, obliterating Mrs Ingram's house and the one next door. In front of them, a beech tree lay uprooted, and further down another, torn apart by the explosion, dripped sap like blood. Looking down, she saw near her feet a broken lampshade which had either rolled or been flung to the edge of the mound of debris, and, next to it, what looked like the corner of a board game. Somehow, those little relics of people's lives seemed more shocking than anything else, and for a moment she thought she was going to cry. Pulling herself together, she blew her nose, said a hasty silent prayer for Mrs Ingram, and hurried on to the Rest Centre.

She hung up her coat in a narrow hallway papered with notices about water restrictions, warnings not to waste coal or paper and exhortations to eat vegetables (cavorting potatoes and carrots with little faces). As she folded her scarf and put it into her handbag for safe keeping, she heard snippets of conversation from the next room. 'Fair knocks you sideways…Expected home any day now…They find houses for them French refugees quick enough, but not for our people…Had me head under the pillow, but the bed was covered in broken glass…Right near you, wasn't it, that one last night…'

The Rest Centre was a school, taken over four years earlier and hastily equipped with trestle tables, rough blankets, pails as extra lavatories and a small amount of first aid. They were rather better off now, thanks to the WVS, the Red Cross and the London County Council, with a clothing exchange and a supply of milk for babies, although the food—soup, bread and marge with occasional jam—was still workhouse fare, and the process of rehousing bombed-out families was often only fractionally less chaotic than it had been in 1940.

Avoiding the general chatter, Jenny spent the morning helping people fill out forms claiming for damage to property, furniture and belongings. Halfway through one of a dozen unvaried and wearying exchanges—'You can get a grant to replace your teeth, Mrs Clayton'—'I don't want sharity'— 'Pardon?'—'*Scharity*'—'It's not charity, they'll take it off your War Damage claim'—'I don't know, sheems like scharity to me'—Jenny looked up to see her sister Doris standing behind the shabby, sunken-mouthed form of Ivy Clayton, looking excited and indicating, by jerks of head and thumb, that she should accompany her outside immediately. Although she would never have admitted it, Doris was Jenny's favourite sister, much closer in both looks—though Doris was taller and darker—and temperament than she and their eldest sister Lilian.

'Will you excuse me for a moment, Mrs Clayton? There's something I need to see to. Shan't be long.' Jenny stood up carefully, adjusting her skirt; the lack of elastic meant that this particular pair of knickers was in constant danger of falling down. Leaving the woman muttering shushily to herself, Jenny followed Doris into what had formerly been the playground. 'Before I forget,' Doris whispered, 'I got some toilet paper. Four rolls each. Mr Bolster let me have it. And he's kept back some soap for you.'

'How did you manage that?'

'My natural charm,' said Doris, striking a haughty, chin-up pose and flicking out one wrist like a mannequin. 'Drop in later, and I'll give them to you. That's not the reason I'm here, though—it's that Mrs Ingram from last night. I couldn't sleep for thinking about the poor woman, all alone like that and with no-one to look after her, so I went to the hospital this morning to see how she was doing. They said she could go, and did I know where her husband was or if she had any relatives near? So I said why hadn't they asked her, and they said she still wasn't up to talking but they couldn't keep her because she didn't have any injuries and they need the bed because they've had so many come in with the new bombs.'

'Where's her husband?'

'Called up, remember? Anyway, there didn't seem to be anyone she knew—well, she's not been here long—and I thought it was a bit much to turn the poor woman onto the street in that condition, so I said she could come and stop with us.'

'There's beds here.'

'I know, but they said she needs someone looking after her. She's in a bad way.'

'Where is she?' Jenny looked round the yard.

'Still at the hospital. I came down here to get some clothes from the WVS so I can take her home.'

'Course, she only had the nightgown, didn't she? You are good.'

'Well...' Doris shrugged. 'Hope someone'd do the same for me if I needed it. I'd better get on—there's her new ID card and ration book to sort out as well, and I don't see her being able to do it...'

Jenny left Doris sorting through heaps of rancid garments in the clothing exchange and returned to the problem of Ivy Clayton's missing teeth. In due course Ivy was replaced by a man with a dangerous air of hilarity about him, as if he had been celebrating his birthday on his own, who kept laughing and waving his arms. 'I've lost everything,' he announced. 'House, ration books, identity card, kiddies' birth certificates...I can't even find my wife. That's why I'm here. Have you seen her?'

What with the bomb-happy man, and several others who needed immediate assistance, Jenny was kept continuously occupied for almost four hours, and had no time to think about Mrs Ingram, or whether she was pregnant, or anything much else.

On her way to Doris's, she wondered whether to bring up the subject of last night's 'mistake' with her sister. Doris was always pretty sensible about these things...All the same, she had a feeling that, if she voiced her fears about pregnancy, it would somehow make it more likely. While this did not make any sort of logical sense, it had far too much of the nebulous, paranoia-inducing power of superstition for her seriously to consider acting against it.

CHAPTER 5

The man, Sam Todd, took the scalpel—filched from the mortuary—from his jacket pocket. Too elated to sleep, he tested its sharpness with his thumb before laying it down on the lace-edged runner that lay across the little table in his dreary room. Next to it was a bundle of newspaper the size and shape of a large cabbage, which he unwrapped carefully, revealing the shiny, yellowy-grey convolutions of a human brain, saved from incineration at the hospital.

He flattened out the newsprint around the brain to protect the runner. Strange, he thought, that this was now merely a piece of obsolete machinery that had once been operated by a conscious force. It was of no more significance than, say, a spent light bulb, and yet it had been the seat of control; the place where decisions were made and challenges were undertaken. It had contained likes and dislikes, and all the things that made its former owner—one Bernard Henry Porteus, auxiliary fireman, killed by falling masonry—what he was. This is what determines us, he thought. It's what dies when we die. He'd no time for God, or souls, or anything like that—those were just inventions to keep credulous fools happy.

He'd smuggled the brain back to his room to study it at leisure. He pulled his copy of Cunningham's dissection manual—stolen from Foyles Bookshop—from his battered knapsack, and found the relevant page. At various times he'd brought back livers, kidneys, hearts and wombs to dissect in this room, but this was his first brain. He prodded it with a fingertip, gingerly, as if he expected it to react. 'Hello there, Mr Porteus,' he murmured. 'Let's find out what made you tick.' He picked up the scalpel and jabbed the brain with the sharp tip. 'Didn't you like that, old chap?' he asked. 'You know, you really shouldn't complain. Just think'—he chuckled —'you're helping to advance the cause of science in a way you could never have imagined.'

After a couple of hours' studying, slicing, and making notes, he dumped what was left of the brain in the basin, then sat back and took stock of his surroundings. The room was where he'd been living since he began his life as Sam Todd, mortuary attendant, back in April (the real Sam Todd, a two-year-old who'd succumbed to Spanish influenza in 1918, was lying in a Gravesend churchyard). It didn't contain much that was his. Most of the few things he owned—the second-hand suitcase with the labels from foreign travels, the expensive cigarette case, and a large quantity of varied stationery—were mere props. For the rest, there was a high, narrow, single bed, scuffed brown lino on the floor, a battered table and chair, and a rickety washstand with a jug and basin of cheap white china. It was not home, merely a place he inhabited, the latest in a long line of many such that he'd inhabited since he had 'died', aged seventeen, in 1932, while on holiday at Camber Sands. He'd left his clothes in a heap on the beach and disappeared as completely as if his body really had slipped beneath the cold grey waves of the straits of Dover. So far, that had been his finest hour: sneaking out of the boarding house at night, depositing on the sand the clothes his mother had last seen him wearing, together with his watch, pocket-knife and wallet, and then donning the new things he'd carefully hoarded and walking away in the night, towards freedom, sloughing off his old self like an unwanted skin.

It had taken years since then to achieve his goal, but now he was in sight of it. His pulse raced and he felt warm all over and aroused with the excitement—the *need*—of it. The mortuary attendant, like all the personas before him, was merely a stepping stone to something better. After the first week in the job he'd taken all his clothing coupons and purchased the uniform of a doctor: black jacket and striped trousers. Wearing these beneath a white coat, and carrying a stethoscope, he'd walked about the Middlesex Hospital after his shift was over, trying out his potential new self. As he'd moved through the building, keeping a brisk but steady pace, looking calm and resolute, he'd enjoyed the deference of the nurses and the respectful looks of the matrons. In the Gents', he had admired his wonderful new self in the mirror.

He'd only dared appear dressed as a doctor once. It wasn't likely that he'd he recognised but, with so much at stake, he didn't want to risk it a second time. Now, he went across to the small square of mirror that hung on a nail above the washstand. Its surface made him think of a river in an industrial town, and gave his sandy hair and moustache and his nondescript features a brown, rather blurred look.

'Who are you?' he asked himself, then stepped back to light a cigarette. There were only six in the packet to last the next two days, but he'd earned it. Squinting through the smoke, he saw, once more, the image of himself as a doctor, an educated man with dignity and authority, worthy of the esteem and regard of his peers. A man who would make his mark and be remembered. He felt a surge of power, like an electrical force, go through his body as he shouted a reply to his own question. 'I am anyone I want to be! Anyone at all!'

He stood for several minutes, watching himself smoke, and then, when the cigarette was finished, he bent over the basin and, very deliberately, stubbed the fag out right in the middle of what remained of Bernard Henry Porteus's brain.

CHAPTER 6

Right from the start, Todd had loved the atmosphere of the hospital: the quiet efficiency, the routine, the firmness of purpose. The stone corridors, swing doors and neat rows of patients tucked beneath their bedclothes were all part of a beautifully ordered world. Even the names of the departments—Radiography, Physiotherapy, Infant Welfare—seemed like poetry. By the beginning of May—after a month working in the mortuary and, satisfied, finally, with the progress of his studies—he had decided to make the next move towards the creation of his ultimate self. This involved the mother of James Dacre, a boy from his first school who, almost five years ago in the early days of the blackout, had been fatally hit by a car a month after graduating in medicine. When Todd had heard about it, he'd realised the importance of the information, and filed it away for use when he was ready. So, one evening in the first week of May, he set to work in his room, drafting a letter on the back of an old envelope.

Dear Mrs Dacre,
I don't know if you remember me, but I was a school friend of your late son, James. I have many happy memories of him, and I was so sorry to hear, recently, of his death several years ago.

I am afraid that we had rather lost touch, which is why this letter has been so long in coming to you. As I have said, it was only recently that I learnt of the tragedy. It is a terrible shame that such a promising young man should be taken so young...

Thus far, nothing but truth—or almost truth...But now he had to think...Nothing too exaggerated about James Dacre's potential. From what he could remember, Dacre was a stolid, unremarkable type who would probably have made a competent physician, but nothing more. So...another sentence about him being a nice chap, a tasteful reference to the Almighty, and a suggestion that, as he was passing that way the following week, he might drop in for a visit. Mrs Dacre, he knew, had long been a widow, and James had been her only child. If she were lonely, she'd appreciate the company. Even if she were not, Todd thought, she'd probably welcome an opportunity to talk about her son. He put the final touches to his letter and then, from the supply of paper he kept in the battered desk, he selected a sheet of fine, heavy bond, and spent a few moments testing his fountain pens until he found one that felt right for the job. He copied the words out neatly with his address at the top, then paused. It was too risky to sign his real name—she'd probably have read about his 'death' in the local paper. Although he had met James Dacre's mother briefly a couple of times—tea after prep-school sports—and had a vague memory of a well-fleshed woman in a flowered summer dress, he did not think she would remember what he looked like. After all, one small boy is much like another...

He was as sure as he could be that she'd never met his own mother who, used—as she herself put it—to better society, would have thought it a comedown to be friends with someone like Mrs Dacre. The Dacres may have had more money than his family, but in his mother's eyes they were vulgar and middle-class, and he was sure that her loneliness would not have overcome her prejudice.

What should he call himself? Nothing too unusual—or too common—as both might prove memorable. Something easily confused, he thought. A surname that was also a Christian name, perhaps? He pondered, tapping the end of his pen against his teeth: Oliver? Thomas? Norman? He jotted down the names: Oliver, Thomas, Norman. Thomas Norman? No, Norman Thomas. Entirely unmemorable. He'd use that.

He found a matching envelope and wrote the address—copied from the post office directory—then he tucked the letter behind the clock on the mantelpiece. Lighting a cigarette, he sat down to rest for a moment before starting work on his next project: an identity card in the name of James Dacre. That was the main thing; a ration book could wait. His landlady kept his—or rather, Todd's—and there was no reason why she should not continue to do so for the time being. As for clothing, he had everything he needed at present. The identity card would be a simple matter. He'd seen to this when, at the start of the war, he'd managed—this time as 'John Watson'—to secure a job as a lowly clerk in the National Registration Office. Over the course of several months, he had purloined a stack of blank identity cards, which had come in very handy, and he knew how to fill them in to look authentic. He tamped out his cigarette, reached under his bed for the trunk where he stored his most important stationery and papers, and undid the brown paper parcel where he kept the blank cards. Choosing a thick-nibbed pen, he filled the cartridge and was about to start writing when he remembered that he didn't know if James Dacre had a middle name. He couldn't afford to make stupid mistakes—completing the card would have to wait until he had seen Mrs Dacre.

He slid the card under the blotter on his desk. In some ways, more paperwork made life more difficult, but in others, it was a godsend. For as long as he could remember, embossed papers had been substitutes for achievement, and nowadays identity cards had become substitutes for personhood, if there was such a word. His new medical qualifications would have to wait until his visit to Mrs Dacre, too; he wasn't going to use counterfeit documents if the real thing turned out to be available. Besides, he needed to find out which university Dacre had attended. In order to create a convincing fiction, it was important to stay as close to the truth as possible. He had an idea that Dacre had studied at St Andrews in Scotland. This, if correct, would be excellent—as far away from London as possible.

He opened the bottle of beer he'd been saving and stared at the end of the envelope that stuck out from behind the clock, praying that the widow Dacre hadn't evacuated herself from Norbury. The sooner the wheels were set in motion, the better. Meanwhile, he'd continue to use his spare time well. Learning, he'd found, was easy, as long as there was a point to it, and he'd always had a good memory. So much for his mother, and the teachers who'd scoffed at his ambitions and abilities. 'MB, ChB,' he murmured to himself. Bachelor of Medicine, Bachelor of Chirurgery. That was the old-fashioned word for surgery. 'MB, ChB'. Lovely, resonant sounds, full of promise, but, for the time-being, they, and everything else he craved, were on the other side of the door of opportunity, and that was locked against him. Life had not given him the key, so he must force his way in by whatever means were necessary. It was as simple as that.

CHAPTER

7

The four days after he'd posted the letter to James Dacre's mother had seemed an eternity, but on the fifth, he came home to find a letter waiting for him on the japanned tray on the stand in the dingy, narrow hall. Beatrice Dacre (Mrs) would be delighted to receive him for tea on the date he'd specified.

A week after that, the train had jolted him towards Norbury, clad in flannel trousers (pressed under the mattress), shirt, tie, and jacket, his hair neatly brushed. He'd given a lot of thought to a suitable present, and finally, with a great deal of luck and even more expense, had managed to obtain an oval tablet of pre-war Elizabeth Arden soap.

The journey was risky—for all he knew his own mother still lived in Norbury. Supposing she spotted him? Would she believe the evidence of her eyes, or would she simply note, with sadness, the young man who so resembled her only child? It was a Saturday, so perhaps she'd be at the Tennis Club—provided, of course, that it still existed, the Croydon area having had it pretty badly. It occurred to him, then—incredibly, for the first time since the war began—that his mother might be dead. After all, he hadn't seen her for twelve years.

How old would she be now? Fifty-something? Sixty? He'd never been entirely sure. He felt no guilt—she'd have thrown his life away if he'd let her, with her grim satisfaction at 'having come down in the world'.

The train pulled into Streatham Common. He stared out at the station, with its taped windows and sandbags piled on the platform, and the desire to jump out and head back into London was so overwhelming that he had to grip the edge of the seat and grit his teeth in order to stop himself rushing for the door. It wasn't the risk—in the past he'd always got a kick out of that—it was being far, far too close to the place he'd once called home.

Norbury, at first sight, seemed the same. Shabbier, but everything was still there: the cinema, the Express Dairy, his old school, and the sweetshop that sold fancy chocolates in beribboned boxes that they could never afford (and now with a cardboard wedding cake and empty cartons in the window).

He walked up the hill towards the avenues of mean, semi-detached villas, identical post-1918 suburban architecture, coated in stucco, with creosoted gates. They looked even smaller than he remembered, and the corner of his old street was upon him before he realised exactly where he was. Catching sight of the road name, he stopped, making sure he was hidden behind a privet hedge. He craned his neck to look down the street. As far as he could see, all the houses were still there.

He stood still, rooted to the pavement. He hated the cheapness of the little houses with their box-like spaces and thin internal walls. His family had been forced to move here from a bigger, better, double-fronted house with a circular driveway, a car, a cook and a maid. His lip curled as he remembered how, as a young boy, his father had introduced him to approving business associates as the third generation. 'One day, son, all this will be yours,' he muttered in mocking imitation. When he was eight, the second generation had managed to lose the family business, and with it the house, the car, the servants and all the money.

The memory of his father telling him they'd lost everything still sickened him. He hadn't understood. 'It's our home,' he'd told his parents, 'they can't take it away from us.' But apparently they could. 'I'll make some more money,' his father had said. 'We'll have our house back again.' His mother had said in a cold, hard voice, 'Don't lie to the boy. The fact is, we don't belong here any more.' The silence after that had been painful, like a piercing high note singing in his ears, making him swallow and run from the room.

They didn't belong in the little house, either. They were no good at being poor—not that it was actual poverty, like living in a slum, but a desperate sort of lower-middle class gentility. Their furniture was too big for the pokey rooms, but there was no money left to buy smaller pieces. As a result the attic and one of the upstairs bedrooms were stacked high, and he was relegated to the box room with its small window overlooking a meagre strip of garden that didn't even have enough space for a proper tree. He thought of the decanters standing empty on the sideboard beside the rows of unused tumblers, and the pathetic fire, never quite catching or going out, but filling the room with smoke.

His mother had never let them forget that they'd slipped several rungs, and his father, growing ever more stooped and miserable, had tried, ineffectually, to 'make the most of it'. His father had finally managed to secure, through the recommendation of one of his remaining friends, a job as a clerk. Then he'd died—a perforated ulcer—when his only child was fifteen. By then, Todd's wish to become a doctor had already been dismissed by both his mother and his teacher.

Remembering his mother's thin smile of wintery contempt, and Miss Dunster's patronising moue ('Perhaps something a little less *ambitious*, dear. Why not learn a trade?'), hot and sickening fury made his stomach lurch. There was nothing more galling in the world than being *expected* to fail. How dare they, the bitches? I never belonged here, he told himself, *never*. He must get to Mrs Dacre; get what he needed, get out, and never return. He spat, savagely, on the pavement, and turned away.

He still felt the rising bile as he stood on Mrs Dacre's small porch, his hand on the ornamental knocker, letting it fall smartly, twice. Hearing footsteps, he straightened his hat, and then the door opened and there she was: a thicker version than he remembered, the curves having solidified to a tubular bulk, with eyebrows raised in delighted surprise. 'Come *in*! I was *so* pleased to get your letter!'

In the time it took for her to shoo him down the hall in a flurry of exclamation marks and almost tow him into the sitting room, Todd decided that the key to success here was innocent flirtation.

He dug into his pocket and produced the cake of soap with a diffident air. 'I bought you this. I thought you might like it.'

'Soap! How lovely! I haven't seen this brand for ever so long. It's terribly kind of you.' She blinked, and, for a moment, he had a horrible feeling that she was about to cry. 'Oh, dear...' She pulled a handkerchief out of the sleeve of her cardigan and dabbed her eyes delicately. 'I *am* being silly. It's just that I don't often...you know, it's so nice to be able...'

'I do understand,' he said. 'I'll go if you'd rather—if it's too...' He looked into her eyes for just long enough, and then down slightly at her lips, and a little further—a gentlemanly way of showing that he acknowledged her as an attractive woman, as well as a nice one. 'Mrs Dacre,' he said, 'I am so sorry. I didn't mean to upset you.'

'No, please,' she said, slightly flustered and blushing faintly, as was his intention. 'Don't mind me. Why don't you sit down, and I'll fetch some tea?'

Another judicious glance—eyes and lips, eyes and lips. 'That would be very nice.'

She bustled off, leaving Todd to look round the room. The first thing that took his eye was a single photograph, framed in silver, in the middle of the mantelpiece: James, in his gown and mortar board, his 27-year-old features already settling into jowly complaisance. For a moment, he stared—the inno-cent, smiling eyes that looked back were remarkably like Mrs Dacre's—then looked away. He noted the brightly polished coal scuttle and the fire-irons on their stand by the grate, the chintz-covered armchairs, the small fumed-oak tables, and the porcelain shepherds and shepherdesses in a glass-fronted cabinet. There was even a selection of mottoes—Bless This House, and the like—executed in hideous pokerwork, hung about the walls. He read them, lips curling, and only just had time to reset his features to an expression of polite anticipation as James's mother returned with a tray, on which sat the tea things and a small cake. Jumping up, he said, 'You shouldn't have gone to so much trouble.'

'Not at all. I had some fruit saved, and it was so nice to bake again. James always loved my cake.' As he moved to take the tray from her, she said, with a little giggle at her own daring, 'Please, don't stand on ceremony. I'll just set it down here, and we'll be quite comfortable,' and deposited it on the pouffe beside his chair.

When he was settled, none too comfortably, with the tea and cake on his knees, and they'd had twenty minutes or so of chat about Dacre, and Todd's memories of school, she said, 'Everything I have left of him is in there,' and gestured towards the sideboard. 'Photographs and memories. Would you like to see?'

This was going to be even easier than he'd hoped. 'Yes, please.' Beatrice Dacre removed a wooden box from the side-board, then, producing a small key from beneath a porcelain yokel, fitted it to the lock.

She sat down again, the box in her lap, and threw back the lid. Catching a glimpse of certificates, Todd hastily drained his cup and craned forward to look.

'Are you sure you don't mind?' she asked again.

Barely managing to conceal his impatience, Todd said, 'No, of course not. I have so many happy memories of James myself.'

'Do you, dear? You know, I've been thinking since I got your letter, and I can't remember him ever mentioning you. Other boys, but not you.'

He had to get hold of that box. 'Didn't he?' He gave her a relaxed smile, as if that was mildly interesting but not important.

'Oh, well, it was quite a time ago...' Mrs Dacre took out a large handful of papers.

On the pretext of leaning forward to put his cup back on the tray, Todd caught a glimpse of the name James Walter Dacre on a school certificate. Dacre's middle name was the same as his own original one! Better and better, he thought, forcing himself to look straight at Mrs Dacre with an expression of restrained anticipation.

'Those are just certificates and things,' she said. 'You don't want to see all those. I've got photographs from when James was at school,' she said. 'I expect you're in some of them.'

'I'd like to look at them, very much—if you wouldn't mind.' He leaned into her, brushing her arm as if by accident. He was sure she'd noticed, but she didn't flinch. 'I don't have anything like that.'

'Haven't you?' Mrs Dacre pulled away from him slightly, sounding surprised.

'Lost in the bombing,' he explained.

'Oh, yes, of course. Dreadful. Ah, here we are.' Leaning towards him once more, Mrs Dacre passed him a postcard-sized photograph of a toddler in a jumper that buttoned at the shoulder, cheeks and lips rosily hand-tinted, grinning against the painted backcloth of a photographer's shop. This image, like the ones in the official prep-school pictures that followed, big boys standing at the back, small ones sitting, cross-legged, at the front, had the doughty sturdiness and the eager, open gaze that he remembered. He stole a glance at Mrs Dacre, anticipating tears, but she was dry-eyed, frowning at the rows of boys in their caps and blazers. 'I can't see...which one are you?'

He saw, too late, that she'd produced a class photograph, this time mounted, with the names of the boys pencilled on the cardboard surround. Todd took a deep breath. He hadn't bargained on that.

'I can't see any Thomas,' she said.

'Let me have a look.' Todd took the photograph from her and puzzled over it. He could see himself—properly captioned, of course, with his real name—in the second row, half-obscured by the boy in front, cap pulled down over his face. 'Do you know, it must have been after I'd broken my leg. I was off school a while that year. My mother wasn't very pleased. Let's see if I can find myself in one of the others. May I?' He picked another photograph off Mrs Dacre's lap, one without captions, careful to have minimal contact with her knee.

'Look,' he said, scanning it. 'There I am.' He was on the end of a row, slightly apart from the others, looking as if he were trying to step away from the picture.

'Are you sure?' said Mrs Dacre, leaning over. 'Only that'— she pointed to the new photograph—'looks more like *him* than anybody.' She pointed to Todd, half-hidden in the captioned picture. 'And that can't be right, because he's called—'

'Perhaps they made a mistake.' Hoping that hadn't sounded too petulant, Todd got up and went over to stand with his back to the fireplace. Things were beginning to get sticky. Why couldn't the silly bitch leave well alone? Seeing that Mrs Dacre's attention was now taken up in comparing the two photographs, he bent slightly at the knees and, stretching one arm down, picked the poker off its stand and hid it behind his legs.

'This can't be right,' Mrs Dacre said. 'I'm sure that was the boy who drowned.' Todd's heart skipped a beat. He adjusted his hand to give his sweating palm a better grip on the iron handle. 'I mean, I don't remember what he looked like or anything'—Todd smiled, quizzically—'but I'm pretty sure that was his name.'

'Drowned?' asked Todd, feeling as if his face had gone numb and the smile was now fixed for ever.

Mrs Dacre nodded. 'Yes, don't you remember? On holiday, I think. Very sad. James would have been...oh, about twenty, at the time.'

'Which one does it say he is?'

'There, look.' Mrs Dacre leant forward to hand him the photograph. 'The one you said was you.' This time, there was no mistaking the accusation in her tone.

Todd stepped forward, the poker still clasped firmly behind his back, and took hold of the cardboard mount with his free hand. He knew his movements must seem awkward but, having come this far, he wasn't going to take any chances. One, perhaps two, quick smashes—he'd have to get behind her, though, so he couldn't see her face. He stared at the picture for a moment, then said, 'That is me, you know, not this other chap. Whoever did the caption got it wrong.'

'James did them himself.'

'Well, it's quite easy to get muddled. Perhaps he just left my name out. That's probably it.'

'I suppose he might have done, but if you were such good friends—'

Surreptitiously, Todd tested the weight of the iron in his hand. Why didn't she just *shut up*? Why did it *matter* to her? She couldn't even remember properly anyway. For God's sake, he willed her, just take my word for it. Leave the subject alone. *Save yourself.*

'It's very easily done,' he continued, as if she hadn't spoken, 'especially if one tries to remember all one's friends' names a few years afterwards...' Shame it was the front room of the house, although the net curtains meant that they were unlikely to be seen by anybody across the way. He shifted the poker slightly again, trying to dry his sweating hand on his trousers.

'I suppose so.' Mrs Dacre looked at him doubtfully, then, picking up another picture—also not captioned, thank Christ—said in a more definite tone, 'This one looks more like you. You're right next to James.'

Todd relaxed fractionally. 'That's a relief. I'd hate you to think,' here he gave her one of his never-fails charming smiles, 'that I was some sort of imposter.'

'Oh, no!' Mrs Dacre laughed—but she was blushing, too. 'What a ridiculous idea!'

Having got her on the back foot, Todd judged it safe to relinquish the poker, which he did with a little bob downwards while she refilled the tea cups. 'Oops,' he said, as the clang of metal on metal made her look up. 'Clumsy of me. Tripped on the fender.'

'That's all right.' She handed him a cup of tea. 'Here you are.'

He rejoined her, leaning towards her once more. 'Heavens,' he said, gazing at the photograph on her lap—it was too soon to reestablish trust by any sort of touching, even the supposedly accidental. 'It does look rather as if the sun was in my eyes, doesn't it?'

'It does a bit. Didn't you like being photographed?' She sounded unguarded now, friendly, almost maternal.

'Not much, no.' He gave her a bashful, boyish look.

'Well, I don't know why. You're very handsome when you smile.'

'You're very kind,' he said, modestly.

'Oh, not at all. Look, there's Billy Powell,' she said, pointing at another boy in the line. 'Do you remember him? He used to come here for tea. Such a funny little boy—always pulling faces...' As she rambled on, Todd's eyes strayed to the pile of paper on the tray. He could see tantalising glimpses of crests and embossing. Those were the things he wanted: documents that validated a life.

'You haven't finished your cake,' said Mrs Dacre. 'I hope it isn't too dry. Would you like some tea to go with it? I'm sure I can squeeze one more out of the pot.'

'Thank you.' He extended his cup as she removed the knitted cosy. 'You're very kind.'

'It's sweet of you to say that, but really, this is so nice for me.' Mrs Dacre poured milk. 'It's kind of *you* to listen to me rambling on like this. I don't often get the chance. Are your parents still living here?'

He shook his head. Might as well start with the truth, he thought. 'I'm afraid my father passed away some years ago,' he said, 'and my mother's in Worcestershire. She moved when the flying bombs started—too much for her, and we have family there, so...' That, he thought, was suitably vague.

'I don't blame her,' said Mrs Dacre, fervently. 'Horrible things. I'm sorry about your father.'

'It was very sudden,' he said. 'A perforated ulcer. He hadn't been well for a while, but we had no idea...' The memories that impinged made it impossible to finish the sentence. In the last weeks of his life, his father had become more withdrawn and depressed, but Todd had simply chalked it up to the demoralising effect of failure, and thought no more about it. When his father had collapsed on the sitting room rug, crying out, his mother's first reaction had been to tut over the upset ashtray and rush for the dustpan. He remembered his father's outstretched hand fumbling, in an agonised crawling motion, towards her feet as she crouched, swishing up the mess with brisk strokes of the brush, ignoring his pain. Despite his protests, she'd insisted they get him upstairs and into bed before calling out the doctor. He'd screamed as they hauled him up the stairs, and died a week later, in hospital, having caught pneumonia after the operation.

'How dreadful.' Mrs Dacre's words sounded extra loud in the charged silence. 'I hope he didn't suffer too much.'

'It was very quick.' As he said it, the excruciating image of his writhing, tormented father came before him so strongly that it took all his self-control not to wince.

'That's what the doctor said about James,' said Mrs Dacre. 'He wouldn't have known.'

He gave her an encouraging smile. 'That's a blessing.'

'Yes...I can't bear to think of him in pain. Oh, dear...' Raising her handkerchief once more to her eyes, she stood up. 'Do excuse me for a moment...' and left the room.

Quickly, he scooped up the papers on the tray and slid them into the inside pocket of his jacket. Gathering up the photographs, he returned them to the wooden box and locked it. Catching sight of his almost untouched slice of cake, he broke it in half and, standing up, stuffed a piece into each trouser pocket, crumbling it with his fingers so that there would be no bulge. Then he drained the last of his tea and went out into the hall in time to see Mrs Dacre, her nose freshly dusted with powder, coming down the stairs. 'I'm sorry,' he said. 'I didn't mean to upset you.'

'No, please.' She put a hand on his arm. 'It's my fault.'

'I put the things back in the box,' he said. 'I locked it. It might be as well not to...'

'You're right. I'll put it away. But I do thank you for coming. You'd think I'd be used to it by now, wouldn't you?' She tried for a smile. 'It's silly, but the war makes it worse. So many mothers losing their sons...'

'Not silly at all,' he said, heartily, covering her hand with his.

'You're very kind,' she said. 'And I am glad you came to see me.'

He said goodbye and hurried back to Norbury station, grinning to himself. Really, he thought, Mrs Dacre ought to be pleased that he was putting her son's identity to such good use. As he waited for the train to arrive, he patted his jacket over his heart, where his new life was folded up, waiting for him.

Now, sitting in his little room, he took stock of his situation. A vacancy, in the shape of Dr Reynolds, had been created, and an identity, in the person of Dr Dacre, secured. Next he needed to engineer a meeting with some of the doctors at the hospital, get himself an 'in'. He'd work on that and he'd have a little fun in the meantime. He needed an appreciative audience, someone to look up to him and admire him, as well as love him: a girl, but it had to be the right girl. A nurse, that was only right and proper. He'd have to have a look round, select a suitable target. Once he was a doctor, he'd be able to have his pick, wouldn't he? That, he thought, rubbing his groin in anticipation, was definitely something to think about, but, in the meantime...He selected a face and body from the harem in his memory (unobtainable girls, these, never girls he'd had), undid his trouser buttons and settled down to satisfy himself.

CHAPTER 8

As he left the police station to look at the body on the bomb-site, Stratton heard the telltale misfiring motorcycle sound and looked up to get his first really decent view of a pilotless plane. So far, he'd seen the damage they could do, but not the machines themselves. He pulled Ballard into a doorway, ducked in beside him, and then, craning his neck, realised that the thing was travelling away from them. A long plume of flame spurted out behind it, vivid scarlet and orange—a dragon's fart, thought Stratton, remembering the picture books he'd read with the kids. Small and demonic, the P-plane went into a glide—somewhere near Baker Street, he guessed—then the noise cut out and it disappeared. Seconds later, they heard a loud, dull trump. 'Christ,' said Ballard, which, Stratton felt, about covered it.

'Let's hope it landed in Regent's Park and not on top of anyone.'

'Know what people are calling them, sir?' asked Ballard.

'What?'

'Doodlebugs. Makes them sound like toys, doesn't it?'

Stratton snorted, thinking of the previous night. 'Some toys.'

They tramped on towards the Middlesex Hospital, and clambered over the damp debris of the bomb-site until they came across the warden, who was squatting over a human-shaped something shrouded in a dusty blanket. He was smoking and swatting at the flies, which, despite the recent rain, had begun to circle.

'What have we got?' asked Stratton.

The warden, his face grimy and exhausted, pinched his fag end between his thumb and forefinger, and flicked it at a pile of bricks. 'Dead bloke, guy. I come across him on my way home—always take a short-cut across here—and I thought I'd better let someone know.'

'Let's have a look.'

The warden drew back the blanket, revealing a clean-shaven face with strong features. About half of it, including the dark hair, was covered with damp plaster dust of a pinkish colour. Blood, Stratton thought, mostly washed away by the rain. 'Was he on his back when you found him?' he asked, pulling the blanket further down to reveal a well-built man in a good—if soaked and grubby—suit. The hands were only superficially dirty, and the nails looked well kept. 'Looks as if the only injuries are the ones to the head.'

'He was lying on his side,' said the warden. 'I turned him over to have a look, and…Well, here we are.'

Aren't we just, thought Stratton, wearily. 'Was he at all stiff?'

'No, he came over quite easy.'

Stratton sniffed at the body, hoping for a whiff of alcohol—if the head wounds could be chalked up to a drunken fall, that would wrap things up nicely. Scenting nothing, he stood up again.

'Must of been last night,' said the warden. 'Like I said, I always come this way, so I'd have noticed. You do see some funny things in this job,' he conceded, 'some of 'em don't have a mark, but this one didn't seem right to me. We didn't get any bombing here last night, or the night before. This lot,' he jerked his thumb at the site, 'come down six months ago, and he ain't dead long enough for that—if he'd just worked his way up to the top, I mean. That happens, too. Things,' he added, vaguely, 'moving.'

Stratton stood for a moment, indecisive. Ordinarily, such a situation would have sharpened his interest, but today...He shook his head, trying to force his brain to life. 'Right,' he said to Ballard, 'seeing as we're so close to the hospital, I'm going to have a word with Dr Byrne. Take some details, and then you,' he nodded at the warden, 'can get off home.'

'Yes, sir.' He left Ballard extracting his notebook from his tunic, and began picking his way through the rubble towards the Middlesex.

After several years' working with Dr Byrne the pathologist, Stratton, though impressed by the man's observational skills, had never got used to his way with the living, which was brusque to the point of rudeness. His manner matched his domain, which was permanently cold and smelt of a mixture of cadavers and disinfectant. The refrigeration—never enough after an air-raid, when sheeted bodies lay in the corridor awaiting inspection— coupled with the damp cement floor and the hard textures of the white porcelain tables, metal instruments, rubber overalls, and the slippery prophylactic feel of recently washed dead flesh, made everything cold to the touch. Everything was impersonal, hygienic, clinical, and bathed in harsh white light.

The odour of decomposition hit Stratton as soon as he opened the outer door. The main room was deserted, save for three bodies lying, covered up, on the tables. From next door came the sounds of bangs and curses, and when Stratton called out, Higgs, Dr Byrne's assistant, wizened and jockey-like, appeared looking flustered. 'What's going on?'

'Bit of a problem, Inspector.' Higgs opened the door to the refrigerator room, and Stratton saw, propped against the wall, a metal tray with a fat woman, wrapped in a paper shroud, stuck to it so that she appeared to be hovering three inches from the floor like some bizarre decoration. An elderly undertaker's man, clad in top hat and black coat, was chipping away at her sides with a hammer and chisel, aided by another mortuary assistant. 'Frozen, she is, Mr Stratton. Stuck fast. We've tried sliding her, but it's no good.'

'Jesus,' said Stratton, revolted. 'Can't you wait for her to thaw?'

'Not likely,' said the undertaker's man. 'She's due in Cricklewood. Funeral's at twelve, and we'll have to tidy her up a bit first.'

'I'll leave to you to it.' Stratton rolled his eyes. 'Best of luck. Where's Dr Byrne?' he asked Higgs.

'Gone up to the laboratory. I'll take you.'

'Does that happen often?' Stratton asked, as they went up the stairs.

'No. Got up like a fourpenny hambone when she come in, with not a mark on her. Nothing to tell who she was, though. Had a hell of a job finding someone to claim her, so she's been with us for a while, and...' Higgs's face, which reminded Stratton of the sort of preserved infant one might see in a Will Hay comedy, puckered in disgust. 'As if we didn't have enough to be going on with. Bodies all over the shop. At least we've got an assistant now.'

'Was that him in there?'

'That's right.' Stratton tried to recall what the man had looked like, but, beyond a vague impression of medium height and sandy hair, couldn't visualise him. 'If you don't mind,' said Higgs, 'we'll use the stairs. Lift keeps breaking down.'

After three flights, neither man was inclined to talk, which suited Stratton, but after five, he was panting, and had to stop and collect himself before Higgs ushered him into the laboratory. Dr Byrne, perched on a high stool, sat squinting into a microscope, surrounded by an array of jars containing, variously, a grotesquely malformed baby, a severed hand, a tapeworm, and something that looked horribly like a tumour. Byrne himself had a sort of specimen quality, being entirely bald, with the thinnest eyebrows Stratton had ever seen on a man, and a greenish-white complexion that made his head look as if it had been preserved in formalin.

'Stratton.' Byrne peered irritably over the top of his instrument. 'What do you want?'

'There's a body I'd like you to see before it's moved. Found on the bomb-site over the way this morning. I'm not sure about it.'

'Making detecting history, are we?'

Stratton, stung by the implication that he was gunning for fame and promotion, said, drily, 'I doubt it's going to lead us to a Crippen or a Ruxton, if that's what you mean. To be honest,' he added, 'I'm hoping you're going to tell me he got that way by accident.'

'Ah.' Byrne managed to work a whole rainbow of meanings into the monosyllable, chief amongst which seemed to be that Stratton's lack of enthusiasm for the chase left a lot to be desired.

'Sorry,' said Stratton, irritated by this. 'Didn't manage a lot of sleep last night.'

'New bomb, was it?' asked Byrne, and Stratton was astonished to see a flicker of something that looked almost like sympathy cross his face.

''Fraid so.'

'Family all safe, I hope?' Stratton was touched to see that, for a moment, Byrne looked concerned.

'Yes thanks.'

'That's good.' The pathologist's face resumed its usual disapproving expression. 'Right, then.' He told Higgs to fetch a stretcher and marched downstairs to collect his bag, Stratton at his heels.

The warden had gone by the time they reached the bomb-site. Stratton had expected Dr Byrne to get cracking as soon as he'd uncovered the corpse, but he stood back, hands on hips, shaking his head. Higgs, next to him, also shook his head, although Stratton felt that it was sycophancy rather than informed opinion that made him do it. 'What's wrong?' he asked.

'That,' said Byrne, 'is Dr Reynolds.' He frowned at Stratton, and shook his head some more. Higgs, whose face had momentarily registered that he had not recognised the corpse and was as surprised as Stratton, immediately narrowed his eyes to mirror Byrne's expression, and added a touch of his own by sucking his teeth.

Turning his attention back to Byrne, Stratton had the impression that the man thought the whole thing was in poor taste—a practical joke, perhaps, set up by himself and Ballard at Byrne's expense.

'You know him, then?' he asked.

'Of course I know him!' Byrne sounded outraged. Jabbing a finger in the direction of the body, he said, 'He's a *doctor*. From the *Middlesex*.' There was no regret in his voice, only the suggestion that Reynolds had somehow let the side down by snuffing it.

'Well, that's given us a head start—at least we know who he is. Are you going to take a look at him?'

'Yes, yes,' said Byrne testily, waving a hand at Stratton. 'Stand back.' Stratton and Ballard withdrew to a discreet distance.

'What a turn up,' Stratton murmured.

'I'd say so, sir.'

'Get everything?'

'What there was, sir. Warden's name's Prior. From Post C. I've got all the details. What do you think Dr Reynolds was doing out here, sir?'

'On his way home, I suppose.'

'Bit dangerous cutting across a bomb-site in the dark, sir.'

'Unless he'd lost his way...or had a skinful.'

'Not if he'd come straight from the hospital, sir.' Ballard sounded shocked.

'That's true. But he might have been off duty. Anyway, there's no point speculating. We'll just have to wait for Laughing Boy to tell us what happened.'

Barely ten minutes had elapsed before Byrne, having finished his notes and sketches, covered the body, straightened up and motioned Stratton over to him. 'Head wound,' he said.

Tell me something I don't know, thought Stratton. 'How was it caused?' he asked.

'Don't know yet. I've done all I can here, so...' On cue, Higgs hurried forward with the stretcher. 'Fetch Todd,' Byrne ordered.

Before Higgs could depart, Stratton said, 'My sergeant can help carry him.'

Byrne looked at Ballard with wary distaste, as if he might violate Dr Reynolds's body in some particularly disgusting way if allowed anywhere near it. 'Todd,' he told Higgs, 'and look sharp.'

Higgs departed, negotiating the uneven ground at a stumbling run, and Byrne turned back to Stratton. 'You'll have my report tomorrow,' he said.

Stratton decided to ignore the air of finality. 'How long has he been dead?'

'Can't say at the moment.'

'An estimate?'

'Six hours, possibly more.'

'Do you think,' persisted Stratton, 'that it was an accident?'

'I can't be sure. I suggest you ask your men to search the area. You'll need to collect all those bricks and so on...' Byrne indicated the area around Reynolds's head, 'and have it sent to the Home Office analyst.'

Bollocks, thought Stratton, that's all I need. Aloud, he said, 'That's necessary, is it, in your view?'

Byrne crossed his arms and pursed his lips. End of conversation. It reminded Stratton of a deckchair being folded away, so much so that he was surprised not to hear an audible snap. 'Well,' he said, 'if that's everything...'

'It is.'

'I'll say goodbye, then,' said Stratton. Byrne gave him a curt nod. Pausing only to tell Ballard to stay put and make sure that nobody else walked over the bomb-site, Stratton strode off as fast as he could without breaking an ankle. Going arse over tit in front of Byrne really would be the last straw. Anyone would think it was his fault that Dr Reynolds had turned up dead. *I suggest you ask your men to search the area.* If only he wasn't so bloody tired…He was going to have enough problems rounding up a team of men, never mind the fact that whatever they found would have been thoroughly washed by the rain which meant it probably wouldn't be much use anyway, and that he'd have to explain himself to DCI Lamb later if the death turned out to be accidental. But if it *wasn't*, and he'd failed to act, then he'd get a strip torn off him, all right…'Jesus,' muttered Stratton.

At the edge of the bomb-site, he glanced round and saw Higgs and his new assistant dashing towards Byrne, jinking from side to side as they staggered over loose bits of masonry. Stratton watched them for a couple of seconds without much interest, then caught sight of Ballard heading off two girls who were about to cross the area. Hearing giggles, he spent the first couple of minutes of his walk back to the station wondering what on earth his sergeant had said to them, or if it was just the effect of Ballard's warm brown eyes. Still, he thought, if it did turn out to be a murder enquiry, it would be a damn sight more interesting than stolen petrol coupons, which was something—or would be once he felt alert enough to deal with it.

CHAPTER

9

Todd did not dismiss Stratton as easily as Stratton had dismissed him. Despite the fact that he'd been expecting the police all morning, it was still a shock. He'd looked up from his attempts to prise Mrs Lubbock away from her temporary resting place—the din of hammers on chisels had been too loud to hear the door to the refrigerator room opening—and there he was. He hadn't said he was a policeman—it was obvious. He was huge: Todd had wondered, several times, what the policeman, or men, might look like, but hadn't imagined that they, or he, would be so bloody *big*. This one looked as if he'd been a heavyweight boxer at some stage—battered, masculine and rugged. He wasn't wearing a uniform—too important. Looking up with those tools in his hands, seeing him towering above them, staring down in horror, he'd felt guilty, and it must have shown. The policeman hadn't seemed to notice; too shocked by the sight of him and the bloke from the undertaker's hacking away each side of the poor woman's bum, no doubt. But the policeman had looked intelligent. Shrewd. He'd only stayed long enough to ask where Dr Byrne was, but all the same, he was someone to watch out for...

When they'd left, the undertaker's man sniffed, and said, 'Copper. Wonder what that's about?' then recommenced his assault on Mrs Lubbock's frozen thigh without waiting for an answer. Todd positioned his chisel under the head and banged away with such ferocity that the other shouted, 'Oi, steady on! You'll have the poor cow's eye out.'

'Sorry.' Concentrating hard, to keep his mind off what the policeman might be doing, he re-applied himself to unsticking Mrs Lubbock from the tray. By the time they'd got her off and packed her up, he was sweating heavily, despite the chill of the room, and so shaky that he felt he must sit down before he keeled over. He was splashing water on the back of his neck when Higgs rushed in, panting.

'Come on!'

'What?'

'Bomb-site—there's a body—Dr Reynolds.'

He kept his face entirely blank. 'Who's Dr Reynolds?'

'Works here. Upstairs. Dr Byrne recognised him.'

That was a shock. If Byrne had recognised Reynolds, he must have more to do with the other staff than Todd had realised. He'd never seen Byrne in the main part of the hospital, but all the same... That wasn't good. Wrenching his thoughts back to the matter in hand, he said, deliberately stupid, 'Do you mean he's dead?'

'Yes.'

'But what's he doing there?'

'Well, he's not admiring the scenery, is he? Come on, look sharp.'

'Mind you,' gasped Higgs, as they galloped down the corridor, 'he's had a bang on the head. Dr Byrne's not happy about it. Said the coppers ought to search the place.'

Todd slowed. 'Search? What for?'

'What do you think?'

'Did someone hit him?'

'How the hell do I know? Bleeding hurry up, will you?'

Despite the fact that Reynolds was covered up, Todd kept his face averted as they loaded his body onto the stretcher and brought him in, bumping clumsily over the mess. Dr Byrne walked silently beside them, and Todd wondered how he might find out how it was that he'd recognised Reynolds. A meeting, perhaps? Some sort of hospital committee? Reynolds had a fairly distinctive face—thick, dark brows and a prominent nose. He was too young to have been at medical school with Byrne. Perhaps Byrne had taught him—but, from what he'd observed of the pathologist, the man wasn't likely to remember his former students, and certainly not to be friendly with them even if he did. Not that recognising someone was an indication of friendship, of course…But it might indicate that Byrne was more in touch with the rest of the hospital than he'd thought. Perhaps he ought to put James Dacre on ice for a while…But that would mean more boredom, more frustration, and he was ready—more than ready—for this. It was his most audacious scheme yet: for that very reason, he told himself, it had a higher than usual chance of succeeding, because nobody would believe it possible.

'On the table, please,' said Byrne, when they arrived at the mortuary. 'I'll attend to him immediately.'

Higgs rushed to fetch the instruments, leaving Byrne staring down at the shrouded form on the table. 'Did you know Dr Reynolds well?' asked Todd.

'Well?' Byrne sounded puzzled, as if the idea of having more than a passing acquaintance with somebody had never before occurred to him.

'Higgs said you'd recognised him, so I thought…I'm sorry if I spoke out of turn. I didn't meant to—'

'No, no,' Byrne interrupted. 'We'd met on a couple of—' He stopped, his lips moving silently, as if trying out words for suitability. 'On a couple of *occasions*.' He turned away and started to remove his jacket.

Todd uncovered Reynolds's body and began, with difficulty since the outer garments were partially caked with wet plaster dust, to strip it. *Occasions*, he thought, as he tugged the trousers over the hips. The way Byrne had said it was significant. The most likely explanation was a post-mortem on one of Reynolds's patients—if there was a suggestion of negligence, perhaps? And if it had happened more than once...?

Higgs bustled in with the instruments and lent a hand with removing the rest of Reynolds's clothes. 'Better make a list of this lot,' he said. 'The police'll need it.' Todd stared down at the stripped corpse: merely the shell that once contained the man. The harsh overhead lamp gave the body a yellow tinge, so that it looked as if it were made of dirty wax.

Dr Byrne took up his position by the table, and his beanpole of an assistant, Miss Lynn (the Forces' Sourpuss) drew up a chair several feet away and hunched, vulture-like, over her notebook. Dismissed by Byrne, Todd took himself out to the basement yard for a breath of fresh air and a smoke. A little curiosity, he thought, would hardly seem suspicious—after all, he'd been told about the blow to the head and the police search. He could ask Higgs later, while they were cleaning up the room. He ought to try and steal a look at Byrne's notes, too—although that would have to wait until tomorrow, when they were typed up, because Miss Lynn's shorthand was incomprehensible. Byrne's office, which was down the corridor, was only locked at night, so it shouldn't be too difficult.

The spectre of the policeman loomed once more in his mind. There's nothing to connect you with Reynolds, he told himself, and no reason for the coppers to be interested in you. And if he *was* questioned, he'd be able to say, with perfect truth, that he had not known the man. He'd seen him, while he was testing out his doctor's uniform upstairs, and made a point of discovering who he was—that was how he'd been able to recognise him, even in the near-darkness. Besides, he told himself, the burden of proof is always on the accuser, even if he is a policeman. That was the most important thing to remember. He was going to be a good doctor, he knew it. Better than Reynolds, if, as he suspected, the man had made some cock-ups...When Byrne went out he'd satisfy his curiosity about that by searching through the records to see if he was right. When post-mortems were on hospital patients, Byrne always noted the name of the doctor at the top, so it would be fairly simple.

He crushed his cigarette out and leant against the wall, eyes closed and face turned upwards to the meagre sunlight. 'MB, ChB,' he murmured to himself, remembering the moment when, in the safety of his room, he'd taken Dacre's papers from his pockets and scattered them across the bed: birth certificate, school certificates, degree certificates—he'd been right about St Andrews. There were even some letters to his mother, written from university. Handy, those, since he'd never been anywhere near either St Andrews or Dundee, which was apparently the home of the medical school. They'd be useful for background colour, if he ever got into a conversation about it. There was nothing a university man liked more, he'd learned, than a good chinwag about the dear old college with another graduate. He'd been caught out that way once before, and he wasn't going to make the same mistake again. He'd send off for a prospectus too, to be on the safe side.

He'd already made up a new ID card for Dacre. The next thing he needed to do was to open a bank account in Dacre's name, and then there was the question of the medical discharge certificate. The hospital was bound to ask why he hadn't been called up—which was ironic, considering that the real reason was because he was, officially, dead, and you couldn't get more medically discharged than that. How to go about it? He heard a creaking noise and, opening his eyes, he saw, slouching through the door from the emergency operating rooms, the rotund form of a hospital orderly. 'Sorry to disturb you, mate. Got a match?'

'Here.' As the orderly bent his head to light his cigarette, Todd realised that the answer had been provided. Had been there, in fact, all along, right under his nose.

'Deep in thought, were you? Looked like you was concentrating on something.'

'Nice to have a bit of peace, that's all.'

'Work in there, do you?' The orderly jerked his head in the direction of the mortuary.

'That's right.'

'Blimey. Wouldn't fancy it myself. That what happened to
your hand?' He gestured at the pink scar that circled the base
of Todd's right thumb. 'One of 'em sit up and have a go at you?'

Todd shook his head. 'Dog bite. When I was a kid. It's not so
bad in there, you know. You get used to it soon enough.'

'You'd have to. Not that it's all fun and games where I am,
mind. Been on my feet all morning...' The orderly rattled off a
litany of complaints and Todd nodded sympathetically, his mind
racing. Something about the orderly's face, with its meaty flesh and
bulbous nose, put him immediately in mind of his landlady's son,
Jimmy, a thickset twenty-year-old layabout with—according to his
mother—a weak heart that prevented him from fighting (or, as far
as anyone knew, doing anything except ambling down to the pub
on the corner). Jimmy must have a medical discharge certificate,
if he could only get hold of it...He hadn't needed one for Todd,
as the Administrative Department had been happy to accept his
explanation of call-up deferred on compassionate grounds (they'd
been so pleased to have an applicant who wasn't either a dribbling
half-wit or as old as Methuselah that a vague explanation about a
mentally-defective brother had sufficed, backed up by the promise
of a confirming letter in the post, which, despite the fact they'd
never received it, was never asked about again).

'...so I told him,' said the orderly, 'it's not my job to bugger
about with nitrous oxide. Those young doctors think they know
it all.'

'Which doctor was it?'

'Betterton. But they're all as bad as each other.'

'Are there many, then?' asked Todd. 'I'd have thought
they'd have been in the army.'

'Only three—Dr Unwin's another, and Dr Wemyss—
though, come to think of it, he's all right, really. Got money, he
has, but he doesn't swank about it. Nurses flirting with him left,
right and centre, though—he could have his pick. Look, mate,
I'd better get back. Nice talking to you.'

'Right you are. See you.'

Todd paused outside the door of the main room. He could hear the sound of people moving about, and Byrne's voice dictating monotonously to Miss Lynn. After a minute straining his ears for details, he gave up and went through to the refrigeration room to clean up after Mrs Lubbock. Betterton, Unwin and Wemyss, eh? He'd be on the lookout for them. His first aim was to find out where they drank. Meantime—through the half-open door he eyed a group of nurses walking down the corridor towards their quarters, discreetly appraising, and rejecting, faces, breasts and legs—there was the matter of choosing the right girl.

CHAPTER 10

Stratton, at the station, stood in front of DCI Lamb's desk while his superior, looking more like George Formby than ever, went through a series of facial contortions. Anyone would think, Stratton reflected wryly, that he'd asked the man to solve some impossible philosophical conundrum, not provide a few blokes for a search team.

'This,' Lamb jabbed his desk with a forefinger, 'isn't officially a murder enquiry, Stratton.'

'No, sir.'

'We're very busy at the moment.'

'Yes, sir,' said Stratton, wearily.

'There's a lot' (jab!) 'to be attended to, and I don't' (jab!) 'want' (jab!) 'anything overlooked.'

'No, sir. But Dr Byrne seems to think it wasn't an accident.'

'*Seems* to think?'

Stratton thought he might as well opt for a bit of arse-covering. 'He suggested the search, sir.'

'What do *you* think?'

'I'm not sure. Not until we have the results of the post-mortem.'

'Yes, but what did it' (jab!) '*look* like to you?'

'It's hard to say, sir, without some more information. Perhaps,' he added, 'you'd like to take a look yourself, sir. Give us the benefit of your opinion.' This was definitely pushing it, and Lamb gazed at him warily for what felt like about five minutes. Stratton, straining every nerve in an effort not to shout 'oh, fuck off', forced himself to meet his superior's eyes with what he fervently hoped was the guileless and sincere expression of one seeking assurance.

'I hope we can trust your judgement,' said Lamb. 'I'm sure we can spare one or two chaps if you think it's important.' The implication that Stratton would be for the high jump if it turned out not to be important buzzed in the air between them like an angry wasp.

'Thank you, sir.'

'Take Watkins and Piper'—two reservists, fair enough—'oh, and,' Lamb gave Stratton a look of pure malice, 'Arliss should be about somewhere.'

Stratton's heart sank. Arliss had such a knack for cocking things up that if there was anything there to find, he'd miss it, and Lamb bloody well knew it. 'Thank you, sir. We'll get started immediately.'

'I take it you haven't spoken to the family yet?'

'No, sir.'

'Better do it yourself, if you can. And be careful what you say—we don't want to alarm them if it's not necessary. Where are they?'

Damn, thought Stratton. 'I'll have to ask the hospital, sir.'

'Do that. If they're out of London, better get the local chaps to have a word. Otherwise...' he waved a hand. 'You know the drill. Use a car if necessary. I need you to sort this out—if there is anything to sort out—as soon as possible.'

'Yes, sir. Thank you.'

Watkins and Piper set off smartly in the direction of the bomb-site, with Arliss trailing them at an unenthusiastic distance. Stratton accompanied them and gave instructions to search the area thoroughly for anything that looked suspicious. Like most people, he supposed, he hated hospitals. He could never enter one without remembering how, when he was six and his mother had died, his father had stood, humiliated, before the almoner, twisting his cap in his huge farmer's hands as he tried to explain how they couldn't afford to pay the bill.

Dismissing his memories with an effort, he went to find the Administrative Department, where he spoke to a woman with thick, round spectacles who kept repeating, 'Dead? Dead?' in outraged tones, as if dying were some particularly disgusting contravention of the Hippocratic oath.

She took Stratton to see the Senior Registrar, a man with a voice so upper class that it sounded as if he were being slowly strangled with piano wire, who had an empty sherry decanter and an antelope hoof with a hinged lid (Stratton thought it might have been a snuff-box) on his desk to denote his vertiginously high status. After explaining the situation four times in slightly different words, he managed to elicit the information that Dr Reynolds was married and lived in Finchley.

On the way back to the station, he paused for a quick word with Ballard at the bomb-site (nothing to report), and, returning to West End Central, asked the desk sergeant to organise a car. After a few minutes of fuss and harrumphing, a Railton saloon and a driver appeared, and Stratton was borne off to North London in the company of Policewoman Harris, chosen on the grounds of her kind face and sensible demeanour.

The late Dr Reynolds's home was larger and handsomer than he'd expected, and Stratton wondered if he'd had a private income as well as his doctor's salary. God, he hated this part of the job: that split second before you said the words when they guessed from your face why you were there, and you'd have given anything not to say it and they'd have given anything not to hear it, then the bewildered denial, the growing comprehension, the wait for the anguished spasm of the face, the tears...The worst thing about it was having to perform the roles of unwilling participant and professional witness at the same time, sympathising while probing at grief to check its authenticity. *Christ.*

Shuddering inwardly, he pressed the bell. As he stood waiting, Harris by his side, he made the necessary mental adjustments, tuning himself, like a wireless, to the right level of spontaneity and compassion. A quick look at Harris, who was staring fixedly at her shoes, told him that she was doing the same.

Mrs Reynolds was a large-boned, fair woman. Her pale blue eyes widened when she saw them, and, before Stratton had a chance to introduce himself, she gabbled, 'It's Duncan, isn't it? He telephoned to say he'd be late—after ten, he said—but he didn't come home. I've been frantic—I telephoned the hospital last night, but they didn't know. What's happened to him?'

'I'm afraid, Mrs Reynolds,' Stratton began, 'that we have some bad news...'

CHAPTER 11

Half-past eight. Stratton checked his wristwatch as he stood in front of the door of the Swan pub in Tottenham. The top part had a panel of multicoloured engraved glass, criss-crossed with tape. Stratton peered between the head of a thistle and the leaves of an improbably solid-looking red flower, hoping not to spot the bulbous form of his brother-in-law Reg Booth. He needed a drink after the sort of day he'd had, but having to endure Reg's company would be too high a price to pay for it. Relations with Reg, which had gone back, more or less, to normal, since his son Johnny's near brush with a spell in borstal, had become sticky in recent weeks. This was partly due to the fact that Reg, ten years older than either Stratton or Doris's husband Donald, persisted in playing the schoolmaster or elder statesman or field-marshal or whichever other authority figure took his fancy, and also due to the reaction of Stratton and Donald to the news that Reg had had his right buttock punctured by a bayonet during a Home Guard exercise. Learning of this, they had choked with the effort of concealing their laughter, and, undeterred by the combined reproving stares of Jenny, Doris, the invalid himself, and his long-suffering wife Lilian, the pair of them had bolted from the room to Stratton's garden shed where they could roar in peace.

It would just have to be his arse, thought Stratton, as he squinted into the gloom. Stratton didn't know the individual responsible, but Reg was so irritating that he wouldn't mind betting it wasn't, as claimed, an accident.

'Is he in there?'

Stratton turned to see the tall, skinny form of Donald, who was peering over his shoulder. 'Christ, you made me jump! I can't see him, but...'

'Want to risk it? Safety in numbers.'

Stratton shrugged. 'Why not?'

'Come on then, before they run out. I'll get them.'

Stratton went in and found a corner table. A few minutes later Donald joined him, looking apologetic, with the beer. 'Halves only, I'm afraid. It is Thursday.' Supplies of beer, which had become increasingly erratic, usually ran out before the end of the week.

'Oh, well. We'll just have to make them last. Cheers.'

There was no point in asking Donald if he had any spare razor-blades, thought Stratton. His brother-in-law being fairer skinned than he, the poor chap's chin had now reached the consistency of raw sausage.

'I'll bet it's watered,' said Donald, peering suspiciously into his glass.

Stratton, who had heard this many times in the past couple of years, wondered if this was actually true, or just part of a general nostalgia for when life's necessities and pleasures weren't rationed, curtailed or simply 'off'.

'Bad day?' asked Donald.

Thinking of Byrne and Lamb and Mrs Reynolds's face and the fruitless search of the bomb-site, Stratton said, 'I've had better. People keep pissing on my head and telling me it's raining.'

'Me, too.' Donald, exempt from the forces courtesy of a perforated eardrum from a childhood bout of scarlet fever, had closed his camera shop the previous year, and was now working for a light engineering firm. (Reg, too old to be called up, never let his two younger brothers-in-law forget he'd served in the Great War, with every third sentence addressed to them beginning, 'Of course, in the *last* lot...')

'Here.' Stratton fished out his cigarettes. He only had two left, so—unless Donald had some—it meant doing without the last one before bed, which he always enjoyed, but it was worth it for the company.

Donald looked into the packet. 'It's all right,' he said, taking out his own, 'I've got a few.' Seeing the look of relief cross Stratton's face, he said, with a sort of gloomy satisfaction, 'I know. Bloody awful.'

They smoked in companionable silence, with Donald, who was facing the right way, keeping an eye on the door in case Reg should appear. After a couple of minutes he glanced over at the non-activity at the bar and said, 'Probably be too late now. He won't get a drink if he does come in, so he'll bugger off.'

'Shouldn't serve him anyway,' grumbled Stratton. 'Not his pub.'

Reg lived two streets away from Stratton and Donald and usually frequented the Marquis of Granby, but patronised the Swan just often enough to make constant vigilance a necessity. 'I didn't expect to see you, though.'

'Bit of a turn-up at home.' Donald grimaced.

'What happened?'

'That woman you dug out last night—Mrs Ingram—Doris brought her back from hospital to stay with us.'

'Why on earth would she do that?'

'No known relatives, apparently, and the husband's in the army. She's in a bad way; Doris can't get anything out of her.'

'Shocked, you mean?'

'She's that all right. Doris said she didn't speak all afternoon, and she didn't seem to understand a word that was said to her. The doctor had a look at her—said she just needs a rest. Then she started repeating things.'

'How do you mean?'

'Well, Doris asked her if she wanted a cup of tea—I was there—and she sort of...screwed her face up, as if she was trying to make sense of it, and then she said, "Cup-tea, cup-tea," like a parrot. Doris asked her if she wanted to lie down, and she came back "lie, lie, lie". And when they went upstairs she went to the bathroom, picked up the nailbrush, and started trying to clean the basin with it. Daft behaviour.'

'Sounds like shock,' said Stratton. 'Takes people different ways. Terrible, losing your house like that—and she's all on her own. Still, she's bound to recover once she's had a bit of a rest. How's Madeleine liking her job?' Donald and Doris's pretty sixteen-year-old daughter, having returned from evacuation in Essex, had started work in a factory that made seats for Lancaster bombers.

'Loves it. So far, anyw— Oh, Christ.'

'He's not, is he?' asked Stratton, whose back was to the door.

'Just come in. He's on his own.' Their brother-in-law, bulging in Home Guard khaki, was making his way to the bar. Donald put his hand in his pocket and, taking out his penknife, weighed it in his palm, then rolled his eyes horribly and let his tongue loll out of his mouth.

'Everything went black, Your Honour, and an impulse came over me,' murmured Stratton.

'Wish we knew the bloke who speared him in the arse,' said Donald. 'I'd buy him a pint.'

'If you could get it,' said Stratton, keeping one eye on the bar. 'Look, she's not serving him.'

Donald followed his gaze. 'She's not put the sign up, though.' The sign was a piece of wood that hung, all too frequently nowadays, above the bar, chalked with the words 'Sorry. No Beer'.

'Look away.' Stratton hastily produced a stub of pencil and a scrap of paper, and both men bent over, pretending to study it.

'Think he's seen us?' muttered Donald.

'Dunno. He might pretend he hasn't now she's refused to serve him,' said Stratton, considering that the loss of face might mean a hasty retreat. 'Don't look up, for God's sake.'

'He might come over to cadge a fag—he's got the neck.'

'He'll be—'

'Evenin' all!' Reg's liver-coloured face, with its drooping grey moustache, appeared between them, and he clapped Stratton on the shoulder in his usual just-too-hard-to-be-jovial manner. Stratton palmed the paper and shoved it back in his pocket, hoping that his brother-in-law hadn't noticed it was blank. 'How's tricks?'

'Fine, thanks. Just talking about the allotment.'

'Got a problem, have you?' Unlike Stratton, Reg knew bugger-all about gardening, but that didn't stop him talking balls by the yard.

Donald, who had been glaring at him, asked abruptly, 'Couldn't you get served?'

'They've just run out. Not had a chance to put the sign up.'

'Hmmph.' Donald gave an upward jerk of his chin that could have meant either 'Wouldn't you bleeding know' or 'I don't believe you.' Reg naturally chose to interpret it as the former, and said, 'I daresay if she'd known I was coming in...'

'I daresay,' murmured Stratton, sardonically.

'Anyway, I'd best be off. Can't really spare the time, to be honest, but I thought it would be nice for us chaps to have a bit of a chat.' Given that Stratton and Donald had decided to come to the pub on a whim and without consultation, this statement was patently untrue, but neither man wanted to prolong the encounter by challenging it. Reg then employed the latest refinement in a battery of mannerisms that were already quite annoying enough, thank you very fucking much. He'd started it in the last year, after, Stratton guessed, seeing something similar in a film; it was a particular intense look, as if he were judging whether or not to let you in on some secret or otherwise important development, but then—regretfully—decided that you weren't quite ready to hear it just yet. This time, he even went as far as opening his mouth, then closing it sharply again before saying with apparent casualness, 'Seeing as I'm here, you don't happen to have a ciga-rette, do you? I've run out.'

'Sorry,' said Stratton, 'I've run out as well.'

'Me too,' said Donald. 'Just smoked my last.'

This was followed by an impasse, during which Reg stared first at Stratton and then at Donald as if attempting some sort of mental X-ray technique, while they stared back with conspicu-ously neutral expressions.

'Well, gents,' said Reg, when it became apparent that neither of his brothers-in-law was going to relent, 'I'll bid you goodnight, then.'

''Night, Reg.'

''Night.'

Stratton and Donald held their positions as Reg walked slowly to the door, and, turning round, gave them a hurt and lingering last look before disappearing through it.

After a short pause, Donald said, 'You know what really gets my goat? That look—*I thought better of you than that*—when you know the fucker's got half a dozen fags in his pocket.'

Hearing the cue for the start of one of their favourite pastimes (only indulged in private, by unspoken consent, because, although enjoyable, it was undeniably childish), Stratton said, 'Yes, but the thing that really annoys me are his feet. Why are they so small? Why doesn't he just fall over?'

'Pomposity,' said Donald. 'Keeps him upright. Especially since he got that sergeant's stripe. I'm surprised he hasn't asked us to salute him.'

'And the way he raises himself up on his toes,' said Stratton, 'as if he's going to fart and wants everyone to know it.'

They continued in this vein for some time, running through Reg's belief that he was a comedian (and underlining it frequently by describing himself as being 'cursed' with a sense of humour); his general buffoonery; his bullying of his wife Lilian, and his air of appearing to know more about everything than anyone else did.

'But you know the worst thing,' said Donald, suddenly serious, 'is that he makes me feel like a complete shit for saying all this, even though he hasn't got a clue that I'm saying any of it.'

'Does he? Make you feel bad, I mean?'

Donald held his gaze for a moment, then grinned and shook his head. 'Naah...Come on, drink up and let's get home. Doris must have Mrs Ingram safely tucked up in bed by now.'

'Good idea. I could do with an early night myself—then I might have a chance of being able to think straight tomorrow.'

12

Todd stopped on his way to work to watch the policemen walking slowly and purposefully across the bomb-site, pausing now and then to inspect the ground. The fact that they were still searching after yesterday obviously meant that they had not, so far, found anything of note, which was good. In any case, they wouldn't find any trace that he'd ever been near the place— he'd been too careful for that. Just as well, since Dr Byrne had pronounced that the death—caused by blows to the head—was suspicious. And the police, clearly, agreed with him.

Across the way, he noticed a gaggle of nurses chattering and laughing amongst themselves, their red capes and white caps standing out, the only clean, bright things in a landscape of dusty greys and buffs. He observed them as an entity, not as individuals, much as he might a group of cows in a field, until one figure, slightly to the left of the centre, drew his eye. He didn't know exactly what it was about her, but he knew—after what? Thirty seconds? A minute?—that he was looking at *his* girl. That it was *now* and it was *her* impressed him with such force that it might have been a thunderbolt. Yet, strangely, it wasn't love that he felt, it was, simply and directly, knowing that this one *belonged to him*. He just knew it. And now he looked more closely, he could see that she was a knockout. Dark hair, dark, almond-shaped eyes, creamy-white skin, nice legs, and, so far as he could make out beneath the cloak, a shapely figure. And she looked as if she were kind—not in a nurse's way, the put-on, professional caring, but really, properly, kind.

He didn't stare. That would be rude, and besides, he did not want to draw attention to himself. Now that she was earmarked, she'd keep. And when he was Dr Dacre, he'd have her. He needed her name, though. That was important: he must know who she was. He moved closer, making as if to walk past the nurses, hoping for a closer look as well as information. As he crossed the road, the group began to break up, leaving his girl standing alone on the pavement. She stared at the bomb-site for a moment, apparently in a dream. Another nurse turned back and called out, 'Come on, Marchant! We'll be late!' and then, in exasperation, 'Fay!'

Fay Marchant. My girl Fay, he thought. He watched her run to catch up with her friend and then, just as he was about to turn away, he heard another female voice, slightly breathless, calling, 'Dr Wemyss!' Remembering that this was the name of one of the junior doctors the porter had told him about, he stopped. One nurse—a coppery redhead with a sharp-looking, almost fox-like face—had broken away from the group going towards the hospital, and was walking back towards (and, judging by her movements and the way she was holding her body, beginning to flirt with) a man of about his own age, tall, with carroty-red hair and a relaxed air. Perhaps the nurse noticed that they were being watched, because she suddenly turned her head and looked straight at Todd. For a moment their eyes locked, and he was sure he saw a flicker of surprised recognition. He turned away, quickly. Had he seen her before? Had they met? Where? His memory, usually reliable, came up blank. Probably nothing, but...Anyway, there was nothing he could do about it, at least for now.

And that was Dr Wemyss, was it? Very useful. Two for the price of one, how about that? Todd glanced back for just long enough—the nurse had resumed the conversation and didn't see him—so that he'd be able to recognise his man again, then took himself off to the mortuary.

Lying on a trolley in the main room was an enormous corpse covered in a sheet. 'Allow me to introduce you,' said Higgs. 'Mr Albert Corner.' As Higgs uncovered him, beginning at the head, Todd saw, first, wispy white hair, then an elderly face with the dull damson blush and smashed capillaries of the dipso, then the mound of a huge belly, and, finally, a vast pair of women's pale pink silk drawers, one leg of which was hitched up by the groin, displaying a pendulous scrotum.

'How the hell...?'

Higgs shrugged. 'Don't ask me. Let's just hope someone claims him before he gets all frozen up like that Mrs Lubbock. We'd never get him off the tray and he looks like he'd take a week to thaw out.'

'Who'd want to claim *that*?'

'Buggered if I know. Landlady found him. Poor woman— must of been a hell of a shock. Divorced, apparently.'

'I'm not surprised. Moral degeneracy, by the look of him.'

'Well, I should think it was a bit more than pissing in the sink.'

Dr Byrne's face appeared round the door of his office, frowning as he caught the last words. 'Not ready yet?'

'Sorry, Dr Byrne.'

'Well, make sure you have those things off him before Miss Lynn arrives.' He withdrew and closed the door.

'Come on,' said Higgs. 'You take the head end.'

They manhandled the fat man onto the table with his head resting on a wooden block and, after a lot of huffing and puffing, managed to remove the silk drawers. Todd tried, as much as possible, to keep his eyes closed while this was going on and think of the girl but the corpse before him kept mutating, horribly, into that of Reynolds. This, combined with handling the loose, clammy folds of skin of the stomach and thighs, made him nauseous.

'For Christ's sake,' said Higgs, 'I know he's no oil painting, but you should be used to it by now.'

'Something I ate,' Todd muttered through closed lips.

'Well, you've gone green, and I don't want him covered in spew, so piss off outside if you're going to throw up.'

'Thanks.' Leaving Higgs whistling 'Nice People', Todd stumbled out into the yard just in time to heave his meagre breakfast down a drain.

Once Dr Byrne had finished, and was removing his rubber gloves in a tight manner that suggested he was skinning his own hands, Todd returned. The cause of death was a heart attack. As he helped sew the body back together with twine and clean up before the next job, Higgs brought up the subject of Dr Reynolds. 'Could be a really good murder. You've not done one of those, have you?'

'*What?*'

'A proper murder. Not just some chap killing his wife. Something with a bit more to it. It can't have been a robbery,' Higgs added thoughtfully, 'or they'd have had his wallet off him, wouldn't they? Or perhaps they didn't mean to kill him and panicked when they realised what they'd done. Dr Byrne found a bruise on the back of his head, remember? He could have been pushed and fell backwards, but I'd say it's more likely he was clobbered from behind.'

'Can you tell that?' asked Todd.

'Not always…Mind you, we've had some very odd things. About six months ago we had a bloke run over by a car. Brought in upstairs, still alive. Not a mark on him, so they discharged him, and he's died the next day. When Dr Byrne opened him up he found a ruptured kidney. You'd think the doctor who examined him would have found something, but no…Come to think of it, that was Dr Reynolds. Dr Byrne was not impressed—said he hadn't examined him properly, but with no bruising I suppose he just didn't think of it.'

Todd's interest quickened. 'That's terrible, sending him home like that.'

Higgs looked grim. 'It wasn't the only time, neither. I don't like to speak ill of the dead, but...' He shook his head.

So it was as he'd thought: Reynolds was in the habit of making a hash of things—and that was with the proper training. He was going to be far, far better. And he'd have his girl. Of course, he hadn't heard her voice yet, but he was sure that anyone who looked like that would speak properly...

He listened with half an ear to Higgs's various theories about Dr Reynolds's death and wondered about the medical exemption certificate he'd filched from his landlady's son Jimmy's room the previous evening. Provided he could get hold of the right paper, the green form would be easy enough to forge, now that he knew what it looked like. The stamps that validated it were a different matter—he'd have to steam off the ones on Jimmy's certificate and doctor them carefully so that they passed muster. That meant, of course, that he wouldn't be able to put Jimmy's certificate back in his room, but there was no reason for him to he suspected of its theft. As far as both his landlady and her son were concerned, he—Sam Todd, that is—had a certificate of his own, because he'd taken care to tell them so when he arrived.

Jimmy's 'weak heart' had turned out to be something called cardiomegaly. Todd had looked this up and found that it meant an enlarged heart, and that the condition could be either pathological (related to significant heart disease), physiological (related to exercise or other physical activity), or idiopathic (with no known cause). The last bit made it sound promising, as was the fact that it was diagnosed by X-ray and couldn't be spotted by eye or some simple physical test. Also, it was only sometimes accompanied by irregular heartbeats—or rather, Todd corrected himself—arrhythmia, and palpitations. This was definitely a bonus because, as far as he knew, his heartbeat was normal. Other symptoms, apparently, might be shortness of breath and dizziness, and they'd be easy enough to fake if necessary. The treatment seemed to consist largely of keeping healthy and visiting the doctor to have one's blood pressure checked, so that wouldn't pose a problem. All in all, it was a lot better than bad eyesight or flat feet.

At the end of the day, when Dr Byrne gave him the keys to his office to take upstairs to the porter, Todd slipped them into his pocket. Alone in the mortuary, on night duty, he waited until the coast was clear, then went down the corridor to Byrne's office to search for his notes on Reynolds, which, by a stroke of good fortune, were on the top of the pile in the tray.

After the usual preamble—*Name, age, height, probable weight...*—came the extent and position of hypostasis. That, Todd now knew, was the discolouration from blood collecting in the lower parts—not to be confused with bruising. There seemed to have been quite a bit of hypostasis, with the bruising and external wounds confined to the head. *Three lacerated wounds— an inch and a half to three inches in length...Bruising to edges and contusion to deeper tissues of the scalp...some cranial damage... fracture...evidence of foreign matter...Inconclusive as to whether wounds were produced by weapon or fall. Wounding may have taken place at separate location and subsequent exertion resulted in collapse.*

Todd sat down in Dr Byrne's chair. It wasn't exactly cut and dried, but nobody had seen him, had they? And even if they had, they couldn't have been close enough to be certain, in the dark, of his identity, otherwise *he* would have spotted *them*. All the same, he ought to keep an eye out for the policeman, who was bound to be back.

He locked the office door behind him and took the keys up to the porter, claiming to have forgotten about it earlier. Then, returning to the mortuary, he went to the refrigerated room, pulled out the smallest, lightest corpse—a skinny teenage girl the colour of tallow, suffocated in bomb debris—and laid her on one of the slabs. She would be tonight's subject. On other nights when he was in the mortuary alone, he practised examining his 'patients' and performing such procedures on them as would leave no trace, or dissecting organs he'd saved from disposal, but tonight was to be his self-imposed weekly anatomy test. He drew back the sheet that covered the body and brandished it in the manner of a matador before bundling it up and throwing it into a corner. Observing her, naked on her back, he mentally superimposed Fay Marchant's features onto the underbred rodent face and *her* curves onto the meagre body. Idly, he cupped the breast nearest to him and rubbed the nipple with his thumb. The flesh was inert, cold and slippery beneath his touch. 'Oh, Fay,' he murmured. 'Fay...' When he was Dr Dacre, he'd have *her* like this, at his disposal, to do with as he wished—though not, of course, in a mortuary...Taking a coin from his pocket, he said, 'Heads or tails?' and flipped it into the air.

'Tails. So,' he said to the dead girl, 'if you don't mind, I'll start with your feet. Muscles, I think. First layer, then...*Extensor brevis digitorum, abductor pollicis, flexor brevis digitorum...*'

He worked slowly and methodically, occasionally, when he forgot something, consulting the dissection manual. After an hour or so he'd worked his way up to the head. 'Epicranial region, one muscle, *occipito-frontalis*...auricular region, three muscles...'

He stopped to think, tapping his fingers on the girl's cheek and frowning. Being alone with the dead at times like this didn't bother him—in fact, he felt an odd sort of kinship with the corpses. After all, he'd died himself, hadn't he, in a way? It was just that he happened to be still inhabiting the same body.

Perhaps, he thought, I should get a book on psychiatry. Maybe he'd find out something about himself. The idea of that made him laugh out loud. As if any of those professors knew—or could even guess—anything about him. Even if they were to interview him, he'd run rings round them. All the same, psychiatry was an interesting—and comparatively new, and certainly underrated—branch of medicine, and he could do whatever he wanted, couldn't he? He might win a prize, one day, for advancing the understanding of the human mind...

Hearing a commotion in the corridor, he covered Maisie Lambert with another bullfighter's flourish, and went out to greet the bearers of the first corpses of the night. Perhaps they'd be jigsaw jobs—a practical opportunity to practise his skills as an anatomist. He hoped so.

CHAPTER

13

Stratton glanced at his wristwatch—five o'clock—and scraped absent-mindedly at his itchy chin with a thumbnail. The day had been entirely unproductive and very frustrating—now he'd had some decent sleep, he wanted to get on. However, those of Reynolds's colleagues he'd spoken to had been just as bewildered as Mrs Reynolds yesterday, though without the tears. The hospital had been co-operative about letting him use a spare consulting room to conduct the interviews, but, beyond telling him that Reynolds had been a valued colleague, none of the doctors had said anything of interest. It wasn't just a matter of not speaking ill of the dead, he thought; it was also the fact that medical folk would be bound to stick together. Stratton couldn't blame them— coppers would do exactly the same. Perhaps tomorrow, when he saw the nurses, the results would be better. The other problem was that, Dr Byrne having been out of his mortuary for most of the day, Stratton was completely in the dark as to the results of the post-mortem. After two days of searching, Ballard and the others had come up with sod-all from the bomb-site, and the Home Office analyst, he knew, would take several days over the bricks and whatnot, but at least if he knew *how* the bloke had died, it would be a help.

By five-thirty, Byrne was back in his office, and insisted on reading out a lot of guff about rectal temperatures and the condition of the natural orifices before giving Stratton the general gist, which was—once you'd stripped away all the medical terminology—that he didn't know exactly how, or even where, Reynolds had died, but he hadn't had any booze on board. 'You mean,' Stratton asked, 'you can't actually tell if someone walloped him or if he simply fell over and hit his head?'

'Not precisely,' said Byrne. 'But I should say he was struck—there are, after all, three distinct wounds, and it seems unlikely that he should have fallen backwards three times at almost the same angle.'

'What if he were pushed? Or if someone rammed his head down repeatedly?'

'That's certainly possible, but it's pretty unlikely.'

'Could the wounds have been made by a brick? I mean, if someone hit him with it.'

'Well, there's not much leverage. It isn't like a cosh or an iron bar. You could certainly knock someone out with a brick, but I should think it would be quite difficult to kill them—an adult, anyway. However, it's a possibility. I take it you haven't had the results of the analysis of the matter found beneath the head.'

'Not yet, no.'

'Well, if the weapon was a brick, or his head was banged down on one, there should be some hairs adhering to it.'

Stratton, who'd worked that out for himself, asked, 'How much force would be needed?'

'Hard to say…A well-nourished woman could have done it, if that's what you mean.'

'But she'd have to be rather tall, wouldn't she? Assuming they were both upright, I mean. The wounds are on the top of the head, and Reynolds was…what? Six foot?'

Byrne glanced at his notes. 'Five foot eleven. But it depends where she was standing. The ground's very uneven.'

'Pretty hard to keep your balance, especially if there was a tussle…But you said Reynolds might not have been killed at the bomb-site. If someone was dragging him around, there's more chance they'd have been spotted, even in the dark. Still…' Stratton sighed. 'What about the time of death?'

'Judging from the temperature, I'd say, with the conditions during the night, he'd probably been dead between four to eight hours by the time we saw him.'

'So...' Stratton did a quick calculation. 'Between two a.m. and six a.m.'

'That would be about right.'

'I suppose that narrows it down a bit. It would have been light at, what...quarter to six?'

'Thereabouts.'

'Surprising no-one spotted him earlier. My sergeant said it was reported at...' Stratton thumbed through his notebook, 'five-and-twenty past eight. If he fell, or was attacked, else-where—when it was getting light—and managed to get to the bomb-site under his own steam before he died, perhaps someone noticed him staggering about.'

'He might not have been staggering,' said Byrne reprovingly. 'He might have been walking normally until the effects of the exertion caught up with him.'

'But he'd have had blood on him, wouldn't he?' said Stratton. 'He wasn't wearing a hat to hide it, was he, and my chaps haven't found—'

A knock at the office door stopped him.

Byrne sighed. 'Come!'

The bespectacled woman from the Administrative Department appeared, looking on the verge of hysterics. 'Inspector, thank heavens you're still here! A terrible thing, quite dreadful...'

'What is it, Miss Crombie?'

'One of the nurses, Dr Byrne—Leadbetter—we've just found her in one of the upstairs operating theatres. One of the porters found her. He fetched me. I told him not to let anyone in there until you'd seen—'

'What's happened to her?' asked Stratton, gently.

'She's dead, Inspector!' For a moment, impatience overrode distress. 'The porter says she's quite cold, and her face is blue—I saw that for myself. You must come at once.'

'We're not using the upstairs theatres at the moment,' said Miss Crombie, as they went up the stairs. 'Everything was moved to the basement when the bombing started. Otherwise she'd have been found immediately.'

'Why was the porter there?' asked Stratton.

'He went to fetch a screen and she was behind it. The room's being used for storage, you see.'

An elderly porter, grey in the face and shaken, was outside the door to the operating theatre, bent over with his hands on his knees. 'Gave me quite a turn, seeing her laying there.'

'I'm not surprised,' said Stratton. 'Why don't you go and get yourself a cup of tea? But not too far away, because I'll need to talk to you later.'

The man looked relieved. 'Right you are.'

'Perhaps, Miss Crombie,' said Byrne, 'you could organise a trolley?'

A similar look of relief passed across the administrator's features. 'Of course, Dr Byrne. At once.'

Miss Crombie having left, Stratton and Byrne entered the theatre. It was full of pieces of medical equipment, and the dead nurse was not immediately apparent. 'Must be over there.' Byrne pointed to a folding wooden screen in the corner. Stratton pushed aside various bits of clinical paraphernalia to make a path through the room.

They saw Nurse Leadbetter's feet first, then a pair of long, slender legs. She was lying on her back with her stockings torn and her uniform rucked up over her knees, stained dark round the crotch where her bladder had emptied itself. There was a red woollen scarf around her neck and the face above it was purple and suffused with blood, the tongue lolling obscenely from the mouth. Bulging brown eyes as big as gobstoppers stared up at the ceiling and tendrils of copper hair had escaped from the cap, which was askew. She couldn't, Stratton thought, have been much older than seventeen—not much more than his own daughter. He turned away from the body, gripped by the mixture of anger, grief and disgust that always threatened to engulf him at such times.

'Strangulation by ligature,' said Byrne, kneeling beside her. 'She was only young, poor lamb.'

Once again, Stratton was taken aback by the unexpected compassion. Byrne had always seemed so dry...Perhaps I've got him all wrong, he thought. 'Let's just hope,' the pathologist continued, 'that she wasn't interfered with, as well.' Very gently, he unwound the scarf from her neck. 'Abrasions. You can see the grooves—horizontal, not very deep, but pretty uniform...some bruising...'

'How long do you think she's been dead?'

Stratton expected the question to be greeted with exasperation, but Byrne said, 'She's cold, and there's some rigor in the face and neck, but...' the pathologist felt the arms and chest, 'not much further, so probably not more than six hours.'

'That would be...' Stratton checked his wristwatch, 'any time after midday.'

'That's right. I'll make some sketches, but I can't do much more here. Do you want to see if the trolley's coming?'

'Right away. Do you mind if I use your telephone? We'll need to lock up the room and put a policeman outside overnight, and I'll have to speak to Fingerprints, too. Although, to be honest...' he glanced around him at the assorted medical clutter, 'if every Tom, Dick and Harry has been hauling this stuff all over the place, I don't hold out much hope...'

'Of course,' said Byrne. 'Help yourself.'

The last thing Stratton saw before he turned away to make for the door were Byrne's fingers gently brushing over the dead girl's face, closing her eyes. 'There we are,' he murmured. 'You poor, poor lass.' Just shows how little I know the man, Stratton thought.

Stratton found the trolley and made his telephone calls, then returned to the Administrative Department with Miss Crombie, where they ascertained that Leadbetter's Christian name was Marian, and that she was an orphan with a brother serving overseas. He then spent ten completely unenlightening minutes with the old porter and a fruitless half-hour going through the dead girl's unremarkable belongings in the nurses' quarters in the hospital basement, before returning to the station for a very unpleasant half-hour with DCI Lamb, who seemed to hold him personally responsible for Leadbetter's death.

In each of the three different buses that took him home—diversions caused by flying bombs—he turned the problem of Reynolds over and wondered if his death, and Nurse Leadbetter's, might be connected in some way. One male, one female, one bashed with a brick, one strangled, perhaps raped; one outside the hospital, one inside. It didn't seem likely, but it was best to keep an open mind...Reynolds's wife had said that she was expecting him back by nine p.m., but hadn't worried at first because he was often kept late and sometimes slept at the hospital. So, as none of the other doctors had seen him after half past eight in the evening, he must have stopped off somewhere en route home. An appointment? An affair? And, if an affair, could it have been with Nurse Leadbetter? Stratton guessed that, in life, she must have been nice—or, at least, presentable—looking. Had Reynolds been taking advantage of the poor girl? Or was it some utterly senseless, random thing—one of the patients going berserk for some reason, but in that case, surely anyone out of bed would have been spotted...? Whatever it was, they'd need to interview everyone at the hospital, and do a house-to-house enquiry around the area for Reynolds, and that would mean putting more men on the job, which would undoubtedly annoy DCI Lamb. He spent a miserable moment reflecting that, whatever happened, he was bound to end up with the wretched Arliss, who could break into a sweat just by standing still. It was just his luck to find himself going arse over tit on the thin ice of half-knowledge, with nothing definite to hold on to. And he'd have to talk to all the doctors again about Nurse Leadbetter, and Ballard would have to do the same with the nonmedical staff...

An Empty Death

He rubbed a hand over his face, feeling depressed. Poor, poor girl. What a waste of a young life...If only someone—other than the usual lunatics and time-wasters who presented themselves at such times—would come forward and tell them something, they might get somewhere...

Todd, who had knocked off before Nurse Leadbetter was discovered, was smartly clad in his jacket and tie, sitting in the Black Horse pub on Rathbone Place. His plan was to go into several pubs in the area and discover, by enquiry, which one Dr Wemyss (and therefore his friends) frequented. With a description—and, by good fortune, Wemyss, being tall and red-headed, would tend to stand out in a crowd—it simply sounded as if he was trying to catch up with a chap he knew, and, if pressed, he could give a false name. This was his first attempt.

The barmaid, fleshy and middle-aged with unhealthily pallid skin and a predatory eye, whose thick slash of scarlet lipstick made her look like a ghoul that had forgotten to wipe its mouth, hadn't recognised his description.

'Well,' he said, 'perhaps I'll wait a bit, and see if he comes by. I'm sure he mentioned this pub.' Tired after only a few hours' restless sleep the previous night on one of the mortuary slabs, he thought that he might as well butter up the woman a bit on the off chance of a second whisky before continuing his search. Taking his newly acquired (or rather, stolen) psychiatry book out of his knapsack, he put it on the bar.

'What you got there, then?'

'This? It's about things that go wrong in the mind.' He tapped the side of his head.

'That doesn't sound very nice, dear.'

'It isn't. It's about senile deterioration.'

'What's that, then?'

'Some people get it when they're older. They lose their mental faculties.'

'You a doctor, then?'

Todd gave her an enigmatic smile. 'In a manner of speaking.'

Concluding, as he'd meant her to, that he was the sort of doctor who was rather more than just run-of-the-mill, the barmaid asked, 'Can you cure that, then? Losing your...' Now she tapped her head. 'Because that's what happened to my mum. She's not been herself for a couple of years, now. Keeps asking for sweets—we give her our ration, but we can't get no more, and she's always making a fuss...And knitting. The whole time. I've been unpicking things she done before, so's she's got enough wool to keep going. She don't *make* nothing, just knits. It gets on your nerves. Can you do anything for it?'

'Not at the moment, I'm afraid. We're looking in to various treatments, but these things take time. The brain is a complicated organ, you know, and we don't understand everything, not by a long chalk. Your mother is very fortunate to have you to look after her with such sensitivity,' he added, gallantly.

Ten minutes' more sympathetic listening and some pseudo-scientific comments got Todd his second Scotch ('This is meant for regulars only, so don't say nothing or my life won't be worth living'), after which he decided it was time to try another pub. As he left, however, he saw Inspector Stratton marching down the opposite side of the road. The big policeman was easy to recognise, being at least half a head taller and several inches broader across the shoulders than anyone else on the pavement. Todd stood watching him for a moment, thinking that even though the man wasn't wearing the uniform, he would have spotted him for a copper; it was something in the upright carriage and the measured nature of the walk.

Stratton tramped to the corner of Oxford Street and turned left. Realising that he wasn't heading back to the police station—

Higgs had said he came from West End Central—Todd decided that it might, on the basis that information gleaned nearly always came in useful, be a good idea to follow him. Besides, he was curious.

It was harder than he expected. For one thing, it was still light, and although the big policeman seemed preoccupied, he got on and off several buses, forcing Todd to dodge about and, on two occasions, duck down so that he was hidden by the seats. They were heading north, but it was a part of London he didn't know. They left the West End and went through the City, and then some of the East End, before Stratton boarded a bus—his last one, it turned out—heading for Tottenham. When he finally alighted, Todd, keeping a cautious distance, followed him down the high street and right into Lansdowne Road, which was full of small, semi-detached mock Tudor houses, built between the wars, which reminded him of the ones in Norbury. How dismal, he thought, to come home every night to *this*, as the policeman did, as his own father had done, and as he himself would have done, if he had not struck out for better things...

He halted abruptly as Stratton stopped, opened a garden gate, and went up a path. A second later, before he'd had time to take out a key, the front door flew open and a woman appeared, talking animatedly while at the same time removing, and then folding, a cretonne overall. Even from a distance of about fifty feet, with his view partially obscured by a privet hedge, Todd could see that she was pretty and slightly plump, and, moreover, she looked delighted to see the policeman who was, presumably, her husband. As he watched, Stratton bent to kiss her on the cheek, then took his hat off and set it lightly on her head. She gave a little shriek and, whipping it off, patted her chestnut hair self-consciously as she followed him into the house.

Todd leant against the hedge and lit a cigarette, disconcerted by the sight of their fond silliness. They are in love, he thought. Of course, there was no reason why they should not be—it was simply that he hadn't expected it. Why, he didn't know, but it bothered him. Troubling, too, was the pang of disappointment he'd experienced when the front door closed, the feeling that he was being deliberately shut out from the light and warmth of a happy place. Even though—and this was truly strange—it was the type of place he despised.

Disturbed by his reaction to the undistinguished little home, Todd walked up the road and, turning a corner, saw that there was a muddy, rutted alley, with high wooden fences on each side, that separated the Lansdowne Road back gardens from the ones of the next street down. He wandered into it, trying to estimate how many gardens he'd have to pass before he reached the Strattons'. When he judged he'd got there, he stood on tiptoe to look over the fence and saw, through a back window, Stratton's wife moving about in what looked like a scullery. The garden was neat, but fairly nondescript: about sixty feet long, with an Anderson shelter and a couple of apple trees on a scrubby-looking lawn, some flowerbeds, a small shed, and a hen house with a run made of wire netting.

He ducked out of sight as Stratton's wife approached the window, and then, gingerly raising himself once more on his toes, he saw that she was standing, her eyes cast down, in front of what must—because he could see a tap—be a sink. Stratton, hatless now, entered the little room and, standing behind his wife (he was at least a foot taller than she was), he put his arms round her and kissed her on the top of the head. Todd saw her look up and smile, and then, as she twisted round to face the policeman, Stratton's eyes met his. An instant later, Todd was sprinting down the alley in the direction of the high street, but it was unmistakable: the man had looked straight at him. He half expected to hear a roar of rage and footsteps pursuing him, but none came. Once he reached the main road, he forced himself to slow down so as not to draw attention to himself by charging down the pavement where there were people milling around. In any case, Stratton had only seen him for a second, and it was pretty difficult to identify someone from a glimpse of their eyes and the top of their head.

Todd found the bus stop and stood waiting, keeping an eye out in case Stratton should appear. After five minutes, when it was evident that this wasn't going to happen, he felt able to relax. A few moments later a bus arrived, and, having ascertained that it was supposed to be going back into the centre of town, he boarded it and sat, elbows on the back of the seat in front, smoking and thinking, as the vehicle snorted its slow way past the houses and shops.

He felt gloomy and rejected, and knowing that this wasn't entirely irrational didn't help. It's all very well for Inspector Stratton, he thought. He can be contented in his own skin, with his house and his wife, because he's only ever been one person, not a whole series of different ones. He wondered what it would be like to have a wife; to love and to be loved without pretence. He thought of his brown-eyed nurse and smiled. She was his, all right. Strange, he'd always recoiled from the idea of love—it was too genuine, too intimate. Now he knew different. *She* had made him feel that way. As for the illusion of intimacy, he could buy it, if only for a short time; barring infection, it carried no risk. The thought of Stratton and his wife lingered in his mind, encased in a sort of nimbus, as the bus trundled towards Stoke Newington, and by the time it had reached Shoreditch, he'd come to a decision. Alighting from the bus at the London Bridge terminal, he crossed the river and walked up King William Street in the twilight, past missing railings, a group of auxiliary firemen herding squealing pigs across a bomb-site, and people hastily doing their blackouts. At the top, he found a bus that would take him to Soho, and boarded it.

It would be easy enough to obtain the brief comfort of a warm body next to his own—at this hour, the place was heaving with tarts, lured there by the promise of easy money from the foreign servicemen. He paused in Old Compton Street, outside the Swiss, wondering if he wanted a drink first—it seemed an odd thing not to know, but he didn't. He opened the door and, glimpsing wall-to-wall khaki and air-force blue, all of it wreathed in smoke, decided it was too crowded. He was about to close the door again when a slender female shape detached itself from the mass and came towards him, jiggling on platform-soled shoes.

She was clearly young—no more than twenty—with darkish hair, hazel eyes and long lashes, but her face had a thick, almost clownish coating of powder, and her mouth was caked in scarlet lipstick. She stopped in front of him and struck a pose, one hip stuck out, and said, 'Looking for someone, dear?'

As the light caught her hair, he saw that it was bright chestnut, like Stratton's wife's, and it was this, more than anything else, that decided him. 'I think I've just found her, haven't I?'

'That's nice, dear. You coming along with me, then?'

'Got a room?'

'Yes, dear. Three quid. More if you want something special.'

'Just the usual, but I want to rent it, not buy it. I'm not some Yank with more money than sense.'

The girl considered him, her head on one side. 'All right. Two pound ten. Unless…' she put her hand on his arm, 'you could manage a few shillings more? I've got a fine to pay, and I've been poorly all week, so I'm short…I'll give you ever such a good time.'

Todd didn't believe the bit about the fine—it was something they often tried—but he said, 'We'll see. Go on, I'll follow you.'

She left at a fast clip and he trailed her, at a discreet distance, to a dilapidated house in Frith Street, where he hesitated for a couple of minutes before following her inside. She was waiting for him in a dirty hall with scabby-looking walls. 'Up here,' she called, from somewhere beyond the stairs.

Bare and grimy, with a few sticks of cheap furniture, and a balding candlewick bedspread, the room had cumulus clouds of damp on all the walls. A couple of canes stood in one corner, one with a red ribbon dangling forlornly from its handle, and there was a cluster of empty beer bottles on the mantelpiece.

'What's your name?' he asked.

'Business first, dear. No kissing, and you'll have to use a French letter. Got the money?'

When Todd handed over the two pounds ten, she said, 'Couldn't manage a little bit more, could you? I'd be ever so grateful.'

Todd took half a crown out of his pocket, holding it up between a thumb and finger. 'If you tell me your name,' he said.

'For one of those,' she said, deftly swiping the coin and dancing away from him, 'I'll be anyone you want me to be. Anyone at all.'

Todd eyed her thoughtfully. 'Your name,' he said, 'is Fay. Now come here and shut up.'

CHAPTER 15

The following morning at half past ten, Stratton, having received the results of the Leadbetter post-mortem—strangled but not raped, which was something to be thankful for, at least—was sitting in the room allotted him by the Middlesex, waiting for the first of the nurses to be brought to him. In a room down the corridor, Sergeant Ballard was preparing to interview the orderlies, porters, and other menials.

Stratton had already re-interviewed the doctors, none of whom had anything interesting to tell him, and seen the matron. Miss Hornbeck was a small, dignified woman with thick spectacles, who had explained that the nurses would be sent to him one by one, beginning with the senior staff and ending with the probationers.

He lit a cigarette and, resisting the urge to swing the swivel chair—a novelty only enjoyed at Savile Row by DCI Lamb—full circle, contented himself with turning it to face the window, which gave him a good view of the hospital's vegetable garden. It was a great deal tidier than his allotment, which was in dire need of weeding. Jenny would be out again this evening, so he'd go and spend a couple of hours up there after supper. That was an odd business last night, thinking he'd seen a man watching them over the garden fence. It was only an impression—one that Jenny said he'd imagined—but he was sure someone had been there, although he couldn't imagine why anyone should want to spy on them.

Probably just kids, messing about. He dismissed it from his mind and was about to go and see if anyone was waiting outside without realising she was supposed to knock, when the door opened, revealing a skinny woman in a dark blue uniform. She had a desiccated look, as if you might be able to reconstitute her into a proper person by adding water. 'Assistant Matron,' she announced balefully. 'I hope this won't take long. We're very busy.'

'Of course not,' said Stratton, rising. 'Please come in and take a seat.'

By the end of the morning, Stratton had finished interviewing the sisters and staff nurses and begun working his way down the hierarchy. The senior nurses, who, whatever their shape or size, seemed to him to be more like monuments than real women, had been replaced by junior ones in stripy uniforms, many of whom wore harassed expressions and arrived in a flurry, adjusting their cuffs and pushing wisps of hair under their caps. All, without exception, spoke of Dr Reynolds with reverence and expressed shock and regret, but none had anything to add to what little the doctors had already told him. They all seemed to know—albeit with varying degrees of accuracy—the results of the post-mortem. That, Stratton supposed, was not surprising; hospitals were just as likely to be hotbeds of gossip as anywhere else. About Leadbetter, they had even less to say—although a competent nurse, the young woman seemed to have formed no close friendships; in fact, she seemed to have made very little impression at all. No-one, apparently, had come near the disused operating theatre all afternoon, and nor had any of the patients gone AWOL.

At one o'clock, with his meagre stock of cigarettes much depleted, Stratton left for some fresh air and a spot of lunch.

At four o'clock, after a scared-looking probationer had scuttled in with a cup of tea and emptied the ashtray, he received Nurse Maddox from the Men's Surgical Ward. She was a flat-chested girl with pink cheeks, who would, but for a calculating expression in her light blue eyes, have been rather pretty. Stratton, who had, by this time, largely given up on any sort of preamble, said, 'So, what can you tell me about Dr Reynolds?'

Nurse Maddox eyed the packet of Weights on the desk and said coquettishly, 'Mind if I have one of those?'

Interesting, thought Stratton. Not only was she the first one who hadn't immediately expressed dismay or sorrow at Reynolds's death, she was also the first who had asked directly for a cigarette, the others having simply cast longing looks at the packet until it was offered. He slid the cigarettes across the desk—'Thanks ever so'—and leant over with a match. Judging from the exhibition she made of it—lots of exaggerated sucking and blowing and fancy wrist movements—she wasn't a habitual smoker. It was, Stratton thought, an attempt to be sophisticated, and matched her voice, which was cockney with a self-consciously genteel overlay, like someone unaccustomed to answering the telephone.

This, he thought, was definitely one who fitted the matron's description of a junior nurse who wanted to make herself important; the first so far. The others had been nervous, shy, or just pleased to have a break in routine and take the weight off their feet. 'Well?' he said. 'When did you last see Dr Reynolds?'

'About three days ago, I think.'

'What were you doing on the evening of Wednesday the twenty-first?'

Nurse Maddox did a bit more wrist twirling and put her head slightly on one side in what Stratton supposed was meant to be an imitation of a film star. 'Let me think…' She batted her eyelashes at him. Come on, darling, thought Stratton. We both know you weren't dining at the Ritz.

'Actually, I was here,' she admitted, clearly disappointed not to be able to give a more glamorous-sounding alibi. 'In the nurses' quarters with some of the other girls.'

'All the time?'

'Yes.'

'Fair enough. Had you much to do with Dr Reynolds?'

'Sometimes. He used to come into the Men's Surgical Ward. It's so much easier,' she added, confidingly, 'nursing men than women. Women are frightful.' The last word came out as 'freightfull'.

'When you say he used to come in,' said Stratton, 'do you mean he was treating the patients?'

'Well,' she ducked her head and tried an up-from-under look on him. 'He was sometimes.'

'I don't understand,' said Stratton. 'He wasn't a surgeon, was he?'

'No, but some of them were people he'd referred from Casualty. Air raid casualties and car smashes and things like that.'

'So he came to see them.'

'That's right.'

'What about the other times?'

She put her head back and blew smoke at the ceiling. 'Other times?'

'You said he was there to see patients *sometimes*. What was he there for the rest of the time?'

'Oooh...' She did the head-on-the-side thing again, but with a lot less conviction this time. 'I don't think that's for me to say.'

'Yes it is,' snapped Stratton. 'This is a serious matter, Miss Maddox. Dr Reynolds is dead. Failure to tell me what you know could have serious consequences, and I don't have time to sit here while you go through your Hollywood movie-star act, so I suggest you pull yourself together and start co-operating.'

Nurse Maddox, flushing, mumbled, 'Sorry,' and bent forward to grind out her cigarette in the ashtray. The humped shape of her shoulders, and the fact that she seemed to be taking a long time about doing it, made Stratton feel uneasy. His words had come out more harshly than he expected. Some chap had probably told the wretched girl that she looked like Veronica Lake or someone, and the poor kid had never got over it.

When she raised her head, Stratton saw fear in her eyes and realised that she'd never meant to say anything but hadn't been able to help herself. It was entirely possible, of course, that she had absolutely nothing to tell. Either way, the thing had clearly gone further than she'd intended, but at this point he couldn't risk passing up any information. 'Tell me what you meant,' he said.

The words came out haltingly, in an almost-whisper. 'Sometimes he came to see one of the nurses. He pretended it was something else, but that's why he was there.'

'Which nurse?'

'Marchant.'

Stratton looked at his paper. 'Fay Marchant?' he asked, without mentioning that she was the next name on his list, and probably waiting outside.

'Yes. She used to work in Casualty. We get moved around, you see, and—'

'Why did he come to see her?' asked Stratton, neutrally.

'He…Look, she doesn't know I know about it. She'd never speak to me again if…It was only a couple of times. I just happened to catch sight of them, and then when he came in another time, I saw her looking at him, and it was, you know…'

'When you caught sight of them, what were they doing?'

'They were in the sluice.'

'Sluice?'

'The sluice room. For the bed pans.' She gave a little moue of disgust.

'Oh, yes. Of course. But a doctor wouldn't normally be in there, would he?'

'No. That's why it was strange. The door was open a little way, and that's when I saw them.'

'What were they doing?'

'He had his arms round her. He gave her a kiss.'

'On the lips?'

Nurse Maddox shook her head—regretfully, Stratton thought. 'On the cheek. But he was embracing her.'

'When was this?'

'A couple of weeks ago, I think. Maybe ten days. I can't remember exactly.'

'I see. Now, how about Nurse Leadbetter? Did you know her?'

'I knew who she was, but...Not really.'

'Do you think she might've had some connection with Dr Reynolds?'

'Like *that*, you mean?' The femme fatale returned as Nurse Maddox tossed her head. 'Hardly!'

'Why do you say that?'

'She was a little mouse of a thing. Never went out or wore makeup or anything like that.'

'Any boyfriends that you know of?'

'No. She wasn't interested in anything like that. Far too serious.' Nurse Maddox leant forward, prurient, agog. 'They're saying she was strangled, Inspector. Is that true?'

'We haven't had the results of the post-mortem yet,' said Stratton.

'Well, I can't understand it if she was—that's a sex crime, isn't it, strangling?'

'Not always, Miss Maddox. Perhaps,' suggested Stratton, gently, 'you should spend less time at the pictures.' He rose to escort her from the room. 'Thank you. You've been very helpful.'

When he opened the door he saw, leaning against the opposite wall of the corridor, a slim young woman with smooth dark-brown hair tucked neatly under her cap. Nurse Maddox saw her too. She turned the colour of beetroot and uttered a little shriek before dashing away. The dark-haired girl stared after her for a moment, then turned to Stratton, eyebrows raised in surprise. He mirrored her expression with his own for long enough to convey that he had no idea why she'd reacted in such a fashion, then said, 'Nurse Marchant?'

She smiled. 'Yes, Inspector.'

Fay Marchant, Stratton thought, was beautiful. Her enormous eyes were deep chocolate brown with long lashes, her complexion was ivory and her lips were full. Stratton cast a discreet glance at her legs as she preceded him across the room. They might have been encased in thick black stockings, but they still looked shapely, and so, beneath the uniform, did the rest of her.

He seated himself in the swivel chair. 'Would you like a cigarette, Miss Marchant?'

That smile again. 'Thank you.'

Once the cigarette had been lit—this time with the minimum of fuss—Stratton said, 'So, tell me about Dr Reynolds,' and, putting his elbows on the desk, rested his chin on his hands in a manner suggestive of one about to hear a confession.

'Well,' Fay (it was impossible to think of her as Nurse Marchant, despite the uniform) hesitated. 'It was a terrible shock, for all of us. And his poor wife...I wouldn't say I knew him, really. Of course, I knew who he *was*, because I was in Casualty before I was transferred to Men's Surgical.'

'You knew he was married?'

'Well, yes...I mean, it's not as if it was a secret, or anything.'

'But your relationship with him—you knew him quite well, didn't you?'

Fay frowned. 'I don't understand what you mean.'

'You were observed in a rather...' Stratton paused deliberately to see if Fay's face would betray anything, but she looked merely puzzled, 'intimate position with Dr Reynolds.'

'Was I? Who told you...? Oh.' Fay, evidently remembering Nurse Maddox's odd behaviour, said, 'Of course. You don't have to tell me. Oh, dear. I didn't realise.' She stared down at the polished wood of the desk for a moment, then raised her head and, looking him straight in the eye, said, 'She saw us in the sluice room, didn't she? I did wonder at the time...Look, I can see why she came to that conclusion, Inspector, but it really wasn't what she thought.'

'What was it?'

'It's hard to explain to someone who doesn't work here, Inspector.'

'Have a go.' Stratton gave her an encouraging smile.

'Well, I was on nights, and one of the patients, an elderly man who'd been smashed up in an air raid—he'd had a couple of operations, but he was in a bad way, and we'd done everything we could...' Fay looked at Stratton as if he might be in some doubt about this.

'I'm sure you did. What happened then?'

'He died. The night sister had called the house surgeon, and we'd all done our best, but it wasn't any good. Dr Reynolds had come up, and—'

'Why? Had he been called for as well?'

Fay shook her head. 'He'd treated the man in Casualty, when he was first brought in, and he knew he wasn't doing well...He did come to see me, sometimes, if he was on his rounds. Not because...what you thought, just...well, we had a sort of affinity.' She gave Stratton a pleading look.

'What sort of affinity?'

'A mental affinity. It was dreadful, hearing he'd died like that.'

'Like what?'

'Being attacked, and on his own. Horrible.'

'You think that's what happened to him?'

'Well, it was, wasn't it?'

'That's what we're trying to find out. Do you know anyone who might have wanted to harm him?'

'No!' Fay sounded shocked. 'Of course not.'

'You said you had a mental affinity. Meaning not emotional or physical?'

'No. Well, a bit emotional, I suppose, but never physical. What I mean is, we got along in a friendly way, not—'

'But he kissed you, didn't he?'

'Yes, but that was because of this patient. After he'd died I was upset, you see, and...I don't usually react like that, I mean, when people die—it's dreadful, but you get used to it, only he'd been there quite a while, and he was such a nice old man. A widower, but his daughter used to visit...'

'At night?'

'No, that was when I was on days.' Stratton made a note to check that this tallied with the nursing rota, and she continued, 'I'd just started on nights, and it takes time to adjust. It can be tiring—I'm not complaining, it's just that sometimes one can get a bit emotional about things. That time just before dawn, you can start to feel worn down, especially with something like that, and everything seems sort of dreary and hopeless. My fiancé was killed at Tobruk, you see, and that's when it's worst. When you see a body—someone you knew—and it looks like them but they've gone and it's not them any more...And Ronnie—that was my fiancé—he must have looked like that, too. It probably sounds stupid, but if you felt something for the patient...and I'd got fond of Daddy Banks. I went into the sluice room, just to be by myself for a few minutes, and Dr Reynolds saw me. He was just trying to cheer me up, that's all. You do believe me, don't you?'

'I can see how such a thing might happen,' said Stratton, sympathetically.

'That means you can't see.' Fay sounded resigned. 'Look, Inspector, I could get into terrible trouble if the matron heard about this. It really hasn't got anything to do with Dr Reynolds dying like that, and I'd hate his wife to think that there was... anything...untoward...between us.' Her words broke up into gulps, and Stratton could see that she was fighting to contain tears. If it wasn't real, he thought, it was a bloody good performance, and he was discomfited, as he always was—no matter how many times it happened, which in his job was rather a lot—by the sight of a woman weeping. He produced his handkerchief—clean that morning, thank goodness—and passed it across the desk. 'It's bound to be distressing, but try not to upset yourself. We can,' he added, with awkward gallantry, 'be discreet, you know. Where were you on the evening of Wednesday the twenty-first?'

'In the nurses' quarters,' said Fay, promptly. 'All evening. With Maddox and some of the others.' She gave him a watery smile. 'She obviously didn't tell you about that.'

'What about Nurse Leadbetter?' asked Stratton. 'Was she there?'

'I don't think so. She was on nights. I've just gone back on to days.'

'So she'd have been asleep during the day?'

'That's right.'

'Did you know her well?'

Fay shook her head. 'I don't think she was a very easy person *to* know. She didn't say much—kept herself to herself. She seemed...well, aloof, really, but perhaps she was just shy. I can't imagine why anyone would have wanted to kill her.'

After she'd left, Stratton sat down to make some notes and collect his thoughts before admitting the next girl. As far as poor little Leadbetter was concerned, Fay's comment was not dissimilar to Nurse Maddox's, or, indeed, to several of the others', in that no-one had considered her significant enough to warrant killing, but then nobody had admitted being sufficiently close to her to have enough of an idea...And if she was supposed to be asleep in the basement, what the hell was she doing in a disused operating theatre several floors up? After staring into space and tapping his pencil on the desk for several minutes, he was forced to admit to himself that he was doing nothing more productive than imagining what Fay's breasts might look like. Regretfully dismissing the delightful image from his mind—it would never do if one of the other nurses, or, God forbid, the matron, came in and found him sitting there with an expression of slack-jawed lust—he applied himself to the probable nature of her relationship with Dr Reynolds. His instincts as a man told him to believe her, because he wanted to, because she was charming and beautiful; and because he hadn't liked Nurse Maddox, the simpering tale-bearer. His instincts as a copper, however, made him question all these things. Admittedly, Nurse Maddox's demeanour had suggested that she was quite capable of making something out of nothing. Perhaps she was jealous of Fay's looks, too, but it did not mean that she was, in this particular instance, a liar. And—a definite point in her favour—she'd held back from describing the embrace she'd witnessed as a full-blown clinch.

As far as Fay herself was concerned, the fact was that women's faces were not the indexes of their souls, and beauty was no guarantee of truthfulness. He recalled the photograph he'd been given of Reynolds, now at the station being duplicated for the men conducting the door-to-door enquiries. He wasn't, Stratton thought, a bad looking man, but he wasn't a matinée idol. Then again, you saw girls who were knockouts with all sorts of ugly men. Rich ones, usually, with influence, but weren't all nurses supposed to want to marry doctors for that very reason? And for an unscrupulous girl, the fact that a doctor was already married would be neither here nor there...

Which brought him full circle: he didn't believe that Fay was unscrupulous. She hadn't returned Maddox's cattiness, either, except for one tiny flash of claws. He wondered about her social life. She'd said her fiancé was killed at Tobruk, which was...Stratton thought back...1942. She hadn't mentioned seeing anyone since then, but such a lovely-looking girl would hardly remain unattached for long—unless she chose to, of course. Nurses, he knew, lived communally, and there were always strict rules about being home before a certain time in the evening. However, he'd bet on the fact that there was a bathroom window or something that they could crawl through if necessary.

The whole thing needed further consideration...something for this evening's stint on the allotment, he thought. He got up and went to the door to usher in the next girl.

CHAPTER 16

By six o'clock Stratton, having checked the nursing rota with the matron and discovered that Fay had been telling the truth about when she was on nights and that Leadbetter had been on nights too, found himself with a good deal more to ponder than just her. Two nurses from the Casualty Department, interviewed back-to-back, had, on being pressed, timidly suggested that Reynolds was not, perhaps, as good a doctor as his colleagues had made him out to be. One had mentioned an incident in which Reynolds had apparently mistaken a diabetic coma for a drunken stupor, and the next girl (nice legs but a squashed-up face that, if it wasn't for the absence of fur, could have belonged to a friendly Pekingese) had, reluctantly, admitted that this had indeed been the case. Stratton remembered that Arliss (who was, admittedly, no doctor, or even averagely intelligent) had done something similar the previous year, and that by the time the police doctor had been called to the cells, the chap was pretty far gone and had to be rushed into hospital.

Having done this, he decided to recall Fay and ask her about it. He found the Men's Surgical Ward, and asked the sister if he might have a word with Nurse Marchant. She looked at him as if he'd just farted and said, '*Another* one?' but she called Fay.

They returned to Stratton's allotted room in silence, Fay looking worried. Once they were settled on either side of the consultant's desk, Stratton asked, 'Would you say Dr Reynolds was a competent physician?'

Fay flushed. 'I don't think I'm qualified to answer that question.'

'Nevertheless, I'd like to hear your opinion.'

'Well...' Fay glanced towards the window, evading his eye.

'Strictly between ourselves,' said Stratton.

'The thing is, we're so busy at the moment, and anyone can...'

'Make a mistake?'

'Well, yes. Someone came in last year, when I was on Casualty. A sixteen-year-old boy. It was after a raid, and he had a cut on his foot. It wasn't too bad—in fact, I don't really understand why they hadn't sorted it out at the warden's post, because there's always a doctor on duty. But they hadn't, and it was a busy night with a lot of casualties. He came in with his mother, and Dr Reynolds treated him and sent him away. He was a bit...well, he pretty much told the pair of them that they were making a song and dance over nothing. Anyway, the boy was brought back two days later in a bad way, and he died that night. Blood poisoning. I felt so sorry for the mother.'

'Were there any other incidents like that?'

'That's the one I remember, but...I did think, sometimes, that he could be a bit...well, dismissive. But anyone can be, when you're busy, and...doctors are human, Inspector. I'm sure that most of them have made the odd mistake.'

'Are you sure you're not letting your friendship colour your views?' asked Stratton.

'I don't think so,' said Fay miserably. 'I'm trying to be fair to him.'

'Did you have an affair with him?'

Fay shook her head steadily, staring at the floor. Stratton still didn't know whether to believe her or not.

When she'd gone, Ballard came in to report on his day's findings—or rather, the lack of them. 'We've located Sergeant

Leadbetter's senior officer and sent a telegram, but we haven't turned up anything of significance, I'm afraid. Oh, and there was a message from Fingerprints, sir, about the operating theatre. Stuff all over the place, apparently, all different, smeared and messed up. They can't make anything of it.'

Stratton, who'd been chewing the end of his pencil in order not to deplete his limited stock of cigarettes further, took it out of his mouth and tossed it down on the desk. 'Bollocks.'

'I'd say so, sir.'

'Oh, well. Same place, same time, tomorrow, then. You off now?'

Ballard nodded. 'Plans for this evening, sir.'

'Oh, yes...' Stratton was aware that Ballard had been seeing Gaines, a shapely policewoman from the Marlborough Street station, for some time, but—such things being forbidden—found it easier to pretend that he knew nothing about it. He assumed, since marriage would have automatically meant Gaines's immediate dismissal, that there were no plans of that sort in the offing. Perhaps they'd decided to wait until the war was over before setting up home. 'Well, I'm not going to ask any more, so you don't have to tell.'

'Thank you, sir.'

'Cheerio then.' Stratton rose to fetch his hat. 'Enjoy yourself.'

'I shall, sir. Goodnight.'

After a solitary supper, Stratton went up to his allotment where he spent a pleasant, if back-breaking, couple of hours hoeing, transplanting leeks, and earthing up the early potatoes. Satisfied with his work, he wrapped some broad beans and the first of the carrots in newspaper to give to Jenny, and trudged off home. He didn't feel any clearer in his mind about either Fay or Nurse Leadbetter, but at least he'd managed to make some discreet enquiries about the misdiagnoses and been promised further information. Tomorrow, he'd get the first results from the door-to-door enquiries, which might yield something...

CHAPTER 17

Talk about a shock! Higgs had told him about the nurse when he'd arrived for work, and, for a horrible moment, he'd thought it was *his* girl and someone else had got there first. Then he'd had a glance under the sheet when no-one was looking, and, even with the swelling and cyanosis, he could see immediately that it wasn't her because of the red hair. He wondered if it was the girl who'd stared at him just after he'd first seen Fay—there couldn't be too many redheads in the hospital, could there? All to the good, if it was—one less thing to concern him. He wondered, for a moment, why it had happened, then dismissed it from his mind.

He'd mentally prepared himself to see Inspector Stratton, and was relieved when, bidden into the room on the second floor, he was interviewed by a sergeant. He thought it was the same man who'd been on the bomb-site when he and Higgs had gone to fetch in Dr Reynolds, but he couldn't be sure.

The questions—he'd compared notes afterwards with Higgs, to check—were of a routine nature: did he know Dr Reynolds, did he know Nurse Leadbetter, what had he been doing at the times of their deaths, had he noticed anything suspicious...The whole business hadn't taken more than five minutes.

It was time, he thought, to put the next part of his plan into action, but it was almost the end of the day before he got the chance. It had been a long one: twenty-one post-mortems in rapid succession. Bomb casualties, mostly, dusty, tattered, shattered and crushed, each to be tagged with an identity disc, and each with a few small belongings which he'd bagged up and tied to the bodies of their former owners. As they cleared up, he told Higgs, 'By the way, I'll be leaving soon. I've been called up.'

'Have you? Blimey, they took their time. To be honest, young chap like you, when you come along I was a bit surprised you wasn't already in the forces. Thought you must have flat feet or something.'

'I've been moving around, see,' said Todd, vaguely. 'They took a while to find me.'

Higgs grimaced. 'Bet you wish they hadn't bothered.'

'I don't know,' said Todd. 'We've all got to do our bit.'

'You *are* doing your bit,' said Higgs. 'To be honest, I don't know how we're going to manage without you. Have you told Dr Byrne? Perhaps he could put in a word for you.'

'No,' said Todd. 'This isn't a reserved occupation and I don't want to duck out of it. Besides, you'll find someone else.'

'Yes,' said Higgs, gloomily, 'and guess who'll have to train the bugger? I never said before, but you cottoned on faster than anyone we've had, and I've been here near on twenty years.' After a pause, he added in a gruffer voice than usual, 'I'm going to miss you, mate.' Paying great attention, he pinched out his cigarette and stuck what was left behind his ear. 'Right,' he said, brusquely, 'back to work.'

'I'll catch you up.' Todd stayed outside to finish his fag. He wanted a couple of minutes by himself. He was flattered by what Higgs had said—it was always nice to leave a job on a high note. He was just savouring it, thinking it boded well for the future, when he heard shouts from the pavement above. 'Unwin! Unwin!' Looking up, he saw by craning his neck the foreshortened form of the red-headed doctor, Wemyss, the wealthy one. Remembering that Unwin was the name of one of the other young doctors, he tried for a glimpse and saw a plump man with a sleek, dark head. Wemyss appeared to be giving him something—money, perhaps, or cigarettes—but Todd couldn't hear what was being said. Then Wemyss moved away, laughing, and the other called out, 'Cambridge Arms, then,' before he walked off.

Neither had seen him. The area was deep, narrow, and pretty well hidden from the street unless you looked directly over the railings. The Cambridge Arms. The only pub he knew with that name was in Newman Street. He hadn't thought it was a 'hospital' place, but maybe that was why Wemyss and Unwin (and possibly the third of the trio, Betterton) chose to go there. If it did turn out to be their usual watering hole, it would make things a lot easier. Assuming that the arrangement was for later on, he'd be able to find out tonight.

He'd finish clearing up in the mortuary, then go and break the news to Dr Byrne. After that, it would be time to concentrate on the next part of his plan.

CHAPTER

18

*...*And *the hens are still laying well. Auntie Doris is coming soon, we are going to the Grove to see* The Man in Grey. *Margaret Lockwood and James Mason are in it. We have not been to the pictures for weeks, so it will be quite a treat.*

Jenny put down her pen, and put her elbows on the kitchen table and her chin on her fists, considering what to write next.

*We are still very busy at the 'Rest Centre', and...*And come next year, you might have a brother or sister. Monica might be pleased, she supposed, and at least she was old enough to help— provided she were here, of course.

She must not think like that. There was still plenty of time for her period to arrive, and if she worried, she'd more than likely make herself late. 'I am not pregnant,' she told herself 'Everything is fine.' In the spirit of belt-and-braces—after all, it couldn't hurt —she put her elbows on the table again, and, clasping her hands together, closed her eyes.

She was interrupted in mid-prayer by the sound of Doris shouting 'Coo-ee!' through the letterbox. A moment later, her sister appeared in the kitchen, looking flushed and patting her hair back into place.

'Jen! Mr Ingram telephoned—he's coming to pick her up!'

'Oh, thank God—at last! That's wonderful. When?'

'Two hours, he said. Dr Makepeace finally managed to get through to his unit yesterday—they're in Southampton, supporting the Navy or something. Mrs Ingram was ever so pleased—I'm sure she'll be fine now he's back. We'll have to go to the pictures another time. I was hoping you could fetch her some better clothes from the Rest Centre. You've seen her—skin and bone—my things would hang off her.'

Jenny sighed. 'So would mine. I'll see what I can do.'

Jenny managed to find a respectable-looking blouse and skirt, and a fairly decent cardigan. Later, standing in Doris's kitchen, she held them up for inspection.

'I hope they fit. I got the smallest ones I could.'

'They'll be fine. I'll take them up to her.'

Doris had just returned to the kitchen and was in the process of making tea, when there was a knock on the door. She went into the hall, and Jenny, curious to see Mr Ingram, followed. Opening the front door they saw, standing on the step, a small, narrow-shouldered man dressed in khaki, holding a kitbag. His face was triangular, broad across the temples and tapering sharply to a pointed chin, his lips compressed, and his eyes a hard, concentrated blue. There was a constrained look to him, as if he might explode at any minute. Even the small, tight knot of his tie looked angry. Jenny stepped back, feeling a flutter of fear.

'Hello, Mr Ingram,' said Doris.

'Thank you for taking Elsie in like this,' said Mr Ingram. Evidently, he didn't think it was necessary to make introductions. 'I've come to fetch her now, so she'll be no more trouble to you.' He smiled suddenly, revealing neat little teeth with a sharp canine at each side. Jenny took another step back. There was definitely something menacing about him, she thought, even though he was clearly trying to be friendly.

'No trouble at all, Mr Ingram. Come in and have a cup of tea. Mrs Ingram's upstairs, resting.'

'I don't want to cause any bother.'

His speech, like his wife's, was a sort of diluted cockney. Ugly, thought Jenny, who sometimes worried—especially when at Mrs Chetwynd's, visiting the children—that she sounded the same.

'No bother at all! We were just having one, weren't we, Jen?' said Doris, too brightly.

'That's right.' Jenny was aware that her voice, like her sister's, was overly enthusiastic. This man can't hurt you, she told herself. He's probably not so bad, just nervous, like we are. She helped him off with his hat and coat as Doris, clearly as rattled as she was, bustled into the kitchen to pour the tea.

He accepted a cup, but would not sit. Instead he stood, leaning against a cupboard, so that Jenny and Doris felt that they had to remain standing too, awkward against the sink and the cooker, not knowing what to say.

They caught each other's eye when he wasn't looking and made an unspoken pact—least said, soonest mended.

'Mrs Ingram is fine,' began Doris, in a chatty tone. 'A terrible shock, of course, but it's a miracle she wasn't injured.'

'I'm sure she'll soon be back to her old self,' said Jenny. 'That's what the doctor said, isn't it, Doris?'

'How much for the doctor?' asked Mr Ingram. 'I'll pay you.' He said this defensively, as if they'd been expecting him not to offer.

'It's all right,' said Doris, taken aback. 'Dr Makepeace said he'd send a bill because you're on the panel. Have you got somewhere to take Mrs Ingram?'

'We'll manage.' This was said with such hostile finality that neither woman liked to ask for further information. 'Did the doctor give her anything?'

Doris shook her head. 'Just said she needed rest and quiet. He said there wasn't anything to worry about, didn't he, Jen?' This wasn't *exactly* what Dr Makepeace had said, but it was near enough not to be a downright lie.

'That's right. In any case, I'm sure that seeing you will be just the tonic she needs. I'm sure she'll be down any—'

Hearing the sound of feet on the stairs, Mr Ingram turned round. He had his back to Jenny but she could see, over his shoulder, that Mrs Ingram was standing in the doorway. Clad in the blouse and skirt Jenny had obtained from the Rest Centre, she'd made an effort to tidy her thin hair, with the result that the small pink rims of her ears stuck through it in a way that made Jenny think of a baby chimpanzee she'd once seen at the zoo. Her dash of lipstick was clumsily applied, and something told Jenny that this had been done, inexpertly, at Doris's suggestion.

For a moment, there was total silence. Mrs Ingram stared at her husband. Her mouth opened in a soundless 'O', and Jenny saw that some of the lipstick had got onto her teeth.

'Here we are, dear,' said Doris. 'All safe and sound.'

Mr Ingram took a step towards his wife, who backed away, her small form huddled in the hall. Doris, puzzled, stepped past Mr Ingram, repeating, 'Here we are.'

'It's all right, Elsie,' said Mr Ingram, stepping forward in his turn. 'I'm here now.'

Mrs Ingram blinked rapidly. 'Who are you?' she asked. The words came out slowly, as if she were new to speech.

'What do you mean, who am I? Eric, of course.'

'Who sent you?'

'I've come to fetch you, dear. We're going.' Was Jenny imagining it, or did his jovial, chivvying tone carry an undercurrent of threat? 'I spoke to you earlier on the telephone, remember?'

Mrs Ingram shook her head. 'I don't understand. Why have *you* come for me?'

'Mr Ingram's come to take you—' Doris stopped abruptly and Jenny could see from her face that she'd been about to say 'take you home'.

'Why?' Mrs Ingram's voice was shrill and fearful. Before Mr Ingram, or anyone else, could reply to this, she turned to Doris. 'You said my husband was coming. And *he* told me he was. He said it himself, on the telephone.'

In the baffled silence that followed, Jenny saw Mr Ingram lean forwards and it seemed to her he moved in slow motion, as if forcing himself to walk through an invisible blizzard. 'Come on, Elsie,' he said. 'Mrs Kerr has done quite enough for us as it is. Let's—'

'No!' Jenny saw her sister wince as Mrs Ingram stepped back and her foot smacked into Doris's ankle. 'He keeps calling me Elsie, and he doesn't know me,' she said to Jenny, her words coming faster now. 'My husband's coming,' she told Mr Ingram. 'He'll be worried about me. He won't like it if you're here. He doesn't like that sort of thing.'

'What sort of thing?' asked Jenny, baffled.

'This,' said Mrs Ingram. 'Strange men.'

Mr Ingram's face flushed a dull pink, and Jenny saw that his fists were clenched at his sides. 'Elsie, come on...'

'My husband,' said Mrs Ingram, 'believes in clean living, and so do I.'

'But I *am* your husband.'

'No, you're not. Whatever gave you that idea?'

This was said with such utter certainty that Jenny turned to Mr Ingram and said, 'You are, aren't you?'

Mr Ingram blinked at her. 'Course I am.'

'Are you?' echoed Doris.

'Yes, I bloody am!' He made a grab for Elsie, who ducked behind Doris. 'Now get moving and don't—'

'No!' Mrs Ingram, sheltering behind Doris now, said, 'Don't let him take me.'

'Look,' said Jenny, directing her words towards the right side of Mrs Ingram, which was all that could be seen behind the larger form of her sister, 'you've had a dreadful shock. It's enough to confuse anybody. Why don't we just sit down, and—'

'We don't need to sit down. Come on, Elsie, these people have done quite enough. We're going now.'

Mrs Ingram's face appeared round Doris's shoulder. 'That man,' she said, in a loud voice, pointing her finger, 'is not my husband. 1 don't want anything to do with him. My Eric wouldn't like it.'

'For God's sake!' said Mr Ingram. He grabbed Mrs Ingram's wrist.

Mrs Ingram took hold of the banister with her other hand. 'I won't go with him! I *won't*! Fetch the police!'

'What?' Mr Ingram let go of her, and Jenny saw that he'd left a red wheal on her arm.

'Look, dear,' said Doris, putting an arm round her shoulders, 'why don't you just—'

'Why are you doing this?' Mrs Ingram flinched away from her and looked at them all with wild, fearful eyes. 'Why are you helping *him*?' she wailed, and Jenny saw that there were tears streaking her face. 'I've done nothing to you! I don't understand. That's not my husband. He's pretending!' Mrs Ingram turned to Doris. 'Why don't you telephone the police? They'll soon get rid of him.'

'Look, dear,' said Doris. 'Why don't you go back upstairs, and we'll sort this out.'

'There's nothing to sort out!' shouted Mr Ingram. 'She's my wife, and we're going!'

'Please,' said Jenny. 'Let her go upstairs.' Mrs Ingram seemed so adamant, and so distressed, that it seemed cruel to force her to leave with Mr Ingram (if indeed he was Mr Ingram—it suddenly occurred to Jenny that he had not produced any proof of this).

There was a moment's silence, during which Jenny and Doris stared helplessly at each other, before Mr Ingram burst out, 'For God's sake, Elsie, that's enough! Pull yourself together and come with me!'

Mrs Ingram cowered away, her hands still firmly clamped on the banister, and began to scream. The sound was unbearable, the shriek of an animal, trapped, uncomprehending and in pain. Jenny took hold of Mr Ingram's arm. 'Don't! You're making her worse.'

'No!' He shook her off roughly, so that she staggered and bashed the back of her head against the wall.

As she winced and blinked, Jenny heard Doris making soothing noises and saying, 'Why don't you come back upstairs, dear? Have a nice lie-down,' while attempting to prise Mrs Ingram off the banister. For such a frail-looking woman, she was surprisingly strong.

'No,' she panted, 'no, please…I won't go with him.'

'It's all right, Mrs Ingram,' said Doris. 'You can stay here.'

'What do you mean, stay here? Of course she can't, she's—'

'Stop it!' said Jenny, with an authority she hadn't known she possessed. As Mr Ingram blinked at her in surprise, she took his arm once more and turned him round to face the kitchen. 'I'm sorry,' she said, 'but you can see she's still confused. It's enough to upset anybody, what she's been through. Perhaps if you wait in there for a moment, we can try and sort it out.'

'All right,' he said, ungraciously.

Jenny shut the door in his face and leant against it momentarily, rubbing her head. Mrs Ingram had retreated upstairs, and Jenny heard the door of her room bang, and the sound of something heavy being pulled, jerkily, across the floor, as if she were trying to barricade herself inside. Doris glanced upwards, raised her eyebrows, and beckoned Jenny down the passage to the back of the house.

'Is your head all right?' she hissed. 'That was quite a whack.'

'I'll live,' Jenny whispered. 'What's going on? Either he's her husband or he isn't.'

'I don't understand it either,' Doris whispered. 'But she can't go anywhere in *that* state, can she? Listen...' There were more sounds of bumping and scraping from above. Doris winced.

'We can sort out the floor later. What are we going to do now? We don't actually know it is him, do we?'

'Well, I'm not asking him for his ID card.'

'That wouldn't prove anything—there's no picture.'

'Jen, it must be him. I mean, why would he come here saying he's Mr Ingram if he isn't?'

'I don't know, but she seems so sure.'

'Well, she's had a house fall on her, hasn't she? She's obviously not right yet. Anyway, I spoke to him, remember? He sounds exactly the same. Mind you, I don't like him at all.'

'Me neither.'

'Nasty piece of work. I bet he knocks her about. And I don't believe he's got anywhere to take her.'

'No...Aren't there any neighbours who know what he looks like? At least we could be sure.'

Doris shook her head. 'The warden was asking, remember? And next door was killed. But it must be him. I mean, Dr Makepeace got hold of him, didn't he?'

'Yes...I suppose so. Unless it's someone else from the unit.'

'Why would they do that? It's ridiculous.'

'So is this. We'll have to put him off.'

'*I* will, you mean. He's probably only got a forty-eight-hour pass.'

'He can come back tomorrow then, can't he?'

'This is mad.'

'You can say that again.'

'Now we're going round in circles. Come on...I'm not going in there on my own.'

They didn't have to. Mr Ingram appeared, seeming to Jenny to vibrate with suppressed violence, told them that he didn't know what had 'got into her' and that he'd be back tomorrow morning, scowled at them both, and left.

'As if it was our fault!' said Doris. 'What am I going to do?'

'Ask Dr Makepeace,' said Jenny. 'He might be able come and see her.'

'If she'll let him into her room ...'

'Why don't you telephone,' said Jenny. 'I'll go upstairs.'

Jenny knocked on the door of Mrs Ingram's room. 'It's me, Jenny. Can I come in? He's gone.' She pushed at the door. As she expected, there was something big on the other side, stopping it from opening. Must be the chest of drawers, she thought, surprised that such a small body had the strength to move such a cumbersome piece of furniture.

'He won't come back, will he? He says he's my Eric, but he's not. He looks like him, and sounds like him, but he's not.'

'Are you sure?' asked Jenny, the side of her face against the door panels.

'Yes! It's not him. I don't know why you think it's him.'

'Well, we don't know what he looks like. Doris says it's the same man you spoke to on the telephone.'

'Yes, but it's *not him*! He's not coming back, is he?'

'No, dear.' Jenny gave up. 'I'll fetch you some tea,' she said. 'I can leave it on the landing if you don't want to come out.'

Doris was sitting at the kitchen table, head in hands.

'What did Dr Makepeace say?'

'He's coming later. What did *she* say?'

'She won't open the door. I said I'd take her a cup of tea, but I don't think she cares one way or the other.'

Doris shook her head in despair. 'I wish I'd never gone to the hospital now.'

'Don't say that. You did the right thing, taking her in.'

'Did I?' Doris stared at her with baffled weariness.

On the way home, Jenny tried to imagine any situation—up to and including having your house destroyed on top of you—in which she was unable to recognise Ted, but failed. Mrs Ingram had said that the man looked, and sounded, like her husband, but wasn't. Unless he *really* wasn't—something along the lines of a hitherto-unknown identical twin, perhaps—none of it made sense.

She'd give Ted his dinner—a nasty-looking piece of haddock that was all that the fishmonger could offer—and then she'd talk to him about it. He was bound to have a sensible suggestion. One of the best things about Ted was the way she could trust his judgement. He was good at listening, he could always be relied upon to keep things in perspective, and he usually did come up with solutions to problems. It was rather a shame, she thought, that she only had a bit of pimply fish to give him in return.

CHAPTER

19

The sound of Richard Tauber singing 'My Heart and I' greeted Stratton when he returned home. He felt dispirited: in the two days since he'd finished interviewing the nurses, the door-to-door enquiries had yielded nothing, and Lamb was breathing down his neck. Jenny was cooking, and the place smelt—not in a particularly pleasant way, he thought—of fish. She kissed him and made him a pot of tea while he went upstairs to wash.

When he came down, and was comfortably settled—Tauber having finished his warbling and gargling—in the sitting room with paper and slippers, she placed his cup on the top of the steel-cage Morrison shelter, and said, without preamble, 'Can you imagine not being able to recognise me?'

Bemused, he replied, 'Course not, silly,' and resumed reading about the progress (or otherwise—the report was suitably vague) of the army towards Cherbourg.

'I mean,' Jenny persisted, 'you would always *know* it was me, wouldn't you?'

'Mmm,' said Stratton.

'But what if you'd lost your memory?'

'Well...' Stratton lowered the newspaper. 'Then I'd be jolly glad there was this beautiful, mysterious woman looking after me, wouldn't I? What are you talking about, anyway?'

'The oddest thing.'

Resigning himself, Stratton folded the newspaper and placed it on the Morrison beside his teacup. 'Tell me.'

'This afternoon we were going to go to the pictures but Mr Ingram telephoned Doris—Dr Makepeace managed to get through to his unit in Southampton. He said they'd given him leave to collect Mrs Ingram. She spoke to him, and Doris said she was made up about it. But when Mr Ingram arrived, she...Well, she didn't recognise him. She wanted us to fetch the police.'

'But she'd recognised his voice on the telephone, hadn't she?'

'Yes!' said Jenny emphatically. 'That's the strange thing.'

'And it was definitely the same man?'

'Well, Doris said the voice was the same as on the telephone, and Mrs Ingram recognised it then, but I really don't understand how you can recognise someone on the telephone and not when they're standing in front of you. Well, unless it's not him at all, but I can't imagine why he'd say he was her husband if he wasn't.'

'A joke?' suggested Stratton.

'Ted, it's serious!'

'I know. But it's hardly likely, is it? Has Dr Makepeace been back to see her?'

'He's supposed to this evening. I told Doris I'd drop by after supper.'

'For God's sake,' said Stratton, irritably. 'Do you have to?'

'I can't just leave her to it, can I? It wouldn't be fair.'

'Oh, all right.' Realising he'd said this with bad grace, Stratton added, 'It's just what with the Rest Centre and this bl— this wretched woman, I never seem to see you.'

'I know, dear. He's got a nasty temper though, Ted. I didn't like him at all.'

'For heaven's sake, Jenny. It's enough to make anyone bad-tempered, what he's been through.'

'No, but this was...Oh, I don't know. He was rude, and... He grabbed her, and when I tried to stop him he pushed me out of the way.'

'Oh?' Stratton sat up sharply. 'Did he hurt you?'

'Just bumped my head on the wall, that's all.'

'Well, come here and let me kiss it.' Jenny sat down on the arm of the chair and allowed herself to be pulled towards him. 'You steer clear of him in future, all right? He'll only have forty-eight hours' leave, so they'll be gone tomorrow and you can both forget all about it.'

'But supposing—'

'There's no point supposing, Jenny. Dr Makepeace'll sort it out, and he'll take her off to wherever they're going and that'll be the end of it.'

'But—'

Stratton laid a finger on her lips. 'No buts. If there's one thing I've learnt from police work, it's never a good idea to get between husband and wife. Not unless she wants you to, and then ninety per cent of the time she decides she's made a mistake.'

'But she doesn't think she *is* his wife, Ted.'

'Look, it's bound to sort itself out in time. Or maybe she'll decide he's a better bet than the old one.'

'For heaven's sake!' Jenny levered herself off his lap, glaring at him. 'I'd better finish the cooking. Will do you the blackouts later?'

Although the whiffy haddock had almost disintegrated, it still needed chewing before it could be swallowed, and trying to breathe through his mouth at the same time in order not to have to smell it was difficult. Jenny was clearly having a similar struggle because, after several minutes, she put down her fork. 'I *am* sorry, Ted.'

'It's all right, love. Can't be helped. Is there anything you could put on it? Bisto or something?'

Jenny giggled. 'You can't put Bisto on fish.'

'Well, what about some of that tomato chutney you made last year?'

'I suppose so.' Jenny looked at him doubtfully. 'There's a jar left.'

The addition of tomato chutney was surprisingly successful, as was the pudding—bottled fruit with the top of the milk and a sprinkling of sugar. Afterwards, while they were drinking their tea and Stratton was having a smoke, Jenny said, 'Do you remember George, Ted?'

'George?'

'Mum's cat.'

Stratton grinned at her. 'I remember. It was the first time I came to your house.'

'That's right, we were courting, and we'd all sat down to tea, and George came in — he'd been wandering about all over the house, miaowing, and none of us knew what was up until you told us he was going to have kittens. We just thought he was getting a bit fat round the middle.'

Stratton laughed. 'Your faces!'

'We couldn't believe it. You helped us make a sort of nest in the garden shed, remember? With old blankets and things. And he went in there, quite happy, and when we looked next morning there were four little kittens. We thought we shouldn't change the name, so we went on calling him George. Her, rather—but we never really got out of the habit of saying "he".'

'I'd forgotten about that.'

'Do you know what Mum said, afterwards?'

'A few sharp things about both me and the cat, I should think.'

Jenny smiled. 'No. I never told you this—didn't want to make you big-headed. She said that you'd make a good husband, because you'd looked after George.'

'Did she?'

'Yes. And you don't do so badly with us, either.'

'Well,' Stratton, pleased but slightly embarrassed, said, 'I've never made you a nest in the garden shed.'

'Silly! You know what I mean. Anyway, I just thought I'd never told you that, and I should. That was it, really.'

'Well, thank you. It's very nice.'

As Jenny washed up before leaving for Doris's, Stratton, watching her move about the kitchen, thought that 'nice' wasn't exactly the word, but he couldn't think of one that really expressed what he was feeling. Flattered, touched, proud...He went up behind her and gave her a kiss on the cheek.

'What was that for?'

'I do love you, you know,' he said. 'I know I don't say it much, but I do.'

Jenny turned her head, surprised, and Stratton saw that she was blushing. 'That's good,' she said, 'because I love you, too.'

'That's all right, then.' Stratton released her, patted her on the bottom, and went off to carry on reading the paper.

Jenny left, and he tried to concentrate on the Russian army's advance on Minsk. After a while, finding himself unable to concentrate for reasons he couldn't quite pinpoint, he turned on the wireless to listen to J.B. Priestley talking about post-war conduct, but that did not engage him, either. In the end, he turned it off again, and sat staring into space, thinking vaguely about Dr Reynolds and Nurse Leadbetter and Mrs Ingram and not coming to any conclusions about any of them. By the time Jenny returned he'd given up and was dozing.

'Mr Ingram telephoned again just before Dr Makepeace arrived,' she said, taking off her scarf and patting her hair into place. 'Doris overheard the conversation—Mrs Ingram recognised his voice and kept asking why he'd sent this other man to fetch her. Then Mr Ingram spoke to Doris. She's sure it's the same voice, and he talked about the visit and everything. She didn't know what to say. They decided it would be best if he didn't come tomorrow—she's too upset.'

'What did the doctor say?'

'Well, when Doris told him about the telephone call, it was as if he didn't believe her—thought she was trying to make trouble or something. When we said perhaps it wasn't her husband at all—'

'You didn't, did you?'

'Well, I did. He looked at me as if I was a complete fool.'

'I'm not surprised.'

'Oh, charming! I know *you* think it's a stupid idea, but no-one's seen him, have they? And he could have *stolen* Mr Ingram's ID card, couldn't he?'

'But why would he?'

'I don't know...Because he's fallen in love with her and wants to go away with her or something.'

'Now you really are imagining things. Look at it logically. If—'

'Oh, men and logic. It's always the same. You look at the state the world's in, because of your *logic*. And it's got to be her who's wrong, not him. It always has to be the woman's fault.' Jenny sounded unusually venomous. Stratton wondered if there was something else bothering her as well, but decided—for the sake of peace and quiet, and also in case it was something that he'd done wrong—not to enquire.

'Steady on,' he said, mildly.

'Well, it does. Dr Makepeace treated all three of us as if we were hysterical.'

'Well, you do sound a bit hysterical at the moment.'

'Thanks.' Jenny, who had been standing with her back to the mantelpiece, took a step sideways and plonked herself down in the other armchair. 'What worries me most is that, for all Dr Makepeace thinks we're idiots, he doesn't seem to understand what's going on any more than we do. He gave her a tonic— something to calm her, he said—and told us it was bound to come right and we weren't to fuss.'

'He's probably right, you know.'

'Oh, you *would* say that. You didn't see her. She kept asking why Mr Ingram hasn't come for her, and she was crying her eyes out. There was *nothing* we could say, Ted. It was horrible.'

'What did Donald say?'

'He'd gone to the pub. Doris said he's pretty fed up about it all.'

'I'm not surprised. Look,' he added, hurriedly, 'I know it's a worry, but it's not *that* bad—I mean, Mrs Ingram knows who *she* is, doesn't she, so the rest is bound to come back soon. The brain's a funny thing at the best of times. Yours must be,' he added, winking at her, 'after all, you married me, didn't you?'

When they went to bed he sensed that a cuddle and a bit of comfort was definitely required. Not that it was any hardship, of course, and Jenny seemed cheered up by it, or at least mollified.

'It's all so peculiar,' she murmured, lying in his arms in the dark.

'I know.' Stratton stroked her hair. 'It doesn't make sense, but neither do a lot of things, do they?'

'S'pose not. But at least I know you're you.'

'That's a relief,' said Stratton, 'because I don't permit my wife to go to bed with strange men.'

'Quite right.' Jenny yawned. After a moment, she said, warily, 'Te-ed?'

'Ye-es?'

'No, it's all right. It's nothing.'

'Sure?'

'Yes.'

'Well, as long as you weren't about to tell me you're planning to run off with the postman or something.'

Jenny snorted. 'The way you've been going on, I just might. Well, I might if he was better looking. 'Night, Ted.'

''Night, love.'

CHAPTER
20

Todd allowed some time to pass after the awkward farewell drink in the mortuary office—a finger of Scotch each in assorted receptacles gathered by Miss Lynn, at least one of which looked as if it might, previously, have contained body fluids, and with Dr Byrne conducting the proceedings as if it were a wake. Todd gave his landlady a week's notice, and found himself some new lodgings—Eversholt Street this time, beside Euston Station. It was depressingly similar to his old room, but nearer to the hospital, which was something.

After leaving both his job and the persona of Sam Todd, he had shaved off his moustache and dyed his hair darker. He'd done this before with a preparation bought from the chemist's but this time it had proved unavailable, so he did the best he could with the remainder of the bottle, supplemented by a spot of boot polish. The result, he thought, wasn't half bad, although he'd have to be careful about getting caught in the rain.

Now, exactly two weeks later, he brushed his jacket and retrieved his trousers from beneath the mattress. This was a red-letter day—or, rather, evening: his first outing as Dr James Dacre, MB, ChB. Already, he looked more substantial; shoulders broader, back straighter, head held higher. He and Fay Marchant, he thought, would look good together—very good indeed…But, he reminded himself, until it was properly established, his new identity was a fragile thing, and must be nurtured carefully. First things first...

'I say,' he said to his reflection, in the smarter, more precise tones of the professional man, 'I couldn't help overhearing...You chaps are from the Middlesex, aren't you?' He offered his hand for an invisible shake. 'Dacre. Trained up in Scotland. I must say, I'm jolly glad I've run into you...'

He clapped his hat on his head, winked at his reflection and left his room. He made his way to the Cambridge Arms, where, in the two weeks since leaving his job, he'd hung around in the evenings watching the three doctors. Now, as Dr Dacre, newly minted, he was ready to join them.

He'd done the necessary research into their backgrounds, and—another good omen, this—none of them had trained at St Andrews. Of course, it was entirely possible that they might know somebody who had, but an indirect connection could be easily managed...In any case, at this first, seemingly accidental, meeting, he'd be the one asking most of the questions.

Once he'd gained their confidence—he'd enough money to buy them drinks—he'd be home and dry, but he mustn't be too cocky. Cracking jokes, he'd found, could help out in sticky situations, as long as one didn't overplay it. He'd have to watch the voice, too; it was important to sound natural, not 'put on'.

The doctors weren't there when he arrived—no bad thing, as it would make the encounter seem more as if it had come about by chance. Perhaps, he thought, they were on duty and he'd have to come back the following evening. That would be irritating, but not disastrous. In the meantime, he'd enjoy his first public appearance as Dr Dacre. He chose a spot at the corner of the bar from which he could easily survey the whole room. Judging by what he'd seen around him, this pub appeared to attract a quieter lot than the raffish types who frequented the pubs of Rathbone Place and Soho. They seemed to be mainly businessmen, some with women—not whores—in tow, a few elderly locals, and, in one corner, two American soldiers clad in short, buff-coloured Ike jackets.

Watching them all through the haze of smoke and the buzz of chatter, seeing their mouths open and close, their hands lifting up and down as they drank, he thought, they are like fish, swimming aimlessly in a murky tank, not knowing where they are going or what they are seeking, operating only on instinct, nothing more. Whereas he, superior, a shark scenting blood and going in for the kill, knew precisely what he was doing.

Within five minutes, Doctors Wemyss, Betterton and Unwin entered and established themselves at one of the corner tables. Dacre waited until they had settled, each with a pint of the suspiciously watery 'Scotch Ale' which was all there was on offer, and began to study them, surreptitiously.

He had worked out, over the course of several evenings' observation of the three men, who would be most approachable. The rich one, Wemyss, was easy to spot, tall and freckled, his red hair already receding at the temples; Betterton was plump, with a shiny face and fleshy, quoit-like lips, and Unwin was long-nosed with a sardonic expression. Dacre had discounted the latter very quickly on the grounds that he looked both impervious to flattery and prone to making sharp remarks. He'd considered Betterton, but after watching him, on several occasions, jabbing a fat finger on the round, copper-covered table as he made some point with eager argumentativeness, had decided against him too. Wemyss, he concluded, was the man to aim for. There was something about the way he lolled in his seat with his head resting against one of the blackout boards that were placed over the windows that suggested a fundamental laziness. Of course, it was possible that the man was simply tired, but his part in the conversation appeared so consistently languid as to suggest he was willing to agree with things because to do otherwise was too much of an effort. Perhaps it was because he was protected by his money against actually having to work for a living, jammy bastard. For casual acceptance into the medical brotherhood without too many questions being asked, Wemyss was definitely the best bet.

Dacre's luck was in. After half an hour, during which the pub had become far too busy for Dacre to have any chance at all of overhearing what they were talking about, Wemyss rose and brought their empty glasses to the bar for more drinks.

Dacre took a quick glance back at the table. Betterton and Unwin were deep in discussion, both looking down as Betterton's finger drew a diagram of something on the tabletop with the help of matches and a crumpled cigarette packet. Hoping it wasn't some medical conundrum that he might be asked to pronounce upon later, he contrived to move next to Wemyss, manoeuvring himself so that the taller man jogged his elbow just as he was raising his arm to take a drink.

Dacre, who was holding the glass in a deliberately clumsy manner, spluttered in an exaggerated fashion as beer splashed over both their sleeves and the lapel of his jacket.

'Sorry, old chap,' said Wemyss, in a drawling voice that managed to be both contrite and condescending at the same time. 'Didn't see you there. Terrible waste of beer—you must let me buy you another.'

'It really isn't necessary.' Dacre looked down at his beer-stained clothes in dismay.

'No, I insist.'

'Well, in that case…' Dacre smiled at him. Thank you. I don't seem,' he patted his pockets, 'to have a handkerchief.'

'Here.' Wemyss proffered his own. 'This should dry it up a bit.'

'This is jolly decent of you,' said Dacre, blotting his clothing.

'My fault entirely,' said Wemyss. The barman was serving another customer, and Dacre saw that he'd have to move the conversation on to the next step before the drink was bought and Wemyss, duty done, returned to his colleagues. He didn't want to have to resort to the line about overhearing their conversation—the racket in the place was such that it simply wasn't credible.

It was the barman, coming momentarily to rest opposite Wemyss and seeing the empty glasses, who saved the situation. Although there was nothing on offer but beer, the habit of years made him say, 'What can I get you, doctor?'

The order given, Dacre said, 'Good heavens. You don't happen to be from the Middlesex, do you?'

'Yes.' Wemyss indicated the table with a jerk of the head. 'All of us.'

'Well, there's a turn up.' Dacre stuck out his hand. 'James Dacre. Trained up in Scotland. St Andrews.'

'Really?' Wemyss's expression shifted from polite but necessary interest to engagement. 'Wemyss,' he said. 'Pleased to meet you. What are you doing in this neck of the woods?'

'Nothing, really.' Dacre gave a self-deprecating grin. 'At least,' he amended, 'nothing at the moment. I'm hoping to help. On the scrap heap as far as the forces are concerned. Wanted to join the RAMC of course, but...' he hesitated to allow Wemyss to prompt him.

'But?'

'Cardiomegaly, I'm afraid.'

Wemyss frowned, and Dacre, realising in a flash that he'd never actually heard the word spoken, wondered if he'd mispronounced it. 'Didn't know myself until the medical,' he continued. 'No arrhythmia or palpitations or any of that, but...' He shrugged. 'Felt a bit of a chump, if I'm honest, when they told me. What about you?'

'They kept us back.'

'Oh?' Dacre injected the monosyllable with a note of surprise.

'Needed some fresh blood.' Wemyss shrugged in his turn. 'You know how it is.'

'Mmm...' Draining the remains of his first pint so as not to have to reply too quickly, Dacre said, 'I suppose they must be keeping you pretty busy over there.'

'I should say so.' Wemyss grimaced. 'We're a man down, actually.'

'Air raid?'

'Poor chap got himself murdered. At least, that's the *on dit*.'

'Good heavens! What happened?'

'Nobody's really sure. Someone seems to have clobbered him on the head in the blackout. And then there was a nurse, managed to get herself strangled. That was actually *in* the hospital.'

Dacre raised his eyebrows. 'Good heavens. Patient run amok?'

'God knows. Look...' Wemyss eyed him for a moment, as if making a decision, then said, 'Why don't you come over and join us? Those two'—he glanced across at Betterton and Unwin, who were now watching him expectantly—'must be getting thirsty.'

Pleased by the small evidence of an alliance between them, Dacre said, 'If you don't mind. I'll give you a hand.'

'All right, thanks.'

Securing the remaining glass as well as his own, Dacre struggled behind him through the throng until they reached the corner table. Betterton and Unwin looked up curiously, and Wemyss, depositing the pints, announced, 'Dacre. St Andrews man. Met at the bar.'

'James Dacre. Hope you don't mind,' said Dacre. 'Whose is this?'

Betterton stood up. 'Me, I think. Betterton. How do you do? This,' he added, as Unwin, who had also risen, showed no sign of speaking, 'is Unwin. Man of few words.'

Handshakes followed, during which Unwin still did not speak. Dacre, deciding not to force the issue, or show presumption by sitting down, said, 'If I'm barging in, do tell me. I shan't be offended. Just that I find myself at a bit of a loose end.'

'You must be the only medico in London who is,' said Unwin. 'How come?'

'Well, as I was explaining, I'm not fit enough for the services, and the job I had in Scotland fell through—some sort of mix-up over paperwork which nobody could get to the bottom of, including me, although,' Dacre laughed, 'I must say, I didn't try too hard.' He'd prepared this little speech earlier. Tales of papers going astray and getting lost or destroyed were so commonplace that, as with bomb stories, everybody had their own and it was a fair bet that they'd be quickly bored with the details of anyone else's misfortune. 'Found myself digs in Euston—bit of a hole, but it'll do for the time being...Anyway, here I am.'

He was right. Unwin rolled his eyes in mute acknowledgement of bureaucratic cock-ups everywhere and said, 'Well, pull up a chair.'

Wemyss, picking up his glass for a toast, said, 'Well, here's how.'

'Cheers,' said Betterton, raising his own. Dacre and Unwin followed suit.

'To the future,' Wemyss added, clinking glasses with Betterton. Turning to Dacre, he said, 'He's just got engaged to be married.'

'Congratulations,' said Dacre. 'Got married myself, last year. Best thing I ever did.' This was entirely unplanned, and as soon as he'd said it he wished he hadn't. Of course, it was another point of difference between his new self and Todd, which was good, and it gave him an added respectability, but if it got about, it would be likely to queer the pitch with his girl. Thinking he'd better do some compensatory groundwork, he said, 'Mind you, I've hardly seen her—she's staying with her parents in Suffolk. Far too many glamorous American airmen up there for my liking.' That was an inspired touch: if necessary, his wife could have an affair with a Yank, breaking his heart, which would appeal to the sympathetic nature he was sure his girl would possess. Rather good, actually. 'Make sure you keep yours close to,' he counselled Betterton, who grinned.

'Oh, I intend to. Sooner rather than later, in fact. Courtesy of Wemyss here.' He fished in his pocket and brought out a labelled key.

Dacre raised his eyebrows in mystified enquiry.

'Lucky old Wemyss has use of a suite at the Clarendon,' said Unwin.

Dacre whistled. The Clarendon was a smart West End hotel.

Wemyss looked slightly sheepish. 'I don't actually live there. My father got it at the beginning of the war,' he said. 'He went back to the country last year but he kept it on for when he comes up. The rest of the time...' Wemyss shrugged. 'Well, let's say I keep the key handy. Might as well put it to use.'

'Absolutely,' said Dacre, filing away this information for use in the future. 'Shame to let it go to waste.'

'I'd be obliged if you'd keep mum,' said Wemyss. 'Don't want everyone to know, or they'll all be wanting it.'

Dacre nodded acknowledgement, and Wemyss turned to the other two. 'I was just telling Dacre here about Reynolds and that poor nurse,' he said.

'Dreadful business,' said Betterton, briskly. 'Not,' he added, 'that anyone knows exactly what happened to either of them.'

'Terrible.' Dacre shook his head. 'When did it happen?'

'About three weeks ago,' said Wemyss. 'Don't want a job, do you?'

'As a matter of fact…' said Dacre, 'I mean…'

'Don't like to step into a dead man's shoes?' asked Unwin.

'Well…' Dacre hesitated. 'There is that, but these things have to go through the appropriate channels, don't they?'

'Probably,' said Wemyss, 'but we're fairly pushed, and with these new bombs…'

'If the Powers-that-Be wait for anything to come through official channels,' put in Betterton, 'they'll be waiting till Doomsday—'

He stopped abruptly as the muffled crump of an explosion somewhere to the north of them made the building shake slightly and dislodged the paint from the ceiling. Putting a hand over his pint to protect it from the drift of nicotine-stained flakes, Unwin said, 'And by the sound of it, Doomsday may be sooner than we thought.'

'So,' said Betterton, '*carpe diem* and all that.'

Hoping that *carpe diem* didn't also have some medical meaning he wasn't aware of, Dacre said, 'I'll drink to that.' Having done so, he said, 'Who's the head man there, then?'

Forty minutes later, Dacre left the pub and—despite the blackout—strode down the street in a mood of elation, waving his torch. He had established that the man in charge was Professor Haycraft, manoeuvred Wemyss into effecting an introduction within the next couple of days, and demonstrated that he was a thoroughly good sort by wheedling another half-pint for each of them out of the barman. The gamble had paid off, and the evening had been a resounding success. He had given just enough information to allow them to arrive at their own conclusions, and found out a fair bit about them, too. He had also produced, in order to jot down the name of Wemyss's ward, a sheet of writing paper with the letterhead of the prestigious Athenaeum Club and, just visible, the words 'My dear James,' in confident scrawl. The paper was stolen and the letter forged, but seeing their glances at it he knew it had done its job: the things people worked out for themselves had ten times the value of anything one might tell them.

As he walked along, he turned the conversation over in his mind. Unwin had described Professor Haycraft as 'a nice enough old buffer', and the other two had concurred. Dacre suspected that this meant that the prof. was a fundamentally lazy person who wouldn't be too bothered about checking up on his carefully prepared references. The fact that he'd be far busier than usual and distracted by recent events would also help.

Past experience had taught him that, whenever possible, one should go to the top by the fastest and most direct route. Not only were the people in charge able to make decisions, but they were accustomed to doing so. They could afford to be more understanding and liberal because they did not need to have second thoughts about how someone lower down might like it. And, once the top man accepted you, everyone else would...And Wemyss, Betterton and Unwin had accepted him already, hadn't they? That meant there were three people who would be able to introduce him as Dr Dacre. Convince A, B and C, and D and all the rest will follow. He was definitely on his way to the top of the tree. He was going to be a doctor! It was a wonderful, heady feeling. And there was Fay Marchant, ripe and luscious, to look forward to...Oh, he was going to enjoy himself, all right.

CHAPTER
21

Ten days after Dacre's encounter with the doctors, Stratton
left DCI Lamb's office with a heavy heart. Even though he'd
managed to sort out his end of the NAAFI robbery, the stolen
army tyres and several other cases in the past three weeks,
Lamb's parting shot had been that his patience was wearing
thin and would Stratton please pull his finger out and conclude
'the business' at the hospital. Sitting at his desk with a tepid
cup of tea, Stratton reflected that Lamb's patience was always
wearing thin, largely because he didn't have much of it in the
first place—a bit like Hitler, really. Although they appeared to
have found the weapon used on Reynolds—much to Stratton's
surprise, the Home Office analyst had reported that one of the
bloodied bricks collected by Ballard had two hairs on it which
matched the victim's—the extended door-to-door enquiries had
revealed nothing, and neither, barring the fact that Reynolds may
have been rather too friendly with Fay Marchant, had his own
interviews at the hospital. Still, thought Stratton, finding that
Reynolds had been hit with a brick indicated that, if it was deliberate, then it wasn't premeditated—whoever had bashed him
had simply picked up the nearest object to hand. The Leadbetter
killing seemed more likely to have been the result of malice afore-
thought, as whoever had killed her had presumably lured her into
the operating theatre first.

After much prevarication from Reynolds's former colleagues at the Middlesex, he and Ballard had compiled a list of the dead doctor's cock-ups and visited the bereaved spouses and relatives in an attempt to rule out the idea of a revenge attack. Leadbetter, it transpired, had never worked in Casualty, so it seemed unlikely that she'd either compounded or covered up any of Reynolds's errors. The previous week, Stratton had been to Euston to see Mrs Beck, the mother of the boy who'd died of blood poisoning. That had been a depressing morning. The mother, with greasy hair and a grey face, was abject and lost in the dirty, cluttered tenement flat with cracked panes and walls stained by soot and brick dust from nearby bombing.

'The doctor said he'd be all right,' she said.

'Was that Dr Reynolds?' asked Stratton.

Mrs Beck looked at him as if she didn't understand the question. 'A doctor said,' she repeated, 'Sammy'd be all right. He told me.'

'But you don't know the doctor's name?'

She shook her head. 'He *told* me.'

'What else did he say?' asked Stratton.

'Just that I wasn't to worry over it, and…Well, they'd bandaged it up, hadn't they? It was a nasty cut, but I never thought…perhaps the badness got into it later, I don't know. I'd have taken him back before, only the doctor said it would get better left to itself and I didn't want to cause any bother.'

'What happened when you took him back to the hospital? Did you see the same doctor?'

Mrs Beck nodded. 'He just took one look at Sammy and took him away. I never saw Sammy again after that. I did ask, but they wouldn't let me. They told me to go home. I come back in the morning, just like they said, and they told me he was dead.'

'Did you see the doctor again?'

Mrs Beck shook her head once more with the same hopeless lack of understanding. 'Sammy'd died, hadn't he? In the night.'

'What about your husband?' asked Stratton. 'Was he there?'

'He's in France. I wrote to him about Sammy. The doctor said he'd be all right,' she said, dully. 'If only…' She gazed at Stratton miserably.

'You did your best for Sammy,' he said, gently. 'I'm sure of it.' He rose from the battered wooden chair. 'Thank you for talking to me.'

Mrs Beck blinked at him and shuffled down the few feet of hallway to let him out of the flat. She couldn't be more than forty, Stratton thought, but she moved like an old woman. He took his leave and was about to descend the stairs when she suddenly said, in an urgent tone, 'He was a good boy. He was never in any trouble.'

Stratton turned. 'I'm sure he was a credit to you, Mrs Beck, and I am very sorry about what happened.'

'Sorry isn't going to make a bloody bit of difference, is it?' he said to Ballard afterwards. 'I'll bet my last penny Reynolds never apologised to her, or even thought of it. The way she said "If only..."—it was the weight of it. She couldn't bring herself to say the rest of that sentence—all those things: if only the doctor had been right, if only the wound hadn't been poisoned, if only she'd taken him back to the hospital earlier, if only she'd had the confidence to make a fuss...'

'That's it, isn't it, sir? People don't want to make a fuss. That's how my lot were, too.'

'Which ones were they?'

'The Greens. Widow and sister of the wrongly diagnosed diabetic. Can't imagine either of them walloping Reynolds with a brick or anything else.'

'Imagine living with it for the rest of your days, though. The thought that if you'd said something...But I suppose it's the same as Mrs Beck not asking me why I was there. She just assumed I had a right to question her about the most painful thing that ever happened to her.'

'People do, don't they, sir? You know, white coat, mortar board, dog collar, any uniform, really. People just accept authority. If someone with a uniform tells you what to do, especially nowadays...Just as well, really. For us, I mean.'

Now, sitting in his office, Stratton was reflecting on this conversation when there came a vigorous battering at the door.

'Come in,' he shouted. The banging continued. Stratton raised his voice. 'I said come in! There's no need to bash the door down.' The door opened, and Arliss—it would be—appeared, standing to attention with the self-satisfied air of one who had vital news to impart.

'What is it, for God's sake?' asked Stratton irritably.

Arliss cleared his throat in readiness before announcing, 'Telephone message, sir. From Mrs Reynolds, sir.' Arliss nodded, smugly.

'Well, what did she say?'

'It's very important, sir. She wants to speak to you. Says it's urgent.'

'In that case, I suppose I'd better get round there straight away. Can you find me a car, and round up Miss Harris, if she's available.' Arliss continued gazing at Stratton, but did not move.

'Go on,' he snapped, 'get cracking before you take root.'

Arliss departed, leaving Stratton to pick up his notebook and put on his hat. Perhaps, he thought, Mrs Reynolds was going to provide the clue he was looking for.

CHAPTER

22

It was a man who answered the door at Mrs Reynolds's. Middle-aged and pinguid, he announced himself as 'Alec Dearborn. I'm Blanche's—Mrs Reynolds's—brother.'

Recognising the name of a well-known manufacturer, Stratton said, 'Hairbrushes?'

'That's right. I do hope you won't make this more unpleasant than it needs be,' he said, officiously. 'Mrs Reynolds is very upset.'

As Stratton hastened to reassure him, he thought, So that's where the big house comes from—the money was hers, not Reynolds's.

Dearborn led them through to the sitting room and hovered, silent and proprietorial, beside his sister, who was standing in front of the fireplace. Stratton could see that, despite her air of forced calm, she had grown gaunt in the past couple of weeks and the room had a neglected air, with soiled antimacassars and unpolished surfaces.

Without preamble, Mrs Reynolds said, 'I found this,' and held out a grubby square of paper.

Stratton examined it. The writing—a round, schoolgirlish hand—was in pencil, and quite faint, but he could make out the words: *Off at 6, essential I see you. Meet back gate. Must arrange something very soon. F x.*

'Where did you find this?'

'In one of his jackets. The inside pocket.'

'I see. Have you any idea who "F" might be?'

'No. But it's a woman, isn't it?'

Stratton hesitated. 'I should say so,' he said, gently.

'She was pregnant, wasn't she? "Must arrange something very soon..." What else could it mean?'

'I don't think,' said Stratton hastily, 'that we should start jumping to conclusions. There may well be a perfectly innocent explanation.'

'1 can't think of one.' From Dearborn's face, it was evident that he couldn't, either. Neither could Stratton, but he wasn't going to admit it. 'It must be somebody at the hospital,' Mrs Reynolds continued. 'It's a clue, isn't it? This F person, whoever she is, she could have had something to do with his death, couldn't she?'

'Well...' Stratton chose his words carefully. 'If she was pregnant—whether or not she was planning to have the child—'

'She wasn't. "Arrange something!" That means an illegal operation, doesn't it?' Beside her, Dearborn, nodding vigorously, made a harrumphing noise. 'She'd got herself into trouble, and she was trying to make Duncan break the law.'

'Not necessarily, Mrs Reynolds. And if she was pregnant, it is, of course, entirely possible that Dr Reynolds wasn't the father.'

'Why else would she ask him? Unless she was going to try and persuade him to run away with her.'

'As I said, I don't think we ought to jump to conclusions. I know this must be upsetting for you, but—'

'I had no idea,' said Mrs Reynolds, bleakly, to her brother. 'I thought we were happy. We couldn't have children—well, I couldn't—but I was a good wife to him...This woman was trying to trap him, wasn't she? To get him for herself. I don't know how people can be so...so...shameless. She must have known that Duncan was married.' She turned and stared at Stratton, hollow-eyed. 'I found it two days ago. I've been sitting here looking at it ever since. I can't think about anything else. He must have been lying to me, saying he was working, and all the time...this...' Her words broke up in sobs. Obviously at a loss for words, Dearborn made feeble calming-down motions with his fat hands and it was left to Miss Harris to put a comforting arm around the weeping woman.

'Don't distress yourself, dear,' she murmured.

Mrs Reynolds gulped back her tears and pawed at her eyes with a handkerchief. 'I'm sorry,' she said, 'but it's the shock. It's as if our life was all a lie—I thought Duncan loved me, even though I couldn't give him a child, but she got her claws into him, and I don't know how long...and it was all just a sham...'

'No, Blanche...' murmured Dearborn, ineffectually. 'No...'

'We don't know that,' said Stratton, firmly.

'But you will find out, won't you?'

'Yes. I'll take this with me, and we'll make some enquiries.'

'I have to know,' she said. 'I don't want to know, but I have to. I can't sleep, since...'

'I understand, Mrs Reynolds. We'll be looking into it. I'm sorry,' said Stratton, 'but I do have to ask you this. On the night that Dr Reynolds...that he died...was there anyone with you?'

'Really!' Dearborn, who had been staring at the floor, brought his head up with a jerk. 'Is that necessary?'

'I'm afraid so,' said Stratton. 'We have to follow the procedures.'

Mrs Reynolds shook her head and then, opening her eyes wide, said, 'I was here. I told you before. I was on my own, but one of the neighbours came round, collecting—Salute the Soldier Week, I think—and I gave her something, but I can't remember what time that was.'

'Can you give me the name?'

Dearborn started to say something, but Mrs Reynolds laid a hand on his arm. 'It's all right, Alec, they have to do their job. It was Mrs Loomis-Browne. Number twenty-four.'

Stratton noted it and, after further reassuring pats from Policewoman Harris and assurances that the matter would be thoroughly investigated, he shook hands with Dearborn and they took their leave.

'You don't think Mrs Reynolds could be involved, do you, sir?' asked Harris, when they were in the car. They'd been to see Mrs Loomis-Browne and confirmed the story about her visit to Mrs Reynolds, which had taken place sometime between half-past six and seven o'clock in the evening.

'Not really,' said Stratton. 'Mind you, women have killed their husbands for less, although the money seems to be hers, not his, so she's got nothing to worry about on that score.'

'I've got a Dearborn hairbrush myself,' said Harris. 'Jolly good, they are. But if she'd killed him, she wouldn't have shown you the note, would she? I mean, it gives her a motive.'

'Exactly.'

'Do you think the woman who wrote it might be one of his patients, sir?'

'Well, she could be,' said Stratton, 'but she's not.'

Harris's eyes widened. 'Do you know who it is, then?'

'Let's just say,' said Stratton, grimly, 'that I've got a pretty good idea.

'Hope you don't mind, dear, but it's as black as my shoe. I'm afraid we've run out of milk.'

Jenny glanced into the cup of stewed liquid presented to her by Mrs Haskins. 'Oh, well. Beggars can't be choosers. Thank you, dear.' She had already spent several fruitless hours at the Rest Centre attempting to get through to the assistance board, the hospital and the mortuary in pursuit of a missing woman and was about to take a well-earned rest when the double doors at the end of the school hall flew open and Mr Ingram hurled himself through them.

'Mrs Stratton!' he bawled, running headlong towards her, pursued by several indignant ladies. He turned to Jenny. 'I've got to see her,' he said. 'Please, help me to see her.' He leant across the table and whispered, hoarsely, 'I'm not meant to be here. I kept asking, but they wouldn't let me, so—'

Jenny held up a hand. He might have frightened her before, but she recognised desperation when she saw it, and this was a man at the end of his tether. 'It's all right,' she told Mrs Haskins. 'I know this gentleman. If you wouldn't mind...' she indicated the man she'd been helping, 'I'll take him to see his wife.'

'Do you know her?'

'She's staying with my sister Doris. They were bombed out.'

Mrs Haskins took her sleeve and drew her aside. 'He came bursting in like a madman,' she said, keeping her voice low. 'Are you sure he's all there?'

'He's worried about his wife,' murmured Jenny. 'She's been staying with my sister Doris and she went a bit funny in the head.'

'He's a bit funny, too, by the look of things...Well, good luck, dear. Rather you than me—be careful.'

Mr Ingram followed Jenny outside, then, impulsively, grabbed her hand.

'Would you mind?' she asked, wriggling from his grip.

'I'm sorry, Mrs Stratton, it's just that I was so worried, after what happened...'

'I'm not surprised,' said Jenny. 'But now—'

'No, that's what I mean, what *just* happened five minutes ago. I've been round to Mrs Kerr's—she wasn't there, else she'd have opened the door herself, so I called Elsie's name through the letterbox and waited a bit until she came downstairs. She was talking to me all the time, asking why I'd been so long, and how she'd thought I'd left her and how glad she was, all this while she's in the hall, opening the door, all excited, and then the moment she sees me she slams it shut. Right in my face, and the minute before she'd been fine...I don't understand. I feel as if I'm going mad.'

'I'm sorry,' said Jenny. 'I don't understand it, either. No-one seems to.'

'You don't think...if you were to come back with me to Mrs Kerr's...?'

Jenny seriously doubted this, but, feeling that she must do *something*, said, 'Well, I do have a key. Let me fetch my things, and I'll come along now.'

As they walked the few streets to Doris's house, Mr Ingram said, 'The doctor said she'd get better. Mrs Kerr told me. She's always suffered with her nerves, but never like this.'

Jenny sighed. 'Well, it's a dreadful thing to happen, especially to someone who's...sensitive.' 'Sensitive', she felt, had more merit than 'nervous', and wasn't so far down the sliding scale of mental afflictions that ended in the black hole of insanity. Doris's daughter Madeleine had repeatedly expressed the view—with a lot of eye-rolling—that one of the pair must be off their rocker, and it was just a case of deciding who; not exactly helpful, but then she was only sixteen...Both Ted and Donald, when applied to, had taken the 'give it time' line (Donald with less forbearance than Ted, but it was his house, after all).

Jenny and Doris, in their wilder moments, had developed a theory, based mainly on the film *Gaslight*, that Mr Ingram was deliberately trying to make everyone think Mrs Ingram was mad by bribing a friend to pretend to be him, so that she'd be locked away and he could get his hands on her money (supposing she had any), and it was this she remembered now. Perhaps, after all, he was just pulling the wool over their eyes. Or perhaps *he* was mad and just *thought* he was Eric Ingram. This idea now seemed so far-fetched that she almost laughed.

'I don't understand it,' Mr Ingram was saying. 'You don't think...' He halted, putting a hand on Jenny's arm. '...that she's punishing me for something I've done wrong? Because I've always tried to be a good husband to her, Mrs Stratton. What if she doesn't get better?' he asked. 'Will she have to go to... to...?' Jenny knew what he was talking about—the big asylum at Barnet. He blinked several times, and said, 'I don't want to lose her.'

'Good heavens, it's not going to come to that,' she said, as breezily as she could. 'Look on the bright side. She recognised your voice on the telephone, didn't she?'

Mr Ingram stood well back while Jenny unlocked the front door of Doris's house. 'Yoo-hoo!' she called. 'Mrs Ingram! It's Jenny Stratton—I've come to see you!'

Hearing no reply, or even any sound, Jenny—not at all sure that she was doing the right thing—advanced cautiously down the hall and peered into first the kitchen and then the sitting room. Finding nobody, she stood at the bottom of the stairs and called again. Still nothing. With a sense of trepidation, she put one foot on the first step. What if Mrs Ingram had done something silly? Several images of just what 'something silly' might entail—the slight body, dwarfed by her sister's dressing gown, hanging from a rope; slumped against the bathroom door, wrists slit and hands gloved in blood; or simply tucked in bed, marbled blue-white and lifeless—crowded her mind. You're the one being silly, she told herself. She went slowly up the stairs, crossed the landing, paused in front of the closed door of the room Mrs Ingram had been using, and then knocked.

When there was no response, Jenny cautiously pushed open the door and looked inside. The blackout curtains were closed, but she could make out the form of Mrs Ingram, huddled beneath the eiderdown, so that only the top of her head and her eyes could be seen. Even in the dim light, she looked terrified.

'*He's* not with you, is he?' she whispered.

'No. It's just me.' Jenny advanced to the end of the bed.

'That bad man was here. He's got my Eric. I know. I heard him talking, and then when I opened the door he wasn't there. He must have done something to him to make him talk, and then when I opened the door they took him away.'

'Who did?'

'The people with that man. They're trying to trick me. They've captured Eric. They're going to do something horrible to him, and—'

'Mrs Stratton?' Mr Ingram's voice came from the hall. 'Is everything all right?'

Hearing the sounds of feet on the stairs, Jenny went to the door of the bedroom and shouted, 'Don't come up!'

'That's Eric!' said Mrs Ingram, pushing away the eiderdown to reveal that, although dishevelled, she was fully clothed. Over the past week she'd lost what little weight she had on her, so that her cheeks had fallen in and her collarbones poked out sharply. 'Is it really him?' she asked. 'Or is it other one?'

Before Jenny could close the door, Mr Ingram came into the room. Mrs Ingram shrieked and clutched at the eiderdown. 'You let him in!' She pointed at Jenny accusingly. 'You're one of them!'

'Elsie, please—'

'For God's sake,' said Jenny, 'get out!' Pushing Mr Ingram out, and muttering, 'Wait downstairs,' she shut the door and leant on it.

'You let him in,' repeated Mrs Ingram. Her eyes, which had been frantic, assumed an expression of fear. 'I trusted you,' she said. 'You and her. I know what your game is. You're the white slave trade. I've heard about people like you. Locking up girls and tricking them.'

Jenny gaped at her. 'No, we're not. We're trying to help you.'

'If you're trying to help me, why don't you call the police and get him arrested?' Mrs Ingram looked at Jenny with sudden shrewdness. 'Or are you afraid they'll arrest you, too?'

'Of course not.'

'Then what are you waiting for? There's a telephone here— they let my Eric talk to me, and—' Mrs Ingram broke off, looking doubtful. 'If it was Eric,' she said. 'It might have been that other man, pretending, and I couldn't tell because I couldn't see him. And they'll be listening. The Germans can do that, you know.'

'The Germans?' echoed Jenny, more bewildered than ever. 'But we…Mr Ingram…I mean, the man who was just here…he's English. You heard him speak.'

Mrs Ingram shook her head. 'You've got people down there to take me away.'

'There aren't any people,' said Jenny. 'I'll show you. I'm going to open the curtains—you can see the front garden and the whole street from here.' She advanced to the window and began to unpin the black curtains in order to pull them back. As she removed the pins, she peered, surreptitiously, through the gap—it would be just her luck if there was some innocent passer-by who could be labelled as 'one of them'. Seeing no-one, she removed the final pin and pushed back the curtains with a flourish. 'See?' she said.

Cautiously, Mrs Ingram uncovered herself and got off the bed. Crouching, she moved towards the window, moving her skinny limbs in a creeping scurry that made Jenny think of a spider with half its legs missing.

The confirmation seemed to deflate Mrs Ingram, who turned and burrowed, rodent-like, under the eiderdown once more. Jenny went downstairs. Mr Ingram was standing just inside the front door, his shoulders hunched, aggression coming from him in waves.

'Well? Is she coming down?'

'I'm sorry,' said Jenny. 'She's not really making much sense. She thinks there are people watching her—waiting to come and get her. She thinks we're...in league with them.'

'That's ridiculous. I want to know what the hell is going on. I know,' he added, hastily, 'it's not your fault, but...' He shook his head, an expression of baffled disgust on his face.

'I know, but...' Jenny gave up. 'I'm going to make some tea.'

As he followed her into the kitchen, she was uncomfortably aware of his tenseness and the way his fists were clenched. Although he was not a large man, his anger and desperation seemed to fill the room, charging the air. He was so close to her that she could smell his hair oil and sweat, and, before she could move to a safe distance on the other side of the table, he grabbed her arm, making her jump.

Jenny tried to pull away, but he held on, hurting her. When she looked down, his knuckles and fingers were white around her wrist. 'Please...' she said. 'This isn't going to help.'

'I just want to show you,' he blurted out. 'I am her husband. Honestly. I can prove it.' He let go of her, and, as she retreated behind the table, rubbing her arm, he thrust his hand into the top pocket of his battledress blouse and pulled out a tatty-looking wad of papers. 'My ID card. And here's a photograph of Elsie.' He pushed them towards her across the table. Jenny bent her head to look, making sure she was out of his reach. The photograph, showing him and Elsie sitting in deckchairs on a beach, laughing, looked as if it had been carried around for a while.

'Whatever she thinks,' he said, 'I'm not this…this other man.'

'I know you aren't,' said Jenny, 'but'—she hesitated, pleased that he looked relieved at this but fearful of angering him again—'I don't think it's a good idea for…well, for you to try and see her again—not today, anyway.'

'What am I going to do?' His pleasure in being believed—acknowledged for who he really was—was gone. Now his eyes were muddy and resentful, with the look of a man who has realised the magnitude of the catastrophe and is about to buckle under its weight. 'I shouldn't be here. They'll be after me. What the bloody hell am I supposed to *do*?' The last word was almost a howl.

Jenny took a decision. She didn't trust Mr Ingram's temper—apart from anything else, said a small but persistent voice in the back of her mind, he was probably feeling frustrated sexually. But it was gone six, so Doris was bound to be back soon, and Donald as well. She'd be able to keep him calm for ten minutes or so. The thing to do was to keep on the other side of the table and talk to him. 'Look,' she said. 'Do sit down. Please. You must be tired.'

'Yes.' He wiped a hand across his face. 'I'm exhausted. I haven't slept properly for weeks…'

Mercifully, Doris and Donald arrived at the same time, about five minutes later. Jenny skirted the table carefully and dashed outside, and the three of them had a hastily whispered conference on the front porch, during which Jenny explained what had happened and Donald muttered 'Christ Almighty' and cast up his eyes. Sweetened by Doris's revelation that she'd managed to obtain new razor blades, he was prevailed upon, after more mutterings, to shepherd Mr Ingram to the pub. This was mainly because they could think of nothing else to do with him, also because he looked as though he could do with a drink.

'I'm sorry,' said Jenny, when the men had gone, 'but I just didn't know what else to do. I didn't want to say this in front of Don, but she was talking about white slavers and Germans and I don't know what else. She really has lost her marbles.'

Doris sighed, and Jenny noticed for the first time how strained she looked. 'I know. She's been getting odder and odder, what she comes out with. You can't keep on arguing when she's making no sense. I'm glad *he's* gone though. Don't think I could manage another of those go's. I've been all day queuing, or that's how it feels. Honestly, I'm so damn tired, Jen, sometimes I just feel like crying. I know there's others worse off, but...' Doris pulled a handkerchief out of her sleeve and blew her nose.

'Are you all right?' asked Jenny, concerned. 'It's not like you to be weepy.'

'I'll be fine,' said Doris, firmly. 'Don't fuss.' She sat down on a kitchen chair and begun fumbling in her handbag. 'Here,' she said, pushing a small package across the table. 'Razor blades. Make sure Ted gets one.'

'Oh, Doris, I don't know how you do it, what with all this... He'll be thrilled.'

'Well,' said Doris, brusquely, 'tell him to make the most of it. I heard a rumour today that the Gillette factory was hit.'

'Mrs Ingram'll be worried,' said Jenny. 'I'll just go up in case she thinks you've parachuted in to ravish her, or something. You just sit there and have a rest.'

'You know,' said Jenny, when she'd returned and they were drinking tea, 'Mrs Ingram asked me to fetch the police again.'

'I really don't think that's a good idea. There's nothing they could do, and she might end up getting carted off to...well, you know where.'

Doris and Jenny looked at each other. Jenny knew that her sister was thinking the same as Mr Ingram had; it had crossed her mind too several times in the last couple of hours. They were both remembering their Aunt Ivy who had been in Friern Barnet Asylum for the last twenty years of her life. As youngsters, the three girls had been pressed into accompanying their mother on her monthly visits. Jenny knew that Doris, like her, was remembering the confusion and despair of the place, their walks around the grounds with her mother struggling to think of things to say and mute Aunt Ivy trying desperately to please them by darting into the bushes and presenting them with handfuls of earth, cigarette ends, and once, appallingly, a dead squirrel.

Auntie Ivy had died before any of them met the men they were to marry. Jenny hadn't thought it appropriate to mention her existence to Ted—her mother, in fact, had advised against it, and had said something similar to both Doris and Lilian. Even now, Jenny found it hard to talk about, and, judging by Doris's face, she felt the same way. 'That's what I thought,' she said, drawing a line under the subject. 'But I did wonder if I should ask Ted to talk to her. He rescued her, after all.'

'Yes, but she doesn't remember it, does she? And think about it: if Ted comes in and introduces himself—"I'm Inspector Stratton"—she'll know he's your husband, and then she'll think the whole *world* is against her. She'll see it as proof...' Doris groaned. 'I can't stand it! And what if Don brings Mr Ingram back? He can't stay here, there's no room—'

'Take him to the Rest Centre. Look, Dor, if this carries on, do you want me to look after her for a while? I mean, if she came to us.'

'Don't be daft. You've got enough to do. It's not fair to expect Ted to be on his own with her. It's bad enough for Don and Madeleine, and I'm *here*.'

'Well, if you change your mind...' Jenny glanced up at the kitchen clock.

'It's all right, dear,' said Doris. 'I'll be fine. I was just being silly. You go on home. I've got the supper to get.'

'If you're sure. Only I'd better get back to the Rest Centre. I did leave them in the lurch a bit.'

Doris rose. 'Course I'm sure. Come here.' Rounding the table, she gave Jenny a hug. 'Thanks, love.'

The only good thing about all this, Jenny reflected after-wards, was that it had stopped her worrying, for a whole three hours, about being pregnant. For the last few days she'd told herself that it was worry and being tired that was upsetting her system, or that she'd got the dates wrong, but now—today, in fact—there was no getting round the fact that she was one *entire week* late.

Not knowing whether Fay Marchant was still on duty, Stratton decided to leave visiting the Middlesex until the following day. It would nice to be home on time for a change even if Jenny wasn't there.

Walking up Lansdowne Road, Stratton was hailed by Donald coming the other way, with someone he did not recognise in tow. 'I called for you,' he said. 'Fancy a drink? Mr Ingram and I were just on our way to the Swan.'

Stratton looked at Mr Ingram, wondering if he was all right, or even all there. Jenny had said he was aggressive, but he could see no evidence of this, unless one counted the fact that the little man had the look of a punch-drunk boxer (flea-weight) who was trying to rise to the occasion without knowing quite what the occasion was. Presumably, there'd been some further upset over his wife. 'How do you do?' he said, playing for time.

Donald, sensing hesitancy, grimaced at him over Mr Ingram's head and telegraphed a 'don't-you-dare-let-me-down-you-fucker' message with his eyes.

'Why not?' said Stratton.

The pub was full to bursting, as it often was nowadays at the beginning of the week before the beer ran out. The pea-soup haze of smoke in the place was even more acrid than usual and made Stratton's eyes smart. Standing beside him in the crush at the bar, Donald managed, between securing and paying for three half-pints, to fill him in about the situation in a series of muttered asides. 'Christ knows what I'm supposed to do,' he finished. 'I'm bloody glad you're here because I haven't a clue what to say to him.'

'Neither have I,' said Stratton. 'But I hope Jenny and Doris have decided he is who he says he is, so they won't be expecting me to interrogate the poor bastard.'

Donald responded to this by casting his eyes ceilingward in a 'women, wouldn't you know it?' sort of way, and said, 'And he's AWOL. But I didn't tell you that.'

'No, you bloody well didn't,' said Stratton, grimly.

They stood in an awkward group with their drinks, and managed, by dint of finding common ground in Tottenham Hotspur, to avoid mentioning the subject of Mrs Ingram for a good ten minutes.

They were in the middle of a good-natured argument about borrowing players from other teams to make up the numbers, when Stratton received a clap on the back that was hard enough to propel him forward several inches, slopping his drink. 'Look out!'

'Oh, wonderful,' Donald muttered, 'bloody marvellous.'

Stratton's heart sank. He'd been trying to keep an eye out, but what with the crowd and the smoke, it was impossible to see properly who was in the place. 'Hello, Reg,' he said, without turning round. Their brother-in-law bustled forward, elbowing him in the ribs. 'What are you doing in here?'

'Fancied a change. How's the long arm of the law?'

'It would be a bloody sight better without beer all over it,' Stratton said, shortly.

'Sorry about that.' Seeing Mr Ingram, apparently for the first time, Reg added, 'I don't believe I've had the pleasure...'

'This is Mr Ingram,' said Donald.

'Aaah...' said Reg, '*aaah...*' Stratton gaped in disbelief as his brother-in-law closed one eye, inclined his head to one side, and regarded the little man as one might on encountering a problem while putting up shelves. At least, Stratton thought, having a pint in his hand, Reg couldn't actually cross his arms.

'Did you hear,' Stratton began, in an attempt to head Reg off, 'we've taken Caen. Monty's army's gone in and—'

He got no further. 'Are you indeed?' said Reg, loudly, to Mr Ingram. 'Having some trouble at home, I hear?'

Stratton felt, rather than saw, the tremor go through Mr Ingram's slight frame. Turning slightly, he saw the man's Adam's apple bob in a convulsive movement and his jaw clench, but Mr Ingram did not speak. Neither did Donald, who was glaring at Reg. Before Stratton could think of anything to say, Reg continued in the same, breezy tone, 'Your missus staying at the Kerrs', isn't she?'

'Yes,' said Mr Ingram in a low voice, and stared miserably into his pint.

'You shouldn't worry too much,' Reg said, apparently oblivious to the waves of hostility coming from Donald and Stratton, which had now reached a halitosis-like intensity. 'They can do a lot with these mental cases now, you know. Learnt it from the last lot. I remember...'

Do something, Stratton told himself. Hit him, knock the beer out of his hand, stamp on his foot, anything. Paralysed, he continued to glare at Reg, who, having assumed a professorial stance, was regaling Mr Ingram with a story about a man in his regiment in the Great War who had lost the use of his voice though shell shock. 'So you see,' he concluded, 'with modern—'

Mr Ingram cleared his throat. Reg looked at him and held up the admonishing finger of one who is not yet ready for questions from the floor, and continued, 'With modern methods, they can—'

'I'm off,' said Mr Ingram, abruptly. Thrusting his glass into Donald's free hand, he said, 'Got to find a place to kip.'

'Why don't you—' began Stratton, but he'd already left them, dodging through the crowd like an eel.

After a loaded silence of about thirty seconds, Donald burst out, 'What the hell were you playing at?' Reg looked at him in hurt astonishment. 'All that stuff about mental cases—what did you think you were doing?'

'Just trying to be helpful, old man. No need to take it like that.'

'Helpful!' said Stratton. 'Why didn't you just come right out and tell him to buy her a straitjacket?'

'There's no need to be—'

'Yes, there bloody is,' said Donald. 'I don't believe you sometimes, Reg. I really don't.'

'All I meant was,' said Reg, looking at the pair of them as if he was attempting to reason with two exceptionally backward children, 'is that if these cases aren't treated, they can become violent.'

'Violent! You wouldn't know this, because neither you nor Lilian have set foot in my house since she's been there, but Elsie Ingram is a skinny little thing who wouldn't say boo to a goose, and she's about as likely to become violent as you are to...to...' Here, Donald's powers of invention failed him. Stratton, who could have supplied quite a lot of appropriate comparisons (buy a round, crack a joke that anyone finds funny, get through an evening without one of us wanting to knock your teeth out, and so on), said nothing, but nodded his head in agreement.

'I see,' said Reg. 'Well, in that case, I really don't think there's anything more to be said. So, if you'll excuse me...'

'Now we're for it,' said Donald, as they watched him go. Doris'll kill me.'

'I don't think so,' said Stratton. 'Not when she hears the whole story. And I'm sure Jenny would think the same. Anyway, you said yourself that Lilian's not been visiting, so...'

'You don't think...What Reg was saying about mental cases...You don't think he could be right, do you? I mean, that she is actually, you know, *mad*?'

There was an uncomfortable pause while both men considered the possibility, and then Stratton said, 'Don't talk cock. Reg has never been right about anything in his life. He's *Reg*, for Christ's sake. Mind you,' he added, 'it has to be more likely than Jenny and Doris thinking the bloke wasn't her husband at all… Look, I don't know about you, but I could do with another drink, and it's my shout. And then,' he added, 'for Christ's sake let's talk about something else.'

CHAPTER
25

The Men's Surgical Ward was in chaos. Orderlies and nurses were hauling temporary bed frames down the length of the room and putting them together, and those patients who were well enough to be moved were being chivvied, pushed and carried to them as soon as they were made. Stratton, feeling sprucer than he had for weeks, thanks to his new razor blade, stood in the doorway and surveyed the scene. They were obviously clearing the beds nearest the door to make room for a new batch of casualties. There were screens around three of the beds, and the pungent stench of burnt flesh and sweat cut through the odour of carbolic. The patients who could sit up were staring, goggle-eyed, as a stream of nurses rushed up and down carrying hot water bottles, blankets, and small trays bearing hypodermic syringes.

Nobody took the slightest notice of Stratton until he put a hand out to stop a small and obviously very junior nurse who was scuttling past with a bucket of dirty swabs. She whirled round at his touch, a blur of stripes, looking so terrified and overwrought that, for a second, Stratton thought she might scream. 'What's going on?' he asked.

'Explosion,' she gabbled. 'Burns cases, all at once. You'll have to leave. Sister Bateman won't—'

'It's Sister Bateman I've come to see,' said Stratton. 'Where is she?'

'She's not...' The girl, who looked hardly more than a child, shook her head wildly.

'May I ask what is going on here?' The sister, a tall, dark-blue column, appeared so smoothly and silently that, if Stratton hadn't been able to see her legs (no ankles to speak of) he would have thought she moved on casters. The small nurse uttered a shrill squeak and shot off in the direction of the sluice room. 'I'm afraid you'll have to leave, Inspector,' said the sister. 'As you can see, we're very busy.'

'Yes,' said Stratton, feeling about two inches high, 'and I'm sorry to disturb you, but I need to speak to Nurse Marchant again.'

The sister gave him a look that could have stopped a clock. 'Is it really necessary to do it now?'

'Yes,' said Stratton, with all the firmness he could muster. 'I'm afraid—'

The sister grabbed his arm to move him aside as a man on a trolley was wheeled past, his face, arms and torso glazed with what looked like an ill-fitting skin of dark purple, and two bright white pads over his eyes. Stratton stared, appalled, unable to help himself. 'Gentian violet,' the sister told him. 'Most of the others are worse. Clothes burnt into their skin.'

'I'm sorry,' said Stratton, again, 'but I do have to—'

'Oh, very well.' She said this with more bitterness and disgust than he would have thought possible for just three words—not that he could blame her, but what choice did he have, with Lamb breathing down his neck? 'Wait here,' she ordered, and disappeared behind one of the sets of screens.

After a moment, Fay Marchant emerged, wiping her forehead with the back of her hand. She gave Stratton a wan smile, and he could see that, although she still looked disturbingly lovely, there were blue smudges of exhaustion under her beautiful eyes. 'You wanted to see me, Inspector?'

'Yes, Miss Marchant.' Stratton moved towards the door. 'If we could just—'

'Nurse Marchant!' The sister reappeared—apparently at the speed of light—beside them. 'Where do you think you are going?'

'With the inspector, Sister.'

'You are about to leave the ward, Nurse. Where are your cuffs?'

Fay's pale ivory complexion turned a dull red. 'Sorry, Sister.'

Sister Bateman gave Fay a look that suggested the poor girl was entirely lacking in human decency. 'There is no excuse, Nurse Marchant. Ever. Put them on at once and do not leave here until you are correctly dressed. *Whatever* you are doing, you do *not* leave the ward without cuffs. How do you expect the public to have confidence in you if you don't look the part?'

Honestly, thought Stratton, as he waited for Fay to fetch and don her cuffs, anyone would think the girl was wearing a negligee or something. Momentarily distracted by the image of Fay in such a garment, he was recalled to his surroundings by a bellow of agony, and felt sheepish.

Fay returned, received a curt nod of approval from Sister, and they left the ward. As they walked down the corridor, Stratton glanced sideways at Fay, who seemed on the point of tears. Bad enough, he thought, to be chewed up by the sister, but worse that he'd witnessed the whole thing. In an attempt to clear the air and establish a friendly atmosphere, he said, 'Phew! Quite a tartar, isn't she?'

'Oh, no,' said Fay, loyally. 'She was right. I should have remembered, it's just…well, I've only had a few hours' sleep. We were meant to come back on duty at eight, but they called us last night when the casualties were brought in.'

'Then I expect you'd like to take the weight off your feet. You'll be able to, in a minute.'

They reached the office, which Stratton had managed to re-requisition for a couple of hours, and settled themselves on either side of the desk. Fay looked very relieved to be sitting down, and Stratton guessed that she was simply too shattered to be perturbed at the thought of anything he might have to ask her.

He produced the folded scrap of paper from his pocket and slid it across the desk towards her. 'Did you write that?'

Fay unfolded the note and stared at it for a moment. Then, in a defeated tone, she said simply, 'Yes.' Pushing the paper back to Stratton, she said, 'Where did you find it?'

'Mrs Reynolds gave it to me. She found it in one of Dr Reynolds's jackets.'

'Oh, no...' Fay leant forward and, elbows on the table, held her head in her hands. 'Does she know...who...?'

'No. At least, not yet.'

'Look,' she said, wearily, raising her head, 'it's not what you think.'

'Isn't it? There was a bit more than a "mental affinity" between you and Dr Reynolds, wasn't there?'

Fay nodded miserably. 'It was just...Oh, dear. Whatever I say it's going to sound pretty sordid, but it wasn't like that.'

'No? Then what was it like?'

'I was lonely, Inspector. After Ronnie—my fiancé—was killed, I just sort of...closed down inside. But after a while, I started to feel that my whole world had narrowed down to being Nurse Marchant, as if I didn't have a name any more, because nobody ever said it, and there was nothing else but the hospital, and all I ever did was empty bedpans and scrub things. Look, I'm not trying to make excuses, but that's all there was...'

'Until Dr Reynolds came along?'

'Yes. But I'd broken it off, Inspector, before...'

'Before he died?'

'About a month before.'

'That's rather vague. Do you remember the date? When did it start?'

'Last Christmas. We give this concert for the patients, you see.' With sudden animation, Fay rolled her eyes.

Stratton, encouraged by this, said, 'As if they weren't suffering enough?'

Fay smiled. 'They certainly suffered when they heard Sister Bateman sing "Goodnight Sweetheart", I can tell you.'

'And what was your part in this entertainment?'

'I was in the back row. We did the "Lambeth Walk" and "Run, Rabbit".' Fay shook her head. 'Dreadful.'

'And Dr Reynolds?'

'He wasn't in it. Some of the doctors were, but he just came along to watch. We started talking afterwards. Some people had to get straight back on duty, but there's this tradition of having a Christmas dinner where the doctors serve the nurses, and we both went to that, and I said something about being desperate to put some normal clothes on and get away from the hospital, and he invited me to have a drink with him in the new year— said we'd go somewhere right away from it all. I thought he was just being kind, but he remembered. He took me out to dinner, and then we went dancing. It was wonderful—like being alive again—and it sort of went on from there. I did have qualms about it, really, but...'

'One thing led to another...?'

'Yes, but it's not what it sounds like. The note, I mean. About arranging something. I know how it must seem, but...'

'How must it seem?'

'As if I was in trouble. I thought I might be, but it turned out I wasn't.'

'You thought you were pregnant?'

Fay nodded, miserably. 'Yes.'

'So when you wrote "arrange something", what did you mean, exactly?'

'Just...talk about what I—we—were going to do.'

'Which was?'

'We didn't...We talked about it, and Duncan told me to wait a few days to be sure, so I did, and...' Fay flushed. 'It was fine.'

'Did you discuss an illegal operation?'

Fay hesitated.

'Dr Reynolds is dead,' said Stratton. 'He can't be prosecuted. Neither can you, if you didn't do anything.'

'I didn't! I didn't need to. Honestly, Inspector.'

'But you talked about it.'

Fay nodded. 'He said, if I was pregnant he could arrange for me to go away somewhere...a nursing home...and they would, you know...'

'Had he done this before, do you think?'

'You mean, other girls?'

'I meant procuring abortions. But yes, that too.'

'I don't think so. I mean, I don't know that he hadn't—girls, or...the other thing—but I never heard any rumours.'

'Do you know the name of the nursing home?'

'I don't even know if it *was* a nursing home. He just said he could make arrangements.'

'When did you write the note?'

Fay thought for a moment. 'I don't remember the exact date, but I know it was quite soon after Easter, because I'd had two days' leave and I'd gone to see my parents. They live in Cheltenham.'

Stratton did a quick mental calculation: April, May, June, July...three and a half months. Had Jenny begun to show by then? He couldn't remember. Fay was shapely, but she was slim as a reed, so...

Fay, who seemed to guess what he was thinking, said sharply, 'I'm not going to have a baby, Inspector.'

Stratton was covering his embarrassment by scribbling something totally unnecessary in his notebook when she added, in a pleading tone, 'Inspector, I know you have to ask about all this, but surely you can't think I had anything to do with Duncan's death?'

This, Stratton remembered, was pretty much what Mrs Reynolds had said. 'I don't know what to think,' he answered, truthfully. 'But,' he held up his pencil for emphasis, 'I shall get to the bottom of it one way or another. Now,' he added, briskly, 'if there's nothing else you'd like to tell me...'

When Fay had gone, Stratton reflected that he still had no real idea if she was telling the truth. Some of the truth, certainly, but all of it? Had she been pregnant? Was Reynolds not only incompetent, but an abortionist as well?

After a moment spent staring into space, considering this possibility but reaching no conclusion, Stratton pocketed his notebook and left for the station.

CHAPTER
26

Dr Dacre, now of the Middlesex Casualty Department, stood inside his self-appointed bolt-hole and mopped his face with his handkerchief. The room had been one of the hospital's linen stores, several floors up and unused for this purpose since its window frame was torn out by a bomb blast and the sheets, coarse and patched but irreplaceable, had been turned to sandpaper by splinters of glass. Now, it was a repository for crutches and prosthetic limbs. Hanging slackly from a hook on the back of the door was a life-sized articulated human model, used by the student nurses for practising splints and bandaging, and Dacre sat—in half-darkness, thanks to a loose board he'd managed to shove to one side—surrounded by the wooden hands and feet that protruded from the edges of the shelves.

Three days into his new job, Dacre had appropriated the key from the head matron's office. Here, secreted in the corner of a cupboard full of callipers, he kept a medical dictionary, which he consulted by torchlight whenever a patient with a tricky set of symptoms presented himself and couldn't be palmed off on his elderly colleague, Dr Ransome. Absenting himself to hare up four flights of stairs wasn't always easy, but the hospital was so busy that, so long as he looked purposeful, no-one, thus far, had asked where he was going. Besides, it gave him the opportunity to look out for Fay. He'd seen her twice, but on both occasions she was with a group of other nurses, and he needed to get her on her own. A chance meeting, or an engineered chance meeting, was what was needed, and, as the days passed, the more frustrated he felt. He didn't want to make his intentions known by asking one of the other doctors about her—that would invite interest, and ribaldry as well, and he wasn't having that: Fay was not to be shared with anyone, even in jest.

Everything else, however, was going nicely. Now, nearly two weeks in, barring one appalling incident when he'd been about to inject a child with a lethal dose of insulin and only just noticed in time, things were going as smoothly as could be expected, and he was beginning to enjoy himself.

After an introduction from Wemyss, the all-important 'interview' with Professor Haycraft had been almost farcically easy. Unwin's description of the man in charge as a 'nice old buffer' had been spot on: absent-minded and with an air of learned helplessness, he was one of the easiest marks Dacre had ever dealt with. After some basic questions about his training and previous experience, Dacre had produced his forged references. This had been the most hazardous part of the interview—if Haycraft *had* decided to contact any of the professors from St Andrews who'd supposedly written them, he'd have been in trouble. However, the old boy had simply nodded and said, 'These seem to be in order. Frankly—' here he'd given Dacre a rueful smile, 'I'm not disposed to look a gift horse in the mouth. Besides, I know McDermott,' he tapped the topmost paper. 'Good man.'

'Indeed, sir.'

'I expect you'd like to see where you'll be working.' Haycraft had risen. 'I'll give you the tour myself. Just let me go and speak to my secretary.' He chuckled. 'She keeps me on rather a tight rein, you see.'

When he'd left the room, Dacre took the opportunity of pinching some headed writing paper from a pile in a tray on the desk: bound to come in useful at some point, he thought. He was back sitting innocently in his chair when Haycraft returned.

'Permission has been granted, but only for ten minutes,' he said. 'Off we go.'

Dacre guessed that the secretary probably wasn't bossy at all, but merely a handy prop to ensure that his new boss didn't have to do much of anything he didn't want to do, and Dacre was more than happy to collude.

As they strolled towards the Casualty Department, Dacre had felt as if he were part of a stately progress. Haycraft walked along like the naval officers he'd seen in films patrolling the upper deck, with his chest out and his hands behind his back. At the sight of him, voices were hushed and everyone stood to attention, and Dacre basked in the reflected glory. 'I must say,' the professor told him as they went down the corridor, 'your arrival is something of a godsend. It's most irregular, but we're absolutely desperate for another pair of hands.'

'I rather gathered, sir. Dr Wemyss told me about poor Dr Reynolds. And Nurse Leadbetter, of course.'

'Dreadful business, dreadful. Never known anything like it before. I really don't know,' Haycraft shook his head in wonder, 'what the world is coming to. Now,' he continued, as they turned the corner and went downstairs, 'we are the key institution in Sector Five, and, as such, we're the main casualty receiving point for the area. We keep two hundred beds for them. As soon as they're fit to travel, they either go home, or we move them to other hospitals in the sector. We have a first-aid post for minor injuries. All the operating theatres are on the lower floors now, of course, and we have an emergency accumulator in case the power gets interrupted...'

They reached the heavy double doors of the Casualty Department, and Dacre smoothly stepped forward to hold one open for the professor. 'Thank you. Now, this is the sharp end, as you might say. As you can see, we have all the—Sister Radford!' A large, pink-cheeked woman of around fifty had hurried past the rows of waiting patients and was hovering by his elbow. She bobbed slightly as Haycraft addressed her, as if barely able to restrain herself from curtseying. 'This is Dr Dacre. He'll be coming to our aid—very shortly, I hope.' Turning to Dacre, he said, 'That's right, isn't it?'

'Oh, absolutely,' said Dacre, heartily. 'As soon as you like.' At that moment, he'd forgotten that he wasn't really a doctor, and honestly felt that nothing would be finer than to step into the breach and heal the sick. He gave Sister Radford a beaming smile and received one in return. To show her that he appreciated her charms as a woman as well as her authority, dedication and whatnot as a nurse, he gave her the quick up-and-down look: eyes, lips, eyes, breasts, eyes, holding each fractionally—but not vulgarly or lasciviously—longer than he normally would. Simple, but, as usual, it did the trick.

'Splendid,' said Haycraft. 'We'll get you, er...bedded down...' he paused to give his listeners a chance to chuckle at this witticism, which they duly did, '...straight away. Is Dr Ransome about?'

'I'm afraid he's rather tied up at the moment, sir. He had to go and speak to the house surgeon.'

'Never mind. Ransome,' Haycraft told Dacre, 'is in charge of this department. You'll meet him later. Anyway, let's have a look round, shall we? Sister, lead the way.'

Sister Radford bustled off towards the row of wooden screens that concealed the patients being treated, and the two men followed.

'We've had to create a sort of overflow, as you might say, in this area,' said Haycraft. 'Now then,' he added, as they approached the first patient, a youngish woman with lank red hair and protruding teeth, who was sitting dejectedly in one of the temporary cubicles, 'what have we here?'

Dacre felt his scrotum shrink and his stomach lurch. Up to now, he realised, his confidence had been that of an actor who had learnt his lines. He'd thought he had prepared himself for the moment when he'd been called upon to display practical evidence of medical expertise, but now, his script gone, he must ad-lib.

'This is Miss...' Sister Radford glanced at one of several charts that were hanging on the wall. Most of them were covered in illegible inky squiggles, but one was blank apart from a name at the top. '...Miss Kendall.'

Dacre, aware that both Haycraft and the sister were watching him expectantly, advanced on Miss Kendall. Apart from the dispirited air, he could see nothing wrong. 'What seems to be the problem?' he asked.

'It's this, Doctor.' Miss Kendall took off her coat and then, to his horror, began unbuttoning her blouse, revealing first the white upper slopes of what were clearly very nice breasts, second, an uplift brassiere, and third, a flaming red rash across the lower part of her chest. Dacre, horribly aware that he was starting to blush, stared helplessly as Miss Kendall removed the blouse entirely and half-turned to show him that the rash was all over her back as well. ''Ad it since this morning,' she said. 'Itching something terrible.'

Dacre tried desperately to keep his eyes on her face, which, he noticed, was thickly smeared with cosmetics. She couldn't be a...Could she? Secondary stage syphilis, perhaps? His mind raced. There was a test, wasn't there, the Wassermann reaction... And he ought to examine her...Oh, God. He must think. Slow down, and *think*. Perhaps it wasn't venereal at all, but some highly contagious plague. The bumps certainly looked angry enough, although—he took a couple of paces forward to study the woman's back—they didn't appear to be actually suppurating, which, he supposed, was all to the good...Maybe it was something simple, like measles or chickenpox, that any doctor worth his salt would be expected to recognise instantly—but surely only children had those? Christ Almighty, he didn't have a bloody clue...His heart was thumping so loudly that he was amazed the others couldn't hear it gonging away in his chest.

'Well?' asked Haycraft, from behind him. 'What do you make of it?'

Keep calm, Dacre told himself. Play for time...*Time*. The professor had said he only had ten minutes, hadn't he? They must be pretty well up by now. 'Well...' Smiling, he turned to look at the professor, who had removed his pipe from his pocket and was busy stuffing it with tobacco. As Dacre began to speak, he discreetly rubbed his arm against his side so that the sleeve of his shirt and jacket rode up over his wrist, then deliberately gestured with his hand, revealing his watch. 'I often think that being a good doctor means knowing when to leave well alone...' Haycraft raised his eyebrows, 'but,' Dacre continued quickly, with another flourish of his watch arm, 'in this case—'

'Good heavens!' Haycraft, seeing the glint of metal flash before him, had removed his thumb from the bowl of his pipe and was looking at his own timepiece. 'I'm sorry, Dacre, but I must get back or,' he chuckled, 'I shall be in trouble. I'll leave you in Sister Radford's capable hands. I'm sure she can give you the grand tour far more thoroughly than I ever could. Come back up when you're finished, and the administrative people can sort you out...' He held out his hand to Dacre, who shook it. 'Wonderful to have you on board.'

Sister Radford, delighted by the compliment, was practically skipping as she escorted Haycraft to the door of the ward. Dacre, left alone with Miss Kendall, breathed a sigh of relief—evidently audible, as she gave him a shrewd look and said, 'Well, he likes you, don't he?'

Taken aback at this lack of deference, Dacre said briskly, 'Button up your blouse.'

'Aren't you doing to examine me, then?'

'You haven't got this anywhere else, have you?'

'No, you seen it all.'

'Well, then.' Now that he wasn't being observed, Dacre's head cleared and he began to concentrate. Diagnosis, he thought. Take a history. 'How long have you had the rash?'

'Since this morning. I told you.'

'And it's itchy?'

'Yes.'

'We can give you something for that,' he said, remembering the calamine lotion that his mother had used for nettle stings when he was a child.

'Have you a temperature?'

'I don't know, do I?'

'Well, do you feel at all hot?' asked Dacre, warming to his role.

'Not really.'

'Have you ever had this before?'

Miss Kendall shook her head.

'Have you had any other symptoms?'

'I was sick.'

'When was that?'

'In the night. Three times. Must have been something I ate.'

'Which was?'

'Tinned lobster and salad. Oh, and some bread and marge.'

Aha, thought Dacre, remembering what he'd read about food poisoning. This was going to be a piece of cake.

'Mum was saving the lobster specially,' said Miss Kendall.

'How long for?'

'Ooh, six months or so, I should think.'

'Did it taste all right?'

'Dunno. I thought it was a bit funny, but then I never had it before.'

'Were you the only one who ate it?'

'Yes. Mum left it for me, for a treat 'cos I'm on leave. I'm on the land, see? I was really looking forward to coming home,' she said, sadly, 'and now it's all spoilt.'

'Don't worry, we'll soon have you better,' said Dacre, heartily. 'What did you do before?'

'Hairdressing.'

That, Dacre thought, explained the face-paint. He wondered if she wore it on the farm. 'Bit different from pigs and cows.'

'You can say that again, Doctor. Horrible smelly things, they are.'

She'd called him 'Doctor'. Dacre glowed. 'You're sure your mother didn't have any lobster?'

'Not as I know of. She might of had some today.'

'Well, when you get home, tell her to throw it away immediately. Now, you're not to eat anything for the next twenty-four hours, but make sure you have plenty of liquids—water or tea, nothing stronger.'

'You're not giving me nothing for it?'

Dacre paused. He didn't have a clue what to prescribe. The memory of a talk by the Radio Doctor made him say, 'No. You see, your stomach and bowel are irritated by what you've eaten, and you need to give them a rest so they can start working properly again.'

'Yes, Doctor.' Miss Kendall sounded disappointed.

At this point, Sister Radford returned and stood, in respectful silence, just inside the screen. 'I think we've found the culprit, Sister,' said Dacre, cheerfully. 'Tinned lobster. Now,' he turned once more to Miss Kendall, 'you won't be eating any more of that, will you?'

'No, Doctor.'

'Splendid. Off you go.'

'What about the itching, Doctor? You said you could give me something for it.'

'Yes, of course. Calamine lotion. You can get that from a chemist.'

Sister Radford summoned a nurse to fetch some paper, and Dacre scrawled Calamine Lotion across a page in large capital letters before presenting it to Miss Kendall. 'There you are. Now, you just remember what I said, and you'll be as right as rain in a couple of days.'

When his first patient had gone, Dacre turned to Sister Radford. Now he'd got the measure of her, he decided that the way forward was to establish himself as a charming maverick, with an easygoing, considerate manner. He'd start by a few more up-and-down looks—all women liked flattery—and by reinforcing what he'd said about too much medical interference (unless vital, of course) being a bad thing. 'As I was saying earlier,' he gave her his brightest smile, 'it's my belief that it's best to let Mother Nature take her own course whenever one can. After all, the old girl knows what she's doing, doesn't she? But, you know, so many of these things could be prevented if people would only look after themselves better. After all, we have enough to do in the present circumstances...Besides,' here, he favoured her with a boyish twinkle, 'there's nothing better than good, old-fashioned nursing. But,' he added, seriously, 'I'm sure you don't have time to listen to me pontificating. Can you be spared to show me the ropes?'

'Of course,' said Sister Radford. 'But,' she took down the chart that was hanging on the wall, 'before I do, you'd better write up the patient.'

'Heavens!' Dacre produced his pen again. 'I'd quite forgotten. Just give me a couple of minutes.'

Sister Radford looked slightly puzzled, and remained where she was.

'I shan't be long,' said Dacre, firmly, praying that she'd leave. This was the moment he'd been most worried about. He'd taken every chance he could to study patients' charts, but the problem was that most doctors' handwriting was illegible, and half of what they put was in Latin. He wanted to look at the other charts hanging on the cubicle wall for inspiration, but he could hardly do that with her watching.

'But—' began the sister, and then—bang on cue, thank God—a nurse stuck her head round the screen. 'Please, Sister, Dr Ransome says can you come? There's a—'

Dacre lost the rest of it as Sister Radford, with a final, quizzical glance at him, hurried off with the nurse. He took a deep breath and leant forward to consult the completed charts. It looked like gibberish to him, with plus signs sprinkled here and there, a few numerals and what appeared to be fractions. The signature at the bottom looked as if it might possibly be 'Ransome', but if he hadn't heard the name mentioned, he wouldn't even have been able to guess at it. What the hell, he thought. He'd come this far, hadn't he? Nearly all doctors had unreadable writing, and he would be no exception. He scribbled a couple of lines across the chart, added two plus signs (if that rash didn't merit a plus, he couldn't imagine what would), then signed his name, indecipherably, at the bottom. Hanging the chart back on the wall, he decided it looked quite as genuine as its fellows—and surely Sister Radford wouldn't have any reason to refer to it? After all, Miss Kendall had been discharged.

He peered out of the cubicle and saw that Sister Radford was on her way back to him, pausing to issue instructions to various nurses en route. He went across to meet her. 'All done,' he said. 'Do remember, Sister'—cheeky smile—'I'm the new boy here, so I'm throwing myself on your mercy.'

'Oh, Dr Dacre!' Sister Radford looked very taken with this notion. 'You'll find it all quite simple really, you know.'

'Well, you mustn't be surprised if I ask lots of questions. I've always found that it's never a good idea to make assumptions about anything.'

He'd spent most of the afternoon being shown around by Sister Radford, and had succeeded, by four o'clock, when they shared a pot of tea, in reducing her to a giggly state of adoration. She had introduced him to the head matron and to the elderly Dr Ransome, head of the Casualty Department, a fat little man who blinked owlishly behind thick-rimmed spectacles and was clearly delighted to see him. After this, he'd gone back upstairs and spent the remains of the day closeted first with Professor Haycraft's secretary, Miss Potter (who, with doe eyes and an apologetic manner, had nothing of the termagant about her) and then in the Administrative Department, where his appointment was made official.

After a final handshake from the professor, he'd gone home to ready himself for his first day's work. That evening, alone in his room with a single, celebratory bottle of beer, he'd decided on a system.

He'd try, as far as possible, to ensure that any patients whose symptoms seemed complicated would be seen by Dr Ransome. Anyone who looked as if they needed to be admitted could—provided he made a tentative stab at diagnosis—be taken care of in the wards and, if in doubt, he'd get a second opinion from Dr Ransome. As the junior doctor, he could not be expected to have seen everything, and besides, the older man would be flattered by such deference. The most important thing with patients, he thought, was to be confident. Indecision, which Dr Ransome would—if correctly presented—take as thoughtfulness and conscientiousness coupled with a slight lack of confidence, would be interpreted by a layman as weakness, so it must not be allowed to show. The fact that a doctor paid attention and cared, he'd decided, was more important than the actual cure. A little more practice with the old stethoscope, and he'd be laughing.

Lastly, he'd decided to establish the private hidey-hole where he could consult his crib and, if need be, compose himself. This was what he was doing now, having just successfully diagnosed a case of appendicitis. He leafed through the dictionary in search of the term 'testicular torsion'. Dr Ransome, before being called away to another emergency, had directed his attention to a patient he thought might be suffering from it, but, beyond thinking that it sounded horrible, he had absolutely no idea what it was. The sight of the poor man writhing on the bed, his face glistening with sweat and twisted in agony, had sent him fleeing for his textbook, according to which he could expect to see swelling, and pain so bad it could send you dizzy and make you spew…

He wasn't much looking forward to inspecting the bloke's balls, but he felt it could be managed. After all, such extremes aside, the people he saw were starting to resemble not human beings, but anatomical sets. He was learning more every day, and studying at night. Quite a lot of medicine, he had discovered, was as much a matter of common sense as of specialist knowledge. Sister Radford worshipped him, he'd noticed adoring looks cast in his direction by several of the nurses, the patients trusted him to look after them, and now, some of the things he was writing on the charts were actually making sense. He'd have a quick smoke—Wemyss had introduced him to a local tobacconist who favoured doctors above all other customers, so he was well supplied—then return to the fray. All in all, he thought, the securing of Fay aside, things were shaping up very nicely: he was valued, respected, and growing more competent by the day.

CHAPTER 27

The following day, Dacre dawdled his way towards the Men's Surgical Ward, where he'd been summoned by one of the house surgeons. He was sweating in anticipation, afraid that there was something he'd failed to spot, or a vital procedure left undone... But, he told himself firmly, medicos always stuck together, didn't they? After all, Dr Reynolds's blunders had been covered up, and surely, being so busy, anyone could make a mistake, couldn't they? He racked his brains, trying to remember all the patients he'd seen in the last forty-eight hours. Reduced, as they now were, to the relevant portions of their anatomy, he could not recall any of their faces. He took a deep breath and pushed open the door of the ward. Nurses moved briskly amongst beds into which men of various ages were tightly tucked. The exception to this was a young man who had a basket to take the weight of the sheets and blankets off his lower half, and it was beside this bed that the house surgeon, Mr Hambling, was waiting. With a sinking heart, Dacre recognised the patient as Doherty, the suspected testicular torsion. The memory of the swollen scarlet scrotum that seemed almost to pulsate in front of his eyes made him feel sick. He directed a queasy smile at Mr Hambling, but it wasn't returned. 'Dr Dacre?'

'Yes.'

'Come with me.'

Dacre followed him outside.

'I've just performed an orchidectomy on that man.'

Dacre's mind raced. Orchid— Oh, *Christ*. That meant he'd chopped Doherty's balls off. 'What...?'

'You should have told us it was an emergency.'

'But I thought—I mean—these cases are always emergencies, aren't they?'

'*I* know that,' snapped Hambling, 'but *you* are supposed to let us know, so that we can prepare.'

'I'm sorry,' said Dacre, humbly. 'He was Dr Ransome's patient originally, but he was called away, and...well, to be honest I wasn't sure, initially, if it wasn't simply an infection. But I thought I ought to send him up and not wait for Dr Ransome, just in case.'

'What were the symptoms?'

'Pain, swelling, vomiting, fever...'

'I see. Well, the testicle was quite dead. I had to remove it.' Feeling faint, Dacre leant against the wall of the corridor. At least, he thought, the bloke had only lost one.

'Gangrene, man,' said Hambling, impatiently, taking Dacre's expression to be one of incomprehension.

'Yes,' said Dacre, feeling as if he might throw up at any moment. 'Of course.'

'I tied the other one to the scrotal wall, so there won't be any repetition.'

Dacre's head was swimming. Feeling actual pain between his legs, he closed his eyes. To his surprise, he felt Hambling's hand on his shoulder. 'It's all right, old chap,' he said, in a softer voice. 'Not seen one of those before, eh?'

Dacre shook his head.

'Bit of a shock, I expect.' Hambling chuckled. 'The old wedding tackle...Not very pleasant. And quite unusual in a man of his age—it's normally boys. Still, no hard feelings, eh? As long as the procedures are followed in future...'

Dacre gulped. 'Yes,' he said. 'Sorry. New here. Feel rather... deep end, and all that.'

'Of course. Quite understand. Not to worry. Leave you to pull yourself together.' Clapping him on the shoulder, Hambling returned to the ward.

Dacre stood quite still. Gangrene. The man might have died, and, if he had, the responsibility would have been his. The image of Doherty's agonised face swam before his eyes. He blinked hard. Stop it, he told himself. All doctors must feel this at some time or other. He must be detached. There was no room for squeamishness, and certainly not for emotion. That was something he'd managed to hold at bay for years—to yield to it now would be to ruin everything.

Quivering, he levered himself away from the wall, and was just about to return to Casualty—with a calming smoke in his bolt-hole on the way—when someone cannoned straight into him and he heard the clatter of something metal hitting the floor. Perhaps because he wasn't entirely steady on his feet, he slumped back against the wall, wincing as his shoulders hit the tiles.

'I'm so sorry, Doctor,' said a sweet, anxious voice.

Looking up, Dacre felt his heart skip a beat. It was *his girl*, glowing before him as if wreathed in light. Close to, she was even more lovely than he'd thought when he first saw her by the bomb-site. Could he pick them or could he pick them? She was *perfect*. Now, her beautiful eyes had an expression of grave concern. 'Are you…all right?' she asked. 'You look awfully white.'

'Yes…' Oh, he'd been right! Fay Marchant was as kind and thoughtful as he'd imagined. And well-spoken—her voice was as lovely as the rest of her. There was no doubt: she was the one. Here, now, the one. 'I'm fine,' he said, in a robust, cheery voice. 'It'll pass off.'

'I don't mean to be rude,' Fay said, 'but don't you think you should sit down until it does?'

'No, no.' Dacre straightened up with a brave smile. 'It's nothing. I'll be fine. Did you drop something?'

'Yes.' He admired Fay's bottom as she bent down and picked up a tray and a syringe. 'Oh, dear. Now it'll have to be sterilised again. And there should be some phials too, somewhere. I hope they're not broken.'

Dacre looked down at the floorboards. 'I can't see anything,' he said. 'What was in them?'

'Morphine. We've got some terrible burns cases.'

'Well, they must be here somewhere. I expect they've just rolled a bit.' As he said this, Dacre spotted, out of the corner of his eye, something glinting beside the skirting board a few feet away. Fay, who was looking in the centre of the corridor, hadn't seen it. On impulse, he said, 'You look on that side,' and pointed her in the opposite direction. 'I'll see if there's anything down here.'

She did as she was told and Dacre bent down to inspect the edges of the wooden boards. There he found two of the small glass bottles intact, and one smashed. Slipping the whole phials into his pocket, he picked up the small amount of broken glass and, turtling to Fay, who was still scanning the floor on the other side of the corridor, said, 'I'm afraid they've gone for a burton. At least, this one has. I think the other two might have gone down here.' Kneeling down, he indicated a narrow gap between the wood and the wall.

Looking dismayed, Fay came over to inspect. 'Sister's going to kill me.'

'Surely not,' said Dacre. 'Anyone can have an accident. Don't I know it?' he added, ruefully, and got a doubtful smile in return. 'What's your name?' he asked.

'Marchant.'

'I meant your Christian name.'

'Ohh...' She gave a little laugh. 'One gets so used...It's Fay.'

'Are you working on Men's Surgical?'

She nodded.

'James Dacre.' He held out his hand.

Fay's eyes widened. 'Ooh,' she said, coquettishly. 'I've heard about you.'

Flirting already! She *knew* she was his girl. This was going to be a piece of cake—if she'd heard anything about his being married, he'd soon be able to turn that to his advantage...He'd give her the sob story, and she'd feel anger towards his faithless wife and pity him. 'Thank you for being a ministering angel.'

'I'm not! I mean, I ran into you.'

'But you ministered afterwards. Or rather, you tried.'

Fay laughed. 'Hardly!'

'Would you like to do a spot of ministering later on?'

She raised her eyebrows, prepared to be comically affronted. 'What do you mean, exactly?'

'Oh heavens...' Dacre permitted himself a nervous chuckle. 'Nothing like that. I didn't mean...' He smiled bashfully, in a way that showed that he was attracted to her, but hadn't meant anything suggestive. 'That came out rather badly, didn't it? What I really meant was, I need some help.'

'Help?'

'Yes. You see, I'm the new boy here, and I've just got myself into trouble with Mr Hambling. So you see,' he added, 'we're both in hot water. A matter of procedure. Don't know the ropes yet.'

'Which patient?'

'Mr Doherty.'

'Oh...'

Seeing Fay's cheeks grow slightly pink, Dacre hurried on. 'Two weeks,' he groaned, 'and I've already blotted my copybook.'

'Oh dear. Mr Hambling can be a bit brisk, can't he?'

Pleased by this small evidence of collusion, Dacre said, 'So, will you help me avoid his wrath in the future?'

'If I can. But—'

'I'm sure you can. What time do you get off?'

'Eight. If I'm lucky.'

'Will you allow me to buy you a drink?'

Fay seemed to consider this for a moment, and then said, 'Yes, I'd like that very much.'

Dacre was about to respond when her eyes widened at something over his shoulder and she whispered, 'Sister's coming.'

'Oh. Right. Are you sure you don't want me to have a word with her? About the...' Dacre indicated the tray.

'No, really. It was kind of you to help.'

'All right then. Main entrance—don't worry if you're late.' He gave Fay a conspiratorial wink and strolled off, deliberately casual, down the corridor in the direction of the stairs. Wonderful, wonderful chance! And he had the morphine as well. It couldn't have happened better if he'd engineered it. Fay Marchant: his girl. At least, she would be very soon, and—

As he rounded the corner, his heart really did stop. Higgs was coming straight towards him.

CHAPTER 28

Eight days late. Jenny put the bowl of eggs down on the step and leant against the back door frame. It was a pleasant, sunny morning—a nice change from all the rain they'd been having—and she always enjoyed watching the hens, or she would if she weren't so worried about telling Ted.

'It's all very well for you,' she told the hens. She'd begun to talk to them quite a bit, but only if no-one else was in earshot. There were five of them, Buff Orpingtons, big fluffy things with pale gold feathers. She wouldn't have had a clue how to look after them but Ted, being a farmer's son, had explained what to do.

They really were dear things, if a bit stupid, and she was getting ever so fond of them. She hoped Ted wouldn't insist on killing one come Christmas, but she didn't want to mention this for fear of giving him ideas. Christmas! If she *were* pregnant—which, unless a miracle happened, was the case—she'd be six months gone by then. I can't face it, she thought. Not all over again, not *now*. It isn't fair.

She took Mrs Chetwynd's letter out of her apron pocket. Since it had arrived yesterday morning, she must have read it a dozen times. Smoothing it out, she looked at it once more:... *thought I ought to tell you that Monica has started her periods. We had a little talk about it, and I have provided her with some sanitary napkins and a belt. She said that you had explained everything to her, and thought that you would wish to know, so I said I would tell you because she felt a little uncomfortable about putting it in a letter...*

Embarrassed in case Ted read it, Jenny thought. Well, that was understandable, but all the same, she'd have liked to hear it from Monica herself. They had had a talk about 'those things' when the children had been at home last year, but she should have been the one there, when it happened, to reassure and explain it was nothing to make a song and dance about but just a normal part of becoming a woman, and...and having babies. Jenny grimaced. She'd heard of gin and hot baths, but she wasn't sure that it actually worked, and the alternatives—elm twigs, syringing, and so on were too dangerous to contemplate. You could die from those.

She shoved the letter back in her pocket and stared hard at the hens, trying to keep the tears back. She didn't often cry, but now...Everything was wrong. Monica was *her* daughter, not Mrs Chetwynd's, and this sort of thing was just— Stop it, she told herself. Monica and Pete are alive and safe: be grateful for that. Hard on the heels of this thought came—as it tended to nowadays—the resentful welling inside, born of so many years of not minding or complaining, of being patient, of making do and hiding one's feelings and counting one's blessings...Not to mention being pregnant from one stupid little mistake. 'It's not fair,' she repeated, out loud. 'It isn't bloody *fair!*'

'Mrs Stratton?'

Turning, she saw her neighbour's head appear above the fence and hoped that Mrs Nairn, who had a bleating voice that reminded her of Larry the Lamb, hadn't heard her swear. It seemed not, as Mrs Nairn's face was wearing its usual bland expression. 'Got a parcel from Bill's sister in America.'

'That's nice.'

'Spam, corned beef, nylons, everything.'

'Ooh, lovely.' Not for the first time, Jenny wished that she or Ted had relatives living in the States. Ted's surviving brother occasionally sent food packages from the family farm in Devon, but that was hardly the same. *Nylons*...She just hoped she didn't look as envious as she felt.

'I could let you have a tin of Spam in exchange for some eggs,' said Mrs Nairn. 'Bill's home on leave tomorrow, and I want to make a cake.'

'Ooh, yes,' said Jenny, eagerness replacing jealousy. 'If you're sure. Take these.' She passed the bowl across. 'Fresh this morning.'

Mrs Nairn dug into her apron pocket and produced the tin. 'There you are.'

'Thank you, dear. Tell Bill to give us a knock, won't you? I know Ted would love to see him.'

Mrs Nairn disappeared, and Jenny stood in the sunshine, turning the tin over in her hands. Spam was Pete's favourite... Something—the brightly coloured wrapper, perhaps—made her remember a seaside holiday they'd had before the war. Monica and Pete at the fair, grinning and waving as they bobbed up and down on the proud but shabby horses of the merry-go-round...

It was nice to think about the happy times. Even poor Mr Ingram had kept that holiday photograph...The photograph! If Mrs Ingram saw that, perhaps she'd be convinced. Presumably, unless Mr Ingram had others, it was the only one left after the bombing—the only actual, physical, pictorial *evidence*. If Mrs Ingram were to see it, to be able to compare it to the man himself...Perhaps they should have a tea party. The only problem was that Mr Ingram, who'd disappeared so abruptly from the pub—thanks to her idiot brother-in-law—appeared to have vanished. No-one had come asking for him, but Ted said there were lots of deserters, so maybe they didn't have time to go chasing after all of them...If only Mr Ingram would ring up Doris, she thought. They could arrange a tea party, and, if Mrs Ingram could be persuaded to stay downstairs for long enough, she could see the photograph and it would all come back—the jokes, the intimate things.

She'd nip down to Doris's later and suggest it. Donald was now agitating for Mrs Ingram to be taken to Friern Barnet. Dr Makepeace hadn't mentioned the subject, but it was only a matter of time before Donald ran out of patience and broached it with him. Doris refused to discuss it, and, Jenny, knowing she was thinking of Aunt Ivy, had backed her up: once they had you in a place like that, the only way you got out was in a box. Ted was so preoccupied with his work that she hadn't liked to bother him... Besides, she didn't see there was much point: he and Donald would certainly have discussed the matter, so, if pressed, he would undoubtedly be on his brother-in-law's side.

The other thing was that she felt cut off from Ted at the moment. Not only because of his work, but because of the pregnancy. There was no point going to see Dr Makepeace about it yet, and she didn't want to tell Ted until she was certain, not just 'possible' or 'probable' or whatever it was they said. With Monica, and then Pete, she'd told him as soon as she knew and he'd been delighted, but this was different. It wasn't what they'd agreed—and it certainly wasn't what they wanted. Jenny crossed her fingers. She'd give it a few more days, yet. There was a slim chance, even now...

Ridiculous how a tin of Spam could make you feel that bit more optimistic. She turned her face up to the sun, enjoying the warmth. Even if she *were* pregnant, perhaps Ted wouldn't mind as much as she thought. After all, he did like children—he'd always been good with the kids, even when they were babies, which was more than you could say for some men. In any case, a trouble shared...Perhaps she ought to mention it to him after all. 'Enjoy the sunshine, ladies,' she murmured to the hens, and went back indoors with a spring in her step.

CHAPTER
29

Dacre gasped, turned on his heel and, opening the first door he came to, stepped inside and closed it behind him. Pitch darkness— a cupboard of some sort, he thought. Heart thudding inside his chest, he stood stock still for a moment and then, hearing no shouts of recognition or banging on the door, stuck out his hands and encountered a splintery wooden thicket of broom and mop handles. As long as none of the ward maids decided this was the moment to fetch a scrubbing brush, he ought to be safe enough. Blood pounding in his ears and soaked in perspiration, he trembled in the carbolic-scented blackness, his mind racing. Higgs couldn't be after him, or he'd know by now. Besides, the man had no idea he was still in the hospital, so, not expecting to see him, wouldn't have recognised him, clean shaven and with black hair…What the hell had he been doing in the corridor? The only time mortuary staff came upstairs was to the laboratory, and there was a separate staircase for that.

Perhaps he'd been delivering a message. Perhaps…for Christ's sake, Dacre told himself, it doesn't matter. Moving gingerly, so as not to disturb the cloths and boxes of soap, he pulled out his handkerchief and wiped his forehead. All the same, if Higgs—or, God forbid, Dr Byrne—had started making a habit of wandering about, he'd have to be on his guard.

As he shoved the handkerchief back into his pocket, his fingers touched something small and hard. It took him a moment to remember what it was: one of the phials of morphine. Why *had* he taken them? Habit, yes—he'd always made a point of picking up anything that looked as though it might be useful. Anything else? That, he thought, was better not examined. The thing was, always to be prepared. He hoped Fay wasn't getting into trouble over it. Still, he'd make it up to her this evening. Their first date...It struck him, then, with a pang of sadness, that Fay would only—*could* only—ever know him as James Dacre. That was who she would love. He could never make a clean breast of things—not only would she despise him, she'd probably go to the police. Getting close to anybody was a risk, but this was definitely one worth taking. Remembering the conversation about Wemyss's suite at the Clarendon, he decided to see if he could purloin the key for use later. Asking Wemyss, at this stage, would be presumptuous. Besides, the man might have qualms about lending it to someone married, and, more importantly, he didn't want anyone to know about his plans for Fay. Wemyss would be bound to tell somebody, and gossip spread around like wildfire. It occurred to him then that if Fay had mentioned their drink to anyone—unlikely, as that sort of thing was frowned upon, but not impossible—she may have already learnt about his 'marriage'. Dacre frowned. That could prove awkward. There was no point in making plans for dealing with it—he'd have to play it by ear.

Wemyss had said he kept the key 'handy', so presumably it was in his jacket pocket—that would be easy enough to extract in the doctors' mess. And he'd also asked Dacre to keep quiet about its existence, which meant Fay would not know about it, and he could pass it off as his own—better and better...

He needed to get moving. Surely Higgs would be gone by now? He took his hand out of his pocket and began, very slowly, to count to one hundred. When he reached ninety-nine, he pushed the cupboard door open a cautious three inches and looked out: coast clear. He took several deep breaths and, stepping back into the corridor, resumed a leisurely pace back to Casualty.

After his fright at seeing Higgs, the rest of Dacre's day had not—apart from a sticky moment when he'd failed to spot a fractured fibula—been too bad, and he was very—very, very—much looking forward to his drink with Fay. Perhaps, he thought, it would be more than just a drink…Normally, he wouldn't consider proposing a hotel room to a nice girl, which Fay undoubtedly was, but, as she belonged to him, then the sooner he enjoyed her the better it would be for both of them. Sliding the hotel room key out of Wemyss's jacket pocket had been the work of a second. He held on to it tightly as he hurried back to Eversholt Street to smarten himself up: in view of the possibility of the Clarendon, he'd better put on a clean shirt and take a brush to his suit.

From the moment Fay had walked up to him outside the hospital's main gate, he'd known, somehow, that it was going to be fine. He'd arrived early on purpose, so that she wouldn't have to wait about and risk trouble if she was seen by the matron, and her gratitude for this put them on a good footing immediately. She'd looked even better with her hair down, and she'd obviously dressed up, because she wearing a smart coat, high heels and lipstick.

She proved quite willing to brave the blackout and the whizzes and bangs to follow the pinpoint light of his torch to a pub near Regent's Park where they weren't likely to be recognised, and where he'd managed to buy two gins.

'You do look lovely like that,' he said, as they settled down at a corner table and she took off the coat, revealing an elegant blue dress.

'Thanks. It's nice to be out of uniform.'

'I'll bet. Are you in awful trouble?'

'A wigging from Sister. I've had far worse. To be honest, everything's been rather at sixes and sevens since that poor nurse was killed.'

'I heard about that. Did you know her?'

'Not well. It was a terrible thing to happen, especially in the hospital.' Fay shuddered. 'I'll never feel the same way about operating theatres again.'

'Well, let's talk about something a bit more cheerful, shall we? Have you been at the Middlesex long?'

'Three years. Since I started.'

'You must know the place inside out.'

'Oh, not really. I've been on most of the wards, though. You know, training.'

'Which do you like best?'

'I don't really mind. The only patients I don't like are the ones who say they'll try not to give you any trouble—they're always the worst. Fetch this, fetch that, sit them up, lie them down, cup of tea...'

'Not quite Florence Nightingale, then?'

'Hardly. Lots of girls do have romantic ideas about it, I suppose, and they get terribly disillusioned. But you must know that.'

'Didn't you ever have a romantic idea about it?'

Fay shook her head. 'My father's a doctor. He was the one who suggested I train. He's the old-fashioned type: nurses should be strong girls who do as they're told. He's quite right, of course, but it's no fun when you get treated like an imbecile child and not allowed out and all the rest of it.'

Dacre laughed. 'If it's any consolation, I get treated like an imbecile, too. Like this morning.'

'That's just Mr Hambling's way. It wasn't your fault that you didn't know.'

'No, but I *should* have known. That's where I need your help, you see...I want you to tell me everything about the hospital.'

'But you already know much more than—'

'Pretend I don't. Do you know, one of our professors used to say that the worst thing a physician can do is to make assumptions. He said that humility and an open mind were the keys to healing. I've never forgotten that.' Dacre, who had gambled that

Fay, being a nurse, wouldn't make enquiries about his training, thought he'd better move on quickly in case she decided to do so. 'The other thing he said was that the patient should be your teacher. Or, in this case, the nurse should. So, you see, you can help me.'

'Well, I'll do my best.'

For the next hour, Fay talked about the Middlesex, and about her work. After a while, she seemed to forget that Dacre was a doctor at all, and even started to talk about various medical procedures. Dacre nodded, encouraged, prompted, and asked occasional questions, and when Fay went to the Ladies, he took out a pencil and paper and jotted down the key points.

'I don't think,' said Fay, as she sat down again, 'that I've talked so much in ages. I hope I didn't bore you.'

'Not at all. I enjoyed listening to you—and watching you. You'd be a wonderful teacher.'

'And you're going to be a wonderful doctor.' She coloured. 'I mean, I'm sure you are already, but—'

'There's always room for improvement. Let's say I hope to be, in time.' He tapped his glass. 'Shall I see if they'll run to two more of these?'

As he put the fresh drinks on the table and was helping Fay to a cigarette, she touched the scar on the base of his thumb. 'What's that?'

'Dog bite. When I was a kid.'

'Must have been painful.'

'It was. I just about yelled the house down. I'd love to tell you that I'd wrestled some huge monster to the ground trying to defend an elderly lady from its fangs, but actually it was just a little ratty thing.'

'They're often fiercer than the big ones, though, aren't they?'

'All the same, it's pretty pathetic, isn't it? I'm not a conscientious objector or anything, by the way. The forces turned me down because I had an enlarged heart, so that's something else that's not very heroic. I thought you might as well know the worst straight away.'

'Well, if that's as bad as it gets, it's hardly very dreadful.' Fay laughed. 'You might have told me you had two wives and five mistresses and fifteen children, or something.'

'Well...' Dacre put his fingers on Fay's hand, which was resting on the table top. 'Actually,' he said, 'I didn't want to tell you this, but it wouldn't be right or fair to keep quiet about it: I am married.' Fay ducked her head and tried to snatch back her hand, but he clung on to it. 'Please hear me out,' he said quietly. 'I'm married, but only in name. My wife lives up in Suffolk with her parents, and I hardly see her. Being apart, I realised I didn't miss her, and, to be honest, I started to wonder if I'd ever loved her. Properly, I mean. In the way she deserved. It was rather a whirlwind sort of thing, and if I'd stopped to think, which I should have...Well, I wouldn't have gone through with it. I feel sad about it, but I'm not sure that we were ever suited, really.' Dacre removed his hand from Fay's and said, 'You can leave if you like—I'll walk you back to the hospital—but I didn't want to start by having secrets from you.'

Fay looked into his eyes for a long moment, as if she were searching for a sign. Finally, she said, 'I'm not going to leave. I know...these things can happen. People grow apart sometimes, and...Shall I tell you something? You said just now about secrets, and I've never told anyone about this before, in fact, I've really only just admitted the truth of it to myself, but...' She hesitated, and Dacre, fearing to break the intensity of the mood by prompting her, sat quite still, his eyes fixed on hers, and waited. 'I was engaged,' she said. 'He was killed at Tobruk. It had been very romantic, because we'd had such a short time together—snatched moments...' She laughed, embarrassed. 'You know the type of thing. And when he asked me to marry him I was so happy…But when he went away, and I was by myself again, I'd try to imagine what it might be like to be married to him, with a family, and I found I couldn't. It was difficult, even at first, but I kept telling myself it was because I didn't know what marriage was like…I'd argue with myself about it. That sounds mad, doesn't it? Arguing with yourself Especially,' she laughed again, 'if you lose the arguments.'

'No,' said Dacre. 'It sounds as if you had far more self-knowledge than I did.'

'That's a generous way to put it, but I'm not sure it's true. If I really had had self-knowledge, 1 would have refused him in the first place. I was intending to break it off, and I tried to write, but it seemed so mean, so I thought I'd wait until I saw him again, and then I heard the news…' Fay lowered her eyes. 'It was a way out, and nobody would know how I was feeling. Oh, I wasn't glad he was dead or anything as horrible as that, but…I felt so guilty because I didn't want to marry him. Was that terrible of me?'

'Look at me, Fay,' said Dacre. She looked up, blinking, and wiped her eyes with her fingers. 'Don't cry,' he said, gently. 'It wasn't terrible at all. I'm honoured that you told me—that you feel you can trust me.'

'Yes, I do. But yours was different. I can't believe that what happened was your fault.'

'Some of it was.' Dacre looked sombre. 'It's never just one person who's to blame, and I certainly don't blame her. But…' His face lightened. 'I'm glad I told you. I'd like us to be honest with each other. You know, I became a doctor because of my father, too. It was how he died, really. A perforated ulcer. He was in agony. I was fifteen—I'd have given anything to have been able to help him.'

'How terrible.'

'It was. We didn't know he was ill, you see, and…Well, I don't think I'll ever forget it.'

'I'm not surprised. Poor man…'

'Yes.' As Fay reached forward and clasped his fingers in hers, giving them a little squeeze, Dacre reflected that there was, actually, some truth in what he had just said. It *was* his father who had made him a doctor, but by the manner of his life, not his death. The wife business had gone down well, too. He'd been right about her not being too inquisitive—a different sort of girl would have asked a hundred questions, but Fay seemed just to accept what he'd said at its face value. He hadn't even had to invent an affair between his fictitious wife and a Yank. She'd believed him because she was naturally sympathetic, and she'd confided in return...Just how sympathetic was she, he wondered, fingering the hotel key in his jacket pocket. After all, she trusted him, didn't she? She'd proved that by confiding in him. Should he try his luck? Even if she declined the invitation, it would show her that he had money and connections, wouldn't it?

He debated the pros and cons of this as they walked back towards the hospital, her arm linked in his, in the darkness. For the most part they were silent, and for once, Dacre thought, the blackout felt like a cocoon, not a menace. The flying bombs were more distant, now—the other side of the river, he guessed—and, but for the odd wedge of light from an open door as the pubs emptied out, a few scuffles and giggles from the odd just-glimpsed couple writhing in a doorway, they could have been entirely alone. It was seeing the clinch that spurred him on to ask. 'You know,' he said, 'it's early yet. Would you like to go somewhere else?'

'Another pub, you mean?'

'I was thinking of somewhere rather smarter. Ever been to the Clarendon?'

'The hotel, you mean?' Fay sounded surprised. 'Heavens, no.'

'Well, would you like to? I've got the key of the door in my pocket. Well, not "the" door, "a" door. Room 135, to be exact. My family keep it on, you see.'

In a single swift movement, Fay unhooked her arm from his and stepped back. For a moment, Dacre thought she would slap him, but she merely said, 'What for?'

'Well, to have somewhere to stay in town…Oh, I see what you mean. A drink, nothing more. I promise to behave like a gentleman.'

'Really?'

'I give you my word.'

During the short stroll to the hotel, Dacre felt his excitement growing. Was it possible that he could actually *have* her, so soon? Painfully aware of her body next to his, her hip brushing against his as they walked, it was all he could do not to drag her into the nearest doorway and pin her against the wall. Wait, he told himself. You'll get what you want…

The lobby of the Clarendon was impressively large and echoing, with marble pillars and groups of leather chairs. Dacre, with Fay on his arm, whisked past the elderly doorman and, leading with his chin, marched across to the lifts. Halfway across, Fay stopped. 'James,' she said quietly, 'I'm not sure about this. Those people…' she inclined her head towards the desk, from behind which several liveried flunkies were watching them with interest, 'they'll know I'm not your wife, and it looks—'

'Don't worry about them,' said Dacre, tucking her arm more firmly beneath his own, 'they know me.'

'That's what I mean! I don't think this is a good idea.'

'Fay…' Dacre drew her behind the nearest pillar, out of sight, leant her against the marble and put his arms round her waist. 'Come on, darling…' he breathed into her ear.

For a second, she seemed to respond, and then, 'No, James, really.' He pressed against her, nuzzling her warm neck and feeling the softness of her breasts beneath her clothing. 'Please stop it.' Fay struggled to push him away, and feeling her strain and wriggle made him more urgent.

'You're so beautiful,' he whispered, hoarsely, pushing his knee between her legs. 'So lovely…Please, Fay.'

'No,' hissed Fay. 'Please stop, James, you're frightening me.' Dacre brought his hand up to her throat and forced her chin upwards. 'Kiss me, darling...'

'Good evening, sir. May I help you?' Letting go of Fay, Dacre whirled round to see one of the hotel servants standing behind him, a deferential but determined look on his face.

'No thank you.' Recalled to his senses, Dacre made his voice casual, as if he were familiar with the place. 'There won't be anything tonight—we were just leaving.' Anxious to avoid further confrontation, he took Fay's hand and led her back outside, followed at a discreet distance by the man.

At the doorway, he turned. 'Goodnight,' he said.

'Goodnight, *sir*. Goodnight, *madam*.'

Once they were clear of the hotel, Fay tugged her hand away from Dacre's. 'What on earth did you think you were doing?'

'I'm sorry, Fay.' Dacre kept looking straight ahead. 'I was carried away.'

'In front of everyone! You made me look like some sort of tart.'

'No-one could ever think that about you,' he said, desperately, trying to win back the ground he'd lost. 'And I really am sorry.' He meant it, too. The genuineness of the emotion surprised him, and he felt lost for words.

'You gave me your word.'

'I know. I forgot myself.'

'You can say that again,' said Fay, lightly. Surprised by her tone, Dacre turned to look at her and saw, by the dim light in the street, that not only was she smiling, but that she had a look of secretive contentment. She's pleased, he thought, and his heart leapt. She's pleased to have such an effect on me. Perhaps she'll let me make it up to her after all.

Fay did not speak again until they reached the hospital, and Dacre, for once not knowing what to say, decided that silent contrition was best. To his surprise, when they arrived, she turned to him and said, 'Thank you for a lovely evening.'

'Except the last part. I know I've said it before, but I *am* sorry, Fay.'

'I didn't like it, what you did in there. I have to trust you, James, and I can't if you're going to behave like that.'

'It will never happen again, Fay, I promise you. Not unless you want it to.'

'I shouldn't think I'd ever want it to…' she said, adding, just as he thought all was lost, 'not in public, anyway.'

'Of course not.'

'Then let's not talk about it any more.'

There was a pause, and he heard her take a breath. Although she was very close to him, he could barely make out her features, but she seemed to him to be frowning slightly.

'Can I see you again?' he asked.

'Yes. I'd like that.' She giggled. 'If you really, truly *promise* to behave yourself.'

'I promise. Honestly.' He put up a hand to touch her cheek. He felt her draw back slightly, so, instead of trying to kiss her, he gave her a little pat.

'I'd better say goodnight before anyone sees us.'

'Will you be all right to go in?'

'Oh, yes. There's a bathroom window we use. Well, it's a sort of bathroom—we don't have a proper one in the basement. It's quite safe as long as you don't land in one of the buckets.'

'Heavens. Better watch your step, then.'

'Yes…Goodnight, James.'

'Goodnight, Fay.'

She left him to walk round the corner, and he stood listening until he could no longer hear her footsteps. Time to go home. Negotiating his way back to Euston, he was aware of an odd, confused sensation, one that he couldn't identify. Relief, yes, that Fay had not rejected him, but something else, too. There was a warmth inside him. Not physical, and not like happiness, which was a fiercer and more sudden feeling that he associated with moments of triumph. Remembering how he'd followed the big policeman and seen him through the window, with his wife—the sense of connection between them—he wondered if he were not, perhaps, experiencing the kind of happiness that others felt. Odd, considering he hadn't had Fay, but that, he knew, was just a matter of time. She was nervous, and worried about her reputation, as any nice girl would be. But she'd forgiven him, hadn't she? And she knew he wanted her, and, for a moment—just a moment—she had responded to him, he was sure of it.

He had an image of the two of them, married, himself a doctor, the father of children, with a home, a life where he was respected and loved...For a moment, it seemed possible. But then the thought returned that it couldn't be, not if it were based, as it would have to be, on a falsehood. Unless there was a way round it...

There must be. He didn't like feeling helpless, it made him angry. Why shouldn't he have what he wanted? Other people did. The big policeman did. But then, with other things he'd wanted, he'd got them, hadn't he? People and circumstances had been the obstacles in his way, but he'd managed to get round them. He'd do it somehow. He didn't know how, but he bloody well would. He'd have the life he wanted—*deserved*—and that would include Fay.

He thought of her as he lay on his meagre bed and pleasured himself, remembering the feeling of her body pressed against his, her warmth and softness, the smell of her. Afterwards, he tried to concentrate on a chapter of Aids to Psychiatry, but he was restless, quickly amorous again despite his climax. Eventually he slept, but woke again at quarter to three. Deciding he might as well use the time, he propped himself up as best he could on his two thin pillows and reached for the textbook. It had to be said that, so far, all this psychiatry stuff hadn't told him much that he didn't already know, even if he hadn't yet seen more than a handful of people who were obviously mentally afflicted. But there must be more to learn…and, as a discipline, it was still in its infancy, and fairly underpopulated. Besides which, there'd be no more physical examinations or worrying about whether one had missed a bursting appendix. Really, the more he thought about it, the more appealing it seemed. And he'd have Fay by his side, wouldn't he? She wouldn't get away—he'd make sure of that.

The following morning in the Gents', washing his hands with enormous concentration after having left a nurse applying Whitfield's Ointment to a man with an appalling case of ringworm, the idea had never seemed so good.

Dacre heard the cubicle door creak behind him, but didn't raise his eyes. He'd read that ringworm was highly contagious, and, having examined the man, was intent on scrubbing himself as thoroughly as possible. He was vaguely aware of a white-coated someone washing his hands at the next basin. He thought nothing of it until the water stopped running and the man's hands stopped moving, but whoever it was remained standing beside him. Turning his head to look, he saw that it was Dr Byrne.

30

Doris always managed to keep her nets lovely, Jenny thought. Even now, with all the dust and muck. She'd got the sitting room furniture really shining, barley-sugar legs and all, and they'd managed a few sandwiches for the tea party, with a tiny scrap of butter and a cucumber Ted had fetched from the allotment. There was even a very small fruit cake. So far, things seemed to be going all right, or at least not actually badly, in that Mr Ingram had telephoned Doris and been summoned to tea, and Mrs Ingram, although initially reluctant to stay in the same room as 'that man', was now perched on the sofa beside Doris.

Mr Ingram, who had been coached in his part by Jenny, was ensconced in Donald's armchair on the other side of the small tea table. He had managed to shave, and kit himself out in civilian clothes—trousers and a saggy jersey that looked as if it had been knitted with walking sticks. She had no idea where he was staying, and he hadn't volunteered anything. He was fidgeting, worrying at the cuticles of his thumbs with the nails of his forefingers, and juddering one leg up and down, apparently unconsciously. 'It won't matter once I know she's all right,' he'd told Jenny. 'Then I'll hand myself over.'

Now, Jenny thought, he looked like a nervous actor in a not-very-good play. Mrs Ingram looked presentable, if dull-eyed, and there was a shakiness about her movements that made Jenny anxious for the china, but she seemed to be following the conversation. Doris, at Jenny's suggestion, had introduced the subject of holidays by mentioning a day trip they'd all taken to Southend on the paddle-steamer before the war, and was now regaling them with a description of the concert party on the pier.

'We did that, didn't we, Elsie?' said Mr Ingram. 'We saw Arthur Askey, remember?'

Mrs Ingram shifted slightly in her seat, but kept her eyes on her cup and saucer.

'Don't you remember, Elsie? They had a train going down the pier.'

Mrs Ingram raised her head. She didn't look into her husband's face, but in the direction of his knees, one of which was still twitching violently. 'I remember it,' she said, 'but how do you know about it?'

'I was with you. We went to Shoeburyness, to the caravan, remember? We'd go into Southend and see the lights all down the front. We even managed Eastbourne one year. Nineteen thirty-nine, in July. They had a bandstand and bowling greens. We took a boat trip to the lighthouse, and we went to Hastings.'

Mrs Ingram's teeth gave an audible click.

'Remember that, Elsie? We saw the fishermen drying their nets on the beach, and you said—'

'How do you know what I said?' asked Mrs Ingram in an agitated voice. 'Who told you?'

'No-one, dear. I was there. We had ice-cream afterwards. Rossi's ice-cream.' And the flowers, Elsie.' A note of desperation had crept into Mr Ingram's voice. 'Remember how much you liked the flowers? It was all beautifully kept. Of course, we loved Southend, too, but they didn't have anything like those displays, did they, dear?'

Mrs Ingram shook her head and glared at him. 'Why don't you show her the photograph?' prompted Jenny.

Mr Ingram held out the picture. 'Look, Elsie, remember this? It was taken on our honeymoon.'

Mrs Ingram snatched it from him. 'What are you doing with that?'

'It's mine, Elsie. I took it to remind me of you, dear.'

She showed the photograph to Doris. 'This is him. This is my Eric.'

'I know,' said Doris. 'He's here, now.'

'No, *this* is him.'

'But they're the same!' said Doris. 'The same person.'

'No!' Mrs Ingram snatched the photograph back and stood up. Gesturing behind her at Mr Ingram, she said, 'Why have you got his clothes? Who gave them to you?'

'They're *my* clothes, Elsie.' Mr Ingram stood up. 'Please, dear...'

'Don't call me that! I mended those trousers with my own hands. You can see.'

'That's right!' said Mr Ingram, pointing at a place on the side of his jumping knee.

'He tore them,' said Mrs Ingram, 'when he—'

'I fell off a ladder,' said Mr Ingram excitedly. 'I was putting up some Christmas decorations, and I came a cropper. Elsie made ever such a good job of mending them, you'd hardly know they'd—'

'I didn't do it for you,' said Mrs Ingram, firmly. 'I did it for *him*. Why have you got them?' Her voice was shrill, quivering with fear. 'Did you take them from him when you stole the picture? What have you *done* to him?'

Seeing that the conversation was about to get out of control, Jenny stood up too and said briskly, 'Another sandwich, anyone? Or perhaps we should have some cake now?'

'Ooh, I think cake, don't you?' said Doris in a gleeful, school-girlish voice.

'How silly!' said Jenny, looking down at the plate. 'I forgot to bring a knife. Shan't be a moment.'

She dashed out of the room, leaving Mrs Ingram wailing behind her. Washing her hands in the kitchen (not that she needed to, but she wanted an excuse to collect her thoughts), she heard Mr Ingram say plaintively, 'I've done nothing, Elsie, I swear to you.' She would have liked to confer with Doris about what to do, but there was no question of leaving the pair of them alone.

Not finding the cake slice in its usual place, she was about to search the other drawers when a clear recollection of putting the thing down on the tray beside the plate, coupled with a sudden cessation of voices from the sitting room, stopped her in her tracks. She shot back across the hall just in time to see Mrs Ingram standing on the rug, photograph in one shaking hand, cake slice in the other, pointing it at Mr Ingram. For a moment, the scene appeared to Jenny like a waxwork tableau: Mr Ingram had his hands up in a placatory 'surrender' gesture, and Doris's mouth hung open in a perfect 'O' of surprise.

'He's not coming near me,' said Mrs Ingram in a loud voice. 'I won't let him.'

Mr Ingram looked so ridiculous standing in front of the fireplace, staring down at the quivering cake slice as if it were a bayonet, that Jenny almost laughed.

'Elsie, calm down,' said Mr Ingram. 'This isn't necessary.'

'Don't you tell me what's necessary!' Mrs Ingram sounded dangerously near hysterics.

Doris put a restraining hand on Mrs Ingram's arm. 'It's all right, dear, he's not going to—'

'Let go!' Mrs Ingram rounded on Doris, throwing her arm off. Doris gave a little scream, and the next moment Jenny saw that a trickle of blood had run down Doris's wrist.

'It'll be fine,' said Doris, looking pointedly at Jenny. 'An accident—just a little nick.'

Jenny didn't know about 'accident' but there seemed to be a fair amount of blood now—some of it had dripped onto Doris's skirt—and it wasn't showing any sign of stopping. Ignoring Mrs Ingram, who appeared to be rooted to the spot, Jenny bound her sister's hand with a napkin. The sight of the bright red blood blooming across the perfectly laundered white linen seemed to concentrate Mr Ingram's mind, because he started forward, just missing the tea table, and grabbed Mrs Ingram's wrist.

Mrs Ingram tried, ineffectually, to push him away and the pair of them swayed backwards and forwards for a moment, sending several cups and saucers smashing to the floor.

'Get—away—from—*me*!' panted Mrs Ingram, fiercely. There was a cry from Doris—Mr Ingram had inadvertently kicked her—and then, as Mr Ingram took hold of Mrs Ingram's shoulders and pushed her back onto the sofa, the cake slice flew out of her hand and clattered onto the hearth.

'I said, that's enough! I've had enough! We all have!' Mr Ingram stood shaking, his face puce with fury. Although small, he towered over his seated wife, who cowered away from him. 'Stop it!' He leant forward and shouted into her face. 'Just stop it! Have you any idea what you're putting me through?' He grabbed hold of one corner of the photograph and jerked it, trying to pull it out of her hand. 'That's me there! Eric! It's me!'

Mrs Ingram clung on, making a little yelping noise as the photograph tore and Mr Ingram, balance upset, took an involuntary step back and collided with the table, making the china rattle. 'I've had enough! Do you understand? I'm not having this nonsense a moment longer. If you want a divorce, you can have one. They're not going to refuse when I tell them what's been going on. And then,' he added, with childish malice, 'you really won't have a husband. There won't be any blessed Mr Ingram, and we'll just see how you like that, won't we?'

Throughout most of this, Mrs Ingram stared at her husband in goggle-eyed terror, not even attempting to turn her head away as his spittle landed on her cheek, but, at the end, she covered her face in her hands and began a high, keening wail.

'You cry all you like—I'm sick of it!'

Doris, clutching her wrapped hand to her chest, got to her feet, staring at Jenny with an expression that was as close to screaming as a face could come without sound actually issuing from it. Feeling that she couldn't bear any of it for another second, Jenny said loudly, over Mrs Ingram's noisy weeping, 'Mr Ingram! Eric! Please…I'm sure there's no need for that.'

Mr Ingram rounded on her, his face working. 'Isn't there? Isn't there? What am I supposed to do? Let her carry on with this...this ridiculous...' His voice died away and Jenny realised that he was trying not to cry. He wiped his eyes on the sleeve of his absurd jersey, then stared at the wreckage of the tea table for a moment before seeming to remember that he was a guest in Doris's home, and saying, in a quieter voice, 'I'm sorry.'

Jenny shook her head. 'I'm the one who should be sorry. I should never have suggested it, but I honestly thought it would work if you reminded her about all the nice things you'd done together, and you showed her the photograph. I can see now that it was a stupid idea.'

Mr Ingram looked round at the wreckage of the tea party with an expression of disgust. 'It's not you, it's *her*. Take this,' he thrust two pound notes in Doris's direction, 'I'm going back.'

'To the army?'

'Yes. I don't care what happens. It's pointless. Look at her.'

Jenny looked at Mrs Ingram, who was still seated on the sofa, now rocking back and forth, her hands over her face. 'She can't help it, Mr Ingram.'

'She could if she tried. And there's nothing I can do.' He put his hands up in a gesture of defeat, and then, hoisting his kitbag onto his shoulder, left the house, slamming the front door behind him.

Jenny and Doris stared at each other. Mrs Ingram, hearing the door slam, peered cautiously at them through her hands. The torn, crumpled photograph, Jenny saw, was by her feet. 'Has he gone?'

'Yes,' said Doris, heavily. 'And I don't think we'll see him again, either.'

'Good.' Spotting the photograph, Mrs Ingram picked it up and sat with it in her hands. Her 'rigid' look had returned, and she sat as unpresent as a piece of furniture as the pair of them gathered up the debris and took it through to the kitchen.

'She'll stay there for a good half hour now,' said Doris. 'Shut off from everything. You know, I'm sure she can control it—it's just when something's gone wrong, or she doesn't like it, then she sort of seizes up.'

'Well, at least she won't disturb us,' said Jenny, fitting pieces of china together. 'Three cups and two saucers, I'm afraid.'

'I'll never be able to replace them,' said Doris, who'd unwrapped the napkin and was running her hand under the tap.

'I'll put that serviette in to soak. Is it hurting?'

'Not much. It was the shock more than anything.'

'I know. Good job it wasn't a carving knife.'

Doris, at the sink, twisted round to look at Jenny. 'You don't think she would have, you know…if it had been? I mean, she didn't say sorry, did she?'

'No, but…' Jenny realised she had no idea what to think. Unwilling to examine this uncertainty, and conscious of the spectre of Auntie Ivy, she took the stained napkin into the scullery and busied herself rinsing it and collecting together soap, Reckitt's blue, and plaster for Doris's hand. So much for having bright ideas—next time, she'd keep her big mouth shut.

'You know,' said Doris about ten minutes later, when they'd washed up the remains of the tea-service and tidied the food away, 'maybe she ought to, you know, *be somewhere.*'

'That's all very well,' said Jenny, 'but don't you remember what Mum said about Auntie Ivy? She said she went right downhill when they put her in the…you-know-where. That was when she stopped speaking.'

'Did she? I don't remember Mum ever talking about it.'

'It was only the once. She said they felt bad about signing the papers, that she and Dad should have taken her in and looked after her.'

'They couldn't, Jen. I am worried, though—what if Mrs Ingram attacks someone else? Madeleine, or—'

'She won't! Why would she do that?'

'She thinks we're all on his side, doesn't she?'

'Well, if he doesn't come back—and if he's going to hand himself in and get locked up for being a deserter, I don't see how he can—it won't be a problem.'

'It will if she thinks we're planning,' Doris dropped her voice to a whisper, 'to lock her up in the you-know-where.'

'Can't we leave it for a more few days?' pleaded Jenny. 'Please? I really can't bear the thought of having her locked away.'

'I suppose so,' said Doris. 'All right, then. But only a few days, mind. And, in that case,' she added, grimly, 'we'd better keep mum about what happened this afternoon.'

It was such a shock that, for a second, Dacre stopped breathing. The air pressure seemed to change around him, and feeling so dizzy that he thought he should faint at any minute, he forced himself to meet Byrne's eyes and return his nod of acknowledgement before bending his head once more and continuing to wash his hands. Just behave normally, he told himself. He's a doctor, you're a doctor—what could be more normal? For God's sake, don't panic. Heart thumping, he saw out of the corner of his eye that Byrne was still standing there, and waited for him to turn away to dry his hands, but he didn't move. The silence was broken only by the gurgle of the water as it ran over his own hands and down the drain, and the clink of the stem of his stethoscope against the porcelain edge of the basin as he bent over it. The tiled walls around them seemed to heighten these sounds, so that they roared in his ears and reverberated in his head. Why wasn't Byrne moving? Go away, he willed the pathologist. Just dry your hands and *go away.*

Byrne did not move. Dacre forced himself to turn his head and saw that he was staring, fixedly, at the scar on his—Dacre's— thumb. Oh, Christ, thought Dacre. This can't be happening. He carried on rubbing his hands violently with the soap, making sure his thumb was hidden from view. It's all right, he told himself. Byrne doesn't know you. He's just taking his time, that's all. But why didn't the man dry his hands, or say something?

Still Byrne remained beside him. Dacre, scrubbing away, started seeing fuzzy grey spots dancing on the porcelain before him. For God's sake, he told himself, keep calm. Feeling as if his head might explode, Dacre gave his hands a final rinse, walked the few steps necessary to dry them on the towel, aware all the time of the silent, watchful presence a couple of feet away, and left the Gents'. This he did at a normal speed, holding his breath and readying himself for the accusation. Byrne, however, neither moved towards him nor called out, and Dacre's last view of him before the door swung shut behind him showed that he was still standing by the row of basins, a frown crenellating his forehead.

Once in the corridor, Dacre walked as briskly as he could without actually running in the direction of the stairs, then felt an uprush of puke from his stomach that made him clap his hand to his mouth and head in the direction of the nearest door, which proved to be—thank God—the ward maids' cupboard where he'd hidden before. Bending over what he hoped was a pail, he vomited violently. He couldn't see, in the near dark, if he'd been right, but judging by the sound as the puke hit the bottom of the receptacle, most of it had gone in there and not over his shoes.

'Christ,' he muttered, leaning shakily against a stack of boxes. 'Jesus.' He was quivering all over, with barely the strength to pull his handkerchief and wipe his mouth.

He attempted to run the moments back in his mind as if they were pieces of film. Byrne had been there, all right—he definitely hadn't imagined that. And it certainly felt as if the man had been staring at his hands for a long time, but perhaps that was just his impression…shock and fear could distort one's impressions. Maybe it hadn't been for more than a few seconds.

Dacre held up his hand in front of him. His eyes now adjusted to the gloom, he saw that the scar on his thumb and the skin surrounding was reddened, irritated by being rubbed so hard with soap. It was, he supposed, the sort of thing that Byrne would remember, and he must have seen it enough times in the last six months when, as Todd, he'd passed over specimen bottles and test tubes and so forth...Byrne always wore rubber gloves to perform his post-mortems, but the shortage meant that there were not enough of them to supply anyone else.

Byrne had certainly been frowning when Dacre had left the Gents'. Was that because he was trying to remember where he'd seen the scar, or one like it? That was fine, provided that he did not remember who'd had the scar, or, if he *did*, simply dismissed it as a coincidence. After all Byrne, like Higgs, wasn't expecting to see him still here, and certainly not wearing a white coat and with a stethoscope round his neck. Of course, his appearance would probably have reminded Byrne of his former assistant, Sam Todd, but the different hair colour and the lack of moustache had probably thrown him off...

What if Byrne challenged him? Could he pretend that he hadn't been called up after all, but had taken a menial job in another part of the hospital? No. That would be far too easy to check, and how to explain the stethoscope? 'Fuck!' Dacre punched the side of the stack of boxes hard, wincing as their unyielding contents sent shock waves through his knuckles.

Perhaps he should just make a run for it now, before Byrne blew the whistle. If he was going to blow the whistle, that is... But he could leave the hospital, collect his few possessions from his digs, stuff them into his trunk and get on a train...Go somewhere else and make a new start. But that meant leaving half of his precious 'Dacre' documents in the hands of Professor Haycraft's secretary. Not to mention leaving Fay—and he was buggered if he was going to relinquish the perfect girl, now that he'd found her.

The thought of this, and of all the work he'd put in, made him genuinely furious. Why the hell should he flee with his tail between his legs? If Byrne challenged him, he'd bloody well go in with both guns blazing. In fact, Dacre thought, that on its own might generate enough doubt in Byrne's mind for him to back off...After all, the burden of proof was on Byrne, not him. And if Byrne was wavering, then he'd have the moral advantage. All he'd have to do was press it home.

Besides, it might never happen. Feeling a great deal calmer, and with a sense of resolve, Dacre left the cupboard and returned to Casualty.

The rest of the morning went smoothly, from a medical point of view, at least. Just as well, because Dacre was on tenterhooks and barely able to concentrate. Every time he stepped out from behind a screen, he expected to find Byrne waiting for him, vengeful and accusing, but as the hours passed and he did not appear Dacre began, very slowly, to relax.

At lunchtime he went to his bolt hole for a quiet smoke. There was no question of eating—his stomach was still churning too much to accept any food. Sitting on the dusty floorboards, cigarette in hand, he tried to convince himself that Byrne hadn't recognised him and that he was suffering from a paranoid delusion. He'd been reading about such states in *An Introduction to Psychological Medicine*. Of course, a general belief that one was being persecuted was not the same thing as he was experiencing, because his fears had a well-founded basis...

He needed to hold his nerve, and, if necessary, to make quite sure that there was no chance of Byrne putting a spanner in the works. To this end, he decided, it would be a good idea to have something up his sleeve, just in case. Remembering Fay's morphine, he took the two small phials, now carefully wrapped in cotton wool, from the inside pocket of his jacket, and weighed them in his hand. After all, forewarned was forearmed...

As the day wore on, Dacre began to feel more secure. His last patient was a fifteen-year-old girl with stomach pains, who'd been brought in by her mother. The girl, moon-faced and vacant, was obviously an imbecile. What was equally obvious, even to Dacre, was that she was heavily pregnant and experiencing the first stages of labour. When the mother, who seemed only fractionally more intelligent than her daughter, finally got the message, she punched him in the face. The blow was as forceful as it was unexpected. Dacre staggered backwards, clutching his cheek, and crashed into Sister Radford who, bristling with outrage, had rushed to intervene.

'Mrs Parker! That's quite enough!'

'Don't you come near me, or I'll have the law on you!'

Dacre, who had landed flat on the floor, was struggling, head spinning, to sit up as the mother—'You're a bloody bitch, that's what you are!'—swinging her capacious handbag in a scything motion, charged forwards, bloodying the nose of an ancient orderly who fell on top of a small table, splintering one of its legs and sending an ashtray tumbling across the floor, spewing fag ends. In an impressive show of strength, Sister Radford, pausing only to instruct the nearest nurse to tidy up immediately, took hold of the woman—who was considerably larger and beefier than anyone else in the place, male or female—by her upper arms, and shook her.

The waiting patients ducked as the handbag flew across the room, bursting open on contact with a bench and scattering its contents in a wide arc. As one of the items was a small bar of chocolate, every child in the place, and several of the adults, miraculously recovered their vitality and made a lunge for it. Mrs Parker kicked Sister Radford in the shins until she released her grip and waded into the brawl, bellowing, while her idiot daughter wailed and clutched her belly.

'Take that, you thieving little bleeder!' Mrs Parker took a swipe at a little boy who'd managed to cram most of the chocolate into his mouth, making him howl.

'How dare you!' The child's mother stepped forward, shaking her fist under Mrs Parker's nose. 'Calling my son a bleeder when your daughter's no better than a—'

At this point the boy, who, unnoticed by anyone but Dacre, had become suddenly and ominously silent, hiccupped once and then vomited copiously. Everyone in the vicinity, including several nurses who had rushed in to try and break up the mêlée, jumped backwards to avoid the splatter of undigested food.

'Disgusting!' yowled Mrs Parker. She made a beeline for her daughter, who was now shrieking at ear-splitting volume, and, clasping her by the wrist, began dragging her towards the door. 'Come on, Iris! We're not staying here to be insulted by a filthy lot of liars!'

A posse of nurses, plus two of the more vigorous porters, charged after her, pursued by a hobbling Sister Radford. At this point, Dacre, who had sat up and was about to go and render what assistance he could, noticed a syringe lying under the nearest bench. All eyes, including those of the puking child and its bespattered mother, were fixed on the scrum in the doorway. The only person near him was the old orderly, who was rocking backwards and forwards on his knees, wiping his streaming nose on the sleeve of his tunic and intoning 'Bloody 'ell, bloody 'ell, bloody 'ell,' as if it were a form of prayer.

The syringe looked empty. Dacre reached out an arm and pocketed it, jabbing himself sharply as he did so. 'Ah, *Christ!*' Fortunately, the cacophony of yells and curses was loud enough for this to go unnoticed and Dacre heaved himself upright and began moving, as slowly as he dared, towards the struggling mass of bodies in the doorway. Fortunately, by the time he got there, Nurse Dunning had got Mrs Parker firmly round the waist and was bundling her, with the aid of the two porters, down the corridor. The rest of the nurses, urged on by Sister Radford, were wrestling the shrieking girl onto a trolley for despatch to Maternity.

Once the racket had receded and order was being restored, Dacre, on Sister Radford's instructions, sat down beside her desk so that she could take a look at him. The sister, though panting slightly and still limping, had, Dacre noted, somehow managed to come through the whole thing without a hair out of place. 'That's going to be a nasty bruise,' she said. 'I'm sorry, Dr Dacre. I don't know what you must think…Some people are no better than pigs.'

'Well,' Dacre grinned at her, 'I hope I never meet a pig with a right hook like that. Anyone would think I was responsible for the girl's condition.'

Sister Radford's eyes widened in shock. 'Of course they wouldn't! That girl ought to be in a reformatory.'

'Bit late for that now.'

'Yes, well…It's absolutely disgraceful, and as for the mother…Now, if you don't mind staying put for just a moment, I'll go and fetch some witch hazel.'

'Shouldn't you be sitting down?' asked Dacre. 'That was quite a kicking she gave you. Would you like me to have a look?'

'Heavens, no.' Sister Radford brushed the suggestion away with a little laugh. 'Just a bruise or two. Nothing to worry about.'

She departed, and Dacre, looking round the room, saw, with a shock that felt like a colossal blow to the midriff, that Dr Byrne was framed in the doorway, scaring straight at him.

CI Lamb made Stratton wait for several minutes, standing in front of his desk, while he read something on a piece of paper in front of him. Or rather, while he sat bolt upright and stared downwards with such a lack of animation that Stratton had the enjoyable fantasy of leaning forward to touch him and watching him crumple over, revealing, in the manner of a detective story, an oriental dagger stuck between his shoulder blades.

It was half past five, and Stratton had been in court most of the afternoon, giving evidence in the hooch case. They'd got a conviction, but he very much doubted that his superior had called him in for congratulations.

Finally, Lamb looked up, and Stratton saw, from his peeved and twitchy expression that he was a) very much alive, b) more like George Formby even than before, and c) just itching to give someone a thorough bollocking.

'Slack!' he barked.

Stratton, involuntarily, looked around him, although he knew there was no-one else in the room. 'Sir?'

'You, man! It's not good enough. It's been over a month now, and no progress on the cases at the Middlesex.'

'We're doing our best, sir. We've got a weapon, and—'

'You've got a *brick*. And you don't have the first bloody idea who killed either of them.'

'Yes, sir, but—'

He got no further. Lamb began his tirade, accompanied by the forefinger jabbing out its usual staccato rhythm on the wooden desktop, leaving Stratton in no doubt that both enquiries were a shambles and a shower and a lot more besides. 'For God's sake,' he finished, 'Dr Reynolds was a professional man! Not some…some hooligan. We need a result, and fast. Is that clear?'

'Yes, sir. But I'm afraid it's rather more complicated than… well, than with a hooligan. There might have been some medical malpractice, sir. Illegal operations.'

Lamb looked outraged. 'The man was a qualified physician, not some old woman in a back street.'

'Yes, but it happens, sir. It's not unknown.'

Lamb made an irritated gesture, as if shooing away a troublesome fly. 'Keep off all that. Doesn't look good, and it's not necessary to blacken the man's reputation. He's got a family. Just solve the case and do it quickly. And get cracking on the nurse, too.'

Stratton left Lamb's office and trudged back to his own, reflecting that the best thing for his career would be to collar some not-very-bright villain with a record for robbery and violence and beat a confession out of him for both cases. And he might as well: the enquiries he'd made to nursing homes about Dr Reynolds had drawn a blank, and he obviously wasn't going to be able to proceed any further down that avenue without Lamb dropping a ton of bricks on him. He was just about to pick up the phone to follow up some information about the forged petrol coupons when he heard the loud report of someone breaking wind behind him.

'Good evening, vicar,' said Stratton, with heavy sarcasm. Turning in his chair, he saw Arliss standing in the doorway. The room was rapidly filling with a pungent odour, like a breeze across a cabbage field. 'Oh,' he said. 'It's you. Perhaps you could think of a different way of announcing yourself next time.'

'It's not my fault,' said Arliss, truculently. 'It's all these bloody vegetables the missus keeps feeding me.'

'Well,' said Stratton, 'tell her to lay off before you asphyxiate us all. What is it, anyway?'

'Message from Dr Byrne, sir. At the hospital. Wants a word.'

'What, now?'

'As soon as possible was what he said.'

'When did you get the message?'

'This afternoon, sir. While you were out. Then you were with the guv'nor,' said Arliss, piously. 'Not my place to interrupt.'

'Oh, fair enough. Now,' said Stratton, seizing his hat and fanning the air with it, 'why don't you bugger off while I can still breathe?'

A telephone call to the hospital mortuary yielded no reply, and Stratton, supposing that Dr Byrne was otherwise occupied, decided, as it was urgent, that he'd better pay the man a visit.

For a long moment, Dacre stared back. Byrne did not step forward or speak, but, lifting one hand with monstrous slowness, crooked his forefinger in a beckoning motion.

Feeling a sudden and violent throbbing from his bruised head that definitely hadn't been there before and a lurch of nausea that made him fear that he was about to spew for the second time that day, Dacre raised his eyebrows at Byrne and, willing himself not to tremble, pointed a finger at his own chest in a questioning manner. Byrne nodded emphatically. With elaborate casualness, Dacre got up, made a show of shaking the creases out of his trousers and dusting himself down, and ambled across to the door.

'I want to see you,' said Byrne.

'Now?' Dacre was aiming for a tone of puzzled enquiry, but it came out as more of a croak. Clearing his throat, he said, 'As you can see, we're rather busy at the moment...' Gesturing towards his eye, he added, 'Bit of an altercation, I'm afraid.'

'Never mind that,' said Byrne. 'My office. Ten minutes.' He tapped the face of his wristwatch. 'I'll be waiting.'

'Very well.' There was no point in arguing. Dacre certainly didn't want his credentials questioned in a public place, and—at this point, at least—Dr Byrne had the upper hand. As he watched Dr Byrne march off down the corridor, he reflected that he could perfectly well use the injury he'd received as an excuse to leave on the dot of six. In a way, the idiot girl and her mother were a blessing in disguise; the staff would be talking about that for days, and nobody was likely to remember seeing his brief conversation with Dr Byrne. Neither Dr Ransome nor Sister Radford—the only two people likely to question the pathologist's unexpected presence in Casualty—were anywhere in sight.

Dacre resumed his seat. Perhaps the sister had gone to fetch him a cup of tea as well as the witch hazel...He could certainly do with one, but, more urgently than that, he needed to be alone to consider his course of action. He'd stick to his original plan— attack as the best form of defence—but if that failed, he'd need something else. Christ, *think*...He'd got the morphine and the syringe, hadn't he? He slid a hand into his inside pocket: neither phial was broken, thank God. Could he? And, even if he could, *how*? He couldn't force the stuff down the man's throat or tie him up, and in any case, Higgs was bound to be somewhere about the place, and then...

Fuck, fuck, fuck. No. It wouldn't come to that. He'd be able to talk his way out of it. He'd always managed before, hadn't he? Or, if he didn't, at least he'd be able to give himself long enough to get clear of the place. Bloody Byrne. Just when everything was going so well, that bastard had to come and screw it all up for him.

'Here we are, Dr Dacre.' Sister Radford poured some witch hazel onto a piece of cotton wool. 'If you'll just look up...' Dacre tried not to wince as she dabbed his face. 'That should do the trick. Nurse Dunning's bringing you a cup of tea—unless you'd like something a bit stronger?'

'No, really. I'm fine. To be honest, sister, I think I just need some peace and quiet. I'm off now, anyway, so unless there's anything else...Why don't you have the tea? I'm sure you could do with a cup.'

Alone in the Gents', Dacre locked himself into one of the cubicles and sat down, fingering the little phials in his pocket. Five minutes. He sank his head into his hands. The pendulum of his feelings swung from anger to despair—perhaps he should just use the wretched stuff on himself and have done with it?—and abruptly back again. Carefully, he filled the syringe and sat staring at it for several minutes. He bloody well wasn't going to give up now and slink away from the life he'd created—from Fay—like a beaten dog. He returned the syringe to his pocket, shook his aching head so violently that for a second he felt dizzy enough to black out, and, letting himself out of the cubicle, stood for a moment beneath the single, shaded light bulb. *Come on, come on...*

You can do this. You will do this. There it was: the sudden, fierce rush of excitement—what he now knew to be adrenalin—that squared his shoulders and straightened his back. If Dr fucking Byrne wanted to play at being his...what was it called? Nemesis, that was it. Well, then, he'd get his comeuppance, all right.

He left the Gents' and strode off in the direction of the basement stairs.

CHAPTER

34

Save for the faint humming of a generator, the basement of the Middlesex was eerily silent. Being late July, it was still light outside, but down here, in the windowless corridor, it could have been midnight. The corridors were creepy enough, lit as they were with faintly glowing bulbs spaced far apart and caged in wire. Together with the sickly green paint on the walls, they gave the place a horribly subterranean feeling.

Stratton was about to turn from the main corridor towards the mortuary when he heard quick, light footsteps coming towards him, and, rounding the corner, found himself face to face with Fay Marchant, who let out a startled 'Oh!'

'Sorry,' said Stratton. 'I didn't mean to frighten you.'

'Good heavens,' said Fay. She gave a nervous laugh and when she continued, it was at a slightly higher pitch than he remembered. 'Inspector Stratton! Have you come to see someone? Only, I don't think there's a soul about. I mean,' she added, unnecessarily, 'apart from us.'

'I do have an appointment, yes. With Dr Byrne.'

'Oh...Well, I hope you find him.'

'I'm sure he's in his office.'

'I don't think there was a light on. As I said, the place is deserted.' Fay gave an exaggerated shiver. 'I don't like it when it's like this. Creepy.'

'Well, I mustn't keep you. I'm sure you're busy.'

'I've just finished, actually. I was going back to the nurses' quarters.'

'I'll say goodnight, then.'

'Goodnight, Inspector.'

Stratton watched her go, and wondered if she'd been telling the truth. After all, she'd come in the opposite direction from the only basement stairs that he knew about...There were outside doors, of course, and yards and things, so perhaps she'd come in through one of those. He suddenly found himself wondering if Byrne had some intelligence about Reynolds and Fay, and, if so, what it might be. Fay had said there was no light on in Byrne's office, but he ought to check. She'd seemed nervous, but perhaps that was the effect of the mortuary corridor, which was bloody creepy. Or possibly bumping into him like that. Policemen had an unsettling effect on some people. He wouldn't have thought she was one of them, but...

Was it his imagination, or was the humming noise louder now? It must, he thought, be coming from further down the corridor—the refrigerated room where the bodies were kept. The thought of all the corpses, lying stiff and blue-white in their individual compartments, made him uneasy.

Stratton set off down the corridor. The sooner he found Byrne, the sooner he'd be able to get out of the place.

'Now then, what's all this about?' Dacre kept his tone deliberately light, as if he assumed it was some minor matter which could be cleared up in a few minutes.

Dr Byrne, standing back to let him enter the mortuary office, closed the door and locked it before replying. 'I think you know very well what it's about.' He paused for a moment, before adding, with hideous emphasis, 'Mr Todd.'

Dacre felt his heart trampoline in the direction of his throat. Somehow, he had not expected Byrne to get to the point so quickly. He raised his eyebrows enquiringly.

'I beg your pardon?'

'You heard me. The game's up, man.'

'What game? What are you talking about? I think you must have me confused with someone else.'

Byrne permitted himself a small smile. 'No. You've confused *yourself* with someone else. Someone, apparently, called Dr Dacre.'

'I don't understand. I am Dr Dacre.'

Byrne shook his head. 'You're Sam Todd, masquerading as Dr Dacre.'

'*What?*' Genuinely furious now, Dacre said, his voice growing louder and deepening with every word, 'Have you lost your mind?'

'I did wonder.' Another thin smile. 'In fact, I've been wondering all day, but there was no mistaking your hand. As you well know, I am trained to remember these things, Mr Todd.'

'Why do you keep calling me that?'

'Because that is your name. Or I assume it is. It may, of course, be something entirely different.'

'Rubbish! I'm not going to stand here and listen to this.' Dacre turned on his heel and started towards the door, with Byrne a pace behind. 'I don't know what you think you're up to, but by God, I'll—'

'Your hand, man.' It was on the handle of the door. Both men looked down. The scar, livid now against the whiteness of Dacre's knuckles, was plainly visible. 'The scar.'

'Yes.' Dacre took his hand off the handle and folded his arms. 'A dog bite, when I was a child. What of it?'

'I recognised it.'

'So you said. Listen, old chap,' here, Dacre injected a patronising note into his speech, as if dealing with a dim-witted child, 'it's just a scar. I'm sure I'm not the only person unfortunate enough to have been bitten by a dog.'

'It's a very particular mark—identical to that on the hand of Mr Todd, my former assistant. I see you've made some alteration to your appearance and your voice, but you are one and the same. Explain yourself.'

'There isn't anything to explain. You're mistaken, that's all.'

'No. Passing yourself off as a doctor, deceiving the authorities, practising medicine without a licence…These are serious matters.'

'Yes,' said Dacre, heatedly, 'they are. But they have nothing to do with me. I've told you, I am Dr Dacre. I can prove it. I don't see why I should have to, but, if it's necessary to defend my good name, I shall. And, believe me, you'll look quite a fool when I do.'

'I'm more than willing to risk looking a fool if it exposes a criminal. I don't know why you're doing this—I can only assume that you are suffering from some form of mental disorder—but I cannot allow—'

'How dare you?' bellowed Dacre. Spittle landed on Dr Byrne's face, causing him to take a step back. 'Who the hell do you think you are?'

'I know who I am.' Byrne took a handkerchief from his pocket and wiped his cheek. The question is, who are you?'

Dacre took a deep breath. This wasn't going according to plan. Instead of beginning to doubt himself, Byrne seemed more positive by the second. 'I am Dr James Dacre. I have a perfectly good medical degree from St Andrews, and I have been practising—'

'In that case,' Byrne interrupted, 'why were you working as a mortuary attendant under a different name?'

'I wasn't! You're deluded. Look,' said Dacre, trying now for a reasonable, both-men-of-the-world, sort of tone, 'I understand how this must have happened. You've obviously been under a lot of pressure, what with...' here, Dacre looked skywards, 'and when one's been working hard, one can sometimes get a bit confused about—'

'There's no confusion, I can assure you of that,' said Byrne, stiffly. 'I have the evidence of my own eyes.'

'How?' demanded Dacre. 'When we've never met before today? How do you account for that?'

An exultant gleam in Byrne's eyes made Dacre realise, with a sudden, sickening oscillation of all his innards, that he had made a terrible mistake. Even before Byrne opened his mouth, he knew what he was about to say.

'If we've never met before,' said Byrne, triumphantly, 'then how did you know who I was? I didn't introduce myself, and you didn't ask, did you?'

CHAPTER 36

In the split second that Dacre hesitated—should he try and flannel his way out of it by saying that someone had described the pathologist to him, or…or what?—he could see that Byrne felt he had won. 'Well,' he began, 'are you going to explain yourself, or do I have to—'

By this point, instinct had taken over from conscious thought, and Dacre gave Byrne a violent, two-handed shove in the chest. Caught off balance, the pathologist, his mouth still open, staggered backwards, slipped and fell, hitting the side of his head against the sharp corner of his desk as he went.

Dacre looked down at the crumpled, white-coated heap before him, one side of the waxy bald pate darkening with blood. 'Oh, God.' Kneeling down, he patted Byrne's face. The pathologist did not respond. After a few seconds, Dacre got to his feet, unsteady and gripping the edge of the desk for support, and stared out of the window into the courtyard. No-one there. No-one had seen. He lurched to the window and pulled down the blackout, then stumbled back across the room in the half-light to turn on the desk lamp.

Still Byrne had not moved. Dacre bent over him. He was breathing all right, just knocked out. This was his chance. Assuming that the morphine did not kill him absolutely on the instant, there was no reason for anyone to think that the blow had come before the injection...It had to look as if he'd injected himself, then fallen over...Was Byrne right-handed? Dacre thought so, but glanced at the desk to verify it. Yes, the pen and ink were on the right side of the blotter, with a piece of paper with writing on it: GER 1212. No name, but GER must be Gerard Street, so it couldn't be far away...Christ! The police station—where was that? Savile Row, so the number might be... And if Byrne had already telephoned them...Checking would mean a call through the hospital exchange, and that was out of the question.

Supposing the police were already on their way? Fuck. He needed to act and get out of there. The door was still locked, which was something, but the bars across the window meant that it was the only way out...Right. Get on with it. Dacre took the syringe from his pocket and, positioning himself behind Byrne, pushed up the left sleeve of the pathologist's coat and jacket as far as he could, then undid the cuff of his shirt and rolled it back above the elbow. He tried to fold Byrne's fingers into a fist but the pathologist stirred and started to mumble something. *Jesus, don't wake up now...*Dacre patted the bare left arm as hard as he dared, attempting to raise a vein, but it was hopeless. He peered at the single blue site he could see in the crook of the elbow, and, aiming the needle, pierced the skin and depressed the plunger. Byrne twitched and made a gurgling noise in his throat. *Don't wake up, damn you, don't wake up...*

Done. Dacre withdrew the syringe and, wiping it with his handkerchief, attempted to put it into Byrne's right hand. The fingers grasped it for a fraction of a second—long enough, surely?—before loosening and sending the thing rolling to the floor. Dacre, on his hands and knees, crawled round to get a look at Byrne from the front.

He saw in an instant that the pathologist's eyes were wide open and focused on him. The lips were drawn back in a grimace, showing yellowed teeth and a surprisingly large top expanse of shiny pinky-orange gum that stood out horribly against the dull white mask of the face. Why wasn't he dead? Dacre drew back, horrified, as Byrne leant towards him and, raising his quivering right arm, made a grab for his lapel. Clutching only air, the arm came down again, the hand thudding against the floorboards, the fingers flexing weakly as if seeking something of their own accord.

Inching backwards to what he judged was a safe distance, Dacre stared at the pathologist, horrified. Byrne emitted a noise that was halfway between a gurgle and a grunt, and continued staring fixedly in his direction. Why wasn't the bloody stuff working? Why didn't he just *die*? Perhaps the injection hadn't been strong enough. Christ…What if Byrne were to recover?

As Dacre watched, Byrne's fingers stopped moving, and his eyes shut as swiftly and finally as if someone had pulled down a blind. His lips returned to their normal position, and his face seemed to settle into the placid semblance of sleep. Dacre could hear his breathing—a stertorous rattle of mucous. What had gone wrong? Why wasn't he dead? Perhaps it just took longer than Dacre had imagined, but he couldn't just sit and wait…

No sounds from the corridor. Maybe the telephone number on the desk was not for the police station, after all. Higgs, or possibly his own replacement—if there was one—must be about somewhere, but, unless the arrangements had changed, they did not have keys to the office. Only Dr Byrne and Miss Lynn had those. Dacre got up and adjusted the desk lamp so that it shone in the direction of the small shelf where Byrne kept a few medical books. *Toxicology*. That was it. He took it down and, dropping once more to the floor, reached up to take hold of the lamp and put it beside him so that he could read. Morphine…Morphine… There it was. *The chief poisonous alkaloid of opium of which it forms five to twenty per cent…*Symptoms, where were the symptoms? *Individual susceptibility varies greatly even amongst adults… Several cases are known in which a dose of one grain of hydrochloride of morphine was fatal…*Well, Byrne had certainly had more than that, so…What else? *Morphine hypodermically injected gives symptoms in three to four minutes…*Good…*A period of excitement*—there hadn't been much of that, thank God, presumably because of the bang on the head—*is followed by incapacity for exertion, giddiness, drowsiness, sleep, stupor, 'insensibility'...respiration becomes slower, pulse is feeble...the muscles of the limbs feel flabby and relaxed, lower jaw drops, sphincters are relaxed, skin is cold...If vomiting takes place before stupor sets in, there is great hope of recovery...*

Dacre stopped reading and, shuffling on his knees, desk lamp in hand, moved over to take another look at Byrne. He certainly looked as though he were in a stupor, but he was still breathing loudly, though more slowly now...What did that mean? Dacre picked up Byrne's hand—it was relaxed, all right, a dead weight—and felt for a pulse: barely perceptible. The stuff was obviously working, but how long would it take? And if he vomited...Wait. Dacre considered Byrne for a moment, his head on one side, thinking, then took hold of his shoulders and pulled him away from the desk so that he was flat on his back on the floor. If he puked, he'd choke on it. Now, it was just a matter of time...

He felt in Byrne's pocket for the office keys—he'd have to take them with him if he wanted to lock up again, but that couldn't be helped. Unless...he was peering beneath the door to see if there was room to slide them back through the thin gap above the floor, when he heard footsteps. He shrank back and crouched, heart pounding and palms clammy, listening. Whoever it was was coming in his direction. Keep calm. Must keep calm. Probably someone going to one of the operating theatres, nothing to do with Byrne. *That's it, go on, keep moving...*

The footsteps stopped and he saw the thin line of light beneath the door darken. He held his breath. The sharp sound of the knock made him jump. 'Dr Byrne? It's DI Stratton from West End Central.'

So Byrne had telephoned, and set him up to walk into a trap, although, presumably, something must have delayed the big policeman, who was now only five feet away behind the door. At that moment, Byrne made a rasping noise in his throat. Dacre stretched out, almost overbalancing, and placed a hand across the pathologist's mouth. Byrne's face was just outside the pool of illumination from the desk lamp. The lamp wasn't pointing in the direction of the door, but what if Stratton saw the light? He couldn't turn it off because that might be more noticeable, or the policeman might hear the click of the switch. *Jesus.* His neck was uncomfortably close to the hot shade, and his calves, unused to the position he was in, were throbbing. *Go away, for Christ's sake just go away...*

He could feel the wetness of Byrne's breath under his right palm, but at least there was no sound other than a faint sighing. He heard a rattle. Stratton must be trying the door handle. 'Dr Byrne?'

He was in agony, but he dare not move. He attempted to ease his legs by taking his weight on the splayed fingertips of his left hand, but they were so damp that he gave up the attempt, fearing to slip. Surely Stratton would go away now? The feet moved a few paces—*yes, yes, that's it, off you go*—then stopped abruptly as a door—the main mortuary room, from the sound of it—opened. 'Can I help you?' Higgs.

What if he had a key, or sent for one? He was trapped. Byrne made another noise, more of a snort this time, and Dacre, his entire body quivering with the effort of control, moved down onto one knee. Reaching out his now free left hand, he pinched Byrne's nostrils closed. Surely, he thought, the man could not be saved now? If they fetched a key, or broke down the door, he supposed he could claim that he had been trying to help Byrne, but that wouldn't explain why the door was locked or why he hadn't called out or answered Stratton's knock. His mind picked its way swiftly across the stepping-stones of a dozen possibilities, but each seemed more implausible than the last.

Sweat was pooling in his armpits and trickling down his brow, stinging his eyes. With both hands occupied covering Byrne's nose and mouth, he couldn't wipe them, and the muscles in his legs felt as if they might snap at any second. He couldn't hold the position—he'd have to move, and then...One second more, he told himself. Just keep still. Then another second, another and another...

37

Stratton stopped outside the door of Dr Byrne's office. Hearing no sound, he knocked. calling out, 'Dr Byrne? It's DI Stratton from West End Central.'

Nothing.

He called out again, less in hope of a reply than to break the eerie silence. 'Dr Byrne?'

Still nothing. Stratton tried the handle of the heavy wooden door. Locked.

'Can I help you?' The door to the main mortuary, several yards down, opened, and Byrne's assistant, Higgs, appeared, clutching a thick sandwich. 'Sorry, Inspector,' he said, indistinctly, 'didn't realise it was you.'

'Is Dr Byrne around?'

'He was in there.' Higgs shook the sandwich in the direction of Byrne's office, causing a piece of lettuce to fall to the floor. 'Finishing up his notes with Miss Lynn. That was about...oh, I'd say an hour ago. I know she's left—I should think he's gone, too, by now.' Higgs bent to pick up the lettuce leaf and, inspecting it, declared, 'Waste not, want not,' then popped it into his mouth.

'You didn't see him leave?'

Higgs shook his head. 'Sorry, Inspector.'

'You don't happen to have a key to his office, do you? I'd like to leave him a note.'

'Afraid not. Dr Byrne's got one, of course, and Miss Lynn—they'll have one upstairs, though. I'd fetch it myself, only I'm not meant to leave in case we get something come down.'

Stratton looked at his watch: it was after seven o'clock. If Byrne had decided not to wait, then perhaps whatever he had to say wasn't *that* urgent, after all. Presumably, if it had been, he'd have left a more detailed message at the station. Firmly shoving to the back of his mind the thought that Arliss—if he'd been the one to take the message—was quite capable of omitting a vital piece of information (or getting it entirely wrong), Stratton told Higgs he'd be back in the morning, and began retracing his steps towards the stairs.

CHAPTER

38

Dacre gasped. As he listened to the mortuary door bang shut and the big policeman's footsteps head away down the corridor, he felt all the muscles in his face and body begin to unclench and relax. When he could hear the feet no longer, he brought his knee round and, sitting on the floor, shaking, aching, and drenched in sweat from head to toe, slowly removed his hands from Byrne's face. For a few moments he was unable to move, and then, turning his upper body slowly towards the desk, he began to haul himself upright. Now, all he had to do was take himself out of the place before anyone caught him. The worst threat was Higgs who might, given today's luck, actually recognise him. Should he, perhaps, remove his shoes? He considered the idea for a moment, then decided it was stupid. To be found padding about in his socks really would look odd, and, after all, Higgs could have no notion of Byrne's suspicions, or he would have said something to Stratton. In any case, from what he knew of Byrne, the man wasn't the type to share his thoughts with his underlings unless it was absolutely necessary. Besides, he was Dr Dacre, wasn't he? He had every right to be in the hospital where he worked: no-one would question that. It was simply a matter of getting as far away from the room as possible.

Byrne was quiet now. This must be the stupor he'd read about. The book! He tiptoed round the desk, retrieved it from the floor, and stuck it back on the shelf, wiping it with his handkerchief as he did so. He wiped the lamp, too, and, holding it in the handkerchief, placed it gently back on the desk, which he also wiped. Stuffing the scrap of paper with the telephone number on it into his pocket, he switched off the lamp, waiting a moment for his eyes to adjust to the dim light before making his way to the door. This was the hardest part—he mustn't be heard. He paused in the almost-darkness, wiping his clammy hands on his handkerchief and trying to control his breathing. So nearly there... He fumbled in his pocket for the keys and almost dropped them. The lack of light and his quivering fingers meant that it took several goes to force the key into the lock, but he managed at last.

*Now then. Don't rush, take your time...*Did the door creak? He couldn't remember. He'd just have to find out. Turning the key, he began, with infinitesimal slowness, to pull the door open. Aaahhh...It was silent. The aperture being just wide enough he slid himself out, and then, closing it—the click of the lock made him catch his breath, but no-one appeared—he locked up, and bending swiftly wiped the keys with his handkerchief then flicked them, in a skimming motion, beneath the door. He heard a tiny scraping noise, then nothing. That, he thought, meant they had probably been stopped by the small rug that lay under Byrne's desk. Good: that would look as if the pathologist had dropped them.

He took a deep breath and then, looking neither left nor right, walked purposefully away, ignoring his brain's panicked instructions to run. He passed the mortuary—no windows, thank God—and kept the same pace until he rounded the corner. No door opening, no-one calling out...Nothing but the steady hum of the generator. Safely out of sight, he sprinted through the rest of the dingy basement maze, up the outside steps, and away into the darkening evening.

CHAPTER

39

Exhausted, Dacre stopped beside a WVS mobile canteen for a cup of tea. He didn't know how far he'd walked or where he was, he'd simply left the hospital and stumbled away as fast as he could through the dusk. It was dark now but he'd continued, more slowly because of the blackout, but just as aimlessly, his only purpose being to get as far away from the Middlesex as he possibly could.

Holding the mug in both hands—the July night was warm enough, but, in spite of his exertion, the sheen of cold sweat on his body was making him chilly—he stared at the bomb-site on the other side of the road. Not a recent one, he thought: there were no demolition men or ambulances in sight, and the humps of rubble had a settled look to them, as if they'd been there for some time.

He looked back towards the canteen and, in the dim light from the hatch, saw a couple of blue-overalled ARP men. 'Two down in the next street,' he heard one say. 'Three unaccounted for. They're still digging.'

How easy, Dacre thought sourly, to kill by firing a doodlebug into the air. He had no idea how the things were launched, but it had to be a bloody sight easier than doing it face to face…if, indeed, he had killed Dr Byrne. Perhaps, right at this minute, the man was recovering, the big policeman beside him, ready to take notes…the alarm being raised, the description circulated…

Surely it wasn't possible? He'd had too much morphine...A score of 'what ifs' buzzed in his head like hornets, and the memory of his hand across Byrne's mouth, the clammy feel of the pathologist's skin against his palm, of pinching the man's nostrils closed and feeling him fight for breath beneath his fingers, made him nauseous, so that he tipped the remains of his tea down a drain.

I shouldn't have done it, he thought. Doctors are there to save life, not to destroy it. Dr Dacre would never kill on purpose...What was he thinking? He *was* Dr Dacre. 'I am Dr James Dacre,' he said, aloud.

'Pleased to meet you.' A man's voice, quizzical. It was the ARP fellows—they must have moved towards him. 'Charlie Horden, ARP,' said the older man. The other hung back, staring at him. 'You're not here for the...' Horden jerked his head, presumably in the direction of the bombed buildings, 'are you? Only they don't usually send—'

'Oh, no. Just...' What? Running away because I think I've killed someone? 'Just wanted a breath of air,' he finished.

'Are you all right? I don't mean to be rude, but you seem a bit...'

What? What did he seem? Was there something wrong with his face? Dacre stared at the man. Was it obvious? Could he *tell*?

'I'm fine,' said Dacre. 'Just felt a bit stifled, that's all, so I thought I'd have a walk...' Even in the faint light afforded by the canteen, he could see the surprise on the man's face. 'I'm afraid I got rather lost. Where are we, exactly?'

'Victoria. Chapel Street, to be exact.'

He must have walked for miles. Squinting at his watch, he saw that it was after midnight. Why am I running away? he thought. There's no need. No-one saw me. Byrne will be dead—of course he will, he must be—and there's nobody to connect the two of us. If I run away now I'm leaving everything I've worked for—Dacre, Fay, all of it.

'Dr Dacre?' Dacre jumped at the sound of the warden's voice. 'I was asking where you come from?'

'Piccadilly.' He'd said the first place that came into his head, but that was all right—he knew the way from Piccadilly to Euston. 'Perhaps you'd be kind enough to point me in the right direction?'

Lips pursed, Horden considered this. 'Well, you've missed the last train. You'd best go up towards the park,' he said. 'Turn left at the end, that's Grosvenor Place, and that'll take you to Hyde Park Corner. Piccadilly's on your right.' The warden looked at him doubtfully. 'You going to be all right?' He glanced upwards. 'You can bet he's not finished for the night.' As if on cue, there was an explosion somewhere in the distance.

Dacre shrugged. 'I'll chance it. The walk might do me good.' He grinned at the warden and went to return his mug to the canteen's serving hatch.

'Or it might not,' Horden called after him. 'Cheerio—be lucky!'

If he really *were* lucky, Dacre reflected as he walked up Grosvenor Place, then Byrne would be dead. He'd already forgotten most of the warden's instructions, but they hadn't seemed too complicated, and besides, there was bound to be *someone* he could ask. He should have paid more attention—the more people he spoke to, the greater the possibility of someone remembering him. He shoved his hands in his pockets and trudged onwards, trying to think of something—anything—that wasn't Byrne's face with its waxy texture and blueish tinge...

CHAPTER
40

Stratton left home early the next morning and decided to go straight to the Middlesex. Unusually, it had been a relief to get off to work, and this made him feel guilty. He'd have to make it up to Jenny somehow, for being tired and uncommunicative—not that she was any better. It had to be that damned Mrs Ingram, causing bother, getting on Jenny and Doris's nerves and making them walk on eggshells. They ought to have a chat about it. Even if it didn't solve anything, it might clear the air a bit—although there was bugger-all anyone could do about the bombs and short-ages and all the rest of the stuff that constantly wore you down.

The basement corridors at the mortuary end were quiet—the only noises to be heard were the generator, which seemed fainter than it had the previous night, and the distant sounds of feet and trolley wheels going to and from the temporary operating theatres.

When he knocked on the door of Byrne's office, Higgs stuck his head out, his wizened face creased with tiredness, and, Stratton thought, some sort of distress.

'Inspector?' He looked alarmed. 'Course, you was here last night. I'm afraid there's been a bit of an accident.'

'What sort of accident?'

'It's Dr Byrne. He's...well, he's dead.'

'*Dead?*' echoed Stratton stupidly. 'Are you sure?' That was all he needed.

'I'm afraid so, sir.'

'Where?'

'In here, sir. Miss Lynn found him this morning. I asked Dr Ransome to come down from Casualty.' Evidently feeling the need for some sort of gloss on the proceedings, Higgs added, 'It's bloody terrible.'

Stratton removed his hat. 'I'd better come in.'

'Yes, sir.'

The first thing he noticed was the smell—relaxing in death, Dr Byrne's body had voided itself. The corpse, one temple dark and bloodied, lay flat on the floor beside the desk, one sleeve rolled back to expose a pale arm. Seeing it, Stratton's first, flippant, reaction turned to pity. However he'd felt about Byrne's punctiliousness and cold manner, the man had, after all, been a colleague—well-valued, if not well-liked, and now he was dead, and in undignified circumstances, and that shouldn't happen to anyone.

The elderly, white-coated doctor bending over the body straightened sharply as they entered. 'I thought I told you that I don't want anyone in here until Professor Haycraft's seen this.'

'It's the police, Dr Ransome. Inspector Stratton.'

'I didn't ask you to call the police.'

'He didn't,' said Stratton. 'Dr Byrne left a message yesterday asking me to come and see him. I came last night, but the office was closed, and I assumed Dr Byrne had gone home.'

'I see.' The doctor held out his hand. 'Ransome.'

'Stratton, CID.' After they'd shaken hands, Stratton asked, 'What happened?'

'Well...' Ransome looked uncomfortable. 'I'm not entirely sure.'

'What, no idea at all? Heart attack? Stroke? Apoplexy?'

'I think it's best to wait for the post-mortem. Then we'll have a better idea of...of...' The doctor tailed off, seeing that

Stratton's eyes had strayed towards the desk blotter, on which lay a syringe. Then, seeing Stratton take out his notebook, his look of apprehension changed to one of alarm. 'Surely there's no need—'

'Was that here when you arrived?'

Dr Ransome nodded unhappily.

'In that position?'

'Yes.'

'No,' put in Higgs. 'It was on the floor. I saw it when I come in. Miss Lynn come flying into the mortuary to tell me, in a terrible state—couldn't hardly get her words out—and when I come in I put it up on the desk there— Didn't want anyone treading on it, sir.'

'And it was where, exactly?' asked Stratton.

'Just about...' Higgs cast around and fixed on a spot equidistant from Byrne's chair, which had been pushed back, and his body, 'there.'

'So it—or what it contained—could have had something to do with his death?'

'Yes.' Dr Ransome looked even more miserable. 'It's possible, but, as I say, we shan't know for certain until—'

'So you said,' interrupted Stratton, understanding that Ransome, assuming suicide, hadn't wanted to contact the police until the post-mortem had confirmed his suspicions. Had Byrne, he wondered, been about to confess to the murder of Reynolds, and, if so, why?

'I don't need reminding that suicide is illegal, Inspector,' snapped Dr Ransome. 'I was thinking of Dr Byrne's widow.'

'His wife's dead,' said Higgs. 'Last year.' Lowering his voice, he added, 'Cancer.'

'That,' said Stratton, 'might have had something to do with it.'

Ransome gave him a baleful look. 'We don't know that.'

'No, we don't. Do you know,' Stratton asked Higgs, 'if he had any children?'

Higgs nodded. 'A son. He's in the forces.'

'Which service?'

'RAF, sir.'

'Does Dr Byrne live alone?'

'I think so.'

'Right. How did he seem yesterday?'

Higgs looked surprised. 'Fine, sir. Same as usual. And, sir—if I might take the liberty of saying...'

'Yes?'

'Dr Byrne didn't approve of suicide, sir. People we've had in here who've done themselves in...He used to say they were weak, sir. In the head.'

'Yes,' said Stratton, recalling that Byrne had several times dismissed suicides as 'neurotic types' in his presence. 'He did, didn't he? Now, what about that?' Stratton pointed at the contusion on Byrne's head.

'I imagine it happened when he fell,' said Ransome. 'It's not enough to kill him by itself.'

'Have you any idea what the syringe contained?'

'Could have been a number of things.'

'Such as...?'

'An opiate, perhaps. As I said,' Dr Ransome sounded irritated, 'the post-mortem should give a clearer indication.'

'Did he leave any sort of note?'

'Nothing,' said Dr Ransome. Behind him, Higgs shook his head in silent echo.

'You're absolutely sure about that?'

'As far as we know,' said Ransome, defensively. 'His secretary found him, so I suppose it's possible that she might have picked up a note, if there was one.'

'I'll talk to her in a minute.' As Stratton knelt down beside the body he could hear the tick of Byrne's watch, a tiny, mechanical pulse. He peered at a dark patch on the inside of the elbow of the bare arm. 'Is that the site of the injection?'

Ransome sighed. 'I would think so.'

'Any other marks like that?'

'Not that I could see,' said the doctor, stiffly. Stratton could see that he knew what was being asked. Addiction amongst doctors and nurses was hardly unknown—after all, they had access to drugs in a way that others didn't.

'Was he found in this position?'

'I certainly haven't moved him.' Ransome sounded affronted.

'Mr Higgs?'

'He was like that when I saw him, sir, and I don't suppose Miss Lynn would have been able to move him, even if she'd wanted to.'

'If he did fall off the chair,' said Stratton, getting up, 'it's a strange way to end up, flat on his back. I don't see how he could have bashed his head on the way down, either.' He peered at the corner of the desk nearest to Byrne and saw a mark on the dark wood near the edge. 'Although...It looks as if he banged himself on this. We'll have to check. Can you get a sample from this?' he asked Higgs. 'If there's enough.'

Higgs looked doubtful. 'I'll have a go.'

'Dr Byrne might have moved, of course,' said Ransome.

'Might he?' Stratton queried.

'It's possible.'

'How long has he been dead?'

'Hard to say. There's rigor in the jaw and neck, but the room's quite warm...over three hours, I should think. Perhaps longer.'

'So, it might have been...' Stratton glanced at his wrist-watch, 'say, quarter to five?'

'Possibly.'

Turning to Higgs, Stratton asked, 'Were you here all night?'

'Yes, sir.'

'Did you talk to Dr Byrne after I'd gone?'

'No, sir.'

'You didn't hear him leave?'

'No, sir. As I said, I thought he'd already left.'

'What about this morning?'

'The office was locked. He was due at the Southwark Coroner's Court at ten, and I thought he must have gone straight there.'

'Wouldn't that be unusual? You didn't give me any indication that he wouldn't be here this morning.'

'Well, it would, but...' Higgs gave Stratton a look that said,
quite clearly, that it wasn't his place to ask questions.

'Did you have a busy night?'

Higgs shook his head. 'We didn't have much come in, so I
had a kip, but I always wake the minute someone comes down.'

'Can't be very comfortable, sleeping in the mortuary.'

'It's all right when you get used to it. We had a chap for the
night duty, but he's gone, too—last week.'

'When you say, "too"...?'

'I mean, as well as Sam Todd. Leaving me on my tod, as you
might say.' The ghost of a smile flitted across Higgs's face.

'When did *he* go?' asked Stratton.

'Oooh...' Higgs screwed up his face with the effort of
recall. 'Best part of five weeks, now. Called up. That's right—I
remember, because it was the day after that poor nurse was
killed, he told me.'

'Hmm...' Stratton, looking round the office, saw a bunch of
keys lying on the floor in the far corner. 'What are those doing
there?' He put out a restraining hand as Higgs started forward
to pick them up. 'Do you recognise them?'

'They're Dr Byrne's. He must have dropped them. Blimey,
Inspector, someone ought to tell them at Southwark that Dr
Byrne won't be coming. I don't think Miss Lynn's in a fit state.'

'Where is she, anyway?'

'She's sitting in the mortuary. I gave her a nip of brandy.'

'I'd better go and have a word with her. You telephone
Southwark.'

'Right you are, sir.'

When Higgs had left, Dr Ransome turned to Stratton. 'It
could have been an accident, you know.'

'People don't tend to give themselves hypodermic injections
by accident, Dr Ransome.'

'No, but he might have been performing an experiment of
some sort, or perhaps he felt unwell and was trying to treat himself.'

'And made a mistake with the dosage?'

'It's possible.'

'So are quite a few other things.'

'But you can't think there's anything suspicious?'

'I don't know, Dr Ransome.'

'You must see that it wouldn't look good for the hospital. Not after Dr Reynolds.'

'I'm sorry, but I'm afraid there's not much I can do about that, other than not advertising the fact. Now, you said that Professor Haycraft was coming down, didn't you?'

'Higgs was about to go and fetch him when you arrived.'

'In that case, I think it would be a good idea if you went and explained the situation yourself.'

'I need to get back to my patients, Inspector. I work in Casualty, and I can assure you that we are extremely busy.'

'I'm sure that one of your colleagues could—'

'I haven't seen my colleague this morning. He was late, and I came down here almost as soon as I arrived.'

'It shouldn't take you very long, Dr Ransome. If you wouldn't mind telling the professor to come and have a word...'

'I'll do that. But then I must get back to work.'

'There's one more thing—would you mind asking Miss Lynn for her keys? I need to lock this room.'

'But...' Dr Ransome gestured towards the keys lying in the corner, then thought better of it. 'Oh, very well.'

He left, and Stratton glanced round the office once more— Byrne's pen was on the right hand side of his blotter, he noted. His pipe, matches and ashtray were on the left, but it would make sense to put them there if he was writing with his right hand. Screwing up his face, Stratton tried to recall the times he'd entered Byrne's office and found him at work. Yes, he'd definitely been right-handed, so it would make sense to inject himself in the left arm...If he'd sent a letter to his son before topping himself, that would clear things up nicely. Ballard could get on to that. Of course, there might not be any connection with Reynolds at all, but if there wasn't, why would Byrne have asked to speak to him urgently? Unless, of course, he'd seen some suspicious-looking corpse yesterday, but Higgs hadn't mentioned anything, so...That should be easy enough to check from the man's notes. Easier than—God help us—thawing out all the corpses for re-examination, anyway.

When Ransome had handed over the keys and hurried off upstairs, Stratton locked the office and went down the corridor to the mortuary. Miss Lynn was sitting, surrounded by sheeted bodies, sniffing into a handkerchief. Higgs was standing beside her, gingerly and ineffectually patting her on one shoulder. She looked up, pink-eyed, as Stratton entered.

'Miss Lynn? Inspector Stratton. It must have been a terrible shock, finding Dr Byrne like that. I'm afraid I'm going to have to ask you some questions—are you feeling up to it?'

Miss Lynn sniffed once more and nodded. 'Perhaps you could get her a cup of tea?' Stratton asked Higgs, who, obviously relieved to relinquish his duty as comforter to a weeping woman, assented immediately.

'Now...' Stratton glanced around the room and, seeing no other chair and not wanting to loom over poor Miss Lynn, leant awkwardly against the nearest slab, which—thank Christ—was bare. 'What time did you enter Dr Byrne's office?'

'I think it must have been about five-and-twenty past eight. That's my usual time.'

'And he was lying on the floor?'

'Yes. He was just...' Miss Lynn shuddered. 'Well, you saw him.'

'He was flat on his back, was he?'

'Oh, yes. I didn't touch him.'

'But you could see that he was dead? Not just fallen over, or knocked out?'

'I thought he was. I see quite a lot of dead people in my job, Inspector. I know how they look.' This was said with dignity and authority and Stratton saw no reason to disbelieve it.

'Was there anything near him?'

'There was a syringe on the floor...And his keys.'

'Where were the keys?'

'Beside the rug. About a foot away from his head. On the same side as the door.'

That, thought Stratton, meant that Higgs, as well as picking up the syringe, must have inadvertently kicked the keys into the corner. Or possibly Dr Ransome had, and in the commotion it wasn't noticed. He wondered if it was possible for someone leaving the office to slide the keys back under the door. 'Did you touch anything?' he asked.

Miss Lynn thought for a moment, then said, 'No. No, I'm sure I didn't.'

'Did you see a note?'

Miss Lynn shook her head.

'Did you look round the room? At the desk?'

'Briefly, I suppose. I must have done. I just remember turning round and going straight back out.'

'And then?'

'I went into the mortuary and told Higgs, and he went in, and then he fetched Dr Ransome.'

'Did you re-enter the office?'

Miss Lynn shook her head. 'I stayed in the corridor. I thought I should wait until Higgs returned, in case anyone else came in and saw Dr Byrne.'

'Quite right. And did anyone else come?'

'No. I didn't see anybody.'

'Now, I'm afraid I do have to ask this—did you have any reason to think that Dr Byrne was a habitual taker of any sort of drug?'

Miss Lynn's eyes widened in shock. 'There was absolutely nothing like that. Nothing at all.'

'Do you think you would have recognised it if there had been?' Miss Lynn looked affronted. 'I do realise,' Stratton continued gently, 'that it's very unlikely, but please think carefully.'

'Well...I certainly would have known if he had been injecting himself, because there would have been marks on his arms. This isn't a very clean job, Inspector, and one finds oneself in all sorts of unpleasant places. I've seen Dr Byrne roll up his sleeves, and wash his hands and arms on many occasions.'

'Of course. But if he'd been taking something in a liquid form? Drinking it?'

'I'm sure I would have known. I can assure you I never noticed anything untoward about Dr Byrne's behaviour. He was absolutely dedicated to his work.'

'Yes,' said Stratton. Seeing that some affirmation of this was needed, he added, quite truthfully, 'We'll all miss him. Were you with him yesterday?'

'Yes, all day.'

'What time did you leave?'

'Half-past six.'

'And you took your key home?'

'Yes. I always do.'

'How did Dr Byrne seem yesterday?'

'The same as usual. We were very busy, and…no, there was nothing out of the ordinary.'

'How long have you—had you—worked for Dr Byrne?'

'Almost five years, Inspector. I believe that I knew him as well as anyone—except his late wife, of course. He wasn't somebody who showed his feelings.'

'Was he upset at his wife's death?'

'Well, of course. He loved her very much. But he never allowed it to interfere with his work. It's probably too soon to ask, Inspector, but do you know who's going to be performing the post-mortem?'

'Not yet, no. One of his colleagues, I should think. From the Home Office.'

'It's just…' Miss Lynn hesitated.

'Yes?' prompted Stratton.

'Well…' The secretary screwed up her face in an expression of discomfort. 'He told me once…He said that he had a nightmare, sometimes, about dying suddenly and Professor Manning being asked to perform the post-mortem. I'm afraid Dr Byrne thought that the way he conducted his work was…well, rather slapdash.'

'Oh. Well, I'll see what I can do about that. Not,' Stratton added hastily, 'that I can promise anything.'

'I understand. But thank you. I know that it would mean a great deal to him. I know...well, that he could seem rather abrupt sometimes, in his manner, but he was a kind man. When my mother died, he was so understanding...I'll never forget it.'

Stratton reflected, as he went to the cubicle that contained the mortuary telephone and asked to be put through to West End Central, that he'd often wondered what went on inside the head of a cold fish like Byrne—clearly, as he'd begun to suspect, there was far more to him, both in terms of imagination and of empathy, than he'd ever imagined. And the business about Professor Manning was, he thought, definitely an argument against Byrne committing suicide—at least, not without leaving very specific instructions.

If it was murder, that brought the total up to three: first a doctor, then a nurse, and now the pathologist. Try as he might, he couldn't see how they could possibly be connected other than by happening to work in the same hospital. Three different methods, and none of the victims, apparently, knew each other well in life...Yes, Fay Marchant had been seeing Dr Reynolds, but she wasn't connected to the others, was she? Except that he'd seen her in the mortuary corridor on the night of Byrne's death. But why on earth should she want to strangle Nurse Leadbetter? Even if Leadbetter had known about her and Dr Reynolds, and was proposing to tell him about it, adultery, whatever else it might be, wasn't a crime...and besides, if that was so, Fay must have guessed, given the speed that rumours got about the hospital, that Leadbetter wasn't the only one who'd noticed something untoward going on. Stratton shook his head: it ought to add up, but it didn't—not at all.

'Are you sure about this, Stratton?'

'No. sir. But I think we should be sure. He did ask to speak to me urgently, sir.'

'And then he apparently went home.'

'That's the point, sir. I don't think he left the hospital.'

DCI Lamb sighed gustily. 'I'll send someone over, and we'll telephone the Yard for Fingerprints. Try and be discreet, will you?'

Stratton suppressed an image of himself stampeding down the corridor tearing at his clothes and yelling 'Murder!' at the top of his voice. Aloud, he said, 'I'll do my best, sir.'

'Good. Anything else?'

'We'll need a pathologist, sir.'

'Pathologist?'

'He can hardly perform a post-mortem on himself, sir.'

'I know that,' snapped Lamb. 'We'll arrange something.'

'I don't know if it's possible, sir,' said Stratton, 'but I understand from Dr Byrne's secretary that he and Professor Manning didn't exactly hit it off, so it might be more suitable...if there's anyone else available...'

'For God's sake! The man's dead, isn't he? He's not going to know anything about it.'

'I know, sir, but all the same...'

'You'll get whoever's available. We can't ask everyone to change their plans at the whim of some wretched typist.'

Stratton couldn't help imagining an interview with Lamb at some future date, should he prove to be wrong about Byrne's death, with himself chewing on an enormous helping of humble pie. Bollocks to that, he thought, accepting a thick china cup of tepid tea from Higgs. With any luck, he wouldn't have to.

He telephoned Ballard and asked him to contact the air force and locate Byrne's son, then asked Miss Lynn to show him the post-mortem results from the previous few days. There was nothing of note in the way of botched abortions, infanticides or anything else, which seemed to put paid to the idea that Byrne had telephoned him about a recent suspicious death.

'How would Dr Byrne get access to drugs or poisons?' he asked Miss Lynn. 'Assuming that you don't keep anything down here.'

'He'd have to go to the dispensary,' said Miss Lynn. 'For morphine, or something like that, he'd have to sign the book. But he wouldn't have any reason,' she gestured towards the covered bodies, 'to request it.'

Stratton was making a note to enquire further about this when a knock on the door announced Professor Haycraft: sparse wispy hair, skewed spectacles set so far down his nose that they seemed to be pinching his nostrils closed, and an air of disengagement. Stratton was not surprised when, at the end of the explanation, Haycraft asked, with the tentative air of a bystander, 'Is there anything you would like me to do?'

'Well, I think we should wait for the pathologist's report— we're arranging for someone to come and do the post-mortem as soon as possible. Depending on that, we may or may not have to interview the staff—'

'Again?'

'I'm afraid so—if it proves necessary. And of course—without wishing to be brutal—you'll need to hire another pathologist.'

Haycraft looked round at the sheeted figures as if he'd only just noticed them. 'Oh, dear. Yes, yes, of course. Well, I'll leave it in your capable hands. And I'm sure you can appreciate that we'd prefer this not to become, shall we say, widely known, especially if there's no necessity to investigate, and so forth...Coming on top of the other matters...I'm sure you understand what I mean.'

'Of course, Professor,' said Stratton, wishing to Christ that everyone would stop treating the whole thing as if it was somehow his fault.

Ten minutes later, Arliss—it *would* be—trudged in and duly stationed himself outside Dr Byrne's office, where, as soon as he thought Stratton's back was turned, he appeared to fall asleep on his feet. Arliss was followed, in remarkably short order, by an extremely apprehensive-looking doctor, who looked, to Stratton, like a schoolboy just grown out of short trousers.

'Can we help you?' enquired Stratton.

The man cleared his long throat. 'Ferguson, to see Dr Byrne. I was sent from Guy's. I came as soon as I could—is he here?'

Bloody hell, thought Stratton. 'Still in his office. I'm Detective Inspector Stratton,' he said, offering his hand.

Ferguson took a step back. 'I don't understand. What's this about?'

'Didn't they tell you?'

Ferguson shook his head. 'They just said to get here as soon as possible.'

'I'm afraid,' said Stratton, as gently as he could, 'that Dr Byrne is dead. We need you to examine him.'

Ferguson turned pale and ran a nervous hand through his hair. 'But...He can't...I mean, I can't...I...Look, Inspector, Dr Byrne taught me. He's...It should be someone senior, someone more...' He gave Stratton a pleading look.

'It needs to be done immediately,' said Stratton. 'You'll have Higgs to assist you.'

Higgs, who had been staring at Ferguson with undisguised horror, now looked down at his shoes. Miss Lynn clutched Stratton's arm. 'Inspector, you don't want...I mean, I can't...'

'It's all right,' Stratton assured her. To Ferguson he said, 'Can you manage without a secretary?'

Ferguson swallowed audibly and turned to Miss Lynn. 'You worked for him?'

'Yes.'

'He was...his lectures...Marvellous. That's why I decided to work in this field.'

'Well, I think that's most appropriate, and I'm sure Dr Byrne would agree,' said Stratton, briskly. 'This way, please. You'll need to examine the body before it's moved.'

Ferguson blinked. 'Oh. Yes. Yes, of course.'

Arliss, who, Stratton noticed, had yellow crusts of sleep at the corners of his eyes, stood aside to let them enter Byrne's office. Ferguson, who went in first, took one look at the prone figure of Byrne, and turned back to Stratton, his eyes imploring. 'I...'

Stratton shook his head and pulled the door shut behind him. Ferguson's Adam's apple convulsed. 'I...Oh, God...'

'It's all right,' said Stratton. 'I'll stay with you.'

'Thank you. Well...Here goes, eh?' He took a notebook out of his jacket pocket and knelt down beside the body.

Stratton gave a brief summary of the situation, and then, fearing a repetition of his conversation with Dr Ransome, only more so, and deciding that a break with etiquette was in order, said firmly, 'There's a syringe on the desk. If you look at his left arm, you'll see that he seems to have injected himself—or been injected—with something. We're going to need a full toxicology report.'

After Ferguson had worked in silence for some minutes, Higgs appeared in the doorway. 'All ready for you, Doctor. I've prepared the instruments.'

Obviously horror-struck by the idea of using Byrne's instruments to dissect their owner, Ferguson looked at Stratton, who nodded encouragement. 'I'm sure it's what he would have wanted.'

'Very good, sir,' said Higgs. 'I've got the stretcher outside if you're ready to move him?'

Ferguson, who seemed incapable of speech, merely nodded. Seeing that the young pathologist was in no state to organise things, Stratton called to Arliss to help with the stretcher. This he did, with agonising slowness, and, bending down to load Byrne's body, let off a volley of small, squeaky farts. 'For God's sake, man!' said Stratton.

'Sorry, sir.' Arliss gazed at him resentfully. 'My stomach's still not right.'

'So we gathered,' said Stratton, acidly. 'When you've finished turning this into a farce, perhaps you could get a move on.'

Miss Lynn stood in the corridor, head bowed, her notebook clasped to her chest in the manner of one presenting arms, as the stretcher, accompanied by grunts from Arliss and tutting noises from Higgs, was borne past her into the mortuary, Stratton and Ferguson bringing up the rear.

CHAPTER

42

Ten days late. Standing in the hall, Jenny gave the knot of her headscarf a final, sharp tug. She'd just taken her coat off its peg when Doris appeared with a basket of shopping.

'I'm so glad I've caught you!'

Jenny groaned. 'Don't tell me. What's she done now?'

'Nothing, really. It's just that Don's not going to be back for a while, and I've been a bit on edge since that wretched tea party…Just a bit of moral support, that's all. I've been queuing all morning, and I really don't think I can bear to go back and face her on my own.'

'That's all right. Being funny again, is she?'

'She won't speak to me.'

'In that case, I don't suppose she'll speak to me, either, but I can have a go. Come on.'

Jenny succeeded in keeping Doris's mind off the subject of Mrs Ingram—after all, what more was there to say about the wretched woman?—until they reached her house. 'She's put the blackouts up in the kitchen, look.'

'For heaven's sake.' Doris unlocked the front door and attempted to push it open, but it remained shut. 'Bloody hell!'

'Doris!'

'Well, *honestly*…Wait a minute, Jen.' Bending down, Doris pushed open the letterbox and peered inside. '*Jen*…I can smell something.'

Putting down her shopping, Jenny leant over and sniffed. 'Blimey. That's *gas*.' The two women put their shoulders to the wooden panels and shoved. After a few seconds, the door began to give. 'There's something in the way. A blanket, by the look of it.' 'Right!' Jenny put her full weight against the door, which, very slowly, started to open. 'That's done it.' She squeezed herself through the crack and threw herself at the kitchen door, which opened easily—the edges of that blanket not being secured—so that she almost fell into the room, with Doris hard on her heels.

The sickly, headachy smell of the gas made Jenny feel instantly dizzy. Taking in the form of Mrs Ingram, clad in one of her sister's nightdresses and lying full length on an eiderdown in front of the oven with a pillow beneath her head, apparently comatose, she said, 'I'll turn it off—you open the doors and windows.'

'Be careful, Jen.'

'Don't worry.' Leaning across the prone body, Jenny switched off the tap and then, bending over Mrs Ingram, began slapping her, none too gently, on her cheek, which, like the rest of her face and neck, was an alarming cherry pink. 'Mrs Ingram! Can you hear me?'

Mrs Ingram moved her head and muttered something, her speech too slurred for Jenny to make out the words. 'We've got to get her into the garden, Dor—fresh air.' Grabbing Mrs Ingram under the arms, and thanking God that there wasn't much of her, Jenny began to pull her towards the door. After a moment, Doris joined her. 'All the windows open?' panted Jenny.

'Downstairs. And the back door.'

'Good. You take the legs.'

They half-dragged, half-carried Elsie Ingram down the passage and into the garden, and propped her up against the tree furthest from the house, struggling to hold her upright as her knees buckled.

'Do you think we ought to walk her around a bit?' asked Doris.

'We can try.' They each took an elbow and attempted to propel Mrs Ingram forward, propping her up on either side. She staggered, as if drunk, her head wobbling. 'She's an awful colour, isn't she?'

'Yes, and she's all cold and clammy. Shall I fetch a blanket?'

'In a minute. I'm not sure I can manage her by myself.'

'All right. Thank God for fresh air. My head…'

'I know. Imagine how she must feel.' As if on cue, Mrs Ingram lurched abruptly to the right and, jerking forwards, vomited into a flowerbed. 'That's a good sign.'

'If you say so.' Doris eyed the puked-on bedding plants grimly. Mrs Ingram sagged between them, spluttering. Over her head, Doris muttered, 'Of all·the stupid…'

'I know, Dor, but she's had a difficult time.'

'Not her, me! I might have known she'd do something silly, after that other business.'

Jenny made a shushing noise, then said, 'Better now?' to Mrs Ingram.

Mrs Ingram leant forward once more, retching, Jenny and Doris hanging onto her arms. 'Don't be daft,' said Jenny. 'How could you know? Come to that, *I* should have known. You can't take this all on yourself, Doris.'

'Yes, well…we keep saying that, don't we? "We couldn't have known…"'

'Well, it's true. Dr Makepeace didn't know, did he? And we're just a couple of housewives, not…' Jenny mouthed the next word exaggeratedly, 'psychiatrists.'

After almost half an hour spent marching Mrs Ingram round the garden, Jenny and Doris decided that, as her face seemed to be returning to its normal colour and she wasn't showing any more signs of wanting to be sick, it would be safe to let her sit down. Jenny propped her against the back door while Doris fetched a deckchair.

'I'm sorry,' whispered Mrs Ingram, as they lowered her into it. 'You won't tell anyone, will you?'

Jenny and Doris exchanged glances. 'No dear,' said Jenny, patting Mrs Ingram on one hunched little shoulder. 'You just stay put there, and I'll get you a cardigan and a nice cup of tea. Don't want you catching a chill.'

By the time they returned to the kitchen, the smell of gas had dissipated somewhat.

'Did you mean that?' asked Doris, filling the kettle.

'What?'

'About not telling anyone.'

'I don't see how we *can*,' said Jenny. 'If we tell Dr Makepeace he'll have to report it, won't he?'

'They wouldn't charge her, though? Not after what she's been through, surely?'

'I don't know. I think it depends whether they think she's fit to plead. That's what they call it—Ted told me. It means you can tell the difference between right and wrong.'

'Right and wrong?' echoed Doris. 'She doesn't even know her own husband!'

'I shouldn't think they would charge her, but they might. And if they don't, it means she'll end up in the you-know-where.'

'Oh, dear…We can't win, can we? Do you think it's safe to light the gas?'

'I don't know. We ought to—'

Hearing the creak of the gate, Jenny stopped. 'Don,' hissed Doris, glancing out of the window. 'I'd forgotten he was leaving work early. Don't say anything.'

'But the door…And your things! We left the basket on the step.'

'What the hell is going on?' Donald appeared the doorway. 'The front door was wide open, and there are blankets all over the place, and…' he spotted something behind the kitchen door. 'What's this?' He reached out and Jenny heard the noise of paper being ripped. 'Beware Gas,' he read. 'It was pinned on the door…'

Jenny and Doris exchanged glances—in their haste, neither had noticed it. 'What's that bloody woman done now? No, don't tell me—that's why you've got all the windows open, isn't it? She's tried to do herself in. For Christ's sake—'

'*Don*, please,' said Doris. 'Keep your voice down.'

Donald jabbed a finger in the direction of the eiderdown, which was still lying on the floor. 'Found her with her head in the oven, did you?'

'Yes.'

'Where is she now?'

'Outside. We thought she ought to have some air.'

'It's a shame she didn't manage to finish the job.'

'*Don!* That's a terrible thing to say.'

Fearing that Doris and Donald were about to have a row, Jenny said she'd better fetch the shopping and left the room. She put the basket in the hall and went back to the garden to see how Mrs Ingram was doing.

Looking even smaller and more frail than before, Elsie Ingram was perched so far forward on the edge of the deckchair in a manner that, had she not been so light, she would have tipped the thing right over. She was staring fixedly at the scrubby lawn by her feet.

'How are you feeling?' asked Jenny.

Raising her head a few inches, Mrs Ingram said, 'I'm sorry... Putting you out like this.' Then she resumed her contemplation of the grass.

How extraordinary, thought Jenny, to be so polite at a time like this...on reflection, though, she'd probably have done the same herself. And she'd left that note, hadn't she? Even though she thought they were all part of some plot against her. People were funny. 'Never mind,' she said. 'These things happen.' Staring at the top of Mrs Ingram's head, she thought, what a ridiculous thing to say—*these things happen*—because they didn't, at least not to anyone she knew. People were just supposed to get on with things, especially now, with the war. But, she thought irritably, what were you *meant* to say? The sheer embarrassment of it was bad enough, never mind all the other stuff.

Mrs Ingram raised her head once more, this time in an uncomfortable-looking corkscrew motion, so that she was staring at Jenny out of one eye in a way that made her think of the hens. 'You're not going to tell him, are you?'

'Him?'

'That man.'

'Oh, yes. I mean no. Of course not.'

'Or the police? It's all of them, you see. No-one believes me.' Straightening up, she looked Jenny directly in the eye. 'You don't believe me, do you?'

'Well...' Jenny, feeling hot, looked away. 'Really...I don't know what to think.' At least, she thought, that was the absolute, unvarnished truth. 'Look,' she said, not wanting, or, in fact, able, to elaborate further, 'why don't you stay out here for a bit, in the fresh air? Then you'll feel better. I'll go and see how the tea's doing.'

'...as if she hasn't caused enough trouble already!' Donald's fury was plainly audible in the hall and, fearing that Mrs Ingram might hear, Jenny closed the back door.

'Still with us, is she?' Donald asked as she returned to the kitchen. 'Not hanging from the apple tree or anything?'

'Don, stop it!'

'She seems a bit better,' said Jenny, as calmly as she could—sarcasm from Donald was never a good sign. 'Do you think it's safe to light the gas yet?'

'Christ!' said Donald.

'Stop saying that!'

'Well, it's come to something when you can't even have a cup of tea in your own house without blowing the place up.'

'There's others a lot worse off,' said Doris, pacifically. 'At least we've still *got* a house.'

'Yes,' said Donald. 'And that's what it's meant to be—a *house*, not a loony asylum. Which is where *she*,' he jerked his head towards the back garden, 'ought to be.'

Wincing, Jenny and Doris exchanged glances. 'She might get better,' said Doris, weakly.

'You've been saying that for weeks. She's as mad as a hatter, and the sooner you face up to it, the better. She's got to go, Doris. I've had enough. She's out of here tomorrow. Otherwise,' he added, giving them a shrewd look, 'I'll tell Ted about this little escapade. I'll bet neither of you were going to do that, were you?'

'Don, you know we *can't*,' said Jenny. 'He'd have to report it, and they'll charge her, or they'll take her off to—'

'Exactly! To the barmy shop, where she belongs!'

'Sssh, she'll hear you.'

'I don't care. I've had it up to here with the bloody woman!'

'Please,' said Jenny, desperately. 'Stop shouting. Why don't *I* take her home?'

'Ted's going to love that, isn't he?' asked Donald. 'He'll be tickled pink to come back after a hard day's work and find there's a lunatic in his house.'

Jenny, suppressing the thought that sooner or later he'd find out that not only was there a lunatic in the house but a baby on the way as well, said, 'I'll just have to cross that bridge when I come to it. And it'll give you a break from looking after her all the time, Doris.'

'But we're still stuck with her, aren't we?' said Donald.

'I don't see what else we can do.'

'I've told you what to do! She belongs in an institution. For Christ's sake, I'll phone Dr Makepeace myself if that'll—'

'No!' Jenny and Doris shouted together.

'What is the matter with you two? A month ago, the woman was a complete stranger, and now, she's—'

'Don.' Doris's voice was quiet, and Jenny knew that she'd decided to tell him about Aunt Ivy. When she looked at Jenny for confirmation, Jenny nodded.

When Doris had finished explaining about their visits to Friern Barnet to see their mad aunt, and how her family regretted committing her, Don, who'd been listening with a grim expression, said, 'And you never thought to tell me any of this before?'

'Well, it wasn't very nice, and...There's no-one else in the family like it, is there, Jen?'

'Oh, no. Just her.'

'Have you told Ted about her?'

Jenny shook her head. 'Our mother always said it was better not to talk about it, and we just thought...well...'

'Oh, for God's sake.' Donald gave them a look of disgust and got up from the table. 'Elsie Ingram's not even a bloody relative. If you want to know what I think, I think you're both mad, and I've had enough.' He started towards the door.

'Where are you going?' asked Doris.

'Out. And,' he added, from the hallway, 'I don't want to find her here when I come back.'

The front door slammed behind him and Jenny and Doris looked at each other. 'That went well, didn't it?' said Doris, sarcastically. 'I thought he might understand. I shouldn't have said anything.'

'It was worth a try.'

'Now he's angry with me for keeping something from him.'

'There's a lot worse you could be keeping from him than that. Look, why don't I take Mrs I. with me now, and then there'll be time to settle her into Monica's room before Ted gets back.'

Walking back home, trying to make small talk as Mrs Ingram trudged miserably beside her like a prisoner, Jenny found herself hoping, for the first time she could remember, that Ted would be late—preferably very late—home.

CHAPTER 43

Stratton despatched Arliss with a chair for Miss Lynn, then stood with his back to the mortuary door, listing Byrne's garments as Higgs removed them. He tried to keep his face averted from the increasingly unclothed body and, noticing that Ferguson was doing the same, and that his hands were shaking as he arranged the instruments, decided he'd better have a word before the man got started: he didn't want anything being missed. When Higgs had finished and Byrne lay naked under a sheet, he said to the young pathologist, 'Perhaps a drop of brandy would help. We won't mention it, of course.'

Ferguson nodded mutely, and Stratton signalled to Higgs to fetch it.

'Here.' Higgs handed over a glass containing what looked like a double-measure. Ferguson put out a trembling hand and despatched it in a single gulp. 'Sister Bateman let me have it.'

The alcohol seemed to fortify Ferguson, at least to the extent of bringing two spots of colour to his chalk-white cheeks. 'Thanks,' he said, returning the glass to Higgs. Squaring his slender shoulders, he added, 'Right, shall we begin?'

Stratton excused himself as Higgs was drawing back the sheet. He went to peer at the gap below Byrne's office door and, using his own keys, satisfied himself that they could be slid underneath it. Then he stood in the corridor, writing notes and wondering how soon the Fingerprint Bureau would be able to send someone. Miss Lynn stood near him, smoking. Judging by her posture and the expression on her face, Stratton was sure that she, like him, was trying not to listen to the rasp of Ferguson's saw as it opened Byrne's skull.

Assuming that Higgs was right about Byrne living alone, there'd be no-one to ask about when, or whether, he'd returned home the previous evening. Unless one of the neighbours had seen him, or the local warden. Stratton made a note to ask Ballard to check up on this. And then there was the business of meeting Nurse Marchant in the corridor. If Byrne's death was connected with Reynolds's, perhaps she'd had something to do with it—revenge, perhaps? She'd seemed calm enough, but... Oh, well. There was no point getting ahead of himself.

After about twenty minutes, the bulky figure of Chief Superintendent Dewhurst, carrying his case of fingerprinting equipment, appeared at the end of the corridor.

'Good morning, sir. I must say, I didn't expect to see you in person.'

The head of the Fingerprint Bureau glowered at him from beneath a pair of bushy eyebrows. 'DI Stratton?'

'Yes, sir.'

'I wanted to come myself. I knew Dr Byrne,' he added, gruffly. 'Good man. Very competent. DCI Lamb tells me that you think this is necessary, so let's get on with it.'

Stratton sighed inwardly. 'I think so, sir. If you'll just follow me...'

Stratton watched as Dewhurst examined the room. 'I assume the desk and chair are the most important, and,' he indicated the syringe, 'this.' Covering his hand with a handkerchief, he picked it up. 'I'll take it away for analysis.'

'Right, sir. I think it would be a good idea if you took those as well.' Stratton pointed to the keys, which were still lying in the corner.

'Very well. And I'll need to take Dr Byrne's prints, of course, and—for elimination—anyone else who came into this office on a regular basis.'

'That would be Higgs—he's the mortuary assistant—and the secretary, Miss Lynn. Dr Ransome from the Casualty Department was down here this morning—Higgs fetched him when Miss Lynn found the body.'

'Well, we'd better do him as well. What about you? Have you been touching things?'

Quelling a sudden and violent desire to inform the man that not only had he fingered all the surfaces but pissed on the rug for good measure, Stratton said, 'No, sir.'

Dewhurst gave a disbelieving harrumphing noise. Christ, thought Stratton, the next thing I know he'll be suggesting that I killed him myself. 'I know better than to do that, sir. There's also Dr Ferguson.'

'Ferguson?'

'The pathologist, sir. He's come to do the post-mortem.'

'Never heard of him. Does he know what he's doing?'

'He's quite young, but he was a student of Dr Byrne's—I'm sure he's competent. If you don't mind my asking, sir, did you know Dr Byrne well?'

'I knew him as a professional colleague. Admired him.'

'Did he strike you as the type of person who might commit suicide?'

'Wouldn't have thought so.' Dewhurst made another rumbling noise, this time indicative of thought, then added, 'Hard to tell. Never know what's going on in a man's head.'

Stratton returned to the mortuary to find out how the post-mortem was going, and found Higgs swabbing the interior of Dr Byrne's chest. 'A fine job, Inspector,' he said, with the air of a connoisseur. 'Neat, quick, clean.' He looked down at the corpse, and gave an affirmative nod. 'Dr Byrne would have been proud of him, sir.'

'Where is he?'

'Gone to the Gents', sir. I think he felt a bit...you know. Don't worry, we've got everything we need.'

Ferguson returned a couple of minutes later, looking pale and wiping his mouth with a handkerchief.

'Well done,' said Stratton.

Ferguson smiled queasily. 'Thank you, Inspector.'

'Can you tell me the time of death?'

'Not precisely, but I would estimate around four or five hours.'

'So...' Stratton checked his notebook. Miss Lynn had told him that she'd arrived at five-and-twenty past eight. 'Between half past three and half past four?'

'I should say that's about right, yes.'

'What else?'

'Well, there was no smell from the stomach, the lungs were engorged, great lividity of the skin to the lower parts—'

'That's usual, isn't it, if the body's been lying about?'

'Yes, but in this case, I can't be entirely sure...'

Stratton looked up from his note taking. 'Can you give me your best guess?'

'Well, given the presence of the syringe and the puncture mark on the arm...It's certainly consistent with an overdose of morphine, but obviously we shan't know that until the samples have been tested.'

'Right. We'll make sure they're sent over to you as soon as possible. Did you find any other needle marks?'

Ferguson shook his head. 'I can see what you're driving at, Inspector, but there's no reason to suppose that Dr Byrne had an addiction to morphine or anything else.'

Stratton could see, over Ferguson's shoulder, that Higgs's eyes had widened and he was shaking his head vigorously in confirmation of this.

'Besides,' continued Ferguson, 'people who are addicts tend to be consistent in their method of use.'

'If...' Stratton hesitated, not at all sure that he wanted an answer to the question he was about to ask.

'Yes?'

Stratton plunged. 'If what you say turns out to be the case, do you think he could have been saved?'

'A stomach wash with permanganate of potash often works. Or if he'd vomited, of course...but then again, he was lying on his back.'

'If it was morphine, how long would it take to work?'

'It all depends on how much was taken, whether it's an adult or a child...'

'In *this* case.'

'Quite a time...Maybe as much as six or seven hours. But that's purely theoretical, of course.'

'Of course. So it could have been administered as early as, say...' Stratton glanced at his notebook. 'Eight-thirty or eight o'clock?'

'Possibly. But as I said, it's only—'

'I do understand, Dr Ferguson. Where,' he asked Higgs, 'did Dr Byrne live?'

'Wimbledon, sir.'

'And what time did he usually leave?'

'No particular time, sir. Depended on what he was doing. Very conscientious, Dr Byrne.'

'So, in all probability,' Stratton thought aloud, 'he didn't go home. Which means...'

Higgs, whose thoughts were clearly tending the same way, finished the sentence: 'If he didn't go home, sir, then he could have been in his office when we were outside. We might have been able to save him, sir.'

'If I'd fetched a key from upstairs,' said Stratton.

'Well, we didn't know, did we, sir?'

'No.' Stratton knew there wasn't anything to be gained by wishful thinking, but all the same...If this were a book or a film, he thought, I'd have had one of those sudden and unexplained feelings that something was wrong, and broken the door down. He'd thought it was creepy, all right, but then it was a bloody mortuary, wasn't it? Oh, Christ—supposing there had been someone in the office with Byrne, who'd let himself out after he, Stratton, had left?

'Did you hear anyone go past before I arrived or after I left? Immediately, I mean?'

Higgs screwed up his face in thought for a moment, and then shook his head. That, thought Stratton, meant that he hadn't heard Fay Marchant, and he must have been awake at that point, because he'd been having his tea. So, either Higgs's ears weren't as sharp as he thought, or what he described as a kip was more of a deep sleep—hardly surprising, since the poor bloke must have been working virtually round the clock for a week, even if his resting place was a hard slab with only a straw-filled sack to cushion it. He only heard me, Stratton realised, because I was calling out and knocking on the office door.

The appearance of Chief Superintendent Dewhurst interrupted his thoughts. 'All done in there,' he said. 'I suppose you'll be wanting to take a look round the place, will you?' This was said in a way that suggested an unwarranted degree of nosiness on Stratton's part.

Stratton nodded, hoping the irritation didn't show on his face.

'No prints at all on the top of the desk,' said Dewhurst. 'Wiped clean. I found a couple of partial prints on the underside of the front edge, but I don't know if they'll be any use. And,' he added, 'I found a couple of things tucked under the blotter. Photographs. Can't see why they'd be of interest, but if Dr Byrne had been looking at them prior to...' he shrugged. 'Thought perhaps you might want to take a look.'

Unable to think of any reply to this that wasn't actually offensive, Stratton nodded again, and, leaving Dewhurst preparing his roller and ink pad, he went upstairs to drag a protesting Dr Ransome out of Casualty to have his fingerprints taken. This done, he retreated into Byrne's office to examine the contents of his desk. The photographs Dewhurst had mentioned—four in number—were arranged in a neat pile by the telephone. The first showed Dr Byrne in the act of dictating to Miss Lynn, who was sitting beside him, pencil poised. The second and third were almost identical. They had obviously been taken in the mortuary itself, and showed a group of people standing behind a sheeted body on a slab: Dr Byrne, flanked by a sombre-looking Higgs and a helmeted and caped policeman who Stratton did not recognise. The only difference between the two pictures, as far as Stratton could see, was the blurred figure on the left-hand side of the second one. Obviously male, with lightish coloured hair, and, he thought, a moustache, the figure was in profile, apparently moving out of the way of the camera.

Unlike the others, the fourth photograph had not been posed—nobody in it was looking towards the camera, but all seemed intent on something (presumably a body) below the bottom of the picture: Higgs, Byrne, Miss Lynn (seated off to the right), and another man, seen in profile, looking quite similar to the blurred image from the third photograph. Perhaps Byrne had thrust them underneath the blotter for safekeeping, but in that case, why not put them away in a drawer? Unless he wanted to hide them from someone coming in…But why? And why wipe the desk?

Stratton glanced at the backs of the photographs, but nothing was written there. He didn't think that the unidentified man looked very much like Reynolds. There was the moustache, for one thing, and the hair didn't seem dark enough. Opening the door, he went to speak to Miss Lynn, who was still sitting forlornly in the corridor, under the eye of Arliss, who was occupying himself by rotating his little fingers in his ears. When Stratton glared at him, he removed his fingers, sniffed them, and wiped them on the front of his tunic. Muttering, 'Give me strength,' Stratton went over to summon Miss Lynn, who reluctantly accompanied him into the office.

'What can you tell me about these?' asked Stratton, proffering the photographs.

'They were for Dr Byrne's book.'

'A textbook?'

Miss Lynn shook her head. 'A book about his work. For the layman. He'd been making some notes. That one,' she pointed at the picture of Byrne and herself, 'was taken in this office. You can see the edge of the bookcase on the right.'

'What about the others? Who's this?' Stratton pointed at the blurred figure.

Miss Lynn peered at it for a moment, then said, 'Todd. He used to work here.' Pointing at the man shown in profile in the fourth photograph, she said, 'That's him as well.' She gave Stratton a wan smile. 'I don't think he liked being photographed much.'

Stratton remembered Higgs saying that Todd had left *the day after that poor nurse was killed*. Had Todd murdered her and Byrne somehow discovered it? Was that why the photographs were hiding there? But if that were the case, why had Byrne waited so long to tell *him* about it (assuming that was why he'd telephoned)? And how would Todd know that Byrne knew? Had Byrne, for some reason, told him, and been killed for his pains? It didn't make sense. Also, why hadn't Todd fled immediately after killing Leadbetter? Ballard hadn't mentioned anyone not turning up for interview. He made a mental note to check with the sergeant.

Miss Lynn contemplated the photographs in silence for a moment, then said, sadly, 'He'll never finish his book, now...'

'No,' agreed Stratton. 'Do you have his home address?'

'I'll copy it for you.' Miss Lynn opened one of the drawers and pulled out a file. 'Would you mind,' she asked, when she'd finished writing, 'if I kept the photographs?'

'I think,' said Stratton, 'that I ought to hang onto them for the time being, just to be on the safe side.' Seeing the look of resigned disappointment on Miss Lynn's face, he added, 'But if the photographer has the negatives, perhaps you could ask him for copies.'

Miss Lynn handed over the address. 'I think I shall,' she said. 'I'd like something to remember him by.'

CHAPTER

44

Dacre dressed himself mechanically, then stood in front of the mirror, gingerly splashing his bruised face with water and wondering if he dared go back to the hospital. After last night's unqualified disaster, he could feel an abyss opening up beneath him, dark and dangerous. Awaking from a tangle of gruesome, confused nightmares, he had a sense of an empty life in empty time, stretching out over days, months, years, until the day came when he looked in the mirror and could not see himself at all, in any version... The compass of his instinct, usually so reliable, was veering wildly between taking flight or risking confrontation by returning to the Middlesex. Burying his head in his wet hands, he shook it to and fro trying to rid himself of doubt, and then, suddenly reminded of the warm dampness of Byrne's mouth against his palm, jerked his face away with a shudder of horror and grabbed the threadbare towel that hung limply from the horse to scour himself dry.

If he was going to run away, why had he not done so the previous night? He'd had the chance. He could simply have carried on walking...Which would have meant, of course, leaving everything behind. *No.* He'd done the right thing by staying—if Byrne were dead, taking flight would look highly suspicious. Closing his eyes, he took a deep breath.

Fay, or at least the thought of her, had helped him last night, hadn't she? Somehow, she'd seemed to personify his intuition, like a beacon, and it was only as Dr Dacre that he could hope to have her. Besides which, he thought, whatever—and whoever—else I may be, I am not a coward.

Already late, he took the stairs two at a time, and rushed out into the street. He could make it in ten minutes, if he hurried. Byrne could not possibly have survived. He'd checked the toxicology book, hadn't he? Unless, of course, Higgs had had some reason to go into the office...He thought back to his own nights on duty in the mortuary—he'd never needed to go in the office, but all the same...He repeated these things to himself all the way down the Euston Road, but still his resolve faltered, and by the time he'd got to Fitzrovia he no longer felt sure.

He slowed and stood, indecisive, on the corner of Howland Street. That ARP man from last night knew his name, didn't he? Or Dacre's name, anyway...Supposing they issued a likeness of him and he recognised it? The light from the mobile canteen had been pretty dim, but...

He leapt a foot in the air as a firm hand clapped him on the shoulder. 'Dacre?'

Spinning round, he saw Wemyss grinning at him. 'Sorry, didn't mean to catch you off guard. What are you doing out here?'

'Just...Rather late, I'm afraid. Bit of a junket last night.' Dacre grinned apologetically. 'Bottle party.'

Wemyss inspected his bruised temple. 'Must have been quite a night.'

'I got that in Casualty.'

'Patient cut up rough, did they?'

'Something like that.'

'But that's not why you're twitching, is it? Nothing like knowing the right people. Well, you've missed quite a hoo-ha.'

'Hoo-ha? Why?'

'Well, I'm sure Ransome will fill you in on the details, but it's Byrne. Poor chap was found dead in his office this morning.'

Dacre felt his insides turn liquid with relief, but managed to convert his queasy smile into a concerned stare quickly enough for Wemyss not to notice. 'Byrne?'

'You obviously haven't killed anyone yet. He is—or rather, he *was*—our esteemed pathologist.'

'What happened?'

'Not sure. There's talk of a drug overdose. Doesn't sound very likely, but I suppose it's possible. Two doctors in two months, eh? Not to mention that nurse. Talk about bad luck.'

'What are you doing out here, anyway?' asked Dacre.

'Tobacconist. Place is in an uproar—most of the nurses seem to think we're all going to be murdered, one by one—so I thought I'd just nip out.' Wemyss patted his pocket.

'Come on, then.' Dacre started in the direction of the Middlesex with Wemyss alongside. In the bubble of his relief, he barely listened as Wemyss told him about the rumours that were buzzing round the hospital.

'...one of our probationers got herself all worked up and started wailing about a maniac going round killing the staff. The sister had to slap her. She was in quite a bate about it, I can tell... You all right, old man? You look a bit...well, queer.'

'Sorry. Bit of a thick head, that's all.'

'As long as you enjoyed yourself. Oh, and you probably don't know this either, but somebody lobbed a bomb at Hitler.'

'Good for them,' said Dacre.

'Missed, unfortunately—but at least they tried. If you ask me, the Nazis are cracking up...You *have* got a nasty one, haven't you? Hair of the dog, that's what you need—better see if you can pinch some brandy...'

Despite Sister Radford's best efforts, the Casualty Department was in chaos. The nurses were either on edge or unashamedly enjoying the drama, and there was an air of barely suppressed hysteria. Rows of patients sat waiting, and Dr Ransome was nowhere to be seen.

'Thank goodness!' said Sister Radford. 'I thought perhaps— that business yesterday—your head...'

'I am feeling a bit under the weather,' said Dacre, glad of the excuse, 'but really, it's nothing to worry about. Who's first?'

Sister Radford indicated an elderly man whose ankle was monstrously wrapped in what looked like a bedspread. 'Ulcer.'

'Right-oh.'

'Before you go, Dr Dacre, I should tell you…There was rather a tragedy last night.'

'So I gather. The pathologist, wasn't it? I met Dr Wemyss on the way in, and he told me.'

Sister Radford, clearly relieved at not having to explain, said, 'It's all rather odd. I've told the nurses they're not to discuss it, but after Dr Reynolds and poor Leadbetter…I'm sure you can imagine.'

'Of course.' Dacre looked sombre. 'I'll try and nip it in the bud. Doesn't do to upset the patients.' He smiled at her. 'At least, not more than one has to.'

'Thank you, Doctor I knew you'd understand. Dr Ransome…' Sister Radford's voice fell to a whisper, 'is downstairs. Apparently, they need his fingerprints.'

'Fingerprints?' said Dacre, alarmed. The big policeman must have come back to see Byrne first thing this morning. Although Dacre had guessed that enquiries would have to be made in the event of the pathologist's death, he hadn't envisaged anything like fingerprints. He tried to remember if he'd wiped everything. In any case, he told himself, there was no reason for them to want his prints—no-one had seen him go down to the mortuary…had they? 'Why on earth do they need Dr Ransome's fingerprints?'

'He was the one who examined Dr Byrne. It's the police—I suppose they have to be sure.' Sister Radford sniffed. 'Really, it's all nonsense. I wish they d leave—it's giving rise to all sorts of stupid rumours…' She appeared to lose her train of thought for a moment, then said, 'You were speaking to him yesterday, weren't you?'

Damn, thought Dacre. He'd been spotted. Playing for time, he put on a baffled expression and said, 'Speaking to Dr Ransome?'

'To Dr Byrne. I saw the two of you over by the door.'

Judging that this was being said in a prompting and not an accusing tone, Dacre said, in the voice of someone who has just recalled something important, 'You're quite right. I was talking to him, wasn't I?' Seeing that Sister Radford was expecting something more, he added, in a puzzled tone, 'Of course, I hardly knew him, but he seemed perfectly all right.'

The sister, clearly torn between deference and curiosity, looked at him enquiringly. 'We didn't see him up here very often,' she said, 'and he'd obviously come specially to see you, so I just wondered...'

Dacre, who had been desperately racking his brains in preparation for this, said, with sudden inspiration, 'It was about that testicular torsion. Mr Hambling told me it had to come off, and... Well,' he gave Sister Radford an up-from-under look, 'I felt I'd made rather a hash of things so I asked Dr Byrne if he wouldn't mind taking a look at the dead testicle—just to clarify things in my own mind, really. I'd not come across one before, you see. I know it's rather irregular, but I didn't want to bother Dr Ransome.'

As he'd hoped, Sister Radford found this thirst for knowledge commendable. 'Of course, Doctor. I quite understand.'

'He was kind enough to give me his opinion,' said Dacre. 'Now...' he looked round the crowded room, 'I think I'd better make a start on these patients.'

Dacre, working with feverish concentration, had finished with the ulcerated leg and was examining a woman with what he thought was probably a broken wrist when Sister Radford put her head round the screen. 'Dr Ransome's back. He'd like a word with you.'

'Very well. If you could arrange for Mrs...Atkins's wrist to be X-rayed, I'll come now.'

Dr Ransome's owlish face was a congested maroon and his small round frame seemed to vibrate with annoyance. 'There you are,' he said, as Dacre approached. 'You're late.'

'I'm sorry,' said Dacre, humbly. 'As I explained to Sister Radford, it was just...' He touched the bruise on his temple.

'Yes, yes,' said Ransome, irritably. 'I know all about that. But you're not *ill.*' His beaky little nose wrinkled in disgust at the idea. 'And of all mornings...You know about what's happened, of course.' He shook his head, then stared headily at Dacre. 'I hear that Dr Byrne came up to speak to you yesterday.'

Relieved that he'd already had a chance to practise his explanation on Sister Radford, Dacre repeated it to Ransome, who blinked and nodded throughout. 'Good, good,' he murmured, and then, 'How did he *seem* to you?'

'Well...' Dacre hesitated deliberately, as if considering how to answer this. 'The thing is, Dr Ransome, I can't say that he seemed himself, because I'd only met him the once, but he appeared perfectly normal to me.'

'Well, there you are,' said Ransome with finality, as if clinching an argument. 'Obviously some sort of ghastly mistake, and the less said about it, the better. Now, for heaven's sake, let's get on.'

As Dacre walked across the room, he felt a balloon of hope rise in his chest. If Dr Ransome had examined the body and thought there was nothing to investigate...Byrne being a fellow doctor, he'd be bound to cover it up if he thought it was self-inflicted. The big policeman obviously disagreed with him, but if the pathologist didn't report anything sinister, then he'd have no evidence, would he? Unless that telephone number...Dacre patted the pocket where he'd put the scrap of paper. He must find out what it was: that could be done from a public telephone box, later. Even if it did prove to be the police station, Byrne couldn't have said anything or the police would have been waiting to collar him, wouldn't they? So all was well—he was Dr Dacre, and no-one knew any different. He rubbed his hands together briskly, and called out, 'Who's next?'

A middle-aged woman rose to her feet. She reminded Dacre of one of those novelty vegetables that get photographed for the newspapers because they bear a passing resemblance to a human face. 'Follow me, please.' Grinning, he led her behind the row of screens.

CHAPTER

45

Miss Lynn having returned to her chair in the corridor, Stratton checked the contents of Dr Byrne's wastepaper basket— several pipe-cleaners and a few scraps of paper, but nothing of interest. Straightening up, he slipped the photographs into his pocket to examine later. Was there any reason, he wondered, for Miss Lynn to lie about not finding a note? Surely there couldn't have been any sort of affair between her and Byrne? The man was a widower, but all the same…She was too skinny, for one thing, and pale as a ghost—but maybe that was how Byrne liked them. Stratton, thinking of Jenny's curves and soft, creamy skin, decided that it would be like having intercourse with an ironing board. And Byrne was no oil painting, either. Well, stranger things had happened…But somehow, he doubted it. Miss Lynn, though clearly devoted to Byrne, had given no indication that she was in love with him. And as far as anything else was concerned, her shock at finding the body had seemed entirely genuine.

Stratton returned to the mortuary to remind Ferguson and Dewhurst that he'd like all the test results as soon as possible, then went up to the dispensary where a short conversation with a bemused pharmacist and a glance at the book showed him that Dr Byrne had not obtained morphine, or, indeed, anything else. Presumably, thought Stratton, as he went back downstairs to collect Arliss, there were other ways of obtaining drugs in a hospital—some things were, after all, kept on the wards—but he did not see how Byrne could have got hold of any from such a source without drawing attention to himself.

He trudged back to West End Central, trailed by a sour-looking Arliss, and sat down at his desk to think.

Sergeant Ballard had managed to locate Dr Byrne's son at RAF Lyneham. 'I spoke to the Adjutant, sir. He says he'll break the news to him and of course he'll get compassionate leave. Home address in Hanwell, which I have. No telephone, but it's a lot nearer than Wiltshire. Do you wish to speak to him, sir?'

'Not just at the moment. But we do need to find out if anyone saw Byrne at home yesterday evening—neighbours and so on.' Stratton handed over the Wimbledon address. 'That's the first thing. Find out how we can gain entry to his home, and then...'

He hesitated, realising that there wasn't really anything else that could be done until he'd heard from Ferguson and Dewhurst.

Ballard, sensing doubt, said, 'Do you think it wasn't suicide, sir?'

'I just don't know,' said Stratton. 'There's something odd going on, but I can't put my finger on it. And if I'm wrong,' he continued, gloomily, 'DCI Lamb'll have my guts for garters.'

If Ballard was surprised by this display of vulnerability, he didn't show it. 'You've been right in the past, sir. Your instinct about—'

Stratton snorted, cutting him off. 'Instinct! Fat lot of good that is, with no facts.'

'Perhaps the pathology report will provide some, sir.'

'Let's hope so.' Stratton sighed. 'Then we might have a clue about what's going on. Oh, and we found these tucked under Byrne's blotter.' He fished the photographs out of his pocket and laid them on the desk for Ballard to see. 'For a textbook he was writing, apparently. Seems an odd place to put them.'

'Who's that?' Ballard pointed at the fairish man with the moustache.

'Todd, apparently. Used to be a mortuary assistant. That's him there, too.'

'I must have interviewed him,' said Ballard. 'After Dr Reynolds died. Don't remember him, though.'

'No reason why you should. You might check, though.'

Ballard took out his notebook. 'It's here, sir. Nothing of any significance.'

'He left soon after Nurse Leadbetter was killed,' said Stratton, 'probably just coincidence.'

Stratton, left alone, began to sort through the detritus on his desk in an attempt to achieve some sort of order before reporting to DCI Lamb. Remembering his meeting with Fay Marchant in the mortuary corridor the previous evening, he tried to recall exactly what she'd said. Something about going back to the nurses' quarters, he thought...That was right, she'd just come off duty. Stratton scribbled this down in his notebook, with the approximate time of their meeting. It was an odd route for her to take, unless she'd been in one of the basement operating theatres just beforehand, which was, of course, entirely possible. Then again, she'd been involved with Dr Reynolds, and, as a nurse, she'd be able to get access to something like morphine fairly easily. He hadn't noticed her name in the dispenser's book, but there were other ways...If Byrne had some medical problem and she'd persuaded him to have an injection...But that was ridiculous. If Byrne had suspected her of something, the last thing he'd do was let her stick a needle into his arm, so how could she have done it? Come to that, how could anyone have done it?

If Byrne had wanted to speak to him about Reynolds—and the absence of anything fishy in the mortuary's recent records made this the most likely explanation—and it had something to do with Fay, then perhaps she'd somehow got wind of it and...

And what? There was no reason for her to kill Reynolds. In fact, if he was going to procure an abortion for her, then she had every reason to keep him alive. But she'd said she wasn't pregnant, hadn't she? Perhaps Reynolds, frightened by the false alarm, had announced that he was breaking it off and she had flown into a temper and bashed him. But she'd said that the note about needing to see Reynolds urgently was written at Easter, and presumably she must have found out fairly soon afterwards that she wasn't going to have a baby after all...So why would Reynolds wait over two months before breaking it off? Dithering, perhaps, trying to find the right time to tell her, or wanting, despite his anxiety, to have his cake and eat it? Could be all sorts of things. And, even if that was what had happened, Stratton couldn't imagine, from the little he knew of Fay, that she'd be capable of killing anyone...Or would she? If there was one thing he was sure of, it was that you could never tell what people might do. And just because a girl had nice legs and velvet brown eyes didn't mean that she was above suspicion. But she was a nurse, for Christ's sake. The way things were going, that made her more likely to be a victim than a murderess. There was something bloody odd about the whole business, but try telling that to DCI Lamb...He stood up, straightened his tie, and forced his unwilling feet down the corridor in the direction of his superior's office.

Stratton was still smarting from Lamb's bollocking when he arrived home, late—his superior had insisted on raking over every tiny detail—and with the beginnings of a nasty headache.

As he opened the front door, he heard women's voices coming from upstairs. Thinking it must be Doris or Lilian, he shouted, 'Hello!' There was a muted scream, then the sound of a door closing, and Jenny appeared on the stairs, looking agitated, with her finger to her lips.

'What's up?'

Jenny shook her head and, running downstairs, bustled him into the kitchen and closed the door. 'Ted, I'm really sorry, but—'

Realisation dawned. 'You've got that bloody woman here, haven't you?'

'Don't call her that! I couldn't help it, Ted. Doris has had her for ages, and she's—'

'I don't see why *anyone* has to have her! She ought to be in—'

'Don't you start, Ted, please. She's all alone, her husband doesn't want anything more to do with her, he's gone back to the army, and—'

'Why didn't you warn me, for Christ's sake?'

'Keep your voice down!'

'Well, why didn't you?'

'I didn't think to telephone from Doris's. I didn't want to bother you with it…Anyway, you're not exactly sympathetic, are you?'

'It's not that, Jenny, I just don't think she ought to be here, that's all. Or with Doris. It's not our responsibility. Next you'll be telling me that she's sleeping in the Morrison with us.'

'Of course she isn't. She'll be fine upstairs.'

'You hope. I certainly wouldn't be if my home had been blown to pieces with me in it.'

'Well, she was at Doris's—she wouldn't sleep downstairs. Insisted on staying up there. The last few weeks haven't been so bad here, anyway—I've put a camp-bed under the stairs, in case she does decide she wants to come down. She hasn't got anyone else, Ted. Look, there's no point fighting about it. She's here now. Just please don't let on about being a policeman.'

'What would be acceptable to her, then? A bus conductor? A bloody toilet attendant?'

'Oh, stop it. I don't know. I'm just saying, that's all.'

'Well, I ought to know, since I'm supposed to be somebody else.'

'Look, Ted,' Jenny's voice cracked, and she looked on the verge of tears, 'I'm not going to turn her out. Why don't you just take your coat off and I'll get your supper?'

They continued to argue while they ate, and then while they drank tea in the sitting room (no wireless, in case it woke Mrs Ingram), and they got ready for bed in bad-tempered silence.

When they were settled, side by side, not touching, in the Morrison, and the light was out, Stratton lay awake, fuming. He'd thought that Jenny was pretending to be asleep, but, after about ten minutes, he heard a snuffle and realised that she was crying. Stratton counted to ten in his head, then to twenty, then thirty. This wasn't fair. None of it was his fault—the war, or Mrs Ingram, or anything else, and yet he was being made to feel as if it was. He hated Jenny being upset, and having the happy atmosphere of his home disturbed like this. Having reached eighty, with the snuffling, still muted, continuing, he reached across to her. 'Come on, love. I'm sorry. But it is a bit much…'

'Everything,' Jenny hiccupped, 'is a bit much.'

'I know…Come here.'

'I need to blow my nose.' Jenny sat up, banged her head on the top of the steel cage, and started crying in earnest.

'Come on, it's all right…we'll sort it all out somehow…I'm sorry…'

'Oh, Ted,' said Jenny, between sobs, 'what are we going to do?'

Get rid of Mrs Ingram, was the first thing that came into Stratton's mind, but he didn't say it. Instead, he kissed the top of her head and said, 'The first thing we're going to do is try and get some kip. It's bound to look better in the morning.' Then he stroked Jenny's back until, eventually, the tears subsided, and she fell asleep.

So much for clearing the air, he thought. They'd had a row, Jenny had cried, and he had a horrible feeling that he still hadn't got to the bottom of things.

46

The following morning nothing looked any better, and Jenny, tight-lipped, was preoccupied with Mrs Ingram. He arrived at work in a bad mood which was made worse by having to deal with an elderly, blue-nosed ruffian, who kept raving that his wife was trying to poison him, when Arliss put his head round the door to announce that Chief Superintendent Dewhurst had telephoned and wished to speak to him. Stratton, who had decided that the old man's symptoms were more likely to be due to delirium tremens than foul play, told Arliss to escort him to the hospital, then went to place a call to the Fingerprint Bureau.

'I've looked at those items,' said Dewhurst. 'The prints on the syringe are right-handed, but they're pretty well smudged...Not good enough for a match, I'm afraid. And nothing on the keys.'

'No prints from Dr Byrne?' asked Stratton.

'No. Perhaps you were right after all,' said Dewhurst, grudgingly. 'We couldn't match the prints on the edges of the desk—not enough to go on. We've eliminated most of the prints from the room—Dr Byrne, Higgs, and the secretary—but there's one set unaccounted for. Only one example—fingertips and partial palm, right hand.'

'Where did you find that?'

'The bookshelf. I'll let you know if we find a match.' With that, he terminated the conversation, and Stratton was left wondering whether he should be glad or sorry about this news. It was strange about the keys—Byrne hadn't been wearing gloves when he was discovered, and none had been found on his person...In any case, why should he wear gloves in his office?

Stratton, because he'd tried it, knew that the keys could have been slid under the door but if someone had done that, they must have wiped them first. He'd just have to hope that Dewhurst could find a match for the unidentified prints. If not, they might have to start looking at the hospital staff. Supposing they turned out to belong to Fay Marchant? Although why she, or anyone else, who was intent on killing Byrne should need to touch the bookshelf, he couldn't imagine. He'd go and have a look at it later. Perhaps he'd missed something.

He was turning this over in his mind when Ballard appeared, notebook at the ready. 'Anything from Wimbledon?' asked Stratton, without much hope.

'The warden didn't see him, sir, and neither did any of the neighbours. We've got a key to his house, though—the woman who does for him...' Ballard leafed through the pages of his notebook. 'A Mrs Evans. Three times a week. I had a word with her, sir, and she said she'd not seen him since last Saturday, but she'd been in to do some cleaning yesterday morning and the place looked exactly the same as usual.'

'What about the bed? Had he slept there?'

'She said it was made up, but then she told me that Dr Byrne often does it himself.'

'Heavens.'

'She did say he was very tidy in his habits, sir. She's a nice old thing—pretty upset when I told her about Dr Byrne. Kept saying how he was one of her favourite gentlemen and she couldn't believe it. She wasn't at all happy about handing this'—Ballard produced a key with a luggage label attached to it—'over to me.'

'We'd better go and have a look round,' said Stratton. 'According to Fingerprints—in the person of none other than Chief Superintendent Dewhurst himself—'

'Blimey!'

'You can say that again. He says they can't get anything from the syringe and the office keys seem to have been wiped.'

'Blimey,' repeated Ballard, unconsciously taking Stratton at his word. 'Have you told DCI Lamb, sir?'

'No. And I'm not going to, either, until we've done a bit more poking about.'

The thing was, thought Stratton, as they crunched up the gravel driveway to Byrne's large and well-appointed residence overlooking Wimbledon Common, being wrong wasn't so bad when people reacted with incredulity and compassion—what was galling was when they took it for granted that you'd cock things up, as Lamb undoubtedly would if Stratton couldn't provide him with a bit more evidence.

'I'll go upstairs,' said Stratton, when they got into the hall. 'You have a look round down here. Anything you think may be relevant, give me a shout.'

'Yes, sir.'

Stratton ascended the stairs and began opening doors—bathroom, three bedrooms, and a room with a large desk and an articulated skeleton, hanging from a stand and wearing a schoolboy's cap, which was obviously Dr Byrne's study. Although tidy and well polished—Mrs Evans was clearly worth her weight in shillings—the house seemed to have an echoey, tomb-like air, and the skeleton didn't help. There were no photographs, no pictures on the wall, no flowers, and no sign anywhere that Byrne had had any interests other than his work. Opening a wardrobe in one of the spare bedrooms, Stratton saw a rail of women's clothing—presumably the late Mrs Byrne's. Had Byrne kept it deliberately, he wondered, or simply forgotten about it? He inclined to the latter view until, examining Byrne's bed, he came upon a framed photograph of a good-looking woman and a boy tucked under the pillow. Wife and son, presumably, thought Stratton, wondering if Byrne looked at the picture before going to sleep, or even kissed it goodnight. Poor chap, thought Stratton.

Cancer, Higgs had said, which probably meant she'd been ill for some time. Poor bloke. He couldn't even bear to imagine life without Jenny, let alone having to witness her suffering like that.

Stratton replaced the photograph carefully and returned to Byrne's office, where he began opening drawers. Everything was neat: the pencils in the brass tray well sharpened, the few piles of papers with their edges squared off, index cards filed in alphabetical order. Stratton stared at the skeleton and wondered how Mrs Evans had felt about it.

His reverie was interrupted by the sound of voices from the hall, and, on going downstairs, he found Ballard talking to a man who looked like a junior edition of Dr Byrne.

'Detective Inspector Stratton,' he said.

'Frank Byrne.' The young man put out his hand. 'I understand you're investigating my father's death.'

'I'm very sorry about it, sir,' said Stratton, adding cautiously, 'I'm afraid there are one or two things that need clarifying.'

'Anything I can help with?' asked Frank Byrne. 'Because,' he added, vehemently, 'I can tell you, my father would not have taken his own life.'

'What makes you say that?' asked Stratton.

'He thought suicide was a selfish act. Wrong. Unlawful.'

'Did he tell you that?'

'On several occasions. He was very firm about it. My father was a principled man, Inspector Stratton.'

Stratton nodded. 'I had the good fortune to work with him on many occasions.' God, he thought, I sound as pompous as he does. Still, judging from the young man's pleased expression, it seemed to be doing the trick.

'Then I'm sure your thoughts will be tending the same way,' said Byrne's son.

'I certainly thought it was worth a second look,' said Stratton. 'That's why we're here. To make sure that there was nothing that indicated any kind of mental fatigue.'

'You won't find anything like that,' Frank Byrne said firmly.

'Had your father written to you recently?' Stratton asked.

'Not for a couple of weeks. He'd certainly never written anything that caused me to suspect he was unhappy. Even after my mother died, he...Well, he never said much about feelings and so forth. He just got on with things—it was his way. He was always...' Frank Byrne screwed up his face in an effort to complete the sentence, then gave up and tried a different tack. 'When he was at home—even before, I mean—he always spent a lot of time in his study. Most of his spare time, in fact.'

Stratton nodded. 'He was certainly dedicated to his work. That skeleton upstairs...' out of the corner of his eye, he saw Ballard raise an eyebrow, 'is that your school cap?'

'That's right. Dad called him Alfie.'

'Alfie?'

'I don't think it was really his name—just what we called him. There's a photograph, somewhere, of Dad sitting at the desk, pretending to dictate notes to him. Mum took it.'

As glimpses of the lighter moments of domestic life went, Stratton thought, that one was definitely bizarre. Ignoring Ballard's quizzical expression, he said, 'We haven't turned that up yet.'

'It shouldn't be hard to find. It's in there.' Frank Byrne indicated the sitting room.

'Perhaps you'd care to show us, Mr Byrne.' Stratton opened the sitting room door.

'Of course. There's a little gadget here...' Frank Byrne crossed the room and poked a little panel of wood inset in the brick chimney piece, which swung outwards, revealing a small space. 'Hidden, you see. He wanted to keep them safe in case there was an air raid—if the house was destroyed.'

'Very neat.' Stratton peered inside. No needles or phials or any of the paraphernalia of the habitual drug-taker, just a single brown envelope. Stratton opened it and took out a number of unframed photographs, lining them up on the mantelpiece. They were family pictures, except for one, which, like the others he'd seen previously, had been taken in the mortuary, and showed Dr Byrne and the man Stratton now knew to be his erstwhile assistant, Todd, in the act of examining some ancient-looking bones.

'It's that man again,' said Ballard.

'I don't know what that one's doing here,' said Frank Byrne. 'Dad must have got it muddled up.'

Stratton, remembering how the photographs in the mortuary office were tucked out of sight beneath the blotter, wondered whether this was the case, but he couldn't, for the life of him, see why the picture was significant. A man as dedicated to his work as Dr Byrne was might well treasure photographs of himself on the job, but why that particular one and not the others?

'That's me, sitting on Dad's knee,' said Frank Byrne, pointing at a picture of a younger but only slightly more hirsute Dr Byrne in the company of a chubby toddler, 'and that's my mother.' He indicated a snap of the attractive fair-haired woman Stratton had seen in the photograph upstairs. 'And, look, there's the one where Dad's pretending to dictate to Alfie.'

'Mr Byrne, this may seem a strange question, but did your father ever take drugs?'

Frank Byrne looked puzzled. 'He never took anything. To be honest...' Byrne hesitated and cleared his throat before continuing, 'he didn't really trust doctors. He never said as much, but I think he'd seen the results of their mistakes too many times to have much faith in the medical profession.'

'I meant,' said Stratton, 'in the sense of an addiction.'

'My *father?*' Frank Byrne sounded incredulous. 'You must be joking. Has someone suggested it?'

'No. But we think his death might have been due to an overdose of some sort.'

'So I gathered,' said Frank Byrne, 'but if that does prove to be the case I find it very hard to believe it was self-administered.'

'I see. But, as I'm sure you'll understand, we need to be certain.'

After receiving permission to take away the photographs, Stratton and Ballard walked back to Wimbledon station to catch the train back to the West End. After several minutes' tramping along in silence, Ballard said, 'Sir, you don't think…that photograph of Dr Byrne with Todd…he might have kept it at home because…well, because of some attachment between them?'

This was something that had not occurred to Stratton. 'You mean…?'

'Yes, sir. Stranger things have happened.'

'I suppose so. It's one explanation, certainly. People have committed suicide for less. And of course being married doesn't preclude that sort of thing, but I shouldn't have thought…'

'One never knows, sir.'

'That's true. Perhaps we ought to speak to this Todd. Still, let's wait for the results of the PM, shall we?' He grimaced. 'I really don't want to go down that particular route unless it's absolutely necessary. The son might be right—Byrne might have got the photographs muddled up, although…' Although, said a voice in his head, that would be uncharacteristic of such a meticulous man. 'Besides, there's that business of there being no fingerprints on the keys.'

'That does seem odd, sir.'

'Bloody odd, if you ask me.'

Returning to his desk, Stratton found a message to telephone Dr Ferguson at Guy's Hospital. 'It's as we thought,' said the young pathologist. 'Morphine, by injection, and a hell of a lot of it.'

'Can you be any more definite about the time of death?' asked Stratton, scribbling notes.

'I'd be guessing,' said Ferguson. 'As I said, it all depends on how long it took to work. I think it would be safest to stay with my original estimate.'

'Which was…' Hunching up his shoulder to keep the telephone receiver in place, Stratton flicked through his notebook, 'between half past three and half past four in the morning, and the injection could have been given as early as eight or eight-thirty in the evening?'

'Yes, that seems reasonable.' Ferguson spoke as if this had been Stratton's supposition and not his own.

'What about the bump on the head?' asked Stratton.

'It looks as if it happened when he fell. There's a match with the blood on the desk.'

'But he ended up on his back...?'

'That is strange, but it's not impossible.'

'Could the bang on the head have been prior to the injection?'

'Impossible to say, but there was some blood flow, and clearly plenty of time for the bruise to develop, so I'd say it happened several hours before death.'

'Would it have been enough to knock him out?'

'I wouldn't be at all surprised. Enough for concussion, certainly. It was quite a blow.'

Stratton thanked Dr Ferguson, replaced the telephone on the hook, then started compiling a list of questions. He'd just written *Fay Marchant*, and added three question marks and a reminder to himself to re-check the dispensary's records for her name, when Sergeant Ballard appeared, bearing two cups of tea.

'Any joy, sir?'

'Thanks. Not really.' Stratton pushed his notebook in Ballard's direction. 'Have a dekko.'

'Hmm...' Ballard scanned the page. 'Hardly conclusive, is it?'

Stratton shook his head. 'Nothing concrete. Just that Byrne tried to speak to me the afternoon before he died, and everyone seems to agree that he wasn't even depressed, never mind suicidal, and that he—or *somebody*—wiped the prints from his desk and his keys. There might be something in what you said about that mortuary assistant—it's as good a place to start as any, so we'd better see if we can find him.'

'Called up, wasn't he?'

'Yes.' Stratton reclaimed his notebook and leafed through the pages. 'About five weeks ago, according to the other assistant, Higgs. Wonder why they left it so late? He wasn't in a reserved occupation.'

'Mucked up the records, I shouldn't wonder. Happens a good deal, apparently.'

'I suppose it must do. And of course we don't know which service.'

'No, but he'll still be doing basic training, won't he? Shouldn't be too hard to find. I'll get onto it right away, sir.'

'Good. I'd better have a word with DCI Lamb,' Stratton rolled his eyes, 'and then I'll get down to the hospital and start asking questions about mislaid morphine.'

Later, Stratton traipsed back to the Middlesex with Lamb's parting shot—'Do try not to turn this into more of a fiasco than it is already'—ringing in his ears.

Stratton went downstairs first, to examine the bookcase in Byrne's office. He didn't really expect to find anything, and, sure enough, it was entirely unremarkable. He then went upstairs to confront the bespectacled lady from the hospital's Administrative Department. When Stratton announced himself, she approached him with all the enthusiasm of a trout confronted by an unbaited hook. On hearing that Byrne's death might not, after all, have been suicide, she raised so many objections to his interviewing any of the staff that Stratton marched off to find the senior registrar with the posh voice, leaving her opening and closing her mouth, looking even more fish-like than before.

Having wiped the controlled sneer off the senior registrar's face by informing him that he was conducting yet another murder enquiry, Stratton secured a room in which to conduct interviews. He asked the man to tell Professor Haycraft, and, leaving him making whinnying noises and fingering what Stratton would have bet a week's wages was a public school tie, he went to check the dispensary records, where he found Fay's signature for three phials of morphine on the relevant date—which, if nothing else, proved she hadn't pinched the stuff—and then marched off to the Men's Surgical Ward.

He found Sister Bateman at the bedside of a chubby, effeminate-looking man who, though clearly middle-aged, had suspiciously butter-coloured hair. It was visiting time, and she was engaging in an animated conversation with a plump and peroxided woman who, judging by the likeness, must have been the man's mother. In fact, Stratton thought, the pair of them could have taken it in turns to be mother, so great was the resemblance. He cleared his throat, causing Sister Bateman's head to swivel in his direction.

'Yes? Can I help? Oh...' she said, in weary recognition. 'It's you.'

'I'm afraid so, Sister. Might I have a quick word?'

'If you must,' she said, ungraciously.

Sister Bateman excused herself from the plump woman, who was still gesticulating wildly, and led Stratton to her desk at the end of the ward. 'I hope this won't take long,' she said. 'I've two nurses off—chickenpox, of all things—and another one's packed her traps and run off home, so we're rather hard pressed.'

'I understand,' said Stratton. 'This won't take long. You've heard about Dr Byrne, I take it?'

'Dreadful business.' said Sister Bateman. 'News spreads very quickly in hospitals, as I'm sure you can imagine.' She glared suspiciously round the ward in case any of the nurses were gossiping.

'What have you heard?' asked Stratton.

'That he took his own life, poor man,' said Sister Bateman in a low voice. 'Was that what happened?'

'We're not entirely sure,' said Stratton, cautiously. 'That's why I'm here. It's about morphine. Have you missed any?'

Sister Bateman raised her eyebrows. 'Was that how?'

'I'm afraid so. Is there any unaccounted for?'

Sister Bateman shook her head. 'We're always very careful about drugs, Inspector. There is a procedure, you know.'

'I realise that, but if you could just cast your mind back...'

Sister Bateman seemed to sag slightly, and Stratton saw that, beneath the starchy carapace, there was a very tired woman. For a second, he was tempted to put his arm round her, but common sense told him that this would be both inappropriate and unappreciated (except of course, by the nearby patients and nurses, all of whom, in their different ways, were going through an elaborate pantomime of not listening to their conversation).

'One of the nurses did have an accident. She was fetching some supplies, and she dropped three phials of morphine. I reprimanded her, of course. We can't afford to waste valuable supplies through carelessness.' The memory of this brought the starch back, and, straightening her spine, she glared at Stratton as if preempting a flippant suggestion about teaching the nurses to juggle with the stuff. 'Nurses are not supposed to run in the corridors.'

'When was this?' he asked.

'Two days ago.'

'What happened to the phials?'

'Lost, I'm afraid. They went down the gap between the floorboards and the wall. The wretched girl wasn't looking where she was going, and...' Sister Bateman spread her hands. 'Gone.'

'Where did this happen?'

'In the corridor outside. It's probably better if you ask Nurse Marchant. She was the one who dropped them.'

Stratton didn't think he'd betrayed himself by so much as a flicker, but Sister Bateman shot him a shrewd look and said, 'You asked to see her before, didn't you? About poor Dr Reynolds. You wanted to interview her again.'

Stratton gave her his blandest smile. 'That's right. A minor matter.'

Sister Bateman looked as if she didn't entirely believe this, but she didn't challenge it. 'I'll fetch her for you, shall I?'

'If you would,' said Stratton. 'It's probably of no importance, but I ought to check.'

She reappeared after a couple of minutes, Fay Marchant in tow. Fay, pale-faced, stared at the floor while the sister told Stratton that she'd leave them to it. He and Fay stood in silence until she'd bustled out of earshot. Fay, he thought, looked tense—more angular, somehow, than she had before—and as he escorted her into the corridor to show him where the phials had been dropped, she seemed to move stiffly, with less grace than he remembered.

She looked around uncertainly. 'It was somewhere down here, I think.' She turned left and moved forward a few steps, Stratton trailing behind.

'How did it happen?'

'Carelessness, really. I was rushing, and I bumped into someone, and the tray just flew out of my hand. It landed over there somewhere,' Fay pointed to a spot a few feet away, 'and the things rolled across the floor.'

Stratton noticed that her pale complexion was reddening, and blotches of pink had appeared on her neck. 'Then what happened?' he asked.

'We looked around for the things, and I picked up the tray and the syringe, but I couldn't see the phials. We found one, but it was broken, and he—I mean,' continued Fay, looking very uncomfortable, 'the person I bumped into, said they must have fallen down the crack over there.'

'Who did you collide with?' asked Stratton, who had remembered Sister Bateman's comments about nurses running in corridors and had an idea that Fay hadn't told her about bumping into anyone. 'Was it a doctor, by any chance?'

'Yes, one of the doctors. He was very nice about it, even though it was my fault.'

Stratton wondered why she hadn't volunteered a name—he was pretty sure she knew who it was. Leaving this aside for the moment, he said, 'And he helped you look for the phials, did he?'

'Yes. He was the one who realised where they must have gone.'

Stratton went to inspect the point she'd indicated, and, crouching down, peered into the gap between the floor and the skirting board, Fay hovering behind him. He couldn't see anything down there, but, he concluded, it would be easy enough to remove the board for a proper look.

'Can you see them?' asked Fay.

'No.'

'I couldn't, either. But they must be down there—as he said, there's nowhere else they could have gone.'

Stratton stood up and turned to face Fay, who stepped back, looking worried. 'I didn't take them,' she said. 'I wouldn't.'

'It's all right,' said Stratton. 'I'm not accusing you of anything. The doctor said that to you, did he? About the phials falling down there?'

'Well...yes.'

'Which doctor was it?'

'Oh.' Fay's colour intensified. 'Dr Dacre. From Casualty.'

'Dacre,' repeated Stratton. Too much to hope that it was Dr Byrne, of course.

'He's new,' said Fay. 'He replaced Dr Reynolds.' Her voice was quite steady, but her discomfort was obvious. Stratton wasn't clear whether this was a result of having dropped the stuff in the first place, or the fact that Dacre was Reynolds's replacement, or their own meeting in the mortuary corridor, or a compound of all of these.

'Ah,' he said. 'Did you tell him what was in the phials?'

'Well, yes.' Fay looked bewildered. 'I wanted to find them. I was worried about getting into trouble with Sister.'

'I understand. Now,' he said, gently, 'I'm going to fetch a porter and get this board up, because we do need to account for anything that's missing. But before I do, where were you going the night before last, when *we* bumped into each other?'

'I told you,' said Fay. 'Back to the nurses' quarters. I'd just come off duty.'

'Rather an odd route to take, wasn't it?'

'I had to take something down to one of the basement theatres,' said Fay. 'A patient's notes, for one of the house surgeons. Sister Bateman asked me to take them.' She glanced around, as if hoping for corroboration. 'I didn't see Mr Hambling—that's the surgeon —but you can ask Sister.'

'I'll do that,' said Stratton. 'Did you hear any noise coming from the mortuary office when you walked past?'

'No. The door was shut.'

'Fair enough. But, just before you go…is there anything else you'd like to tell me, about any of this?'

Fay stared at him for a moment, wide-eyed, then shook her head. 'It's nothing to do with me,' she said miserably. 'None of it.'

Stratton, though strongly tempted to do just what he'd told Fay about getting the floorboard up, was perfectly aware that Lamb—quite rightly, in this case would have him on toast if he did any such thing, and went back to Savile Row to see about a warrant.

'Search the hospital?' Lamb, who having given up on the patience-wearing-thin routine and adopted an air of one bearing up bravely under bad news, now raised his voice an incredulous semitone. 'Take up floorboards? Have you any idea how much disruption that will cause?'

'Of course, sir, but I don't see any other way.'

'In case you haven't noticed, *Inspector*,' Lamb said, acidly, 'we've got quite enough on our hands with the flying bombs, without you demolishing things as well.'

'Unless you have any advice about how it might be managed, sir…' said Stratton, knowing full well that Lamb didn't. 'I thought,' he added, humbly, 'that if you could put in a word, sir, it might speed things up a bit. For the warrant, sir.'

Lamb, resuming his stoic-courage-under-fire voice, said, 'Oh, very well. You'd better wait outside.'

Stratton, who was buggered if he was going to pace up and down the corridor outside Lamb's office like a man awaiting the arrival of his first-born, decided to nip out and see if he could get a packet of fags. The tobacconist on the corner, who knew him, conjured twenty Players from under the counter

('Your favourites, sir'). Stratton returned to the station, where his cigarette-brightened mood was soon dispelled by having to hang about for the best part of half an hour before Lamb stuck his head out of his office to summon him.

'Warrant's at Marlborough Street. You can collect it on your way back to the hospital. Take Arliss, and for God's sake try to be discreet.'

'I'll do my best, sir,' said Stratton, with an air of meekness that caused Lamb to narrow his eyes suspiciously. 'Thank you, sir.'

Arliss and the warrant collected, Stratton returned to Miss Fish-Face in the Administrative Department, who looked even less pleased to see him—although with Arliss grinning horribly at his elbow, this was hardly surprising. Thrusting the warrant under the woman's nose, he asked for assistance in taking up the floorboards. Help arrived about twenty minutes later, in the form of a doddery porter armed with a claw hammer and an air of stoically borne but well-deserved failure. He refused to allow Stratton to do the job himself (and no chance of Arliss, who stood well clear with his hands clasped behind his back, lifting a finger). Holding Stratton back with an outstretched arm and wheezing about it being ''orspital business', the old boy took a further ten minutes before managing to remove the board.

'Nothing there,' he said, as the three men peered down at the thick layer of dust. Thrusting his hand into the gap, Stratton found nothing more than a playing card and a stub of chewed pencil. There were no phials, and no evidence of broken glass.

The porter nailed the board down again while Arliss sucked his teeth and Stratton paced the corridor, checking the floorboards nearest the walls for more gaps. He found a couple about fifty yards down, and decided that these might as well come up, too—Fay hadn't seemed certain exactly where the collision had taken place. Grumbling, the porter complied with his instructions, which resulted in a great deal of interest from a gaggle of passing nurses who stood about exchanging banter with the old man while he made valiant, but none-too-surreptitious, attempts to look up their skirts. This eventually caused him to wheeze so much that he doubled over in a paroxysm of coughing, whereupon Stratton took advantage of the situation to seize the hammer and do the work himself.

Finally, his hands and cuffs grey with dust, he had to concede that there was nothing there. The nurses having gone on their way, giggling, the porter recovered himself enough to yawn massively, causing his top denture to fall with a faint clopping sound and expose a set of shrunken gums, and tell Stratton that there was bugger-all to see and the whole thing had been a waste of time. Stratton thanked him and, leaving him to return the boards to their proper places and instructing Arliss to render assistance (some hope), went downstairs to Casualty to see if he could find Dr Dacre and clarify the situation.

'You're that policeman, aren't you?' Sister Radford looked quite as harassed as Sister Bateman. She eyed him warily, as if he were an unpredictable dog she was expected to pat.

'Detective Inspector Stratton.' He held out his hand. 'I'm sorry to barge in here like this, but I'd like a word with Dr Dacre, if he's available.'

Sister Radford frowned for a moment, then her face cleared. 'Of course—Dr Ransome must have told you.'

'Told me...?'

'About Dr Dacre being one of the last people to speak to...' she lowered her voice dramatically, 'poor Dr Byrne.'

'Oh? When was this, exactly?'

'The afternoon before he...before it happened. Dr Byrne came up here— Isn't that why you've come to see Dr Dacre?'

'Well,' Stratton prevaricated, 'with cases like this, we do need to make sure...' This being said in the reasonable tone of one professional person appealing to another for discretion, Sister Radford said briskly that she quite understood and would fetch Dr Dacre straight away.

Stratton gazed about him at the rows of people waiting, with patient resignation, to be treated. Hearing their low murmurs, punctuated every now and then by a hacking cough, and seeing the grey, worn faces, running noses, lank hair and drab, patched clothing, soiled by brick dust, the rough attempts at bandaging cuts and wounds with anything to hand—the only real touch of brightness being the occasional angry red of a boil or sore—he thought, we can't go on much longer. None of us can; we're exhausted—there's no colour or spirit or jollity left. How can we bring up our children in a world like this? Monica and Pete, he thought, could quite well round on him one day and say, 'Why should we listen to you?' and he wouldn't have an answer. After all, their generation could hardly do worse than his, or the one before it—two world wars and half the country in ruins...Thinking of the children reminded him of his and Jenny's argument last night, over the fact that that bloody woman was stopping at their house. He could see her point about Mrs Ingram having no friends and relations, but all the same...He agreed with Don that she ought to go to the bin, but Jenny had seemed so on edge, so...what was the word...*fragile*, that was it, that he was glad he hadn't pushed it. They'd have to discuss it again later. Stratton turned his mind to why Byrne had wanted to speak to Dacre. If it were a case of negligence, like Reynolds's, which had resulted in the death of a patient...He heard someone say his name and looked up to see a dark-haired young man of medium size standing before him, white-coated, with a stethoscope around his neck and a bruise on his temple. 'Dacre.' The man smiled and offered his hand. 'Sister Radford said you wanted to see me.'

'Inspector Stratton, CID. I can see you're busy, so I'll try to keep it brief.'

'Be glad of the respite, to be honest.' Dacre grinned. 'Rather a full house.'

'What happened there?' asked Stratton, indicating the bruise.

'Bit of an altercation, I'm afraid. A rather large lady with a powerful left hook who took exception when I told her she was about to become a grandmother.'

'Ah,' said Stratton. 'And the father?'

'Heaven knows. The mother-to-be wasn't entirely with us, if you know what I mean.' Dacre tapped his head with a finger.

'Don't I just.' Stratton found himself grinning in response. People—women—would like this chap, he thought. Not because of self-confidence or urbanity or matinée-idol looks—the charm was the self-deprecating type.

'Oh, well.' Dacre shrugged. 'One born every day. How can I help you?'

Stratton, realising that he should be taking the lead, collected himself by clearing his throat and said, 'I understand that you were involved in a bit of an accident a couple of days ago, when some morphine went missing.'

Dacre frowned. 'Accident?'

'Upstairs. A rather attractive nurse by the name of Fay Marchant.'

'Oh, yes.' Dacre smiled. 'Couldn't forget her in a hurry, could you? It's just that rather a lot's happened in the last forty-eight hours, Inspector. Let's see…Well, we bumped into each other— entirely my fault, I'm afraid—and she dropped the things she was carrying. A tray, with a hypodermic syringe and morphine. I found one of the phials—smashed to pieces—but the others disappeared, and we thought they must have gone under the floorboards.'

'We pulled them up to have a look,' said Stratton, 'but we couldn't find anything.'

Dacre raised his eyebrows. 'Very thorough. But I don't understand why they weren't there. I mean…' he looked baffled, 'there's nowhere else they could have gone.'

'You didn't pick them up?'

'Heavens, no! If we want morphine, all we have to do is…' he held out his hand and made an eager schoolboy face, 'please, Sister…We don't have to pinch the stuff.'

'And you're sure they went into the crack between the floor and the wall?'

'Pretty sure. To be honest, I was rather distracted by meeting the lovely Nurse Marchant, Inspector, and. I'm afraid I took advantage of the situation by inviting her out for a drink with me that evening.'

'She didn't tell me that,' said Stratton, privately acknowledging that, in Dacre's shoes, he'd have done exactly the same.

'Well, she wouldn't. It's strictly against the rules, you know.' Dacre grinned again. 'A very nice time we had, too. But I'm sure you're not a bearer of tales, Inspector. I'd hate to get her into any trouble.'

Stratton, thinking of Sergeant Ballard and Policewoman Gaines, and pleased that Dacre hadn't taken the both-men-of-the-world line, said, 'No, of course not. But it doesn't solve the problem of where the morphine ended up.'

Dacre looked thoughtful. 'I haven't been here long, but I think the building's taken a fair old hammering—not necessarily directly, but all this,' he looked skyward, 'does tend to make the old foundations shift about a bit. There might have been a crack below the crack, if you see what I mean.'

'Possibly,' said Stratton, 'but there was a hell of a lot of dust down there, and I would have thought...'

'You're probably right. But short of taking the whole place apart...As I said, my attention wasn't fully on the matter, so I suppose they might have just rolled away and been picked up by someone else. It's not impossible. I know it doesn't sound good, and I'm sorry not to be more help.'

'Oh, well...' Stratton gave a deliberately heavy sigh. He wasn't so drawn in that he'd failed to notice Dacre's assumption that Stratton thought he'd stolen the morphine phials rather than just pocketing them accidentally and forgetting about them. And he'd begun to feel that there was something not entirely right behind the easiness of manner—the man was holding his gaze for just a fraction too long. 'Now,' he continued, 'the other matter.'

'Other?' Dacre frowned.

'I understand that Dr Byrne came up here to speak to you on the afternoon before his death.'

'Oh…yes. Yes, that's right, we did have a few words.'

'Why was that?'

'A medical matter.'

'Which was?'

Dacre hesitated, staring at his shoes, then smiled in a rueful, schoolboyish way. 'You might not wish to hear this, Inspector.'

'Why's that?'

'It was about a testicular torsion.'

'A what?'

'Well, without going into too much detail, it occurs when the cord that takes blood to the testicle becomes twisted, which cuts off the supply. Prolonged torsion can result in the death of the testicle and surrounding tissue, which is what happened in this case, I'm afraid. It's agonising, of course, no fun at all, and—'

'Right. I get the picture,' said Stratton, hastily. He'd started to feel sick fairly early on in Dacre's description, and definitely did not want to hear any more. 'And Byrne spoke to you because…?' he prompted, not at all sure that he wanted to hear the answer.

'I'd never seen one before, you see—the poor chap was in terrible pain, but I hadn't quite appreciated the urgency of the situation. Of course, the testicle had to come off—gangrene, you know, although they did manage to save the other one—and I'd asked Dr Byrne if the dead one could be kept, so that I could have a look at it. Then, next time, I'd be—'

'Next time?' asked Stratton, faintly. 'Does it happen often?'

'Only to children and young men—usually under twenty.' Dacre gave him a sympathetic look. 'No need for you to worry, Inspector, although a hard blow in the right place might—'

Stratton, who was fighting the impulse to clutch his groin, held up his hand.

'Sorry,' said Dacre. 'But as I said, I was worried, because obviously it's important to get the diagnosis correct, and—'

'You can say that again,' said Stratton, adding hastily, 'but please don't. How did Dr Byrne seem to you?'

'It's difficult to say. I'd only met him once, you see. He certainly didn't seem agitated or anything like that. Inspector, are you all right?'

'I think,' said Stratton, who was unable to rid his mind of the vile images Dacre had conjured, and horribly aware of what could—surely to God—only be a sympathetic pain between his legs, 'that I'd better get some fresh air.'

'Good idea. Don't worry, it'll pass off.'

'Thanks,' said Stratton. 'I'll leave you in peace.' Stuffing his notebook in his pocket, and clapping his hat on his head, he made a hasty exit and, hurrying outside, leant against the nearest wall and took deep breaths, while focusing his attention as hard as he could on an ancient poster—FOR YOUR THROAT'S SAKE, SMOKE CRAVEN A—on the opposite side of the road. 'No fun at all,' he muttered to himself. That was what Dacre had said. 'Christ!'

After several minutes, the feeling that he was about to puke receded enough for him to light a cigarette and make some jottings in his notebook. He suddenly had a feeling that the whole business was like a game of chess in which he was ignorant of the moves. Was he missing something obvious? If so, what the hell was it?

He glanced at his wristwatch. Half past five. He'd had more than enough for one day. He'd collect Arliss, look into the station to see how Ballard was getting on with tracing Todd, then go home for supper and an hour on his allotment. Fuck this, he told himself: I've earned a bit of peace and quiet.

Then, with a sinking heart, he remembered Mrs Ingram. Peace and quiet was exactly what he wasn't going to get, at least not in his own home. It would have to be the allotment, then the pub. He was buggered if he was going to have another evening like last night.

CHAPTER

48

Dacre felt pleased with his performance. His deliberately elaborate description of the symptoms of testicular torsion had done its job even better than he'd expected. Besides, Inspector Stratton had liked him; he could tell. After the shock of going into a public call box yesterday evening, and discovering that GER 1212 was, indeed, the number of West End Central police station—he'd put the receiver down pretty sharpish when he heard that—he'd spent a profitable couple of hours rehearsing exactly what he would say when interviewed, and it had all come out word-perfect, with just the right amount of spontaneity.

He watched the big policeman out of sight, then spun on his heels to face the rows of waiting patients. 'Now then,' he sang out, 'who's next?'

A couple of hours later, Dacre had finished work and returned to his lodgings. Apart from his failure to understand *plumbum oscillans*, which earned him a *very* funny look from Dr Ransome, he'd had an unexpectedly good day. It wasn't in his medical dictionary—which he'd removed from his special hidey-hole in case a full search was instigated—but, when he discovered that plumbism was the medical term for lead poisoning, a dim recollection of chemistry lessons at school allowed him to work it out: *swinging the lead*. Malingering. Of course.

Guessing that Fay would come off duty at about the same time as he did, he'd wondered if he ought to nip upstairs to talk to her, but decided against it. It wouldn't do to make himself conspicuous—for all he knew, Inspector Stratton might still be sniffing about the place. He'd see Fay tomorrow. He wanted to hear about her interview with the inspector. There was no reason to imagine that their stories hadn't matched, but it was best to check. Besides, it would give him something to look forward to—it was high time he had her to himself again. Constantly thinking about her was distracting him, and that was no good at all. She must be secured, he thought, properly, and the quicker that happened the better, although, after the fiasco at the Clarendon, he'd need to go carefully with the sex stuff.

On his way home, he'd stopped at a cafe for a supper of tea and sausage rolls, and now he was settled in his single armchair with his pitifully thin pillow doubled up at the small of his back, a bottle of beer and glass to hand, and the *Psychological Medicine* textbook in his lap. He'd been reading for a couple of hours—some of it mundane, obvious, some fascinating, when he came upon a section about delusions and found something that made him laugh out loud.

> *French psychiatrist Joseph Capgras (b.1873, Verdun-sur-Garonne), gave his name to the Capgras delusion. First described in a paper in 1923, using the term 'l'illusion des sosies' (the illusion of doubles), this is a rare disorder in which a person believes that an acquaintance, usually a family member, has been replaced by an imposter of identical appearance, despite recognising familiarities in appearance and behaviour. It is most commonly found in patients diagnosed with schizophrenia. Less often, it may be the result of trauma to the head (brain injury)...*

He read about the Capgras's patient Madame M., who insisted that her entire family had been replaced by imposters, then put the book down and took a swig of his beer. Whatever the opposite of Capgras Syndrome might be, everyone—sane or otherwise—in thinking that he, the false doctor, was real, was suffering from it. That should be Dacre's Syndrome—or, more properly, it should be called by his original name. He mouthed this silently for a few moments, the sheer audacity of it making him laugh again.

There was no mention of how the Capgras problem might be treated. Perhaps nobody knew. If there could be people out there who thought that real people were imposters, then perhaps he—well, Dr Dacre—was just as real as a 'real' doctor, after all. What a strange idea…But then, even by his own standards, he'd had a pretty strange week. Stratton, he thought, was persistent, but he wasn't a mind reader, and as long as he suspected nothing, then he, Dacre, would be in the clear. He'd fooled him, hadn't he?

Psychiatry was definitely the way forward. He'd be capable of understanding others in a way that no ordinary person could hope to do. In comparison to him, ordinary people were blindfolded and blundering. He could break new ground. Father of modern psychiatry—that sounded good. Bringer of a new dawn in the understanding of the human mind…No, the human spirit. That sounded better. He'd become a professor. He'd be revered, consulted by committees and governments, decorated…

Dacre leant back in his chair and closed his eyes, enjoying the image of a medal conferred by a grateful monarch, and, watching with pride and decked out in furs and finery, Fay—Mrs James Dacre, wife to the eminent professor…

How could he have thought he'd be content with being a mere doctor? This, he thought, clutching the psychiatry textbook, this was the future…Away from the Middlesex with its meddling policeman to a place far from filthy old Euston Road, to live in a fine detached house with a couple of acres of garden, and Fay, his wife, by his side. The sooner he started laying plans, the better. The first step would be to tell Fay that he was asking his 'wife' to divorce him. Better leave it for a week or so, though, wouldn't do to spring it on her too soon…

'Not much luck tracing Todd, sir, I'm afraid.'

'Oh?' Stratton, who had just informed Ballard about the progress—or lack of it—made the previous day, squinted at the sergeant through the dusty, smoke-clouded shaft of morning sunlight that had managed to penetrate the dirty office window.

'According to the hospital's Administrative Department,' said the sergeant, 'he was born in May 1912, which makes him thirty-two years old.'

'Why isn't he in the forces?'

'Call-up deferred on compassionate grounds, apparently.'

'Why?'

'Don't know, sir. They couldn't find the information.'

'Well, there must have been something official.'

'Yes, sir. To be honest, they were rather vague about it. I got the impression they'd lost the document.'

Stratton shook his head in disgust. 'That's just what we need...Anything else?'

'Well, I've discovered that there were two Samuel Todds born in May 1912. One in Gravesend—died at two years old— and one in Bristol. He was killed on active service in 1941, when the Repulse went down.'

'Nobody else?'

'No, sir.'

'Well, you'd better try the rest of 1912, and, if nothing comes up, 1910 to...I don't know...1918, just in case. He might have falsified the date for some reason.'

'Yes, sir...Or—it's just a suggestion, sir...'

'Go on.'

'It might not be his name at all, sir. After all, it's happened before. There was that chap we arrested a couple of months ago who was passing himself off as an RAF flight lieutenant, and the bloke last year who said he was a brigadier.'

'Oh, yes. Thompson, wasn't it? But he was mad as a hatter. And in any case, even if he'd been normal—impersonating a member of the services is one thing, but why would anyone want to lie in order to become a mortuary assistant, for Christ's sake?'

'An unhealthy fascination with corpses, sir?'

'Interfering with dead women, you mean...Jesus, that's all we need. I suppose it might explain why Byrne hid those photographs—the call-up story was eyewash, and he'd sacked him for improper behaviour but he was keeping them just in case...but why didn't he say anything to us?'

'Wanted to keep it quiet, sir. Bad for the hospital's reputation if it got out—and after all, they were dead, weren't they? And he wasn't sacked, he left. The Administrative Department said he'd been called up and it was all above board.'

'Had they seen his papers?'

'They couldn't find any record of those, either.'

Stratton raised his eyebrows. 'I see. Have you got his last address?'

'Yes, sir. And I asked one of the local coppers to check with the landlady. A Mrs...' Ballard leafed through his notebook, 'Barnard. She said Todd left on the twenty-fifth of June. Told her he'd got a job up north somewhere.'

'She didn't know exactly?'

'No, sir. But she seemed to think he was exempt from the call-up because of bad health.'

'Did she indeed? Well, that does make it sound as if he left under a cloud for some reason or other. Of course, it doesn't explain why the photographs were tucked under Byrne's blotter. Unless he just happened to keep them there.'

'Odd place, though, sir. And one of them was at his house.'

'Yes…And we need to get to the bottom of this missing morphine, too.' Stratton sighed. 'I suppose it means taking the rest of those floorboards up, but we'll need a general search, as well. I'll see who I can round up for that, and then I'd better go back to the mortuary and see Higgs—find out if he knows anything about Todd, or if he'd seen him do anything…' Stratton rolled his eyes, '*unusual* to the dead.'

A further application to Lamb, who had now added deep, rumbling sighs to his bearing-up repertoire, resulted in permission to take Piper, Watkins and Policewoman Harris with him to the Middlesex.

After another dismal encounter in the Administrative Department, Stratton took his search party, now augmented by the old porter, to Matron Hornbeck. To his relief, she proved far more helpful than old Fishy upstairs, and agreed to conduct an inventory to make sure that no other phials of morphine had gone missing. After issuing instructions, Stratton felt confident enough to leave the others to pull up the rest of the floorboards in the corridor and conduct a search, and went to find Sister Bateman. When she had confirmed that Fay had been sent to the basement operating theatre with a set of notes on the evening of Dr Byrne's death, he thanked her and went down to the mortuary.

'They're sending us that Dr Ferguson for the time being,' said Higgs, nodding approvingly. He was squatting against the wall in the main mortuary room, holding one of Stratton's cigarettes pinched between his thumb and forefinger so that it pointed into his palm. The harsh, greenish light on his wizened features and jockey's frame made him look like the Artful Dodger a week dead. 'He's coming over this afternoon. And Miss L's agreed to stay.'

Stratton, opposite him on the only available chair, said, 'That's good. I wanted to ask you about Sam Todd.'

'What about him?'

'Did he talk much about himself?'

Higgs sucked on his cigarette and stared into space for what seemed like several minutes, two very thin trickles of smoke emerging, eventually, from his nostrils. 'Not a lot. But I never give him my life story, neither. What's he done?'

'Nothing, so far as we know. What *did* he tell you?'

'Said he'd been moving about a fair bit—that's why they only just cottoned to him for the call-up—'

'That was the reason he gave?'

'Yes. Nothing wrong with that, is there? Long time, mind, but then they didn't get onto the older ones until a year or so back.'

'How old was he?'

'Dunno. Twenty-seven? Twenty-eight? Something like that, I reckon. They'll have all them details upstairs though, won't they?'

'Did he tell you anything else?'

'Not that I recall...' Higgs took another drag. 'Wait, though. He said he'd worked for the government. Some department or other.'

Stratton made a note. 'Where was that?'

'Haven't the foggiest...' Higgs gave his earlobe a pensive tug. 'No. If he did tell me, it's gone.'

'Was it in London?'

'I should think so. He told me he used to live at Shepherd's Bush.'

'When was that?'

'Before he come to work here, he said. But he was a good bloke, Inspector—one of the best we've ever had here.'

'How did he get on with Dr Byrne?'

Higgs looked mildly surprised. 'Same as anyone. You knew Dr Byrne a bit, didn't you? More time for the dead than the living. We was used to it.' Exhaling, he added, 'I miss him, you know. A real expert, he was. Best pathologist we've ever had.'

'Did you ever notice Todd behaving strangely with any of the bodies?'

'What, dirty?'

'Yes.'

'Never. Nothing like that. I know the sort of thing—we had a bloke like that when I was working at Southwark, years ago. Found him at it. Reported it straight away. I won't have nothing like that in my mortuary.' He glared proprietorially towards the sheeted shape that lay on one of the slabs, as if daring some invisible pervert to lay a finger on it. 'And Dr Byrne would have had him out on his ear.'

'And as far as you know, Dr Byrne had no reason to be in any way dissatisfied with Todd's work?'

Higgs shook his head. 'Anything like that, and you'd have known about it, Inspector, straight away. Dr Byrne always respected the dead, and he expected everyone else to be the same...I don't understand, Inspector. Has Todd done something wrong—I mean, I don't see how he could have had anything to do with...Well, with what happened. He's gone, hasn't he?'

'Yes,' said Stratton heavily. 'He's gone. And you haven't heard from him since?'

'No. I mean, I liked the bloke, but I don't see why he'd write to me.'

'Who would he write to?'

'I don't know. He never mentioned anything about personal matters.'

'And you never asked?'

Higgs spread his hands. 'None of my business, was it?'

If two women had worked together for almost three months, Stratton thought on his way back to West End Central, they would have got to know all about each other—provided they liked one another, of course. That made him think of Jenny and Doris. He'd arrived back late the previous night having had rather too much in the Swan, and Jenny had ticked him off about making a racket, which had led to another whispered argument. She thinks she's doing the right thing, he told himself, but it's ridiculous. We can't call our home our own. Mrs Ingram would have to go—he'd make it plain this evening.

Higgs had said that Todd had worked in a government department—could be quite tricky to find out about that. Since the war, they'd tended to be pretty tight-lipped about disclosing information, even to the police, and of course any suggestion that one of their employees might have been using a false name would be bound to cause a flap about security, which would make things even worse. Stratton turned over an idea that had popped, unbidden, into his mind the minute that Higgs had said that he didn't know the name of the department: to ask Colonel Forbes-James of MI5. Their last meeting, back in 1940, hadn't been an easy one: Forbes-James had made it clear that if Stratton ever disclosed, or voiced his suspicions about, anything that had happened during that particular investigation, his career would be over before he could blink. In a futile attempt to salvage a scrap of pride, Stratton had indicated that he knew something about Forbes-James that could sink him, too—not that he could prove it, of course. Straight afterwards, he'd wished he hadn't done it, but there had been no repercussions—in fact, DCI Lamb had been forced, with very bad grace, to commend him. And now, he thought, perhaps—without Lamb's knowledge—he might be able ask for Forbes-James's help…

Turning it over in his head, he made his way to the station, passed Arliss, who was leaning on the front desk jawing with Cudlipp, and went to find Ballard, who was in the Charge Room, attempting to referee a slanging match between two irate prostitutes, both of whom Stratton recognised from his days on the beat: Big Red and Little Annie.

'She says I give her the money, but I never!' shouted Annie. Squaring up to the bigger woman, she screamed, 'I wouldn't give yer the steam off my piss, you dirty thieving cow!'

Big Red, whose hair was an improbable shade of magenta, and who had, at that moment, a face that almost matched it, yelled, 'Don't you put your filthy hands on me, you lying bitch! I wouldn't wipe my arse with your money—I'd catch something!'

'That's enough!' Stratton grabbed hold of Big Red's arm. 'Either you keep civil tongues in your heads, or you take it outside and we'll have the pair of you for disorderly conduct.'

'Ooh, DI Stratton,' said Big Red, with a horrible attempt at coquetry. 'I'm so glad to see you,' she simpered. 'I'm sure you'll understand my feelings.'

'No time for that, I'm afraid,' said Stratton. 'But I know a man who will.' Striding back to the door, he yanked it open and bellowed, 'Arliss!'

PC Arliss lumbered reluctantly down the passage. 'Sort this out, will you?' said Stratton, gesturing at the two women, who were, despite Ballard's efforts to separate them, still trying to claw each other's faces. 'I need Sergeant Ballard to come with me. That's it,' he added, as Arliss, groaning, advanced on the pair. 'Come on, Ballard.'

Leaving the three of them glaring at each other, Stratton and Ballard headed towards the office. 'I'd have put my money on Red, sir, but the other one's quite a scrapper.'

'I take it you haven't had the pleasure of our Annie's company before, Sergeant.'

'That I haven't, sir. It was quite an experience.'

'Now you know what's been missing from your life all these years...' Indicating that Ballard should sit down, Stratton settled himself behind his desk.

'Thank you, sir,' said Ballard gratefully, pulling out his handkerchief to wipe his face.

'Now, how did you get on? Anything to report?'

''Fraid not, sir. Records no help at all. One Sam Todd born 1914—he's a miner, works in Wales, somewhere I can't pronounce—one born in 1917, family emigrated to Australia in twenty-eight, and that's it.'

'Any chance he came back?'

'Looking into it, sir. Might take a bit of time.'

'Fair enough. Well, Higgs didn't have much to say for himself—nothing irregular about Todd's behaviour. Said if Dr Byrne had known, he'd have told us about it.'

'Unless Todd had something on *him*, sir.'

'That's true...' Stratton rubbed his jaw. 'Leaving aside that possibility for a moment, Higgs also said that Todd told him he used to work in a government department.'

Ballard frowned. 'That might be a bit tricky, sir. They don't give out information at the best of times.'

'No, they don't. And I don't want to involve DCI Lamb unless I have to. However, I've had an idea how to find out about that.' Rummaging in his desk drawer, he came upon the photographs he'd deposited there the previous day. Fishing them out, he said, 'You know, this chap,' he tapped the picture of Todd, 'looks familiar, but I can't think why.'

'You've seen him, sir.'

'I know, but I don't think it's that.'

'Well, he's pretty ordinary, sir. I didn't remember him, and I interviewed him.'

When the sergeant had left, Stratton looked again in the drawer and, at the bottom of a mound of papers, found what he was looking for. Painfully aware that his motives in taking this course of action were decidedly mixed, he hesitated for a few minutes—the length of a cigarette—before picking up the telephone.

'TATE GALLERY 2346, please.'

'Yes, sir.'

After a moment, Stratton heard the number repeated by a clipped, aristocratic female voice.

'I wish to speak to Colonel Forbes-James, please. It's Detective Inspector Stratton, West End Central CID.'

CHAPTER

50

'I'm sure he thinks I took it.' Fay sat hunched over the corner table in the Regent's Park pub, chewing her bottom lip. Her teeth, Dacre noticed, were white and even.

Looking into her worried brown eyes, he said, 'It was an accident. I told him that. There's no reason for him to suspect you of anything.'

By dint of a bit of judicious hanging about outside the Men's Surgical Ward—where he'd been disconcerted to find the floor-boards being taken up—he'd managed to see Fay on her own and arrange a meeting for the same evening.

'I was sure he'd just find the stuff,' said Fay. 'I thought it would be there. I was almost certain that I pointed out the right place—where we collided, I mean.'

'I told him it was an accident, Fay.'

'I'm sorry he bothered you,' said Fay, miserably. 'He asked me who I'd bumped into, and I had to tell him.'

It clearly hadn't occurred to her that *he* might have pocketed the phials. All she feared was that she might be at fault, or blamed. Silently blessing both her and his own good judgement—she had not once reproached him for the incident at the Clarendon—he said, 'You didn't bump into me, I bumped into you. And you were quite right to say.'

'It was chaos all day,' said Fay, 'with those floorboards up. Sister Bateman was beside herself.'

'Has she been giving you a rough time?'

'She blames me.'

'Would you like me to have a word with her?'

'Oh, no! It's very kind of you, but it would just make things worse. She'd think I'd been...you know...running to you for sympathy. It's bad enough already with all the other nurses talking behind my back. I don't suppose they mean to be nasty— well, not all of them—but it's so hard to concentrate on what I'm supposed to be doing...' She blinked a few times, and stared hard at the grimy surface of the table.

'Fay...' Dacre hadn't expected this. When he'd pocketed the morphine, he never meant that she should be suspected of the theft and, now that she was, he was taken aback by the intensity of his feelings: long-buried guilt rising up inside him, as if a shipwreck was surfacing in all its terrible devastation. For a moment, it seemed overwhelming and he knew that it wasn't only about Fay, but about his father, his mother...everything he'd ever done.

He groaned, and Fay looked at him in surprise. 'I'm sorry,' she said, 'I didn't mean to burden you with all this.'

'Heavens...' Forcing a smile, Dacre made a supreme effort and suppressed the rising tide of his emotions. Such things must not be allowed to interfere, not now, not *ever*. 'I'm very glad you have. Who better? Remember what we said about being honest with each other? Besides, you're having a horrible time, and it's entirely my fault. It was just a sudden twinge...my head.' He fingered his bruised temple. 'I meant to take an aspirin before I came out.'

'I think I might have some.' Fay rooted in her bag. 'You were going to tell me what happened to your face...Here.' She produced a small bottle and shook two tablets into her palm.

'What a good nurse you are.' Dacre knocked them back with the last of his drink. 'Well...' He told the story of the half-witted pregnant girl and her mother, imitating all the voices and adding a few touches of his own. By the time he'd finished, she was laughing so much that she had to wipe her eyes.

'Oh dear...How extraordinary that the woman hadn't realised— even if the daughter didn't know what was up, you'd think...'

'I know. The woman never imagined that her daughter might be pregnant, because she wasn't the full ticket. Somehow, people never seem to imagine that the mentally defective have any sort of sex urge.'

'Perhaps she didn't. Perhaps someone took advantage of her.' Fay looked upset. 'If that's true, it's a vile thing to do.'

'Yes,' said Dacre soberly, 'it is. Particularly as a girl like that wouldn't know the difference between right and wrong. Not that I can pronounce on that,' he added, hastily. 'People in glass houses, and so on.'

'Oh, that doesn't matter,' said Fay, dismissively. 'It's not the same at all. But...' Suddenly, she was looking distinctly uncomfortable. 'The mother should have looked after her better. Kept an eye on her. With so many soldiers about.'

'I think that was why she was so angry. With herself, I mean. Except that she didn't know she was, and she seemed the sort who'd always tend to blame someone else. It was just unfortunate that I happened to be the bearer of the bad news. Anyway...' Seeing that Fay's cheeks were flushed, Dacre decided to change the subject. 'How about another drink? If we're going to become regulars, I ought to butter up the barmaid, don't you think?'

Fay, who had her back to the bar, turned to glance at the bony, lank-haired female of indeterminate age who was, at that moment, listlessly polishing a glass with a grubby-looking cloth. Turning back, she gave Dacre a doubtful look.

'I shall compliment her,' said Dacre.

'On...?'

'That's something of a poser,' he admitted. 'I know—I'll pretend she's you. Then it'll be easy.'

Satisfied that Fay's flush was now one of pleasure, Dacre got up and took their glasses to the bar, returning a few minutes later with more drinks.

'Heavens,' said Fay. 'What did you say to her?'

'That's my secret. You'll have to wait and see. Cheers!' They clinked glasses and Dacre made Fay laugh again by telling her about the old man who'd come to Casualty that afternoon with a bandaged hand and his wife carrying the severed top of his fore-finger in a jar of vinegar. 'Completely pickled. She'd preserved it, thinking we'd be able to sew it back on. They were so disap-pointed. After we'd fixed him up, she said she wanted to take it home with her. I expect it's in the middle of the mantelpiece right now, under the King.'

'Oh, dear...' Fay held his gaze for a moment, bright-eyed and cheerful, and then her smile wavered and her face turned serious.

'What is it?'

'The thing is...' Fay hesitated.

'Would a cigarette help?'

She nodded, and watched intently as Dacre took two from the packet, lit them, and passed one over to her.

'What I said about the other nurses talking behind my back—it's more than just the morphine. When Dr Reynolds was...when he died...you weren't here then, but the police inter-viewed everyone, asking them if they'd seen him and where they'd been...I'm sure you know the sort of thing.'

'I've seen it in films.' Dacre smiled, and added, 'Oh, so you won't talk, huh?' in an approximation of an American accent.

Fay gave him a faint smile in return. 'Well, something like that. I don't particularly want to tell you this, because it doesn't reflect very well on me, but I do want to be honest, so...'

Dacre opened his mouth to speak, but Fay held up a hand. 'Please. Let me try...When Inspector Stratton asked me about the morphine, it was the third time he'd talked to me. He asked me to go back, you see, because...Well, because I was friendly with Dr Reynolds.' Fay stopped to see how Dacre was taking this. 'James? You look...'

Dacre felt as if he'd been hit. He swallowed. '*Friendly* with him?'

Fay flushed and looked down at her lap. 'Yes.'

'Well,' Dacre stared at her, hardly aware of what he was saying, 'I suppose it's not surprising he took a fancy to you.'

'Yes, but not right. He was married. I mean, *properly*.'

It flashed through Dacre's mind that that explained Fay's distressed look when he'd talked about knowing the difference between right and wrong. 'We all make mistakes, Fay,' he said, automatically. 'I made one when I got married, and I made one last time I saw you. Nobody's perfect. And a beautiful girl like you is bound to have more temptations put in her way than most.'

'You're being very kind, but...' Pink-eyed now, Fay fumbled in her bag for a handkerchief, then said, 'Excuse me,' and left the table.

Alone and with a chance to think, Dacre found himself wanting to laugh. How ironic! Reynolds's job *and* his girl! That really was stepping into a dead man's shoes. He took another pull on his pint, then almost choked: If Reynolds had *had* Fay... The idea of it nauseated him. How could he find out? He could hardly ask her directly. It was better not to know. He'd put it out of his mind. He needed her to be fresh, as if she'd just stepped out of a box. His, and only his, and that was how she must remain. Anyway, Reynolds was dead, past, and did not matter because he was no longer a threat. However, if she confessed intimacy to him and was contrite, that would be no bad thing for the future—the moral high ground was harder to assail, and had a better view. Yes, Dacre thought, that was it: if that were the case, he would be magnanimous, and she would love him all the more for it. But he wouldn't press her for information: he must establish himself in her mind as an understanding person, not a bully.

But supposing Inspector Stratton knew about it? The idea nearly made him choke again. That, potentially, could complicate things a great deal. Still, forewarned was forearmed. He'd have to find out.

'All right now?' he asked, as Fay, looking more composed, returned to the table.

'Yes. I'm sorry.'

'No need to be.'

'I hope you don't think...'

'...the worse of you?' Dacre shook his head.

'Because honestly, you couldn't think worse of me than I do of myself. Having temptation put in your way is no excuse.'

'You mustn't think like that. It wasn't your fault, Fay; Reynolds should have known better. That said, I doubt our friend the inspector would see it like that. You haven't told him, have you?'

'I had to,' said Fay, miserably. 'I wouldn't have, but one of the other nurses noticed there was...well, something going on, and she told him about it. Then Dr Reynolds's wife—I mean, his widow— she found a note from me in one of his pockets. He must have forgotten to throw it away...I felt so terrible about her knowing. I mean, it's bad enough that he died, without *that* happening.'

'How serious was it? Your friendship?'

'Well, it was...quite. But we hadn't talked about him leaving her or anything like that.'

'Did you want him to?'

'No! It was just having dinner, and drinks, and...you know the sort of thing. I liked the attention, but...Oh, it sounds terrible. There isn't any way to excuse it. When he died, well, I'd broken it off by then, but I was very upset, and having to pretend I barely knew him...And Maddox—that's the one who noticed the two of us together, she must have mentioned it to some of the others, and I'm terrified that Sister Bateman'll find out, and what with that and the morphine, I'll probably lose my job.'

Dacre put his hand over hers. 'Fay, they're looking for the morphine because of Dr Byrne, not Dr Reynolds. And I'm quite sure the inspector doesn't think you had anything to do with either of their deaths, despite him knowing about your...friendship with Reynolds. I didn't meant to alarm you, I just mean that policemen are paid to have suspicious minds.'

'I met him in the mortuary corridor,' said Fay, miserably. 'The night before they found Dr Byrne.'

'But—' Dacre was so taken aback by this he almost said, 'But I didn't hear you,' and hastily changed it to, 'But what was he doing there?'

'He said he had an appointment, so he must have been going to the mortuary. I mean, there wasn't anywhere else he *could* have been going, except to the operating theatres. He asked me where I was going, and I told him—back to the nurses' quarters. I'd just delivered something downstairs for Mr Hambling, you see, so I had to go that way. But he asked me about it again yesterday, and I don't think he believes me.'

Dacre was thinking about the fact that Fay must have walked straight past the office just as he was pushing Byrne down onto his back—which must have been why he'd missed her footsteps, which, not being made by high heels, wouldn't have made a telltale click-clack noise. 'Did you hear anything? From Dr Byrne's office, I mean.'

Fay shook her head. 'Inspector Stratton asked me that. Not a thing.'

Reassured, Dacre squeezed Fay's hand and said, 'I'm sure he does believe you, you know. He'd have to be mad to think you could hurt anyone.'

'How can you say that? You hardly know me.'

'I know you well enough to know that.'

'Look,' said Fay, awkwardly, withdrawing her hand from his, 'I'm sorry I burdened you with all this. None of it is your problem, and—'

'Don't, Fay, please. It may not be my problem, but I care about you. I know we've only met a couple of times, so we can't be said to know each other *well*, but that isn't how it feels. And I think you must feel the same way, or you wouldn't have told me all this, would you?'

'No. It's quite a relief to tell someone, to be honest. Someone who's not suspicious of me, I mean.' The ghost of a grin flitted across Fay's face.

'That's better. I'm sure none of this is as bad as you think.'

The smile faded. 'I don't know...It's so horrible, being suspected, and...'

'And...?' prompted Dacre, sensing that there was something else.

'Oh...' Fay's eyes suddenly had a look of opacity, as if shuttered, and Dacre wondered what she'd been about to say. 'It's nothing,' she continued. 'I'm probably being silly. It makes you feel guilty, somehow, having all these policemen around.'

'I know what you mean,' said Dacre, with feeling. 'You feel like confessing everything you've ever done wrong, stealing pennies from your grandmother's purse, or pinching your kid sister's toy monkey…'

'Have you got a kid sister?'

'No, actually, I haven't. Or a grandmother.'

'I have. She's in the ATS. My sister, I mean, not my grandmother. Though I'm sure she'd like to be.' Fay chuckled.

'Game, is she?'

'Oh, yes. She organises sales of work for the Red Cross. She's made lots of money—people don't dare refuse.'

'Come on,' said Dacre, 'drink up and I'll walk you back. Don't want you to get into any more trouble for sneaking in late, do we?'

'Heavens, no,' said Fay, ruefully. 'That really would be a disaster.'

The walk back to the Middlesex was pleasant—a few distant bangs, but nothing to alarm them as, arm in arm, they followed the pinpoint light of Dacre's torch down the pavements. They stopped outside the basement entry and stood facing each other.

'May I kiss you?' asked Dacre. 'I promise I won't do anything more than put my arms round you.'

Fay hesitated.

'Please believe me, Fay,' said Dacre. 'We haven't known each other long, but I care about you too much to jeopardise our friendship.'

Fay put her hands on Dacre's shoulders and her face up to his, and let him kiss her on the mouth. Her lips were soft and slightly scented, and afterwards she stood quite still, not speaking. Her breath on his neck reminded him, for a fleeting moment, of the feel of Dr Byrne's breath on his hand, and he drew back, repulsed.

'What is it?' she murmured.

'Thought I heard someone.'

Fay listened for a moment, then said, 'I can't hear anything, but I'd better go in, just in case.'

'Will the bathroom window be open?'

'Oh, yes. We always leave it ajar.'

'Good.' Dacre kissed her again, this time on the cheek, and said, 'Goodnight, Fay. Thank you for a lovely evening—and for confiding in me. Tomorrow will be a better day, I promise.'

'You can't promise that,' whispered Fay. 'You can only hope. Goodnight, James.' She turned away, into the darkness.

Dacre walked slowly towards the Euston Road, where he decided he was tired enough to treat himself to a bus ride home. He sat in the gloom of the blacked-out vehicle, remembering Fay's mouth on his. Stupid to think of Byrne and spoil it, when she was so lovely...Had he somehow known—deep in his unconscious—when he'd singled Fay out, that she was compromised by Reynolds? Had he picked up some signal from her that he wasn't aware of? She said she'd broken it off before he died...perhaps that was because he was putting pressure on her to go to bed with him. That would make sense—look how she'd reacted to him in the Clarendon. Just as well Reynolds was dead, then. He wondered where she'd been on *that* night. The fact that she'd been so close, right in the mortuary corridor while he killed Byrne, was horrible. Surely the inspector couldn't really suspect her?

She was innocent. She was Fay. And she made him feel real: a real person. Sometimes, 'Dr Dacre' seemed to him like a garment he was wearing, and at other times—as in Fay's company tonight—Dacre became inseparable from himself, as if they had merged into a single entity. But now, here, Dacre seemed to alienate him from his real self, which seemed more pitiful and unworthy than ever. He hadn't killed in the person of Dacre, had he? He'd killed so that he could go on being Dacre... And Fay's feelings were for Dacre, not for him. And, if necessary, he'd kill again, to protect them both...No, to protect *all three.*

Feeling a tap on his shoulder, he almost jumped out of his seat, but it was only the clippie—who, both in looks and demeanour, could have been twin to the sour Regent's Park barmaid—asking for his fare.

CHAPTER
51

Colonel Forbes-James did not work at MI5's headquarters, but ran his division, B5(b), from a flat in Dolphin Square, down the Thames from the Houses of Parliament. The following morning, Stratton went straight there, and, after crossing what was left of the garden, climbed the stairs, and was welcomed inside by a slender blonde telephonist. A different girl, he thought, from the one who'd been there four years before, but so similar in her haughty, glacial beauty that he could not be entirely certain. Forbes-James must have access to a job lot, he thought, sitting down to wait as bidden on a flimsy-looking gilt chair.

He eyed the girl, surreptitiously, as she went to the little kitchen to fetch him a cup of tea. Her hair, upright carriage, the long, elegant legs in silk stockings and the merest whiff of expensive scent brought a painfully clear memory of Diana Calthrop, the beautiful agent with whom he'd worked in 1940. For a moment, he was tempted to stop the girl and ask Diana's whereabouts, but decided that such a question might seem strange or even impertinent.

He closed his eyes for a moment, willing Diana to appear. Hearing the office door open, he opened them, hoping against hope…But it was Forbes-James who stood in the doorway.

'Stratton—come in.'

The man before him was as dapper as Stratton remembered, and, except for the fact that his dark hair was beginning to grey at the temples, little changed. The round eyes, though still bright, looked wary. Standing back to allow him to pass, Forbes-James said, 'You mentioned a missing person...'

'That's right, sir. I'm very grateful to you for seeing me at such short notice.'

'Not at all. Do sit down—if you can find anywhere, that is.'

Forbes-James's office was as chaotic as ever, with piles of paper stacked precariously on every surface, including the sofa. But —Stratton's eyes slid, involuntarily, towards the place where the painting of the naked boy bather had hung—there was one change: it had been replaced by something that, to him at least, looked like an innocuous country landscape, dotted with some rather oddly shaped cows. It wasn't quite as large as the painting it had succeeded, and you could still see where the other picture had hung because the wallpaper was a different shade. Stratton saw Forbes-James's eyes flick towards him, noting the direction of his gaze, before he bent over his desk and began sifting through the heaps of documents.

'They never tidy up,' he grumbled. 'I should just move those...' he indicated some cardboard folders on the armchair, 'onto the floor and take a seat.'

Stratton did so, and there was a short pause while the telephonist brought in the tea tray and provided Forbes-James, who was, in a fashion Stratton found immediately familiar, ineffectually patting his pockets and peering under things on the desk, with a light for his cigarette.

'Help yourself,' said Forbes-James. 'There's a box on the mantelpiece.'

'Thank you, sir.' Stratton rose and negotiated his way across the cluttered room to get a cigarette.

The girl having distributed the tea and left, Forbes-James said, 'The man you mentioned on the telephone—what have you got?'

Producing his notebook to refresh his memory, Stratton explained the situation, then, taking a deep breath, said, in the most neutral tone he could manage, 'Also, we did wonder, sir, if there might not have been some sort of…attachment between Dr Byrne and Todd. It would explain the presence of the photograph hidden in his home, sir.'

Forbes-James stared at him for a moment, his mouth tightening almost imperceptibly. 'Yes,' he said, blandly, 'I suppose it would. But then again, it might be evidence of something entirely different.'

'Of course, sir. It was only a theory.'

Forbes-James, said, 'I see.' The two men gazed at each other intently for what could only have been a few seconds but felt, to Stratton at least, like quite a lot longer. He wasn't sure if he should say something, or wait for Forbes-James to speak, and hoped that his silence would not be construed as either offensiveness, or—worse—some sort of implied threat. Before he could come to a conclusion about any of this, much less act on it, Forbes-James said, 'Anything else?'

'Only these.' Stratton produced two of the mortuary photographs from his pocket and handed them over.

'Hmmm…Not very clear, are they? Could be anybody.'

'That's the trouble, sir.'

'Yes…Does your superior officer know about this visit, Stratton?'

'No, sir.' Stratton permitted his eyes to stray over to the left, in the direction of the landscape painting that had replaced the nude boy.

The silence that followed was even more uncomfortable than the previous one. Stratton, feeling Forbes-James's eyes boring into him like gimlets, was on the point of saying that he knew it was a long shot and he was sorry to waste the colonel's time, when Forbes-James said, 'And you want my help, do you?'

'I would appreciate it, sir, yes. Government departments— as I'm sure you know, sir—can be reluctant to give information, especially in circumstances like this, where a false name seems to have been used.'

'And not necessarily the name Todd. You've checked his last known address, have you?'

'Yes, sir. He told his landlady he'd got a job in the north somewhere. She was under the impression that he was medically exempt from the forces.'

'Was she, indeed? Clearly didn't trouble to get his story straight...I can see that it might be rather delicate for you to get the information—no smoke without fire, and so on. You don't suspect anything of that sort, do you?'

'Subversion? No, sir. I can't imagine he'd have got himself a job in a hospital mortuary if that were the case—it's hardly the place for that sort of thing.'

Forbes-James put his head on one side and regarded Stratton for just long enough for him to start feeling twitchy again. 'That rather depends,' he said, 'although I grant you that it does seem unlikely. I am,' he added, 'prepared to help you—although it sounds as though it won't be easy.'

'Thank you, sir.'

'If you discover anything else, you'll let me know immediately. And—at least for the moment—I shall regard it as a matter for this department only. I'll have some discreet enquiries made, show these,' he tapped the photographs, 'around the place. You'd better telephone me in a week's time.'

'Yes, sir. Thank you.'

'Very well.' Forbes-James's gaze lingered on Stratton for a moment, before he turned his head away, as if in dismissal.

Stratton rose. 'I'm very grateful to you, sir.'

'I'd save your gratitude, if I were you. We've not come up with anything yet.'

'No, sir. But thank you.' Stratton knew that it was time to leave, but, for a wild moment, his desire to ask after Diana proving stronger than his common sense, he remained where he was.

'Yes?' said Forbes-James, with a touch of asperity.

'Well, sir...I hope you don't mind my asking, but how is Mrs Calthrop?'

Forbes-James's smile, which did not reach his eyes, had a masklike quality that was somehow far more of a warning than the menacing bonhomie exhibited by any gangster, and served to remind Stratton that, whatever the man did, his manners would remain impeccable. 'You were rather taken by her, weren't you?'

'Well, sir, I did wonder—I mean, it must have been a dreadful shock, finding that body.'

'I'm sure it was. But—to the best of my knowledge, at least—she is very well.'

'She's not here, then?' As he spoke, Stratton realised quite how much he had wanted to see Diana, and hoped his disappointment did not show on his face.

Forbes-James shook his head. 'In Hampshire. Living with her mother-in-law. I believe,' he added, in careful tones, 'that she is starting a family.'

'That's splendid, sir,' said Stratton, aware, as he said it, that the words were too loud, too hearty.

As he clattered down the stairs, Stratton reflected that he'd just put himself, irrevocably, into Forbes-James's debt. He'd just have to hope it was worth it. He cursed himself for asking about Diana, but she'd seemed so close there, in Forbes-James's office, almost a tangible presence...

And now she was in Hampshire, having a baby. He couldn't imagine Diana pregnant, it seemed too...too what, Stratton wasn't sure, but the idea of it made him uncomfortable, somehow. He wanted to remember her as she was. Not that there was anything wrong with being pregnant, of course, as long as she was pleased about it. Stratton wondered if the father was her husband, or Claude Ventriss who—four years ago, at least—had been her lover. None of your business, pal, he told himself. Head down against the spiteful wind that gusted across the river, he began trudging down Grosvenor Road towards Westminster.

What a mess...Todd, Byrne, Reynolds, Nurse Leadbetter, Fay, and thoughts of Diana obscuring any clarity of mind he might hope to achieve...The whole thing was tangled up in his head like a...the idea of something tangled brought back Dr Dacre's description of torsion of the testicle so suddenly and powerfully that Stratton felt sick. Deciding that he needed somewhere out of the wind to sit down and straighten himself out, he veered down a side street and found a small, sheltered square with a couple of benches facing a battered equestrian statue.

As he lit a cigarette, it crossed his mind that he might write to Diana. It would be easy enough to discover her address—just go into a library and look it up in one of those directories of posh people, Burke's or Debrett's or whatever it was. But what would he say? *I've been thinking about you and I hope you are well...* What a stupid idea! She probably doesn't even remember me, he thought.

He forced his thoughts back to his conversation with Colonel Forbes-James, and he wondered if he—or his department—would be able to turn up anything on Todd. He supposed he ought to feel sorry for Forbes-James, having to go through life trying not to be found out. Eyeing a pretty, slender girl who was sashaying across the other side of the square, Stratton tried to picture himself looking at a man in the same way, but failed. So difficult to imagine things which were entirely outside your experience, especially when they were of an emotional nature.

Sometimes, Stratton thought, it was as if the world around him had turned into a place that—though much like the one he was used to, at least in terms of general appearance—had a different sort of logic from normal, or no logic at all. If only his intuition would point him in a particular direction, instead of just giving him a feeling that things were askew...

He looked again at the pretty girl—back view, now, and very nice, too. She reached the edge of the pavement, and was about to cross the road when, apparently sensing his gaze, she turned and gave him a modest smile that reminded him of Fay. Pregnancy, he thought. What about pregnancy? He smiled back at the girl, then pulled his notebook out of his pocket and thumbed through the pages until he came to the notes he'd made during their second interview. She said she'd written the note—in the belief that she was pregnant—'quite soon after Easter'. Stratton read the words *FM had 2 days' leave at or near Easter, went to see parents nr Cheltenham*. He had just assumed that this was the truth, and never checked. He ought to, and the sooner the better.

He flicked his cigarette end onto the ground, trod on it, and, sighing heavily, got to his feet and marched off to catch a number 24 bus to Tottenham Court Road. From there, it was a short walk to the hospital.

52

Twelve days late, and she still hadn't got round to making a doctor's appointment. He'd only tell her to wait it out, anyway. She'd had morning sickness with both Monica and Pete, but she couldn't remember when she'd started to feel it. There had been a definite point when she'd felt different—pregnant—but when?

Jenny stared at the pile of socks at her feet, then glanced over at Elsie Ingram, who appeared to be dozing on the sofa. She picked up another pair and sat back in her chair. She was darning over darns, now, so that no matter how careful she was the socks always ended up with lumpy bits on the toes and heels. Ted had always been tough on socks—it was worse when they were first married and he'd been on the beat, but at least then it had been easier to buy new ones. As long as she could make the wool last out...

At least you could listen to the wireless while you were darning. It was music now—jazzy stuff. The kind of thing Ted liked better than she did, but it was company of a sort. She hadn't got it very loud, but all the same, she thought, if Mrs Ingram can sleep through this, then I'm a Dutchman. She glanced again at her guest and thought she saw an eyelid flicker. It was horrible, being watched, surreptitiously, all the time. Made you feel like you were being spied on in your own home. I'm sure she's trying to guess what's in my mind, Jenny thought, she's reaching out invisible feelers like some sort of insect. And Doris had put up with it for over a month! Jenny didn't feel as if she could manage another *day*. She felt guilty about being irritated with the poor woman, but honestly, it was enough to drive you round the twist. The letters to Mr Ingram, sent care of the army—three, so far—had got them nowhere at all. Ted had told them not to bother—said they wouldn't give them to him if he was being punished for deserting.

Having her here meant it was impossible to talk to Ted properly. It was worse than when the children were small—at least she'd known what to do when they started crying. Mrs Ingram, with her slow, hopeless, *endless* tears was a different thing altogether. Not to mention the fact that Ted had arrived home late last night smelling strongly of beer, made a great racket in the hall and argued with her when she'd tried to shush him. She'd been surprised—and not a little upset—by how belligerent he was. Being tipsy usually made him happy, then sleepy, not angry.

She sighed, and looked again at Mrs Ingram, whose head was now slightly angled towards her. She was convinced that the moment she looked down at the sock in her hand, the wretched woman would open her eyes and stare at her. Honestly, you couldn't call your thoughts your own...

She supposed it was her fault for agreeing to have her here in the first place, but what was she supposed to do? Other than talk to Dr Makepeace about the you-know-where...As far as that was concerned, Jenny could feel her resolve weakening already, Auntie Ivy or no Auntie Ivy.

She'd go round and have a word with Doris about speaking to Dr Makepeace. She felt bad about it but Mrs Ingram seemed to be getting worse, not better, and if she pulled a stunt like that gas business here and Ted found out about it, it would have to be reported. She'd go round there later on—there'd be plenty of time to get the dinner when she got back.

She selected another sock and resumed her darning. Dr Makepeace, having confessed surprise that Mrs Ingram wasn't 'pulling out of it' on several occasions, had started talking about 'persecution mania' and how the workings of the mind were not fully understood. Adjusting the heel on the smooth wooden surface of the mushroom, Jenny thought that 'persecution mania' wasn't a very good name for Mrs Ingram's problem—really, if people who'd had their homes destroyed on top of them *weren't* entitled to feel persecuted, then who was?

The term wasn't in her 'Home Doctor' book, although Insanity and Mental Disease were. She'd spent an unhappy half an hour reading about how women could be affected by what they called the 'crises of life'—puberty, the change, and pregnancy. Mrs Ingram was too old for the first, two young for the second, and, her husband having been away for months, unlikely to be experiencing the third. There was stuff about syphilis, and drinking too much, and tumours, and physical exhaustion, but 'brain injury' was the only one likely to be applicable, and if that had happened, surely they wouldn't have let her out of hospital? The thing that made most sense was a cross-reference to Monomania. *The patient's whole interest is centred around one delusion or false belief...*Nothing about how to cure it, though, and—

'Ouch!'

Jenny dropped the darning onto her lap. A red bubble of blood had appeared on the pad of her left forefinger where the needle had slipped. She stared at it for a second, and then, deciding that a plaster was unnecessary, sucked it instead. Like Sleeping Beauty, she thought. Right now, falling asleep for 100 years seemed quite a nice idea, if only Ted would wake her with a cup of tea at the end of it. Jenny took her finger out of her mouth, examined it, then resumed sucking. She'd have to get a plaster after all. Time to stop, she thought. Then she'd have plenty of time to give the hens their mash and have a bit of a chat with Doris before she went to do her stint at the Rest Centre, and still be back in time to do Ted's supper—if she was lucky.

She stood up and began gathering all the unmended socks into her sewing basket. 'I'm going out for a while, Mrs Ingram,' she said, brightly. 'You'll be all right, won't you?'

Mrs Ingram, eyes open now, gazed at her fearfully. '*He's* not coming, is he?'

'No, dear. He's far away now, he can't hurt you. You'll be quite safe, I promise. Now,' Jenny looked at her pointedly, 'you won't do anything *silly*, will you? I want you to promise me.'

'Oh, no,' said Mrs Ingram, slowly. 'Nothing *silly*.'

CHAPTER

53

*S*tratton found Savage, the old porter, nailing down the last of the boards in the corridor outside the Men's Surgical Ward, aided by a slack-jawed, pimply dullard of about sixteen who was wielding his hammer with unnecessary violence.

''Ad the whole lot up, both sides,' Savage said. 'Sweet FA. You don't want us to pull up no more, do you? Only I got things to attend to. You can have *him* if you want him,' he added, jerking his thumb at the youth, who had now stood up, hands in his pockets, and was occupied in kicking the radiator.

'I'm sure we can manage by ourselves,' said Stratton. 'Where are my men?'

'In the wards. One in there,' he indicated Men's Surgical. 'One's in Lister, and the woman's downstairs in Sophie Jex-Blake.'

'Right,' said Stratton. 'Thank you very much.'

Stratton went downstairs to Matron Hornbeck's office, where he was assured that all the rest of the morphine in the place was accounted for. 'I hope your people will conclude their search as soon as possible,' she added. 'All this poking about is very unsettling for the patients. And as for the racket upstairs...I hope you have found the missing drugs.'

'I'm afraid not,' said Stratton. The matron's eyebrows rose above her horn-rimmed glasses. 'I'm sure there's an explanation,' he added.

The eyebrows rose another half inch. 'I'm sure there is, Inspector. The question is: what is it?'

He found first Watkins, who, on the pretext of examining a stack of bed pans, was chatting animatedly with a couple of the prettier nurses and then Piper, who was prodding listlessly through a pile of sheets in one of the linen cupboards. Harris he fetched from Sophie Jex-Blake, where she was examining the bedside cabinet of a dropsical woman in a tartan bed-jacket. None of them had found anything suspicious. Stratton, having ascertained the extent of the search so far, told them to continue, and went to the Men's Surgical Ward to speak to Fay Marchant. He'd decided not to mention this to the matron, at least for the moment—Sister Bateman would undoubtedly mention it, and, given the nature of the conversation they were about to have, he didn't want to get Fay into further trouble if it could be avoided. Nevertheless, the fact remained that, if the morphine wasn't under the floorboards, then either Fay or Dr Dacre must have taken it. Unless, of course, someone entirely different had chanced upon it beneath a radiator or something, and pocketed it…And that would mean re-interviewing every single person in the bloody place, as well as any mobile patients— *Christ*.

Sister Bateman, frowning, sent one of the probationers to fetch Fay from the kitchen. On seeing Stratton, she paled and looked fearful in a way that he thought was something more than the normal discomfort and obscure guilt that people—however innocent—tended to feel in the presence of a policeman.

'Let's go for a walk, shall we?' he said.

Fay looked at Sister Bateman, who nodded grimly. 'Cuffs, Marchant.'

'Yes, Sister.'

Fay having gone to put on her cuffs, Sister Bateman said to Stratton, 'This is the fourth time, Inspector. Perhaps you'd care to tell me what Marchant is supposed to have done?'

'She hasn't done anything, Sister. I just need to ask a few more questions about the matter of the…accident, when the morphine was lost.'

'You mean you still haven't found it?'

'I'm afraid not.'

'But surely you can't think that she took it, Inspector?'

Stratton was saved from having to answer this by the reappearance of Fay, now clad in a dark blue cloak. They left the ward, and went down to the hospital garden. 'Would you prefer to walk, or sit?' Stratton indicated a wooden bench.

Fay looked startled. 'I don't mind.'

'Let's walk, then. You've got a very impressive vegetable garden here. Puts my allotment to shame. Smoke?'

'Thank you.' Fay took a cigarette from the proffered packet, and gave Stratton a weak smile. There was a tautness to her movements, as if she were poised to flee at any moment. As he drew closer to her to give her a light, he noticed that her hands were trembling slightly.

'We haven't found the morphine,' he said.

'But it must be there.' Fay's voice was a wail, and her face had a look of uncomprehending panic.

'Must it?'

'I didn't take it, Inspector. You have to believe me.'

'Someone did,' said Stratton. 'And why should I believe you? You haven't been entirely straight with me about other things.' He was whistling in the dark, but she—clearly—did not know that.

'What do you mean?'

'Your relationship with Dr Reynolds.'

'But I *told* you.' The lovely brown eyes were pleading.

'Everything?' asked Stratton. 'I don't think you did, you know.' Fay turned away from him and gazed miserably at the rows of brassicas. 'This is a very serious matter,' he added, gently. 'And I can't help you if you don't tell me the truth.'

Fay put her cigarette to her lips. She wasn't just trembling now, but actually shaking. Praying that he was aiming at the right target, Stratton said, 'You fell pregnant, didn't you?'

Fay's nod was almost imperceptible.

'What happened?'

'Duncan...' Fay whispered.

'Dr Reynolds?'

'Yes.' The next words were spoken in a flat, hard voice, through clenched teeth. 'He took care of it.'

Jesus, thought Stratton, repulsed. What sort of man could abort his own child? Even if he was a doctor and knew how it was done...Stratton was all too aware of the things people would do when they were pushed, hut the man could have got her into a nursing home, for God's sake, and told them it was for her health or something. This, Stratton knew, wasn't supposed to happen unless it was an exceptional case, but there were ways. He supposed Reynolds must have panicked, or wanted to save money, or...whatever it was, the man was a bastard. Keeping a determinedly neutral expression, he fished out his notebook. 'Was this in the hospital?' he asked.

Fay shook her head. 'Where we used to go, to be together... A flat belonging to a friend of his who's serving abroad. It's in Holborn. He took things...instruments...from here.'

That was even worse, thought Stratton. Squalid. Poor, poor Fay...'And then you went to stay with your parents?' he asked. 'At Easter?'

'Yes. I didn't want to—my father is a doctor, Inspector. I thought he might realise, but I couldn't come back here, and I couldn't stay at the flat on my own, in case something was wrong. So I thought, I mean...of course my father wouldn't approve, but if I was ill, at least he'd be able to...you know.'

'When Dr Reynolds performed this...operation, was anyone else there?'

'No.'

'Was anyone else involved in any way?'

'No.'

'Did anyone else know about it?'

'No.'

'Is that the truth?'

'Yes! I may have lied to you before, Inspector, but that is the truth, and I did *not* take that morphine.'

'Did Dr Dacre take it?'

Fay's eyes widened in shock. 'No! I'm sure he didn't, Inspector.'

'Sure because you were looking at him all the time and didn't see him do it, or sure because you've been getting to know him rather well and you don't think it's the sort of thing he would do?'

Fay flushed. 'He invited me out to have a drink with him, that was all.'

'So I gather. Have you seen him since?'

'Yes. Yesterday evening.'

'A mental *affinity*?' asked Stratton, feeling mean.

'If you like,' said Fay, stiffly.

'So, what's the answer to my earlier question?'

'Both.'

'But you were looking for the phials yourself, weren't you, so you couldn't have had your eye on him all the time.'

'That's right, but there was no reason for him to take them. If I knew what happened to them,' she added, in an agitated voice, 'I'd tell you. Honestly, I would. But I don't.'

'I see.' Stratton stood silent, staring at the vegetable plot, while Fay fidgeted beside him. After about a minute, she said, 'Are you going to arrest me?'

'No, I shall have to report what you've told me.' Thinking of Lamb, he added, 'I can't imagine, under the circumstances, that action will be taken, but you will need to come down to the station and make a formal statement. Tomorrow will do.' Looking her in the eyes, he added, 'If you're thinking about bolting, I'd advise against it.'

'I wasn't, Inspector.'

'Good. Now then.' Feeling it best to leave no stone unturned, Stratton put his hand inside his jacket and pulled out his remaining photograph of Todd in the mortuary. 'I want you to look at this. Do you recognize the people in this picture?'

'That's Dr Byrne,' Fay pointed.

'What about the other man?'

'It's not very good.' Fay peered at it. 'But it looks like...Well, there's something familiar about it, I'm sure there is. Does he work in the hospital? I suppose I must have seen him, but I don't know...' She tailed off, biting her lip. Stratton notice that two blotches of colour had appeared on her neck. 'I don't know the lady, either,' she added. 'Who is she?'

'That's Miss Lynn. She's Dr Byrne's secretary. Are you sure you can't remember this chap?' Stratton pointed at Todd's image. 'You started to say it looked like someone. Was it someone he reminded you of?'

'Not really. For a moment I thought perhaps I did know him, but...' She shook her head. 'He must have reminded me of one of the patients. We do have a lot of people coming and going, and I'm afraid I've never been terribly good about remembering faces.'

'Very well.' Stratton returned the photograph to his inside pocket. 'You'd better be getting back to your ward.'

'Yes...' Seeing that he made no move, Fay said, uncertainly, 'Aren't you coming?'

'No. I think I'll stay here for a while. Remember what I said about not going anywhere, Nurse Marchant.'

Stratton watched Fay walk across the garden at such a fast pace that he thought she was making a supreme effort to restrain herself from breaking into a run. When she'd disappeared from view, he pulled out his notebook and spent several minutes adding to what he'd already written and turning things over in his mind. There was the matter of Reynolds's death, which he'd not asked her about, but, more interesting—at least at the moment—was her reaction to the photograph. 'He looks like...' was what she'd said, then stopped. Had she been about to say a name? What she'd said about him reminding her of a patient was clearly untrue—it was obviously someone she knew. And she wasn't the only one who thought Todd looked familiar. He'd thought so himself, hadn't he—but *why*?

CHAPTER

54

Reaching a decision, Stratton went back inside and made for the Casualty Department, where he found Sister Radford talking to a woman whose hands and arms were covered in a splotchy red rash, raw and bloody from continual scratching.

'Bad case of scabies,' said Sister Radford, once they were out of earshot. 'Highly contagious. Don't get too close—I'll have to wash my hands.'

While he was waiting, Stratton extracted the photograph once more, and stood staring at it. Was it simply an association of ideas, like the one that was, at this very moment, making his skin feel appallingly itchy? Judging from Fay's behaviour when she'd looked at the picture closely, it was more than just that, although she did tend to colour easily—he'd noticed that before. But it didn't make any sense—and, in any case, as Ballard had remarked, the chap in the picture looked like a lot of people...

'Inspector.' Sister Radford was once more at his side. 'How can I help this time?'

Stratton, affecting not to notice the heavy emphasis on the last two words, gave her the photograph. 'Could you tell me who you recognise here?' he asked.

'Well, Dr Byrne, of course, and that's his secretary—I'm afraid I don't know her name. As for the other one...' Sister

Radford put her head on one side and pursed her lips in concentration. 'Hmmm...No. Sorry, Inspector.'

'Why did you hesitate?' asked Stratton.

Sister Radford looked surprised. 'I was thinking.'

'What were you thinking?'

'Well, I know it's silly, abut I just thought the man had a look of Dr Dacre. Without the moustache, and the hair's too light. It isn't him, of course—I told you it was silly.'

'Are you sure it's silly?'

Sister Radford looked at Stratton as if he'd got a touch of the sun. 'It's impossible. What would he be doing there? It was just a fanciful idea, Inspector, and now I look again, I can see that it's nothing like him. I'm sorry not to be more help, but surely the mortuary attendant can tell you who it is.'

'I wasn't able to find him,' said Stratton, 'so I thought I'd ask you.' It wasn't a very good lie, and Sister Radford received it with an old-fashioned look. 'Where is Dr Dacre?'

'Oh, he's here, but surely—what I said—I mean, it's ridiculous.'

'Don't worry, Sister. It's nothing to do with that.' Stratton sat down on a bench. 'I'll wait for him here, if you don't mind.'

He lit a cigarette, and, tilting his head back, closed his eyes. That, he was pretty sure, made two of them—Sister Radford and Fay Marchant. Not that Fay had said so, but it would certainly explain her behaviour and explain, too, the nagging feeling he'd had. But, as the sister had said, it was—if not impossible—then very unlikely. Stratton opened his eyes, took out the photograph again, and studied it, trying to remember exactly what Dr Dacre had looked like.

In any case, what would he be doing pretending to be a mortuary attendant? But then again, if Fay hadn't taken the morphine—and, on balance, Stratton thought she was probably telling the truth about that—Dacre might well have. But, testicular torsion aside (Stratton tried to ignore the way that his stomach, and everything below it, seemed to clench as if squeezed by a fist), he'd seemed...well, likeable. A bit of a charmer, in fact.

They could be the most dangerous of the lot. If Todd or Dacre or whoever he was had killed the nurse, he might be lining up Fay as his next victim…Byrne must have kept those photographs hidden under the blotter—and the one at home—for a reason… Was that what it was?

Wait, he told himself. Don't jump to conclusions. It was probably just coincidence—two men who looked alike.

Fay had been seeing Dacre before Byrne's death—Dacre had said so. If the pair of them knew each other better than they were admitting, perhaps they'd been in it together. But, taking the position that Leadbetter's death had nothing to do with either of them, where did Reynolds come into it? He'd aborted Fay's child—his own child. Perhaps, despite what she'd said, she'd hoped that he would leave his wife and marry her, but he'd refused. Maybe the experience had affected her mind. But what did any of that have to do with Byrne?

Try as he might, Stratton couldn't see how the pieces fitted together. Perhaps, he thought, they didn't: far more likely that the nurse was killed by a maniac who'd got away and Reynolds was killed by a stranger in the course of a botched robbery…Which left Byrne.

There was no point going round in circles. If he was going to make an arse of himself, Stratton thought, he might as well do it on the evidence of his own eyes, right now. He walked to the back of the room, checking behind screens, and spotted Dacre talking to a man with a bandaged head. He stood back so that he could not be seen, and, on the pretext of waiting until the consultation was finished, studied Dacre's face against the photograph. The hair was darker, but that was easily done, and there was no moustache, but he could see what the two women had spotted. If it had been just his impression, he'd have dismissed it immediately, but it wasn't just him…

The bandaged man shuffled off in the direction of the dispensary, and Stratton saw Dacre's face dull and seem to close down, as if some inner light bulb had been switched off. It was farfetched, what Stratton was thinking, but it wasn't impossible. He remembered something he'd once read about a doctor in Victorian times who'd been discovered, after death, to be a woman. And then there was that American bloke who'd pretended to be a Red Indian Chief and been in films and things...

Turning, Dacre saw him, and, sure enough, his face lit up. 'All finished,' he said. 'Did you want me?'

'I'm looking for one of my men, PC Watkins. Have you seen him?'

'Not in the last hour, I don't think. Found the dope yet? I heard you taking up that corridor.'

'No luck, I'm afraid. But, as you said, these old buildings...' Stratton grimaced and turned to leave, but Dacre laid a hand on his arm. 'Inspector, I know it's none of my business, but I'm sure that Nurse Marchant has nothing to do with this. It was an accident, pure and simple. Could happen to anyone.'

Stratton nodded. 'As you say.'

Dacre beamed at him. 'I know she's been worried about it, Inspector. She's a good nurse. Very conscientious.'

'I'm sure she is.' Stratton gave Dacre a knowing look. 'Well, I shan't detain you any further.'

On the way up to Professor Haycraft's office, Stratton paused to look at the photograph once more: there was a definite similarity. Not that it proved anything, but all the same...

He found Professor Haycraft's secretary, Miss Potter, in the outer office. 'Can I help you?'

'Inspector Stratton, CID.'

Ah, yes. Did you wish to speak to Professor Haycraft?'

Recalling the disengaged individual he'd met in the mortuary, Stratton said, 'Goodness, no. It's a minor matter. I'd like to take a look at the details for Dr Dacre.'

'The new man?' Miss Potter frowned. 'Is there a problem? Are you sure you wouldn't like to talk to the professor?'

'It's just something I need to check. I'd ask Dr Dacre himself, but they're very busy down there. Rushed off their feet, by the looks of it. I'd also like to see the details for Samuel Todd—he was a mortuary assistant here until the end of June.'

'Of course, Inspector. If you'd like to take a seat, I'll fetch them for you.'

Stratton copied down information about Dacre—*James Walter Dacre, 1938, University of St Andrews, Conferred. References: Professor R. F. McDermott, Dr L. K Synott. Address, 28 Eversholt St, N.W.* He paused, tapping the end of his pencil against his teeth, then turned to Todd's file, which gave his address as 14 Inkerman Road, Kentish Town. His last day at the Middlesex had been the twenty-third of June. If he'd been called up, thought Stratton, he wouldn't be in Kentish Town any longer, but it might be worth checking with the landlady again, just to be on the safe side.

Miss Potter, he thought, would be able to produce a copy of the Medical Register for him to look up Dacre's name, but he didn't want to put the cat amongst the pigeons at the hospital by appearing to doubt the credentials of its doctors. What he needed was a public library. The nearest one he could think of in the right direction was just off Leicester Square—if he walked fast, he'd just get there before it closed, and then he'd head back to the station and find out how Ballard was getting on with his enquiries.

Stratton took the large, leather-bound ledger from the library shelf and started leafing through it: *Curnow, Currie, Dacie, Dacombe, Dale*...But no Dacre. The certificates he'd seen had looked genuine enough. Stratton looked at the spine of the volume to make sure it wasn't out of date, then checked again. As he stared at the page, willing the words, *Dacre, James Walter,*

to appear, it dawned on him that he might have got things arse about face: what if Dacre, instead of being a doctor masquerading as a mortuary attendant, was a mortuary attendant pretending to be a doctor? Was that possible? Surely, anyone like that would be rumbled within a few minutes...wouldn't they? Of course, if there really had been a Dr Dacre, and he'd died, then that would explain why his certificates existed, but his name had been taken off the register, wouldn't it?

It would certainly explain why 'Dacre' was still working, and why Sam Todd didn't appear to exist. But, if the man now working in the Middlesex Casualty Department wasn't Dacre and he wasn't Todd, then who the bloody hell *was* he?

55

Stratton went back to the station, where he found Ballard leaving a note on his desk. 'What's that?'

'About the Mr Todd who emigrated to Australia, sir. He's still there.'

'Oh, well. I've got another job for you. Dr James Dacre. Here.' Stratton found the relevant page in his notebook and showed it to the sergeant. 'We need to find out about him. He graduated from university in 1938, which probably means he was born in 1912 or thereabouts. Medical degrees take a fair few years, don't they?'

'Yes, sir. May I ask why?'

'Yes, of course. I should have said. Dr Dacre seems to be as much of a mystery as our Mr Todd, who, incidentally, he rather resembles, so I think he's our best hope at this point. And he isn't in the Medical Register—I've checked. I suggest that you telephone the university first—find out if they had a student called Dacre who graduated in 1938. Might speed things up a bit.'

Ballard raised his eyebrows. 'I'll get cracking immediately.'

'Before you do, there's something else. Fay Marchant has admitted that Dr Reynolds did perform an abortion on her.'

'He killed his own child?' Ballard looked queasy. 'My God...What sort of person does that?'

'Beats me. But it does give rise to all sorts of possibilities.' Stratton stood up. 'I suppose I'd better go and say all this to DCI Lamb.'

'Best of luck, sir.'

'Thanks. I've a feeling I'm going to need it.'

'The thing is, sir, there's rather a…question mark, shall we say, over one of the doctors.'

'Oh?' Lamb frowned. 'Which one?'

'A chap called Dacre.'

'What's he got to do with it?'

'Well, sir…' Stratton gave Lamb a potted history of his findings, omitting any mention of Colonel Forbes-James. 'Sergeant Ballard's looking into it, sir.'

'Good. Perhaps you'll make some progress at last. Not very good for the hospital, though. I hope you're being discreet.'

'Of course, sir.'

'What about this nurse you mentioned…Merchant, was it?'

'Marchant, sir. Fay Marchant.' Might as well take the plunge, thought Stratton—he'll have to know sometime. 'You might recall, sir, that I mentioned the possibility of Dr Reynolds having performed an illegal operation.'

'I haven't forgotten,' said Lamb, 'but *you* might recall that I told you to keep off that sort of thing.'

'Yes, sir, but the problem is that it appears Dr Reynolds did perform such an operation, on Nurse Marchant.'

'Promiscuous type, is she?'

Bloody typical, thought Stratton. 'I wouldn't say so, sir. But she had been…involved with Dr Reynolds.'

'For God's sake!' Lamb's face contorted in disgust. 'Are you telling me it was *his* child?'

'I'm afraid so, sir.'

'Are you *absolutely* sure about this, Stratton? It sounds… Well, frankly, it sounds depraved.'

'Yes, sir. But it appears to be the case.'

'Do you think it has a bearing on Reynolds's death?'

'It might if someone found out about the operation and blackmailed him, sir.'

'It obviously hasn't occurred to you,' said Lamb, acidly, 'that blackmailers tend not to kill the people who are providing their bread and butter.'

'No, sir, but if they'd met on the bomb-site, late at night, for Reynolds to hand over money, there might have been a disagreement which led to a fight.'

'That's possible, I suppose. Who told you about the operation?'

'Nurse Marchant, sir. I did wonder if Nurse Leadbetter had something to do with it, but Marchant denies it.'

'She's downstairs, is she?'

'No, sir.'

'Why not?'

'I didn't like to bring her in in the middle of her shift, sir.'

'So you've left her to run away? What were you thinking of?'

'She won't do that, sir.'

'How the hell do you know?'

'Well, sir, it's not as if we're going to charge her with anything, is it? I don't have anything on her as far as Leadbetter's concerned —and it's pretty unlikely, given that, even if she knew about it, it would simply be one girl's word against the other's; hardly a cause for murder, sir. Also, Marchant said that, as far as she knew, Reynolds wasn't in the habit of performing such operations, and—'

'Oh, she did, did she? And I suppose you believed her. Good-looking girl, is she?'

Stratton, deciding to ignore the last question, said, 'As a matter of fact, I did believe her. Besides which, sir, Reynolds is dead, so we can hardly—'

'That's not the point! If Reynolds was in the habit of doing that sort of thing, then this blackmailer—who may or may not exist—might know of other women he's operated on.'

'Yes, sir.'

'For all we know, this Nurse…'

'Marchant, sir.'

'Marchant…for all we know, she's in it with this Dr Dacre. One of them must have pocketed those drugs.'

'That would point to Dr Byrne as the blackmailer, sir. And if Byrne killed Reynolds, why didn't he tell us that the death was an accident, sir? He was the one who first suggested searching the bomb-site for suspicious material. From what I know of Dr Byrne, sir, I'd say he'd be far more likely to report such a finding than to try and profit from it. And he had photographs of the man Todd—one of them was in a hidey-hole at his home. That could be a result of pictures getting muddled up—a mistake— but on the other hand, it might be that Byrne knew something about him or was suspicious for some reason.'

'And you say the Marchant girl has been seeing this man Dacre?'

'Yes, sir. Also,' said Stratton, reluctantly, 'I did see Nurse Marchant on the night Dr Byrne was killed. She was in the mortuary corridor. I bumped into her on the way to speak to him.'

'Then what are you playing at, man? You see a pretty face and a nice pair of legs and your brain turns to porridge. Bring her in!'

'And charge her with what, sir?'

'Charge her with procuring an abortion and keep her overnight. That should soften her up a bit—and I'll interview her myself in the morning, see if I can't get something out of her about this Dacre chap and what he's up to.'

Balls, thought Stratton, as he went to fetch his hat. Balls and bugger and fuck. He should have guessed how Lamb would react, but what else could he have done? He hated those sorts of conversations—it was like throwing all the pieces of a jigsaw puzzle up in the air and hoping they'd sort themselves into a recognisable picture on the way down. Then you had to try to make it stick together by bullying people...The worst thing was, though, Lamb had a point—he did have a tendency to treat people's faces as the index of their souls, at least where women were concerned. Like most men, he supposed. How much we depend on appearance and trust, he thought. Even if it's your job to be suspicious, you still depend on those things.

CHAPTER
56

Dacre glanced at his wristwatch: ten to six. Fay would be finishing her shift. If he nipped upstairs, he might just catch her. Having Inspector Stratton and his policemen sniffing about the place all day made him nervous, and he wanted to know if she'd been interviewed again. Not that she could tell them anything about him, but he didn't want her involved. He needed to see her, reassure her—after all, it was his fault about the morphine—and make a date, as well. He'd take up some notes to make it look official, in case someone noticed. He tucked a set of notes under his arm and strode through the Casualty waiting area with a purposeful air. He was almost at the doors when Sister Radford appeared. 'Dr Dacre, would you come? There's a boy with a nosebleed, and it won't stop. We've tried everything, and Dr Ransome's not—'

'Of course, Sister.' Dacre gave her an apologetic smile. 'I'll be straight with you, but I'm afraid I really must answer a call of nature first.'

'Oh, I see. Yes, of course.' This evidence that doctors had bladders too caused the sister to flush slightly, as he'd known it would. 'But the notes...'

'Oh, yes. Don't know what I was thinking of.' Dacre handed them over. 'All at sixes and sevens, I'm afraid, but don't worry, I shall be right back.'

Damn, he thought, as he took the stairs three at a time. Still, it wouldn't matter, as long as his conversation with Fay didn't look too intimate—he rounded the corner, and was about to walk down the Men's Surgical corridor when he saw her emerging from the ward with Inspector Stratton. Flattening himself against the wall, and hoping like hell no-one came up the stairs and spotted him, he watched as the big policeman took hold of Fay's elbow. It wasn't done roughly, and Fay wasn't resisting, but there was something about the gesture that told him that she was being taken away...He's taking her to the station, Dacre thought. He's going to charge her with stealing the morphine, or...God, if it was something to do with Reynolds—and there was that business of her bumping into him in the mortuary corridor on the night of Byrne's death...Dacre's stomach lurched. Surely, he thought, they weren't going to charge her with *murder?* He shuddered, feeling sick. They couldn't...'Oh, Christ, *no*,' he muttered, peering round the corner at their retreating backs. It was all his fault, he'd got her mixed up in it...*His* girl...

Fay couldn't have heard him—too far away—but perhaps she sensed that someone was watching, because she suddenly looked round, and he saw, in the split second before he withdrew, that her face was stark white, rigid with fear. A second later, he heard footsteps running up the stairs, and one of the Casualty probationers came pounding towards him, her eyes wide with alarm.

'Oh,' she panted. 'Dr Dacre, please...Sister Radford sent me to find you. It's the boy there's blood everywhere, and—'

'Calm down,' said Dacre, severely.

'Sorry, Dr Dacre, but Sister Radford says it's urgent.'

'I'm coming. Tell Sister Radford I shall see her in a moment.'

Left alone once more, Dacre leant against the wall and took several deep breaths, trying to compose his thoughts. He'd have to go and look at the boy, and then...then what? He peered round the corner into the corridor once more, but Stratton and Fay had gone. One thing at a time, he told himself. He couldn't go chasing after them—the last thing he wanted was a public scene, and if he didn't return to Casualty immediately, Sister Radford might smell a rat. He'd finish his work, then go to the station and tell the big policeman...tell him...what?

It was no good. He couldn't think straight, not now. First things first: the boy with the nosebleed. Then he'd work out what to do about Fay. I am Dr Dacre, he told himself as he went downstairs, sounding one word in his mind each time his foot touched a step: I. Am. Dr. Dacre. I. Am. Going. To. Treat. A. Patient. As long as I do not panic, everything will be fine.

An agitated-looking boy of about fourteen was sitting on the edge of a bed. The instant Dacre saw him, his whole attention was concentrated. He didn't think he'd ever seen so much blood—the boy's face, clothes and hands and the surrounding linen were soaked in it. Nurse Dunning, who stood over him, ineffectually pinching his nostrils with her fingers, was gloved in blood to the elbow, and her once white apron looked like a slaughterman's. A pail containing bloody swabs in the corner showed that either she, or Sister, had already tried stuffing the boy's nose, but to no avail.

'I'm sorry, Doctor,' she said, 'it's not working. If I hold it too tight, he chokes.'

'Are these the notes?' Dacre indicated some blood-spattered pages at the end of the bed.

'Yes, Doctor.' Nurse Dunning automatically moved to hand them to Dacre, but he forestalled her.

'For God's sake don't let go of him.'

Picking up the notes, Dacre saw that—blood aside—they were almost blank. 'Charlie Mortimer? That's you, is it? Don't try to speak, a nod or shake will do.'

The boy nodded.

'How long has he been bleeding like this?' Dacre asked Nurse Dunning.

'He came in about quarter of an hour ago.'

'And the bleeding hasn't let up at all?'

'No, Doctor.'

Charlie Mortimer made a snorting noise. His eyes bulged, and he started coughing. Dacre passed Nurse Dunning a bowl. 'Let go for a moment.' She did so, and, instantly, as if a tap had been turned on full, there was a violent gush of blood.

Charlie ceased to splutter, and, lifting a hand to wipe the blood away from his mouth, attempted to speak.

What is it?' said Dacre.

'B-Bl—,' the boy began to splutter again.

Nurse Dunning tutted.

'Bl-bl—'

'Bleeder?' asked Dacre, triumphantly, and Charlie Mortimer, looking relieved, nodded vigorously. 'He's a haemophiliac, Nurse. Put your fingers back on his nose, and *keep them there.*' Putting his head round the screen, he bellowed, 'Sister!'

Sister Radford appeared from behind one of the other screens to join him.

'Yes, Dr Dacre?' she asked, reprovingly.

'This boy's a haemophiliac. Why wasn't it on his notes?'

'We didn't know, Doctor. He didn't tell us.'

'I imagine that's because you were too busy pinching his nose to give him a chance,' snapped Dacre. 'This needs cauterising immediately if we're to have any chance of stopping it, and he'll need blood.'

Sister Radford blanched as if she'd just lost a couple of pints herself. 'I'll send for Dr Colburn at once.' She departed, moving faster than Dacre had ever seen her move before.

Dacre returned to the cubicle. 'Right, Charlie, we'll get you sorted out. I'll need to take a sample of your blood, so that we can make sure it's compatible with the blood you're given...Do you know if anyone came with him, Nurse Dunning?'

The nurse, who had clearly heard the fiercely whispered conservation on the other side of the screen, stared at him in alarm. 'Mother?' said Dacre. 'Father? Anyone?'

'I think he was on his own, Doctor.'

Charlie Mortimer, whose skin—where it was not bloodily crimson—seemed to be growing paler by the minute, nodded.

'How long were you bleeding before you got here? Hold up your fingers.'

Charlie hesitated, then held up both hands, then his left hand again, then waved it to-and-fro in a give-or-take gesture. 'Fifteen minutes or so?'

A nod.

'Do your parents know where you are?'

A shake.

By the time Dacre managed to get a note of the boy's address, a porter had arrived with a wheelchair. A few more minutes brought Dr Colburn, and Charlie Mortimer, nose still firmly clamped by Nurse Dunning, was taken away for treatment.

Left alone in the cubicle, Dacre pulled the screen back into position and sat down on the end of the bed—the only part that wasn't either soaked, or splattered. He was trembling, limp, and drenched in sweat, as if some inner dam had broken. Relief, fear, exhaustion: everything seemed to flood him at once.

He straightened up as Sister Radford put her head round the screen. 'I'm very sorry, Dr Dacre,' she said meekly. 'I can assure you it won't happen again.'

'Please don't apologise, Sister.' He gave her a weak smile. 'I'm sorry I was so brisk, but those things…Well, they're rather dramatic. If I'd known how serious it was, I wouldn't have left, but in the event you acted very swiftly so let's hope all's well.'

'Yes, Doctor. Thank you.' Sister Radford looked at him with new respect, and left the cubicle.

'Christ,' he muttered, and put his slippery palms to his soaked forehead. 'Oh, Christ…' I'm not pretending any more, he thought. I acted on instinct—but instinct with knowledge. I didn't have to sneak away and consult a book: I knew what to ask, what to do. I have, in all probability, saved a life. I am *real*. This is who I am—I've been working towards this moment all my life.

He sat on for a few minutes, staring down at the blood on the sheet: a large stain, surrounded by spatters and smears. There was some on the screen, too, and on the wall tiles beneath the dado. Now, he must save Fay. He must go to the police station. Dacre's mind, usually so agile, seemed to have seized up, and all he could think of was her terrified face as Stratton took her away, of how frightened she must be.

He had to rescue her. He must fetch his hat, and go down to the station. Yes, that's what he must do. He was a doctor, and Fay was going to be his wife. Stratton *must* listen to him. He didn't know yet how he would persuade the big policeman—he'd work it out on the way. But somehow he would make him see that Fay was innocent. And if that failed…Well, he'd managed before, hadn't he? He'd find a way.

CHAPTER

57

Dacre crossed Oxford Street and walked through Soho, heading for Savile Row. His body was humming like a tram wire, but he had no idea what he was going to say when he got there, and, as he grew closer, nothing presented itself. Finally, on the corner of Poland Street and Broadwick Street, he halted and stood staring around him, biting his lip. A couple of tarts were chatting on one corner, beneath a torn poster of the Squander Bug, a satanic-looking insect whose bloated body was covered in swastikas. Diagonally opposite, men were going into the Railway pub. It's all very well for them, Dacre thought: they may have lives that let them in for a gutfull of boredom and misery, but at least they knew what was going to happen next, which was a damn sight more than he did. He must *think* himself back into control. It was all a matter of psychology. Reynolds, Byrne, the morphine…It must have something to do with one, or both, or *all*, of those. If it was only the morphine, he could admit he took the phials himself…but what reason could he give? That he was in pain because of the bruising he'd suffered at the hands of Mrs Parker? Inspector Stratton had seen the marks, but nobody needed morphine for mere bruises. He'd have to up the ante a bit…cracked ribs. That would do it. Of course, an X-ray would prove that they were nothing of the sort, but Stratton would be bound to take the word of a doctor. And they were painful, especially if people were moving about, and of course he had to keep working. 'Didn't want to let the side down, Inspector,' he murmured to himself. 'In the eyes of the public, doctors aren't human. We don't get ill—or rather, we're not supposed to. Feeble. Very poor form.' He'd say he'd only taken small doses, to keep him working and allow him to sleep. Yes, that sounded plausible enough, especially if admitted ruefully, with the right amount of awkwardness. It ought to do the trick, except...

Wait. He'd pinched the morphine *before* the business with Mrs Parker, hadn't he? That was going to he more difficult to get out of. 'You see, Inspector, I just pocketed them. Absent-mindedness, I suppose. And, as I believe I told you, I was rather distracted by Nurse Marchant, not to mention the business with the torsion—that was why I'd gone upstairs in the first place, because Mr Hambling wanted to see me about it.' Mention of the torsion, he thought, had worked so well before—Stratton had practically turned green before his eyes—that it was bound to forestall further questions. Given the seriousness of the matter, Stratton would undoubtedly ask why Dacre hadn't mentioned all this when asked before. What should he say? 'Well, Inspector, as I said, I'd used some of it by that time'—here, the cracked ribs would come into play—'and I was rather...I am sorry, Inspector. I know that it's a serious matter. When I realised that Nurse Marchant might get into trouble, I was horrified, because really, this is entirely my fault...' The plausibility of this, thought Dacre, would rely far more on the way it was said than the substance. He practised again, mouthing the words to himself, trying out different hesitations to give a convincing demonstration of charming muddle-headedness, as he crossed Regent Street and turned down Burlington Street towards Savile Row.

By the time he opened the door to West End Central, he was feeling exhilarated by the challenge ahead. He couldn't alibi Fay for the night of Byrne's death, but if he admitted taking the morphine, surely the fact that Stratton had bumped into her in the mortuary corridor that night would pale into insignificance? As for Reynolds, there wasn't anything he could do about that, because he (or, rather, Dacre) hadn't been working at the Middlesex at the time...Unless she'd been somewhere with Reynolds on the night of his death, before...Dacre shuddered. He didn't want to think about that. It was a miracle that no-one had seen *him*, because then he'd have had some explaining to do.

He'd rescue Fay, and she'd be grateful. Of course she would. He'd apologise to her, over as nice a dinner as could be got, for not owning up before, and he'd say he really hadn't dreamt she'd be in such trouble, and she (from relief as much as anything) would be bound to forgive him immediately.

An ancient policeman with a pendulous lower lip, who surely would have been retired but for the war, stood behind the desk. Approaching, Dacre caught a whiff of rancid hair oil, and, coming closer, took in the man's ponderous air and dull eyes, the whites of which were an eggy yellow. 'I've come to enquire after a Miss Fay Marchant,' he said. 'Is she here?'

'Why would you want to know that, sir?'

'I'd like to speak to the policeman who brought her in— Detective Inspector Stratton. It's a matter of some importance.'

'DI Stratton has left, sir. If you wish to speak to him, I suggest you come back tomorrow.'

'Might I speak to Miss Marchant?'

'I'm afraid not, sir.'

'But she is here, is she?'

'Are you a close relative, sir?'

Dacre almost said yes, but realised that this lie would seem horribly suspicious to Stratton, who would undoubtedly hear of it. 'No,' he said.

'Then I'm afraid I'm not at liberty to say, sir.'

Stupid old fool, thought Dacre, you've as good as told me she is here. That must mean, he told himself, as he thanked the desk sergeant and left the station, that they're planning to charge her with something in the morning.

He wasn't going to let that happen. He needed to go some-where and think. Retracing his steps in the direction of the hospital, he went into the Black Horse. If the friendly barmaid was on duty, she'd see he got a drink—or several.

She was on duty. Four brandies down, he felt his mind begin to clear. All of this was Stratton's fault. Why couldn't he just leave things alone? What he, Dacre, had, was too precious not to be fought for. All his life, he'd been working towards this, and now some bloody flatfoot was trying to take it all away—take Fay from him, maybe even take *Dacre*, and leave him with nothing. Worse than before, because now he'd had a taste of how his life ought to be. And the thought of Fay in some filthy cell, surrounded by prostitutes and God knows who else, made him furious. It wasn't supposed to happen like this. It wasn't right, or fair. Nobody ever gave him anything—all they did was try to take it away. Well, he wouldn't have it. He'd fight for it...More than fight, if he had to. He'd done it before, hadn't he? Well, then. He'd damn well do it again.

He necked the remains of his fourth drink, slammed the glass onto the table and rose unsteadily, heading away from the smoke, noise and sweat into the fresher air of the street. *I know where you live, you bastard.*

Walking mechanically, his body deadened by the fug of brandy in his brain, he set off towards the bus stop. *I'll fix you, you wait.*

58

With a heavy heart, Stratton left Fay to the mercies of Cudlipp and Policewoman Harris. It was his own fault—he'd been an idiot to tell her that she'd only have to make a statement. Fay clearly felt betrayed, and he couldn't blame her. The fact that she'd accepted it all, and allowed herself to be led away by Miss Harris without fuss just made it worse. He stood in the lobby of West End Central, rubbing his eyes in a futile attempt to erase the image of her reproachful face, and decided that it was time to call it a day before he cocked up anything else—not that home was much of a prospect with that bloody woman mooning about the place. He'd said goodnight to the desk sergeant and had just walked out of the door when Ballard appeared on the steps, breathless and waving a piece of paper.

'Thank goodness I've caught you, sir. It's about Dacre. I managed to get hold of someone at St Andrews. A James Walter Dacre did train there, and he graduated in 1938, *but*'—Ballard's eyes gleamed with excitement—'he died in thirty-nine. Car smash, sir.'

'So our man,' concluded Stratton, 'must have taken his identity. But those certificates looked genuine enough.'

'He might have stolen them, sir. The St Andrews people gave me the next-of-kin: his mother, Mrs Beatrice Dacre, of 16, Buckingham Gardens, Norbury, SW.'

'We'll see her tomorrow,' said Stratton. 'Let's just hope she's still there. Right now, we'd better get round to the hospital and see if we can find the man himself. Come on.'

At the Middlesex, an irritable and exhausted Dr Ransome told them that Dacre had left for the day. They trooped back outside, and Stratton consulted his notebook. 'According to the hospital's records, he lives in Eversholt Street, by Euston Station. We'd better go and see. Too late to do anything about a warrant to search his rooms, but we might be able to find him. I'm beginning to think,' he added, 'that it's just as well Fay Marchant is in custody. At least she's safely out of his clutches.'

'Quite, sir.' As they began walking towards the Euston Road, Ballard added, 'Bit run-down for a doctor, sir. You'd think he'd live somewhere smarter.'

'Except that he probably isn't a doctor.'

'That's true, sir, but all the same...'

Stratton knew what the sergeant meant. Eversholt Street was dingy and, even before the war, uncared for, with the anonymous air of transience common to places near large railway stations. The landlady at number 28, Mrs Draper, was a large woman in a low-cut dress, with a three-string necklace of creases round her throat and more at her tightly squeezed cleavage. She ushered them into a dark hallway that smelt of damp and paraffin. Having ascertained that Dacre—or whoever he was— wasn't currently on the premises, Stratton asked when he had moved into the house. 'Only a few weeks ago, Inspector. Just before the end of June. Paid a month in advance.'

'Could you check the exact date, please?'

'Why? What's going on? This is a respectable house.'

'I'm sure it is, Mrs Draper. If you could just consult your book for us...?'

Mrs Draper disappeared down the hallway and returned a moment later carrying a ledger. She licked her finger and grubbed up the corners of pages until she found the right place, then thrust the book under Stratton's nose. 'There you are...Dr Dacre arrived on the twenty-fifth of June.'

'Two weeks before he started work at the hospital,' said Stratton, when they were back on the pavement, heading towards the Euston Road, 'and two days after Todd left the Middlesex. We'd better go to Kentish Town...' Stratton consulted his notebook. 'Inkerman Road.'

Inkerman Road turned out to be another dingy street of flat-fronted Victorian terraced houses, many with boarded-up windows. Number 14, although it had retained most of its glass, was decorated by a small wrought-iron first floor balcony slewed at such an extreme angle that it looked as if it might fall off at any moment.

A thickset young tough answered the door. 'We're looking for a Mrs Barnard,' said Stratton.

The man looked them up and down, turned and bellowed, 'Ma!' then disappeared.

'I don't think he liked us, sir,' murmured Ballard.

'Evidently.'

'What do you want?' The waistless, bulbous-nosed woman who stood in the doorway, wiping her hands on her overall was, fairly obviously, the man's mother.

'Mrs Barnard?'

Taking the grunt which greeted this question as assent, Stratton said, 'I believe you had a Mr Todd lodging with you until recently.'

'I already told the other copper about that. He's not here any more. What's he done, anyway?'

'Nothing, so far as we know,' said Stratton, blandly. 'When did he leave?'

Mrs Barnard pursed her lips, then said, 'Ooh...somewhere round the middle of June, it was...no, I tell a lie—it was the twenty-fifth.'

'You're sure about that, are you?'

'Yes. I remember it because my Jimmy was took bad with his heart. It's a weakness. The doctors can't do nothing for it. I was ever so worried—he was laid up for three days.'

'That was Jimmy who came to the door, was it?'

'That's right.'

By the look of Jimmy, thought Stratton, he was more likely to have been laid up by a brawl or a hangover, and milked it for all it was worth. 'Well,' he said, 'he seems to have made a good recovery. Did Mr Todd give a reason for leaving?'

Mrs Barnard thought for a moment, then said, 'Got a new job, didn't he? Somewhere north.'

'You're sure he hadn't been called up?'

'Oh, no. He had a medical exemption certificate, same as my Jimmy. He told me.'

'Did you ever see the certificate?'

Mrs Barnard looked nonplussed. 'What would I want to see it for?'

'Can you show us your son's certificate, please?'

Mrs Barnard narrowed her eyes. 'What do you want to see that for? My Jimmy's a good lad.'

'I'm sure he is, Mrs Barnard. If you don't mind...'

'All right,' she said ungraciously. 'It's in his room.'

She returned a couple of minutes later carrying a battered cake tin, with Jimmy lowering behind her. 'In here.' She prised open the lid. The tin was empty.

'Interesting,' said Stratton, as they headed off. 'Unless Jimmy Barnard sold his certificate to someone—which I suppose is possible, if unlikely—then I think our friend must have pinched it for his own use. Mind you, we'd better play safe and check that it actually exists.'

'I'll do that tomorrow, sir.'

'Good. Now...' Stratton thought aloud. 'According to Higgs, Todd was called up. Mrs Barnard has just confirmed that he left here on the same day that the false Dr Dacre moved into Eversholt Street. Quite a coincidence, don't you think? If Dacre and Todd are one and the same, that means that he was at the Middlesex when not just one, but all of the deaths occurred. Now, I'm not sure there's any more that we can do tonight, and as Nurse Marchant is in safe hands, I suggest we both cut off home and we'll see what Mrs Dacre has to say tomorrow morning.'

Stratton looked at his watch. If he went home now, he'd be in time to collect Jenny from the Rest Centre. It would be a gesture of goodwill—she'd like that—and perhaps he could persuade her into the pub for a short while. She wasn't usually keen, regarding it as a male preserve, but perhaps this time she'd agree, and they could have a bit of a chat away from Mrs Ingram. Try to persuade her that the bloody woman would be better off else-where before she drove them all mad. It needn't be long, and there'd still be time for her to get supper...It was a good plan. Things were starting to move on the investigation and now, with luck, they'd get back to normal at home, too. Stratton, suddenly cheerful at the thought of inveigling Jenny into the pub, clapped Ballard on the shoulder and bade him goodnight.

CHAPTER

59

The bus ride sobered Dacre, not to the extent of diverting him from his chosen course, but enough to make him realise that he had no actual plan for what to do when he arrived at Stratton's house. Stepping down from the platform he stood for a moment, uncertain, in Tottenham High Street. The people passing, heads down, jostled him. It's all right for you, he thought, glaring after them. You've got your lives, your women. No-one's trying to take them from you.

Still, no plan came into his mind, just the desperate, repeated thought that he must regain control of his life. Now to find the house...Before, when he'd followed the big policeman home, he'd got off the bus, crossed the road, and...that's right, they'd passed this bakery, and the house with the tall hedge—he remembered that—and then a right turn, and then...

Here it was. Number 27. He opened the gate, went up the front path, grabbed the door knocker and beat it down, hard, several times. He could hear the noise reverberate through the small house, but no-one came. *He must be here, he must...*He was a married man, wasn't he? Where else would he be at the end of the day? The pub, perhaps?

He deliberated. He could hardly walk about trying to find Stratton and making himself conspicuous. He chewed his lip, coming to no conclusion, then, at last, hearing quiet footsteps coming down the stairs, knocked again. What if Stratton's wife were there? He hadn't considered that...He was wondering whether to call through the letter box or just wait, when he saw a woman waving from the other side of the garden gate. 'Are you all right?' Her voice had a thready, bleating sound. 'I saw you out here—I'm from next door. Mr Stratton's not home yet—he's a copper, works all sorts of hours. Mrs Stratton'll be at the Rest Centre, if it's her you're wanting.'

'I was looking for Mr Stratton.'

'Well, I don't rightly know what to suggest—never know when he'll be back. I could give him a message, if you like.'

'I'm afraid it's rather confidential.'

The woman looked disappointed. 'Well, I suppose he might be at the Swan, or up at his allotment. If you're wanting to speak to him urgently, then I'd try the Rest Centre first, see if Mrs Stratton knows where he is.'

'I will. Thank you. If you could point me in the right direction...?'

Dacre set off in the direction indicated, and found the Rest Centre—a converted school—without difficulty. Seeing no-one around, he wandered into a classroom where a woman was sorting through heaps of clothes. 'Can I help you?'

'I'm looking for Mrs Stratton.'

'She'll be in the kitchen. Go down the corridor, right at the end, through the big room and turn left.'

'Thank you.'

Dacre followed her instructions, and found himself in the big room, which, judging by the wood panelling, the crest and the row of dreary oil paintings of stern-looking men in academic garb, had previously been the school hall. He crossed the parquet floor and was about to exit in the direction of the kitchen when the door he'd come through flew open and a small, dishevelled-looking woman rushed towards him.

'Can you help me? Please?' Her voice was shrill and distressed, and, as she came closer, Dacre saw that the thick woollen coat she clutched tightly round her was—as well as being too warm for the season—far too large for her tiny frame. Her hair had fallen down at one side, and her eyes were frantic.

'What is it?' he asked.

'Have you seen her?'

Must be a flying-bomb victim, Dacre thought, searching for relatives—her children, perhaps. 'If you're looking for someone,' he said, gently, 'there's a lady down the corridor who might know. Shall I take you to her?'

'No, no. She might be one of *them*.'

'Them?'

'Yes. Will you help me? *Please?*'

'I'll do my best,' said Dacre. It wouldn't hurt, he decided. Stratton's wife wasn't going to go anywhere, and the big policeman was bound to come home at some point, so he could always go back to the house. Besides, the woman looked so pitiful, so afraid and bewildered, that he couldn't just leave her.

'Oh, thank you. Thank you.'

'Why don't you come and sit down?' Dacre indicated the line of hard wooden chairs at the side of the room.

'Yes,' said the woman. 'Thank you.'

Perched on the edge of one of the chairs, shivering, knees squeezed together, she said, 'Will you help me? There's no-one else.'

She's obviously lost everyone, thought Dacre. Staring at this pathetic scrap of forlorn humanity that trembled beside him, he said, 'What's the trouble?'

'It's her. Them. All of them.'

'All of who?'

'These people. They keep sending him back.'

'Sending who back?'

The woman stared at him, seemingly paralysed by fear. Start at the beginning, Dacre told himself. Try to get some sense out of her. Perhaps she was concussed—it would certainly account for her state. 'I'm Dr Dacre,' he said. 'What's—'

'You're one of *them*.' She drew back, her eyes flicking between the doors at either end of the room, measuring the distance, wondering if she could make a run for it.

'No,' said Dacre. 'I'm not. I can help you.'

'How do I know that?'

Perhaps she wasn't concussed, Dacre thought. Perhaps it was more than that. 'Because I'm only pretending to be a doctor. I had to, to get away from them. What's your name?'

'Ingram. I can see you're not really a doctor, now. You don't look like the other one. He kept asking me questions.'

'Tell me about the other doctor,' said Dacre.

'Makepeace. He's *their* doctor. *Her* doctor. Keeps giving me stuff, but I've not been taking it. I know his game.'

'Very sensible,' said Dacre. 'I'd have done exactly the same.'

'I put it down the lav,' she said conspiratorially.

A *him*—the one that *they* kept sending back—and a *her*. Paranoid delusion, thought Dacre, play along with it. 'Good,' he said. 'They don't fool me, either. I've managed to escape from them, you see. That's why I can help you.'

'It started when my house was bombed,' she said. 'Or that's what they told me. I remember something, but I'm not sure what it was. Horrible. They said it came down on top of me, but they tell lies, so I don't know if that's what happened. Then they started with all this, saying they were trying to help me, but they've taken Eric, and I don't know what they've done with him.'

'Who's Eric?'

'My husband. He's in the army, or he was, before…There's this other man who looks like him. They hired him because he looks like Eric. I don't know how they thought they could fool me, because you always know, don't you?'

'Of course you do. This man, he claims to be your husband, does he?'

'That's right. But I wasn't born yesterday, you know. Do you understand what I'm talking about?'

'Yes, I do. Does he sound like Eric?'

'Oh, they've got everything right. They're very clever with what they can do nowadays. Perverted science, that's what Mr Churchill called it. I don't know why they want to behave like that when I've done nothing to them.'

Dacre remembered the psychiatry textbook. *A rare disorder...* *A person believes that someone has been replaced by an imposter of identical appearance and behaviour...* Something like that, at any rate. What was it called? 'Who got everything right?' he asked.

'Them.'

Cat-something? No, that wasn't it. 'What are their names?'

Mrs Ingram's eyes narrowed suspiciously. 'I thought you knew them.'

Cat...Cag...What was it? 'I do. But they use different people. Agents. You can see why—from their point of view, I mean.'

Cap...Capgras, that was it. The Capgras Delusion. It must be. His first diagnosis. He bet no-one else knew what was wrong with her. If he were a psychiatrist, he'd be able to write it up. He could make a study of it. He imagined himself lecturing to a hall full of students.

'Mr and Mrs Kerr, it was. Now it's Mrs Stratton.'

'And Inspector Stratton?'

'Inspector? Do you know him? How do you know him?'

Dacre's mind raced. Her agitation was such that he felt afraid of going near her in the same unhappy, unreasoning way that he was afraid of birds when they got into rooms and beat up and down trying to get out: an absolute, visceral terror. 'They've been after me, too.'

'They didn't tell me he was a policeman. Oh...' Mrs Ingram shook her head. 'Very clever. A policeman. We've got to find her.' She stood up, and, as she did so, one side of the heavy coat fell open and Dacre saw, concealed inside, something long and thin, wrapped in newspaper, a wooden handle protruding from the top. Jesus...Dacre felt sick. What was she going to do?

'Come on,' she hissed.

'We don't know where she is,' said Dacre, desperately. 'She may not be here at all.'

'She is. She said she was coming here. She *told me*. I think she's in the kitchen.'

'Well, she's not there now,' lied Dacre. 'No-one is. I've looked.'

'She's probably just gone outside. We'll go in there and wait till she comes back.'

'Wait!' Dacre grabbed the woman's wrist. 'It's not safe,' he whispered. 'There's others around—more of them—they might be expecting us.'

'They don't know I'm here. And I've got this.' She shook him off, took out the parcel and began to unwrap it. Dacre stared—it was a carving knife. 'It's hers. I took it from her kitchen.'

'Stop! No—' As he raised his hand to take hold of her arm once more, she slashed at him, a movement so swift he didn't register it properly until he felt a stinging pain and saw a line of blood appear across his knuckles.

Seeing the blood, Mrs Ingram backed away from him, holding the knife out in front of her. 'If you're one of them...' Her eyes glittered. 'If you are...'

Dacre shook his head frantically, and put his hands up in a gesture of surrender. 'No...I just think it may not be safe...not yet...'

They stared at each other for a second, panting slightly, then turned, in unison, towards the door as footsteps echoed in the corridor outside. Mrs Ingram shoved the knife back inside her coat, and, in an instinctively feminine gesture that made her seem even more deranged than before, reached up to adjust her wonky hair. For a moment, they stood side by side, erect and tense, like soldiers awaiting inspection by a general.

The doors swung open, framing the big policeman, and, in that instant, Mrs Ingram swung round and ran for the doors at the opposite end of the room. 'Wait!' shouted Dacre, vainly, rushing after her. Two steps later, he felt himself hit in the back by a heavy weight which sent him sprawling to the floor. 'Stop her!' he shouted. 'You've got to stop her!'

CHAPTER

60

The washing-up water was greasy and cooling rapidly. Lifting out the last of the plates, Jenny decided she'd better boil the kettle before she tackled any more of the dirty crocks on the table. Every time she looked there seemed to be more cups and dishes, although she knew this couldn't be possible because Mrs Haskins had brought them all through before she'd left for the evening. It's because I'm tired, she thought, wiping her hands. They were so rough and red nowadays—last winter, the skin on her fingertips had split painfully, and her wedding ring had actually begun to chafe. She hadn't taken it off, though. She never had, ever since they'd got married. Staring ruefully at her hands she thought, They look as if they belong to an old woman. A pair of decent gloves would help—her last pair of cotton ones were almost beyond saving. Where on earth would they get baby clothes? she wondered. She'd given Monica and Peter's away long ago, and the crib. They'd give you extra coupons, she thought, but how far would they go...? The memory of Monica and Peter's baby clothes suddenly made her smile. So small it scarcely seemed possible they were for a living breathing baby, not a doll. Unbidden, her hands went to circle her stomach.

Shaking her head at her own sentimentality she set the kettle on to boil and scraped the few scraps left on the plates into an enamel bowl, ready to take outside to the pig bin. Looking at the squalid leftover crusts and bits of cabbage, she found herself thinking longingly, as she did very often, of the wonderful Sunday teas they'd had before the war: tins of salmon, watercress, white bread, jam tarts and a big fruit cake...Catching herself, she thought that if anyone had told her that, at thirty-four, she'd find herself daydreaming of food as she'd once dreamt of romance, she'd have told them they were barmy, but there it was.

How marvellous it would be to go into a shop and get anything you fancied—money permitting, of course—with plenty to go round! And nice material to make frocks for her and Monica, and some more hand lotion, and eau de Cologne there was only half an inch left in her little bottle of Coty, now...Pete needed new clothes too, he was growing so fast...He'd be like Ted when he grew up, she thought, tall and broad-shouldered. Amazing when he'd been such a tiny baby, only five pounds when he was born.

She transferred some more plates to the sink and stood back, wiping wisps of hair off her forehead with the back of her hand. At least she and Doris had come to a decision about Mrs Ingram. They'd speak to Dr Makepeace about finding somewhere for her to go. Then, when that was sorted out, she'd tell Ted about the baby. They'd manage somehow...There was a crash from somewhere down the corridor, and the sound of running. Jenny sighed. So much for no emergencies and getting off home—it was probably just children messing about, but most of the other helpers had already left, so she really ought to check. She turned off the gas under the kettle, and went towards the door. The footsteps were louder now, and she could hear shouting somewhere in the background, though not the words. Honestly, kids were so out of control these days, especially— the door flew open, crashing against the wall.

'Mrs Ingram! Are you all right?'

Mrs Ingram seemed to fly towards her in a blur, her face contorted, something—a knife—gleamed in her hand. Instinctively, Jenny put her hands up to protect her face, and, as she did so, felt a sharp stabbing pain in her stomach. 'No, no please—' Screaming, she doubled over, clutching herself, and saw blood on her apron, her hands, the lino...And it hurt so much. *The baby*...Holding her stomach, she collapsed.

Flat on his face, pinned to the ground with his arm forced excruciatingly upwards behind his back, Dacre fought for breath. 'She's got a knife! She's—'

'You must think I was born yesterday, chum.' Stratton's flat voice betrayed no hint of exertion.

'Please.' Dacre forced breath into his compressed lungs. 'She's going to—'

'Listen, *Doctor* Dacre,' Stratton's voice was heavy with sarcasm, 'it's time we had a little chat. I must say, I didn't expect to see you so soon, but now you're here—'

'Please! You've got to—'

'I haven't *got* to do anything. Apart from arresting you, that is.'

'*No!*' Dacre began to struggle desperately, thrashing and kicking out, but it was useless. He might as well have had a ton weight on top of him, and each time he jerked, the big policeman pushed his arm up higher, until it felt as if it were about to snap.

'I'd keep still if I were you. Otherwise, I'll thump you so hard you'll be shitting teeth for a month.'

'She's...got...a...knife!'

'Don't waste my time, chum. James Dacre, or whatever your fucking name is, I'm arresting you for impersonating a—'

A piercing scream from the direction of the kitchen sliced across Stratton's words. Dacre felt the big policeman relax his grip slightly, and straighten up. 'What the hell——?'

The rest of his words were swallowed up by another scream of nerve-shredding intensity, followed by rising shouts of 'No, no, please!'

'Jenny?' Dacre felt Stratton release his arm. 'Jenny!'

'I told you,' said Dacre, elbowing him out of the way and staggering to his feet. Stratton reached the doors ahead of him, and looked wildly up and down the corridor.

'This way,' gasped Dacre. 'The kitchen. I told you, she's got a knife!'

'*No*!' Another shriek, and then a thump, as of a body connecting with something hard. Stratton, tailed by Dacre, reached the end of the corridor and barged the door open, barrelling into the room. There, lying on the floor, was a woman, clutching her stomach, aproned in blood which streamed down her skirt, her legs, her shoes...

Dacre stood blinking, while Stratton rushed towards her. 'Jenny! Christ! What happened? What's happened to you?'

Out of the corner of his eye, Dacre saw a figure rise from a crouching position beside the cooker and stagger towards Jenny and Stratton, now together on the floor. He saw her raise up the knife in both hands and start to bring it down towards the big policeman's chest, and, without thinking, rushed at her, knocking her sideways so that the knife plunged into Stratton's upper arm. Mrs Ingram, on all fours now, seemed to scuttle away from him horribly, like a human crab, and, in a moment, she was upright, through the door, and running away across the yard.

Dacre righted himself. Stratton was before him, cowering on the floor, cradling the bleeding woman in his arms. He was bleeding, too—Dacre could see the dark stain blossoming on the sleeve of his jacket.

'Jenny, oh, Jenny...' Stratton looked up and stared at Dacre for a moment as if he'd never seen him before, then said, 'Don't just stand there! You're the one who's been telling people you're a doctor—fucking *do something*! Help her!'

She was so heavy against him, her blood so warm and sticky, unceasing. 'It's all right, Jenny, I'm here, it's going to be all right, I'm sorry I swore, love, I promise I won't do it again, it'll be all right...' Stratton scarcely knew what he was saying—this couldn't be happening, it couldn't. But it was. Dacre was bundling things at them, tablecloths and tea towels, pressing them against Jenny's stomach, saying something...

'Hold them there, press down...Press hard.'

Stratton tried to obey with his right hand, but his arm wouldn't move. He stared at it in surprise, and saw that there was a knife sticking out of it. That must have been the blow I felt, he thought, stupidly. He reached across Jenny to pull the knife out, but Dacre knocked his hand away.

'Leave it! Use your other hand,' he shouted. 'I'll see to that in a minute. Just got to fetch some more cloths...'

'Yes...yes...it's all right, Jenny, it's going to be all right...' Red blooms on the faded linen, spreading out, it wouldn't stop coming, and now the blood dripping down his arm was mixing with hers, and Jenny was groaning, over and over. He pressed down hard with his left hand, as Dacre had told him to, but it seemed to make no difference. 'I don't want to hurt you, love, but we've got to stop it...'

Jenny's voice, thin and reedy, in his ear: 'It hurts...Ted.'

'I know, sweetheart, but we'll soon have you better, I promise...I'll look after you, I'm here, it's all right, I'm here...'

Jenny began to shake, jerking against Stratton's arms and chest. Dacre was talking again: 'Shock. She's haemorrhaging. Keep pressing down as hard as you can...'

'I am. Isn't there anything else I can do?'

'I—'

The kitchen door banged, and there was another scream. Looking up, Stratton saw a woman standing on the threshold, her hand before her mouth. The man rushed towards her and they disappeared in a blur. 'Ambulance!' he heard the man shouting. 'Police! *Now!*'

'Oh, Jenny, Jenny...' It should be me, not her, thought Stratton. I should have stood between them, protected her...

The man was beside him again, tugging at the shoulder of his jacket, brandishing a pair of scissors. 'What the fuck are you doing?' shouted Stratton. 'Look after her!'

'You first. She's hit something big, or you wouldn't be bleeding like that. Keep still.' Working fast, Dacre cut through the sleeve of his jacket, then his shirt, and then, ripping a tea towel in two, made a tourniquet just below his armpit, yanking the cloth tight and knotting it. 'That ought to do the trick. For Christ's sake leave that knife where it is.'

Then his hands were at Jenny's lap again, scrabbling at the wadded-up cloths. 'No!' bellowed Stratton. 'You said—'

'I need to have a look...Be ready to put them back... Right...' Dacre pulled Jenny's apron aside and Stratton heard material ripping. Jenny began to struggle, weakly, in his arms.

'What are you doing?' Stratton snarled, pushing him away. 'You're hurting her!'

'Her skirt...I'm sorry, but: we need to do this. Wait...' Dacre grabbed the scissors again. 'Now, I'm just going to...Keep her as still as you can.'

'All right, Jenny, it's a doctor, he's going to help you, it's all right, love…'

Dacre's arms were concealed by the bundle of soaked linen on Jenny's lap, but Stratton could hear the snip of blades through material, and, a moment later, Dacre removed a sodden, blackened piece of cloth and threw it on the floor, and then another. 'Her clothes…that's better…Now…Oh, Christ!' Stratton caught a glimpse of something pinkish, shiny, and gouts of dark red blood, momentarily unstaunched, welled out, before the linen was grabbed from him and pressed again into Jenny's lap, Dacre's arms taut and shoulders bowed as he forced his weight downwards.

'What's happening?'

'Haemorrhage,' panted Dacre. 'Won't stop. Got to keep this on here. Keep talking to her.'

'Yes…' Stratton, who was beginning to feel faint, struggled to make words come. 'Jenny…'

Jenny's head flopped against his shoulder, and she groaned again, and made a stuttering noise.

'What? What did you say, love? Say something…talk to me…'

'Pete…Monica, say…say…Oh, Ted. The bay…'

'Ingram,' cut in the man. 'Her name's Ingram.'

'How do you know?' asked Stratton. 'Do you know her?'

'No. She told me her name before you arrived. She had a knife.'

'Why didn't you stop her?'

'I tried,' said the man. 'Then you came.'

'Yes…' said Stratton weakly. 'I'm sorry…Oh, Jenny, I'm so sorry…I didn't know…' It's my fault, thought Stratton, helplessly. He'd do anything to help her, anything, but there nothing he *could* do, and it was all his fault. 'She didn't want me to go down the hole…the bomb…She didn't want me to go…'

'It's all right, mate,' said Dacre. 'Talk to her, not to me.'

'I shouldn't have gone,' said Stratton. 'I should have left the bloody woman where she was. I'm sorry, Jenny, I'm sorry…'

Jenny murmured something, but he couldn't make out what it was, or if it was words at all.

'What is it, love?'

'I'm going to...'

'No, you're not. You'll be all right, just keep very still now, let the doctor do his job...'

Stratton's eyes met Dacre's. But he's not a doctor at all, he thought. Somehow, he'd forgotten this. But he seemed so competent, so much in control...

As if guessing what was in his mind, Dacre said, 'This is the only thing we can do—first aid. We have to stop the bleeding. Stomach wounds are the worst.'

'Yes...' This chimed with something vague in Stratton's memory. 'You're right.'

'Put your hand back on this,' said the man. 'Press as hard as you can. I'll get more cloths.'

As the pressure was momentarily released, Jenny made a mewing noise and twisted against Stratton's arm, her feet drumming weakly on the floorboards.

'Keep still, love, just try to keep still...I know it hurts, but you're a brave girl...'

Dacre rose and turned away from them, and Stratton heard the sound of drawers being yanked open. He looked down at Jenny, whose face was now turned upwards, towards his. Her eyes were closed and he saw—had he ever noticed it before?—the delicate mauve colour of her eyelids. 'Beautiful Jenny, please, love, please...'

'Baby, I'm going...'

'Ssh, Jenny...'

'No, listen...Please, Ted...I'm g-g—' Jenny's lips parted slightly, in a sigh, and Stratton saw that they were losing colour, turning a purplish blue, and, as he watched, a bubble of bright blood appeared at one side.

'Her mouth! She's bleeding from her mouth!'

The man was beside him again, a bundle of roller towels in his hands. These'll be better,' he said. 'Take your hand away, and

I'll just…there…" Another blur as the bunched-up tablecloths were thrown aside, landing in a puddle on the floor, stripes and patterns and lace edges stained red, and replaced by the towels, their fibres obliterated immediately by yet more blood.

'Make it stop,' implored Stratton. 'You've got to make it stop…'

'I'm doing my best,' said the man, grimly. 'Where the hell's that ambulance?' he muttered, through gritted teeth.

'Jenny…Oh, love…Jenny…Jenny…'

CHAPTER

63

He knew she was leaving him. She'd lost too much blood. He must be losing blood, too, he thought, because he could feel his strength ebbing away so that it was harder and harder to hold her. She was dying and he was helpless, so helpless... She'd stopped moving and lay limp now, in his arms, but still he hoped—if she would only open her eyes and look at him, if the ambulance would come, if...'Please,' he begged Dacre, who still knelt at Jenny's other side, his arms rigid, blood welling up—the threadbare towels were saturated and would absorb no more— around his outspread fingers.

The man, head bowed, shook his head slowly. 'The ambulance will be here soon,' he muttered.

'Jenny...'

'Soon...'

'Jenny, love...They'll be here soon, I promise...'

'Keep talking to her...'

'Jenny...'

More blood, now, from her mouth, trickling languidly down her chin and meandering across her neck, as if it didn't matter, as if she didn't need it...She made a sudden retching noise, as if trying to expel something in her throat, and, the next moment, vomited blood. 'Push her head forward,' said the man, 'don't let her choke.'

Stratton did his best to obey, watching as the blood issued from Jenny's mouth in a thick stream, splattering down the front of her frock. He felt as if his heart were being pulled from his chest. 'Jenny...' He pressed her head against his neck. 'Jenny, don't...'

'For Christ's sake, give her some air!'

'Sorry...I'm so sorry, love...'

'That's more like it.' The flow of blood abated a little. 'Keep her like that—there'll be more.'

'Please...Please stop it...Make it stop...'

'I'm sorry, mate. I can't.' Dacre jerked his head up. 'Listen!'

Stratton could hear, faintly, the sound of a siren.

'That's the ambulance,' said Dacre, urgently. 'Now, listen to me.' He grabbed Stratton's left wrist and pushed his hand into the pile of towels against Jenny's stomach. 'Hold these here. Don't let go.' Dacre released his grip and, still kneeling, leant towards him to check the tourniquet, his face so close that Stratton could see the pores of his skin. 'Listen...Mrs Ingram is dangerous. She's deluded. She mentioned a Mr and Mrs Kerr. Tell the police to go to their house...Do you understand me?'

Stratton stared at him.

'Tell them to go to the house. They need to find Mr and Mrs Kerr. Make sure they're safe.'

Stratton nodded.

'Are you sure you understand?'

'Yes.'

'Good.' Dacre straightened, and stood up. 'I'm leaving now.'

'Yes.' Stratton continued staring at Dacre. 'Wait,' he said.

Dacre backed towards the door. 'I've got to go.'

'You saved me, didn't you?'

'Never mind that, just keep talking to her, and—'

'Why are you here?'

'I came to kill you.'

'But...you saved me...'

'Keep talking to her. Tell her you love her.'

'Yes...Wait...'

Dacre shook his head. The noise of the siren was louder, now. 'I can't. They'll be here in a minute. I've got to go.'

'But...who are you?'

A strange expression passed across the man's face. It was only later—months later—that Stratton, recalling it, was able to identify it: puzzlement.

CHAPTER 64

Jenny died just as the siren stopped. Stratton tried to smooth her hair as a deep gurgling noise welled in her throat, and she expelled a final, fierce plume of blood. He saw her eyelids flicker, he whispered to her that he loved her, and then she left him.

He stared, unseeing, at the ambulance men as they burst into the kitchen, followed by the woman he'd seen before, her hand once more in front of her mouth. He tried to shake them off when they wanted to take Jenny away from him. Someone put a coat over her, and eventually they brought a stretcher and prised her from him and took her away. Perhaps he fainted, then, because the next thing he recalled was someone holding a glass of brandy to his lips and urging him to drink, but he retched it back up, and then he was helped to his feet and taken to a different room where his arm was examined. Then he was taken to hospital, where they treated him and gave him something, so that he woke up later, in a bed in a bright white room. There, he tried to talk to an inspector— Doug Watson, from the local nick, a man he knew a little—about Mrs Ingram and Doris and Donald. Watson said he already knew, and then Stratton half remembered telling him before, at the Rest Centre, while they were looking at his arm. 'Don't worry,' said Watson. 'We'll find her, all right. Don't you worry.'

Stratton tried to explain about Dacre but the words didn't come out right. It was still a jumble in his head, too much to explain, and he kept feeling himself sliding away into dark emptiness. He managed to tell Watson to contact Sergeant Ballard at West End Central, and tried to give a description of Dacre, but he couldn't remember what the man looked like, only the blood all over his jacket and cuffs and hands. 'Don't worry,' said Watson, again. 'I'll see to it. By the way,' the inspector turned in the doorway, 'this bloke, whoever he was, he saved your life, you know.'

A young PC was standing at Stratton's shoulder, and there were footsteps in the corridor outside, hushed conversation and someone crying. Then, how much later he didn't know, Lilian and Reg were there, mute and pale-faced, standing at the foot of his bed. Lilian's eyes were red. 'Ted,' she said, 'Ted,' and got no further. Stratton fell asleep as she wept and Reg patted her on the shoulder.

Then Donald arrived with Doris, who hugged Stratton and wept while he lay numb, like a block of wood. Donald pulled her away and said, 'Come on, Doris, he needs to rest.'

'Jenny's dead.' Stratton locked eyes with Donald.

'I know, mate. I'm sorry.'

'Where did they take her?'

'She's here.'

'She's dead.'

'I'm sorry, Ted.'

'It's my fault.' He closed his eyes and rested his head back against the bed.

'No, Ted, don't say that.'

'It's all my fault. If I hadn't pulled Mrs Ingram out of that hole. Jenny didn't want me to. She told me not to.'

'No...You couldn't have known...'

'And we saved her,' wept Doris. 'Jenny and me—when she tried to gas herself. We saved her life...If we hadn't got there in time...If only...And we didn't tell you. We thought we were doing the right thing, but...' her words dissolved into sobs.

'I should have told you,' said Donald. 'I shouldn't have let them persuade me.'

'It's not your fault,' said Stratton. 'Either of you. You couldn't have known.'

'I told you that woman was dangerous.' It was Reg speaking. Stratton thought he'd gone, but he was standing a few paces behind Donald, who turned on him.

'Can't you keep your mouth shut for once in your life?'

Reg took a pace back. 'There's no need—'

'Yes there is,' spat Donald. 'Shut up.'

'Reg is right,' said Stratton dully. 'He said she was dangerous.'

'Forget it, Ted,' said Donald. 'You weren't to know. None of us were.'

'I should have known,' Doris burst out. 'I'm sorry, Ted...I'm so sorry.'

Stratton stared at her hopelessly. 'No, Doris. It's my fault. I was late back from work,' he said. 'I went to fetch her. I thought we could walk home together. I thought we could go to the pub...talk...but then I saw the man. If I'd listened to him, we'd have gone after her, we'd have been in time...But I didn't. It's all my fault.'

CHAPTER

65

Dacre fled the Rest Centre, stopping only to grab a woollen pullover from the pile of clothing he'd seen when he'd asked for Mrs Stratton, and ran for it. When he'd left the sirens far behind, he found a park and pushed his way into a clump of trees where he stripped off his bloodstained jacket and shirt and yanked the jumper down over his head. It was a little on the small side, and stank of mothballs, but it would do. Then, he boarded a bus back to the centre of London and found his way to the Black Horse in Fitzrovia, and, under the maternal eye of the friendly barmaid, finished the—very much interrupted—process of getting extremely drunk. In a packed pub, surrounded by rowdy men—some uniformed and some not—who barely apologised when they jostled him, and brazen girls who ignored him completely, he sat, thinking of the dying Jenny Stratton and trying to block from his mind the expression on the big police-man's face. He'd failed. If he really had been a doctor, Stratton wouldn't have been intent on arresting him, and would have gone to his wife at once, and she would not have been killed. He'd done everything he could think of to save her, but it wasn't enough…If only he could have saved her…Then he would have proved himself, once and for all, and everyone would know… But he'd saved Stratton, hadn't he? That had been automatic, pushing the madwoman out of the way then binding up his arm. He should have let Mrs Ingram do it for him, then grabbed her, kept her there—he'd have been the hero of the hour and Stratton would have been dead, with his wife. But he couldn't. It hadn't even occurred to him. Even though it would have meant the chance to keep Dacre, to keep *Fay*...Funny, he thought, how well you think you know yourself, but, in a crisis, you never really know how you'll behave...If only—

There was a crash of glass from somewhere behind him, and shouts, and a young RAF corporal with a whore staggered into him, almost knocking him over. He mopped the beer from his jacket, deposited his sodden handkerchief on the bar, and walked away from the pub, stiff with squinty-eyed concentration. His life was in ruins. Any job that he could legitimately expect to hold, with no qualifications, would be far beneath him, and there was no hope of 'going straight' because, officially, he was dead. If he tried to resurrect himself he would, in all probability, get caught.

Lurching down the street in the dusk, heedless of the crowds that surged around him, he cast a sour look at a soldier and his girl—or somebody else's girl—embracing in a doorway. He'd never see Fay again—he couldn't. There was nothing he could do for her, and nothing for it but to collect his belongings from Eversholt Street, and—provided of course, that the police weren't waiting for him—then...what? At that moment, he found he really didn't care whether they were waiting for him or not. In some ways, it would be a relief. If they weren't, he could spend the night in an air-raid shelter, and in the morning...? He'd leave London, anyway. There was nothing here for him but prison, if he were caught. As Dr Dacre, he'd had a position, responsibility, self-respect. Now, he had nothing. Before, whenever he'd had to make a run for it, it had been a blow, but not like this. Never had he fallen so far. Now he was empty and rotten, through and through.

He made it back to Eversholt Street, and was attempting to tiptoe up the stairs when he lost his balance and fell, heavily, against the banisters. Mrs Draper, voluminous in a candlewick dressing gown and spiky with curlers, appeared in the corridor below and peered up at him from between the spindles. 'I've been waiting for you,' she hissed. 'I've had the police here.'

'I'm sorry, Mrs Draper.' Feeling unable to conduct a conversation while remaining upright, he sat down on the stairs and gave her what he hoped was a winning smile through the banisters. 'When did they come?'

'This afternoon.' Mrs Draper glared at him. 'What have you done?'

'Nothing. They wanted to speak to me about,' Dacre hiccupped, 'one of my patients.'

'Then why were they asking about you? They wanted to know when you'd come to stay here.'

'A matter of routine, Mrs Draper.' Dacre hiccupped again. 'That's all.'

Mrs Draper shook her head. 'You're drunk. And there's something going on, I know there is. I won't have my name dragged into it.'

'There's no risk of that, Mrs Draper. I'm leaving.' Producing a fistful of notes from his pocket with a flourish, he said, 'I'll give you an extra week, so you won't lose out.'

The landlady sniffed. 'That's all very well, but I don't want another visit from the police. This is a respectable place, and—'

He held up a hand. 'Mrs Draper!'

'Keep your voice down. There's people trying to sleep.' She had to raise her own voice for the last part, to make herself heard over the crump of a distant doodlebug.

'For Christ's sake. Take this,' he thrust a couple of notes at her, 'and let me go upstairs and pack.' Clutching the banister he hauled himself, unsteadily, to his feet.

'I'm coming with you,' she said.

Mrs Draper stood in the doorway of the room, arms folded and radiant with disapproval, watching, eagle-eyed, in case he tried to pack anything that wasn't his. He collected his things as quickly as he could, closed his case, and carried it to the door, where Mrs Draper barred his way. He moved half a step forward, but she failed to retreat so that they stood face to face, or nearly (her hairline was on a level with his nose).

'You stink of beer,' she said.

He averted his face and his mind raced, gunning like an engine that fails to spark, trying to produce some appropriate words. 'I'm sorry to have caused you trouble,' he said, slowly. 'I'm afraid I am not…able…to explain. It's nothing terrible, I can assure you of that. Now, if you wouldn't mind…'

'Your keys, Dr Dacre.'

He fumbled in his pocket. 'Sorry. There you are.'

'Thank you.' The landlady moved aside, and followed aim across the landing and down the stairs to the front door.

He turned on the threshold, and found her directly behind him. 'I'll say goodnight, then,' he said, awkwardly, backing into the street.

'Goodnight. And don't come back.'

He made a sketchy, forlorn gesture, half wave and half salute, and began lugging his case towards the Euston Road.

Waking at dawn, stiff and sour after a night spent in fitful sleep on a hard bench in a shelter, with a foul mouth, a queasy stomach and a thudding head, Dacre felt as if his brain had been shrunk to the size of a walnut, and, with every move, was banging against the inside of his skull. He sat, fearing to move, while the other occupants of the shelter packed up their belongings and trudged out into the morning. After a another couple of hours half-drowsing in hideous dreams, the nausea was starting to recede, and, finding himself alone, he took his remaining money from his pocket and began to count it. There was, he thought, enough for a train ticket out of London, and a couple of weeks' board and lodging somewhere. After that…

He'd worry about 'after that', he thought, getting slowly and gingerly to his feet, once he'd got settled somewhere. Euston was the nearest station—he'd make for there and see where the trains went. North, he thought. He'd board one, and then he'd consider his next move.

At Euston, he obtained a cup of coffee—pretty filthy, but he kept it down—from the station buffet, together with a bun, which he put in his pocket for later. Queuing at the ticket office, he found, when it came to his turn, that he had no idea of where he wanted to go, and said the first place that came into his head, which was Northampton. 'Train's in ten minutes,' said the clerk. 'Change at Bletchley.'

He stood amongst noisy groups of soldiers in the corridor, flattening himself against the window as harassed-looking women towed protesting children past him, their luggage banging against his legs. Sweating in the prickly woollen jumper, he felt as if he were in the muzzy horror of a nightmare. As the coffee settled on his stomach, the action of the train made him nauseous again, and he wondered if he would be sick, and whether he could manage to find his way to the lavatory in time, or if he should try to open a window.

A soldier, attempting to turn round in the cramped space, whacked him on the chest with his rifle. 'Sorry, mate…Here, you all right? Had a skinful?'

He nodded, afraid to open his mouth, and pushed towards the WC at the end of the carriage, where he vomited. He managed to wrench open the small window and stood, sucking in the fresh air, until somebody started banging on the door. It occurred to him that this would he as good a place as any to lose Dacre, so, holding his ID card and ration book, he thrust his hand out of the window and let the wind snatch them away. He opened his case and checked for anything else that might reveal his identity. There were two medical textbooks, so, reluctantly, he launched them from the window, too. They hung in the air for a moment, covers wide open like stiff, ungainly birds, and then, craning his neck, Dacre saw them plummet to earth as the train roared on. Now, emerging from the WC into the cramped corridor, he was nobody: just a face in a crowd.

At Bletchley, he was waiting on the sparsely populated platform, staring at the advertisements—Bovril, dried eggs, Bile Beans—when an old man in a worn suit limped up and stood dejectedly beside him, as if standing in line for some unwelcome parade. He had the ammoniac stink of an unwashed body and sweat-rotted socks, one fixed and one moving eye, and one corner of his mouth was uplifted in a snarl, as if pulled by an invisible hook, exposing rotten teeth. 'Got a fag, mate?'

'Here.' Trying not to look at the man, Dacre pulled his cigarette packet—only two left now—out of his pocket, and offered it. 'Thanks, mate…Got a match?'

'Yes.' Dacre produced a box and handed it over.

The old man lit up, took a pull on the cigarette, and grinned horribly. ''Ere,' he said, 'I know you!'

Dacre took a step back. 'I don't think so.'

'Don't you remember me?' the old man's voice was wheedling. 'I remember you.'

'I've never seen you before.'

'But I know you,' the man insisted. 'I do. Wait a minute… No, that's not it…'

Gripped by a sudden, bowel-clenching panic, Dacre said, 'I don't know you.'

'Yes…' said the old man. 'Let me think…I know you, all right.'

'No!' Dacre was backing away, almost shouting now, and heads were swivelling in their direction. 'I. Do. Not. Know. You,' he muttered.

The old man shuffled towards him again, and thrust his face upwards, into Dacre's. The vile lips opened, and a fetid cloud seemed to engulf him. Vomit rose once more in his throat and he clapped one hand over his mouth.

'Man is born to trouble,' said the old man. 'Born to trouble as the sparks fly upwards.'

Dacre just managed to swallow back the contents of his stomach. He gasped. Was this some sort of message? An angel—a devil—a portent? Feeling a fresh bloom of sweat break out on his skin, he turned on his heel and, feeling that he might faint at any moment, walked away as fast as he could down the platform. The old man pursued him, plucking his sleeve, the voice querulous now, plaintive, 'I do know you, I do, I know—'

Dacre looked down at the hand with its yellow nails, long and thick, like horns, that clutched at him. 'Leave me alone!' he said, jerking his arm away. 'You've got your fag, now *go away*.'

'Oh no,' said the old man, head on one side and grinning atrociously. 'I can't leave you, because I know what you are.'

'What do you mean?' Dacre was shouting now. 'Get away from me!'

'Born to trouble,' said the old man. 'Born to trouble...'

'No!' Dacre shouted. 'No!' He was feeling dizzy, he couldn't hold himself up, his balance had deserted him, he was falling... The old man's face fell away, too, a sheer drop into darkness, and then—quite suddenly—nothing at all.

Part II

April, 1945, nine months after Jenny's death: Stratton stared into the small fire in Mrs Chetwynd's sitting room without really seeing it. It was ten o'clock, and Monica and Pete had gone to bed, Mrs Chetwynd having declared it more sensible for them to remain in Norfolk overnight and return to London with Stratton the following morning. After a miserable winter of ice, burst pipes, chilblains and incessant doodlebugs, not to mention the time it took for his arm to heal and his and Ballard's frustration that Dacre appeared to have vanished off the face of the earth, the last bomb—a V2 rocket—had fallen at the end of March, and it was deemed safe for the children to return home. Doris and Lilian had promised to help keep an eye on them, and in any case Monica, at fifteen, and Pete, at twelve, would be able to do a great deal for themselves.

Mrs Chetwynd entered, carrying a tea tray. Her elderly housekeeper having died the previous year and the servants long departed, she was, as she put it, 'learning to fend for herself'. A raw-boned, angular woman, she had, Stratton thought, grown thinner since they'd first met almost five years earlier, when she'd taken the children to live with her. There were more lines on her long, rather horsey face, and more grey in her hair—things, Stratton thought, that were true of him, also. It occurred to him that, after Monica and Pete departed, she might be lonely, all by herself in her great house. As if reading his thoughts, Mrs Chetwynd said, 'You know, it would be a relief to sell up and move into one of the cottages, but nobody wants these big places nowadays.'

'Someone might turn it into a school,' suggested Stratton.

'Too much work to do,' said Mrs Chetwynd, briskly. 'They'd have to change everything, and the roof is in a terrible state. It's a white elephant, really.' Eyes down, concentrating on pouring tea, she added, 'It's been lovely having Monica and Peter here, you know. They've kept the place alive.'

'I'm very grateful to you,' said Stratton, and then, feeling that this sounded automatic, he said, 'You've been so kind to them, especially since...'

Mrs Chetwynd put down the teapot and looked directly at him. 'Since Mrs Stratton died. I am so sorry, Mr Stratton. It was a terrible thing to happen.'

'Yes, it was,' said Stratton, abruptly, and turned back to the fire, unable to bear the kindness in her eyes.

'People never talk about the dead, do they? They don't want you to talk about them, either.'

Stratton, reflecting on how few conversations he'd had about Jenny, even in the first days and weeks after her death, said, 'No, they don't.'

'It's not because they've forgotten, you know. It's because they're embarrassed, and they don't want to upset you.'

'I know.' Stratton sighed. 'Everyone has been very good.'

'But it's not good if you want to talk about them, is it?' Mrs Chetwynd handed him a cup of tea.

As he stared at the pale liquid, Stratton realised quite how much he did want to talk about Jenny, as well as thinking about her. It wouldn't make him miss her any less, he knew that, but it would be...comforting. Even with Donald, he hadn't really— he'd kept hoping that his brother-in-law would mention her name, or that there might be an opportunity...Not to go over how it had happened, because that was not only pointless, but beyond his ability to discuss without lifting the lid on a great reservoir of fury and self-hatred that seemed to lodge, like a physical thing, inside his chest. But he would like to be able to talk about her, how she looked and was, and things they'd done together, and laughed about. 'No,' he said, 'not if you want to talk about them.'

'Well,' said Mrs Chetwynd. 'I'm listening.'

Stratton blinked. He didn't know what to say. Then a picture of Jenny in the yard at Mrs Chetwynd's home farm came into his mind, and he said, 'She was a London girl. When we first met she'd never been further from home than Southend...We used to go and stay at my brother's farm in Devon sometimes, when the kids were small—that's where I come from. I grew up on the farm, but Jenny was always scared of anything bigger than a dog. She worried about the children getting too close to the cows, even when they were here. When we first met, she used to laugh at my accent—it was stronger then. But it wasn't unkind—she never mocked people. That was one of the things I first noticed about her, how kind she was. If anything went wrong, she worried in case it was her fault, and tried to put it right...and she was a wonderful mother, right from the start, the way she looked after them... all of us...I miss her being there. In the same room, or knowing she's somewhere in the house...I used to walk through the door at the end of the day, and even if things weren't going well at work, it didn't matter, because there she was and everything was all right, somehow...' Stratton found he couldn't speak any more, and suddenly an enormous, gulping sob was in his throat and he couldn't hold it back. He put his head in his hands and, for the first time since Jenny died, wept.

Mrs Chetwynd left the room quietly, and returned a couple of minutes later with two large white handkerchiefs. 'Here you are.'

'Thank you. I'm very sorry about that.' Mortified by his outburst, Stratton blew his nose, hard, and attempted to rally sufficiently to bid her goodnight before he disgraced himself any further.

To his surprise, Mrs Chetwynd sat down opposite once more and said, in a conversational tone as if nothing had happened, 'Yes, that was how Mrs Stratton struck me, you know. A very good mother. Not that I have children myself, but one can sense these things. My husband was killed in the Great War. I was eighteen when I married. Nineteen-fourteen. We'd known each other since we were twelve, and Edward never seemed to mind that I wasn't beautiful.' She chuckled. 'My parents must have been amazed to get me off their hands so quickly, because I had no money coming to me. Edward was killed in September 1915. The Battle of Loos. His brother, Alfred, was killed about eighteen months later, at Arras. His mother never really recovered—they were her only children.'

Understanding that this confidence was kindly meant, Stratton said, 'And you were never tempted to marry again?'

Mrs Chetwynd shook her head. 'Edward was...well, he was *it*, if you see what I mean.' There was no self-pity in her voice, just the flatness of one stating a fact. 'But I had the consolation of knowing that Edward had died for his country...' Her face darkened. 'For some years, at least. When I heard Mr Chamberlain's broadcast announcing that we were at war again, I thought, Edward died for nothing. They all did.'

'Yes,' said Stratton. 'I thought the same about my eldest brother. He was killed at Passchendaele.'

'It's different, though,' said Mrs Chetwynd. 'They were soldiers. It's harder for you. The way Mrs Stratton died...The children haven't talked about it much—or not to me, anyway. It's difficult for them to understand—well, for anyone. So... *pointless*. I'm sorry,' she said, hastily, 'if I'm speaking out of turn, but I think that's why it's so hard for them. If it were a bomb, they would understand it better—the apparent random-ness, I mean, but this...'

'Yes,' said Stratton. 'A bomb would have been easier. I don't know,' he added, on an impulse he didn't quite understand, 'how I shall ever explain it to Monica and Pete, because it wasn't really as random as...well, as I told them. The woman was looking for Jenny, and...' He stopped and stared for a moment at Mrs Chetwynd, whose eyes made him feel that he could say it, before continuing, 'it was my fault.'

'How?'

Stratton launched into an explanation of the events which had led to Jenny's death, from the beginning—his words tumbling over each other and the things he'd known and hadn't known coming out as a jumble, so that he had to go back several times and clarify what he meant—to Elsie Ingram's eventual arrest. 'The worst thing is that everyone blames themselves for it. Doris says it's her fault because she should have listened to Donald and asked for Mrs Ingram to go to the asylum, and because she saved her when she tried to gas herself. Jenny didn't want to bother me, you see. Donald was all for telling me about Mrs Ingram's attempt to commit suicide, but Jenny and Doris persuaded him not to, because they thought I'd have to report it, so he blames himself for that...And I knew Jenny was worried about the woman, but I was so taken up with what was happening at work that when she didn't say anything about it I was relieved, to be honest. I should have asked her. Made her tell me. And at the Rest Centre, if I'd just paid attention—a few moments earlier, and she'd be here now. She was pregnant. I only found out afterwards. She hadn't told me. The baby would have been due last month. I wish she'd told me. She was trying to, at the end, but I didn't listen...didn't understand.' Stratton shook his head. 'Before, she must have thought I'd be angry, because we'd always said we'd only have the two...' Stratton stopped, shaking his head again, in despair. 'I can't tell Monica and Pete I rescued the woman who killed their mother. I wasn't to know, but I think it would he hard for them to understand. They might end up hating me.'

'I don't think they will,' said Mrs Chetwynd, 'but I think you should wait until they're older before you try to explain all that to them. I doubt if even a mental specialist would understand the woman's condition.'

'I'm sorry that you had to be the one to break the news to them,' said Stratton, recalling how it had been when he'd arrived, a week later, to see them: Monica weeping, Pete, white-faced and silent. 'I did wonder if I should have taken them back with me, for the funeral, but...'

'It was probably for the best, Mr Stratton. Having to return here afterwards—away from your family—that would have been very hard for them. Monica has started to talk about her mother in the last couple of months, but not in front of Peter. I think...being rather younger, I suppose...he isn't ready to talk about her yet. Monica was very worried about you, you know. She kept saying that they ought to go home because you'd be lonely by yourself.'

'That's so like Jenny,' said Stratton, touched by this in an enormous, but entirely inexpressible, way. 'Thinking of other people. She's a good girl.'

'They both are. You should be very proud of them, Mr Stratton. It always seemed to me—if you don't mind my saying so—that you had a very happy marriage, and I'm sure that Monica and Peter are aware of that...of your love for their mother.'

'I'd have given anything to save her.'

'I think the children will understand that. Now, as there won't be much time tomorrow morning, there is something I'd like to say: I shall miss Monica and Peter, very much. If they wish to visit me—to stay, in the school holidays—I should be delighted to see them.'

'That's very generous—' began Stratton, but Mrs Chetwynd raised a hand to cut him off.

'Nothing generous about it. Pure selfishness on my part. I like their company. Besides,' she twinkled at him, 'if they come in the summer, they can help with the harvest. And you are very welcome too, of course, if you can spare the time from your work. If you can't, the children are quite old enough now to travel on their own.'

'Thank you,' said Stratton. 'And thank you for...for listening to all that,' he finished, lamely, feeling that it wasn't quite what he'd wanted to say, but he couldn't think of a better way to put it.

'Not at all.' Mrs Chetwynd rose from her armchair and picked up the tray. 'Goodnight, Mr Stratton.'

CHAPTER

67

The children were subdued on the train home, staring out of the window and saying little. Stratton watched them, covertly, from behind his newspaper. Monica, now she was older, looked heartbreakingly like Jenny, except for her black hair, inherited from him. Pete had Jenny's colouring—green eyes and chestnut hair—but the face and build were more like his own. What would the new one have been? Boy or girl? And how was he going to look after Monica and Pete? It wasn't the practical things that bothered him—Doris and Lilian would see that they were fed and clothed—but getting to know them again. When they'd returned in forty-two, it was Jenny who had smoothed their transition back to life at home, not him. They'd had their own war, up in Norfolk, experiences that he did not know about, other than the things they'd put in their letters, and, in the eighteen months since they'd been re-evacuated, they'd changed again, grown up...

Jenny would have known what to do, how to behave with them. His thoughts moved into the futile repeating loop of asking himself why she hadn't told him about how bad Mrs Ingram was—the suicide attempt and the other erratic behaviour—and answering himself, as he always did, that it was because of his job. She'd seen him then as a policeman, not a husband: no wonder, when he hadn't been behaving like one—distant, not listening to her, belittling her fears, not asking her what was wrong...If he'd been able to report the suicide attempt, Jenny would still be alive.

But being a policeman had nothing to do with why she hadn't told him she was pregnant—he couldn't kid himself about that. It was possible that she was waiting until she was certain—they'd said it was very early—but he knew, in his heart, the real reason was that she thought he'd blame her. That, he supposed, was true, but now— Oh, Jenny, he thought, I wouldn't care if we had *ten* more children, if you were only here.

As the train drew nearer to Liverpool Street, Stratton watched his children stare at the ruins of the City, the massive craters left by the V2 rockets, the gaping cellars and rubble where whole streets had been razed to the ground, punctuated here and there by the burnt-out shells of churches. It was far worse than it had been the last time they were in London. Staring out at the devastation, he thought of the reports he'd heard on the wireless from Buchenwald and Belsen, of the open mass graves and socket-eyed, barely-living skeletons. It was as if God were saying, 'If you think that's bad, chum—war, deprivation, bombing, losing your wife—just you wait and see what I'm really capable of.'

So much grief...How can we ever recover? Things can never be the same again for anyone, thought Stratton. He'd seen a fair bit in his time, but if someone had told him, five and a half years ago, that human beings could do such things to one another, he would not have believed them. Now, he felt, he could believe anything of human beings, however brutal, degraded or senseless it might be. How can we build a better world from *this*, for our children? Where do we *start*? At that moment, grieving for Jenny, for the family life they would not now share, and, by extension, for the human race itself—he could not imagine.

Doris was waiting for them at home, with tea ready on the kitchen table. She'd even managed to scrape together the ingredients for a sponge cake. Monica and Pete seemed pleased to see her, but they behaved like visitors, quiet, minding their manners and careful not to eat too much. The house, which Doris and Lilian had cleaned and polished, seemed on its best behaviour, too, as if, Stratton thought, it was holding its breath.

After they'd eaten, he asked Monica and Pete if they'd like to see the allotment. Pete refused, claiming that he was tired, but Monica said yes. On the way, she talked about Mr Roosevelt and what a shame it was that he'd died before victory was announced. 'We said prayers for him at school,' she added.

'Do you say prayers for Mum?' asked Stratton.

Monica looked at him, surprised. 'Of course I do.'

Stratton showed her the rows of leeks and spring cabbages. 'Not as good as the ones at the farm, I'll bet,' he said.

'It's different there,' said Monica. 'They have manure, and it makes things bigger. But these are good.' This was so kindly meant—and so like Jenny—that Stratton felt a lump rise in his throat.

'Have to plant the potatoes soon,' he said, gruffly. 'They're sprouting.'

'I can help you,' said Monica, looking up at him. 'If you like, I mean. I know what to do because I helped Mrs Chetwynd.'

'Did she grow the vegetables herself?' asked Stratton, surprised.

'Oh, yes,' said Monica. 'When the gardener left. She asked him to teach her how to plant the seeds and things. I don't think he thought she'd be able to do it by herself, but she did. Not as good as you, though,' she added, loyally. 'Can I see if the radishes are ready?'

'It's a bit soon,' said Stratton. 'I only put them in a month ago.'

'That one looks ready, said Monica, pointing at a clump of leaves larger than the rest of the row.

'Go on, then.'

Monica pulled it up, carefully, by the base of the stalks, dusted the earth off the root with her handkerchief and held it up. 'See?'

'Oh, yes. Not bad.'

'Would you like it, Dad?'

Stratton shook his head. 'You have it.'

'All right.' Monica tugged off the leaves and bit. 'Hot,' she said, spluttering.

'It's all right,' said Stratton. 'You don't have to finish it.'

Monica chewed and swallowed. 'No, I want to.' She popped the rest of the radish into her mouth.

'Here,' said Stratton, pulling a bar of chocolate out of his pocket, saved specially for the occasion and, until that moment, forgotten. 'Wash it down with this.'

Monica took the chocolate, and broke off two squares. 'Thanks, Dad.'

'Keep it,' said Stratton.

Monica, her face serious, almost scandalised, shook her head. 'It's for you and Pete.'

'All right, then.' Stratton pocketed the chocolate. 'Bossyboots.'

'I'm not!'

This was the nearest she'd come to the Monica he remembered. 'Of course you're not. Not *really*.' I'd do anything for you, he thought, ruffling her hair.

'Da-*ad*! Get *off*!'

'Sorry.'

'Now it's all messy.' Monica smoothed her long black waves.

'No, it's not.' Stratton walked round the edge of the bed towards the rhubarb. 'This really could have done with some manure,' he said. 'It should have been ready in March.'

Monica, joining him, eyed the clump critically. 'It's not pink enough,' she said.

'Not yet...You'll miss Mrs Chetwynd, won't you, love?'

Monica hesitated. 'Well...'

'It's all right,' said Stratton, deliberately not looking at her. 'It would be odd if you didn't.'

'Yes. But we can write to her, can't we?'

'Course you can. And she's invited you to stay in the holidays...It's bound to be a bit strange at first, without your mum, but we'll muddle along somehow, won't we?' When he'd prepared this in his mind, Stratton had thought he'd be able to say it naturally, but now he was aware of a note of entreaty in his tone that he hadn't intended. For all the sensible grown-upness, Monica was still a child who had lost her mother, and he mustn't burden her with responsibility for their fragile future happiness.

Still staring hard at the rhubarb, Monica said, 'Yes, Dad.'

Stratton decided it was too soon to talk about Jenny—there was still too much rawness between them all. And God forbid that he should cry in front of them...For the time being, it was best left alone. And as for the brother or sister who'd died with Jenny, that, he thought, would be best not mentioned at all. Aside from Mrs Chetwynd, he'd told nobody about the baby. It was too much, somehow. He needed to contain it within himself. He looked down at Monica. I mustn't burden her, he thought, and I shan't. Not now, not ever.

CHAPTER
69

On the way to work the following morning, Stratton found himself noticing a girl's legs for the first time in months. It was entirely instinctive—a reflex—but, catching himself doing it, he felt uncomfortable and slightly guilty. Not because it was a sign that he was forgetting Jenny—after all, he'd done it often enough while she was there and thought nothing of it—but because it was a sign of his being alive when *she* wasn't. And—the realisation brought Stratton to a halt—it was the first time he could remember in months that the underlying feeling, now always with him, of anger and bitterness, had seemed to abate. He'd worked hard to keep it at bay, and yet, at the same time, he cherished it, knowing that it was that hard core inside him, even more than the children, that was keeping him going. At times, when he woke up in the night and lay rigid, staring into the dark, the rage seemed to fill his mind so completely, and with such ferocity, that there was no room for conscious thought. Sometimes it happened during the day, as well. He knew he must keep it in check, yet, standing in the street, he clutched it back to him in a physical movement, clenching his fists, knowing that he could not manage without it.

Mrs Ingram had been judged unfit to plead and incarcerated in Broadmoor. Doug Watson, the DI from Tottenham, had been apologetic about this, but Stratton had decided that it was probably for the best. Despite his feelings, simple humanity told him that it would be both senseless and barbaric to hang a woman so obviously deranged, and besides, it wouldn't bring Jenny back...

It was bad enough that Reg, despite repeated warnings from Donald, had persisted, for several months afterwards, in reminding them all of how he'd said that Mrs Ingram might be dangerous. Eventually, he seemed to understand how close he was coming to losing his teeth, and shut up about it...And it was hard for Doris, too, because she'd lost not only her sister but her best friend. How many times, when Jenny was alive, had he walked into a room and found the pair of them in peals of laughter, wiping their eyes?

He'd been more grateful than he could ever have expressed for Donald's—largely unspoken—support in the last nine months, the trips to the pub and the visits to White Hart Lane to watch football on his rare Saturdays off.

Sergeant Ballard, too, had been rock-like, patient, unintrusive, and picking up the slack without fuss. It was he who had searched the room at Eversholt Street—to no avail, as 'Dacre' had fled, leaving no trace—and who had visited Beatrice Dacre at Norbury to enquire about her son. This had yielded the information that the person who had visited her, claiming to be a school friend of her son, and walked away with the real James Dacre's certificates, had called himself Norman Thomas. Enquiries at the local school—which had taken some time, since it was still evacuated and the records had to be traced to a dusty basement in the town hall—hadn't turned up anyone of that name, and, of the register for Dacre's year, all were accounted for. The boy that Beatrice Dacre had picked out of the class photograph turned out to be one John Walter Strang, who had drowned off the Kent coast in September 1932. Stratton would have let it go at that, despite the coincidence of their middle names—he'd seen the class photograph, and the boy, his face partially covered by a pulled-down school cap, and partly by shadow, could have been anyone—but Ballard, acting on his own initiative, had followed it up and discovered that, although a death certificate had been issued, no body had ever been recovered from the sea.

If John Walter Strang hadn't died, he certainly had disappeared—his mother, who they had traced from 7 Ena Road, Norbury, to an address in Henley-on-Thames where she was living as a paying guest, believed him dead, and, when Ballard had visited her, had seemed genuinely puzzled by their questions. She'd given them a photograph of her son as a boy, but, although there was some resemblance, it could—in the phrase they seemed to keep coming back to—'have been anyone'. Ballard had reported to Stratton that Mrs Strang seemed to find it difficult to describe her son, other than to explain that the family had lost all their money but that he had retained 'ideas above his station'. The sergeant's observation about the woman—that she seemed to accept her descent down the social and economic ladder with a sort of miserable satisfaction—was, Stratton thought, a lot more revealing. As for his description of her jigsaw puzzle, which she was completing with all the pieces turned face down so as not to have the advantage of seeing areas of colour or the outlines of forms...it was as good a symbol of a resolutely joyless existence as he'd ever come across. Unfortunately, as Strang's father was dead, and he had no siblings, and apparently no other relatives than an aunt and uncle in Canada, there was no-one else to ask.

As for 'Dr Dacre', he'd disappeared from the Middlesex Hospital as suddenly as he had from his lodgings. At the hospital, general disbelief (the consensus amongst the staff was that he'd been rather good), gave way first to red faces (the staff quickly revising their opinion of him), followed by acrimony and a lot of hasty arse-covering. Fay, who'd been released without charge by an exasperated DCI Lamb, and gone home to her parents, had, when questioned, denied any knowledge of the man's whereabouts.

Colonel Forbes-James, who Stratton had telephoned on his return to work, had told him that the description he'd given of 'Dacre' appeared to correspond with that of one John Watson, who had worked at the Ministry of Health as a clerk to the National Register from October 1939 to January 1941. He had then left, 'apparently under something of a cloud', and had not been heard of since. As Forbes-James pointed out, this would certainly have given him the opportunity to pocket blank identity cards, and Stratton wouldn't have minded betting that was exactly what he'd done.

DCI Lamb had asked him, when he'd returned to work, if he wished to remain on the investigations, and Stratton had said that he did. But as far as 'Dacre' was concerned, the trail had gone cold, and the enquiries into the deaths of Reynolds and Leadbetter were no better. At first, the shock of Jenny's death had consumed him entirely, so that he could not think of anything else, and then came the rage which churned within him, the tight knots in his chest and stomach, the taste of bile in his mouth, any possible outlet dammed up by the utter lack of progress on the cases. Stratton wasn't sure how much he blamed Dacre, or for what, and these considerations took him round in ever tighter, more bitter circles, so that he couldn't tell who he hated more, Dacre or himself. Ballard certainly thought that the imposter had killed all three people at the hospital, but Stratton no longer trusted his own professional judgement where Dacre was concerned. All he knew was that he could have no peace until he found the man.

When he arrived home that evening, there was a letter sitting on the kitchen table next to a plate of salad. It was after ten, and Stratton had just returned after a long, dispiriting day. The children, as usual when he worked late, were sleeping at Doris's, and there was nothing to welcome him but the cold supper left by Lilian, for which he had no appetite. Pushing it aside, he set the kettle on to boil and slit open the envelope.

Inside was a single sheet of paper, dated the previous day, with no address and no signature.

> *Dear Mr Stratton,*
> *I am sure it will come as quite a surprise, my writing to*
> *you after such a long time, but I have long wished to tell*

you that I am sincerely sorry for what happened, and it is only now that I have felt able to set pen to paper. I did all I could to save Mrs Stratton. I cannot suppose it will be of much consolation, but I have spent some time in studying the treatment of wounds similar to those your wife received, and I truly believe that I could not have done more without the aid afforded by a hospital.

In spite of our hasty exchange, you are, doubtless, wondering how I happened to be at the Rest Centre at that particular time. The cause of it was my desire to speak to you personally about Nurse Marchant. I saw you escort her from the Middlesex, and was concerned that she would be charged with stealing the morphine. I can assure you that she had nothing to do with it: the fault was mine, and only mine. Fay Marchant is entirely innocent of any wrongdoing.

My reading on the subject of mental illness leads me to suspect that your wife's assailant, Mrs Ingram, was, at that particular time, suffering from a form of delusion. Before you arrived, she told me she believed that her husband had been replaced by an imposter. She thought that Mrs Stratton, yourself and your sister-and brother-in-law, were working as part of a conspiracy against her. I am afraid that, by telling her that you were a policeman (which she appeared not to have known before), I unwittingly reinforced this idea. I have seen this type of acutely confused state identified as Capgras Delusion or Syndrome. It is, mercifully, rare.

Words cannot express how much I regret that I was unable to save Mrs Stratton. Please believe that, despite what I said to you when we parted, I acted in good faith.

The envelope was stamped Northampton...*by telling her that you were a policeman...I unwittingly reinforced this idea.* The sentence jumped out from the rest of the words as if it had been written in scarlet. It was all his fault. If Dacre, or whoever the bastard was, hadn't told Mrs Ingram that he was a policeman, Jenny might still be alive. Mrs Ingram had had the knife with her, Dacre had said so, and Doris had confirmed that it was one of Jenny's, but she wouldn't have been so quick to act...He could have reasoned with her, overpowered her, taken the knife away... Except that he'd been too busy trying to arrest bloody Dacre, hadn't he? The recollection of those frantic minutes came back to him as strongly and horribly as if they'd happened yesterday, and he sunk his head in his hands and groaned.

The kettle shrieked, and he got up and made tea like an automaton, scarcely registering what he was doing. I must find him, he thought. Whatever happens, I've got to find him.

CHAPTER

70

The Yard's fingerprint men, acting at top speed for one of their own, came up with nothing from the letter, but the handwriting expert compared it to a sample of Dacre's notes from the Middlesex Casualty Department, and to a sample of Todd's writing, obtained from the mortuary records, and declared all three to be by the same author. Mrs Dacre, unfortunately, had destroyed the letter written to her by 'Norman Thomas' so there was nothing available for comparison there.

The following afternoon Stratton was trying to finish a report on a gang robbery at a jeweller's shop, during which the owner and his wife had been tied up and menaced with guns. He'd been at it for ages, but his mind kept drifting back to Dacre's letter. Finally, he gave up on the report, took the piece of paper out of his drawer, and read it again. He must try to stand back from it—pretend he wasn't involved. Emotion, however justified, only served to cloud things. What could he glean from the letter?

Firstly, that Dacre was moved to write to him: partly because of Jenny, and perhaps because he felt some sort of connection to Stratton himself. God knows, thought Stratton, I feel one with him—or I would if I knew who the hell he was. He came to kill me but he saved me when he deflected that madwoman's knife and bound up my arm. Had the doctor's instinct taken over? After all, he'd stayed to try and save Jenny, hadn't he? But it wasn't the instinct of a doctor that had brought him to the Rest Centre. The letter said that his initial motivation was to exonerate Fay Marchant, so he obviously cared for her. But— Stratton's pencil skated across the paper as his hand tried to keep pace with his thoughts—he didn't care enough to come forward later when, for all he knew, Fay could have been languishing in Holloway prison. So, he cared about Fay, but his urge to flee was greater. Stratton spent several minutes wondering if Dacre felt guilty about that. After all, he must realise that there was no actual proof, and the penalty for stealing drugs, while severe— she certainly couldn't have carried on nursing—was not fatal...

Stratton paused to reread the letter...*I have spent some time in studying the treatment of wounds similar to those your wife received, and I truly believe that I could not have done more without the aid afforded by a hospital.*

That was professional pride. He minded what Stratton thought of him—didn't want Jenny's death to reflect on his competence. He'd written *I could not have done more* not 'a qualified physician could not have done more'. Had he come to believe that he truly was a doctor? Or was he just unprepared to admit that he was a fraud?

Stratton tapped the end of the pencil against his mouth. In the next part, there was the business of saying what he thought was wrong with Mrs Ingram. *I have seen this type of acutely confused state identified as Capgras Delusion or Syndrome*...Why the hell should I want to know what you think was wrong with her, thought Stratton. 'Can't resist showing off knowledge', he wrote. But surely that type of stuff wouldn't be in an ordinary medical textbook, would it? Delusions were the province of trick-cyclists.

Where would he have come across such knowledge? Could he be a patient in a mental hospital? After all, Dacre, in his own way, was just as mad as Mrs Ingram. That was the obvious solution...But, Stratton felt, not the right one. After all, Dacre had fooled the staff at the Middlesex, hadn't he? Fooled Stratton, too, if it came to that. And he'd felt secure enough to write the letter—if not to sign it —and was keen to present the best possible view of himself: the conscientious, knowledgeable physician. He must have found a new role somewhere. And if you'd spent your life fooling people, you must, like any confidence trickster, be a dab hand at working out how others ticked. *My reading on the subject of mental illness...* That suggested an interest in the subject, didn't it?

Stratton wrote a final sentence and then began to recap what he knew, scribbling down the names in order:

John Walter Strang, schoolboy (to September 1932)
John Watson, clerk to Nat. Register (Oct 1939 to Jan 1941)
Sam Todd, mortuary attendant (April 1944 to June 1944)
Norman Thomas (name on letter to Mrs Dacre—used before?)
James Walter Dacre, doctor (July 1944 to August 1944)

There was no particular pattern, just a lot of gaps. If all these were the same person, what had he been doing between the time of his 'death' in September 1932 and October 1939, and from January 1941 to April 1944? During the latter period, he'd have needed an identity card in order to obtain a ration book, although both, as Stratton well knew, could be obtained off the back of the same lorry as everything else, if you had the money. In terms of status and salary, it was definitely an upward progression. Knowing enough of such people to realise that such knowledge as they gained was rarely, if ever, wasted, Stratton was wondering whether, at this moment, in a hospital somewhere in England—Northampton?— there was a doctor who wasn't all that he seemed...

Satisfied with his deduction, he was about to pick up the robbery report once more—Lamb had been making noises about why it, and a host of other reports about black market whisky, cigarettes, hams and the rest weren't on his desk—when Ballard stuck his head round the door. 'Cup of tea, sir?'

'Thanks. Come and sit down for a minute. I've been looking at this,' he brandished the letter, 'and I've had an idea. I think we ought to be looking at asylums.'

'You think he's a mental patient?'

Stratton shook his head. 'I think he's become another type of doctor. A psychiatrist.'

'Why? If you don't mind my asking, sir.'

For answer, Stratton pushed his notes across the table and talked the sergeant through each point.

Ballard looked dubious. 'The only thing is, sir, that he must have known about James Dacre, mustn't he? That he'd died, I mean. Otherwise, he wouldn't have gone to see the mother like that. That's why I thought it must be Strang. If he'd wanted to take another doctor's identity, he'd have to find one first, wouldn't he? To know of one who'd died, I mean. Do you think he killed Reynolds in order to take the position at the Middlesex, sir? It would make sense.'

Stratton sighed. 'I'm not sure that it fits...But I think he killed Byrne in order to protect his identity as Dacre, and when he discovered we'd arrested Fay—his girl—he felt as if he was beginning to lose control of it. That was why he came to kill me. He was confused by then, everything was unravelling. I wonder if he hadn't had a bit to drink, too. And something tells me that he might not hesitate to kill in the future if he sees it as a means to an end. Anyway, coming back to my original point, a mental hospital is an institution, and he seems to like those. I think it makes him feel that he belongs somewhere.'

Ballard raised his eyebrows. 'Who'd want to belong in a loony bin?'

'If I'm right,' said Stratton, 'the lunatic who took over the asylum.'

'How would you feel, Ballard, if you'd employed a man like Dacre and then discovered he was a fraud?'

'Bloody embarrassed, sir.'

'Exactly. Remember the way Professor Haycraft was talking about him, at the Middlesex? I had the impression that he'd almost rather not have known Dacre was an imposter. And after that, he was unwilling to admit that the man had been any good as a doctor at all.'

'Yes, he did. But he must have been, mustn't he, sir? Good, I mean. With not being trained, he'd have had to learn all that medical stuff in a very short time. His memory must be excellent—all those facts.'

'So there's no reason,' said Stratton, 'why he shouldn't do the same with psychiatry. And people like him,' he added, remembering his own response on first meeting Dacre, 'trustworthiness, common sense...He'd be able to get into a position of power without making enemies, I think. Let's start with the asylums near Northampton, seeing as that's where the letter was posted. Doesn't necessarily mean anything, but you never know. We need the names—full names—of every single member of staff, and we're looking for Dacre, Thomas, Todd, Watson or Strang in the first instance. If you make up a list and get started, I'll just—'

The telephone rang and Stratton paused to pick up the receiver. Cudlipp's voice announced that a Mrs Strang was on the line wishing to speak to Sergeant Ballard. 'He's with me,' said Stratton, 'you can put her through.'

'John Strang's mother. Wants to talk to you. Let's hope it's useful.' Stratton handled over the receiver.

'Good morning, Mrs Strang. How may I help you?' said Ballard, and then, after a pause, 'No, not at all. Quite the right thing.' After a second, longer, pause, during which he scribbled in his notebook, he said, 'I see. And when was this?' then 'That's very helpful. Thank you...Yes, of course we shall. Thank you very much.'

When he'd replaced the receiver, Ballard said, 'That was interesting, sir. She said she'd been thinking about her son, and she remembered how he'd got bitten by a dog when he was a kid, on his right hand. Left quite a scar, apparently. Said she wasn't sure if she ought to let us know, only when she spoke to her friend, *she* said she ought to talk to us.'

'Good for her friend,' said Stratton.

'It was strange,' said Ballard, 'but she seemed quite...well, diffident about it. As if she didn't really care one way or the other. I think it's because it's too much, really, for her to adjust to—I mean, there she was for all those years thinking he was dead and now it turns out he probably isn't. I reckon she's sort of stopped minding. They say mothers aren't supposed to, but—'

'But everyone's different,' said Stratton. 'And anyway, bearing in mind that he deceived her, you can't blame her for not rushing out to buy a fatted calf.'

'Sorry to ask, sir, but do you remember seeing a scar, when you met him?'

'Mmm...' Stratton grimaced, trying to picture Dacre's hands, but the images this gave rise to—the piles of bloody towels, Jenny's poor white face so near to his own, her last, labouring breaths—made him push the subject away. 'Can't think. I'll telephone Fay Marchant and see what she can remember. And you'd better get started on all those loony bins.'

Ballard left the office and Stratton found the number for Fay's parents' house and asked for the call to be put through. A smart-sounding woman answered.

'Good morning,' said Stratton, consciously elevating his accent. 'Might I speak to Miss Marchant, please?'

'Certainly,' said the woman. 'Who is calling?'

'It's Detective Inspector Stratton, from West End Central.'

There was a sharp intake of breath at the other end. 'Good heavens. There's not...she isn't...there's nothing *wrong*, is there? I mean,' continued the woman, thinking aloud, 'she wasn't involved with that business at the hospital...'

'Goodness, no,' said Stratton, easily. 'Am I speaking to Mrs Marchant?'

'Yes...I'm sorry.' The woman sounded flustered. 'It's just that...oh, dear...Such a horrible business, that doctor being hit over the head, and that poor nurse, and then the other one...'

'There's nothing to be alarmed about, Mrs Marchant.' Fay's mother, he thought, was obviously the anxious type—probably patting her chest with a fluttery hand right at that moment. 'Miss Marchant has been most helpful to us over that...unfortunate matter,' he continued, in his most avuncular tone, 'but I'm afraid that I do need to trouble her with another question. Incidentally, who told you about the doctor being hit over the head?' This wasn't something that had been released to the newspapers—they knew only that Dr Reynolds had died in suspicious circumstances.

'My daughter, I suppose. She won't have to appear in court, will she?'

'I'm afraid there's a possibility of that,' said Stratton, adding, with what he hoped was a reassuring chuckle, 'but only as a witness, of course.'

'Oh, dear...' Stratton heard a female voice in the background, and Fay's mother, evidently recollecting that this conversation was taking place on the telephone, said, 'Just a moment,' and handed over the receiver.

'Hello?' said Fay. 'Can I help?'

'It's Detective Inspector Stratton, Miss Marchant.'

'So I gathered,' said Fay, and then, guardedly—Mother was clearly at her elbow, 'what is it?'

'It's about Dr Dacre, Miss Marchant. Perhaps you could tell me…did he have any distinguishing marks? I mean,' he added, 'on his face or hands?'

'Oh, I see.' Fay's relief was audible. 'Well, there was a mark on his hand. A scar, from a dog bite.'

'Which hand?'

'I'm just trying to picture it…The right, I think.'

'Are you sure?'

'Yes.'

'What did it look like?'

'A sort of crescent shape. At the base of the thumb. Going up towards the forefinger.'

'Thank you, Miss Marchant. I'm sorry to trouble you at home.'

'That's quite all right, Inspector. I probably shouldn't ask this, but have you found out who he is?'

'Not yet, but you've been very helpful. By the way, where did you hear about Dr Reynolds being hit over the head?'

'Dr Dacre told me. With a brick, he said.'

'Did he say how he came by that information?'

Fay thought for a moment and said, 'No, I've no idea. Perhaps Dr Byrne told him. Is it important?'

'Not really. Thanks very much for your time, Miss Marchant.'

'Not at all. Well, goodbye, Inspector.'

Fay put the telephone down, and Stratton imagined her on the receiving end of a lot of breathless questions and exaggerated fuss. Probably a few palpitations, too, if he wasn't mistaken. Wherever she got her sangfroid from, he thought as he went to the Communications Room to find Ballard, it wasn't her mother.

He stuck his head round the door and motioned the sergeant to come outside. 'Did Strang's mother describe the scar?'

Ballard pulled out his notebook and flicked through the pages. 'A half-circle, she said. Near the right thumb.'

'Fay Marchant said that Dacre had a crescent-shaped scar at the base of his right thumb. And he gave her post-mortem information on Reynolds, so it looks like we might be getting somewhere. You got that list?'

'Just coming up, sir. I'll bring it through.'

They divided the list of mental hospitals into two and started work. After two and a half hours Stratton, who had ticked off most of his, and whose hand ached from taking down all the names, hadn't come across a Strang, Watson, Todd, Thomas or Dacre. He was beginning to wonder if it hadn't been a completely hare-brained idea when Ballard came in, looking unusually pleased with himself.

'Which name is it?'

'None of them, sir. There is a Professor Thomas, but the Christian name is Oliver and he's been working in the same place since 1929, so it obviously isn't him. However,' Ballard slid his notebook under Stratton's nose, and indicated a name ringed in red pencil. 'Look. And again...' he flipped through the pages, 'here. Two Dr Christopher Rices, one at the Maudsley Hospital, working with children—they've all been evacuated to the country somewhere—and one at the Northfield Military Hospital, near Birmingham. You know how we were just talking about taking real people's identities, sir—I thought that might be a possibility, but the person concerned wouldn't necessarily have to be dead. I know it's a pretty small field, but he could have dreamt up a different background from the original chap, and what with all the ad hoc arrangements and changes of address and so on, it's easy for things to slip through the gaps. Besides which, Rice isn't such a common name, sir, so when I came across the second one I asked when he'd taken up the post. It was the middle of December, sir. Then I telephoned the first lot again, and asked about *their* Dr Rice, and they said he'd arrived the week before, on the fifth. Odd, wouldn't you say?'

'Either that or it's a mighty coincidence. I suppose that's possible, but...' Seeing that Ballard's grin was widening to Cheshire cat proportions, Stratton said, 'You've got something else to tell me, haven't you?'

'Yes, sir.'

'You're enjoying this, aren't you?'

Ballard nodded enthusiastically.

'Out with it, then!'

'Well, sir, once I'd got that far, I thought it might be a good idea to telephone Northfield—that was the first place I tried—back, and ask about Rice's paperwork. They got very sniffy at the suggestion that it might not be in order, but they checked, *and*... this is where it gets interesting...' Ballard paused for effect.

'Ooh, you little tease,' said Stratton, in an atrocious imitation of an old roué. 'Get on with it.'

'One of his references was from none other than Professor Haycraft of the Middlesex Hospital.'

'My God. What about the other one?'

'There isn't another one. The secretary got all flustered when she realised and told me it must have been lost in the post. You know the sort of thing—enemy action.'

'I do indeed. Well, well, well. How very convenient. I don't know what I did to deserve you, Ballard, but it must have been something good. See if you can locate the real Dr Rice, will you, while I have a word with Professor Haycraft.'

CHAPTER

72

'Not more trouble, I trust?' Professor Haycraft sounded more detached than ever as if he expected Stratton to tell him he'd lost his dog, or his aunt had had a bilious attack.

You bloody old fool, thought Stratton. If you'd got off your arse and checked Dacre's references in the first place, Dr Byrne would still be alive, for a start. 'Just a question, Professor,' he said, as smoothly as he could manage. 'It's about a Dr Rice—Christopher Rice—at the Northfield Military Hospital. A psychiatric doctor.'

'Ye-ess…?' Haycraft spoke cautiously, and Stratton pictured him holding the telephone receiver as far from his ear as possible, as though it were a grenade that might explode at any moment.

'I believe you wrote a reference for him.'

'You're asking me if I wrote a reference?'

No, thought Stratton, I'm asking if you dressed up in a gymslip and spanked the man with a hairbrush. 'Yes,' he said.

During the umming and aaahing and paper-shuffling noises that followed, Stratton realised that he was grinding his teeth, and hastily moved the receiver away from his mouth.

'What did you say his name was?'

'Dr Christopher Rice.'

'And you say he specialises in psychiatry?'

'Yes.'

'I don't know him.'

'Well, apparently you wrote a reference for him in late November or early December last year, for Dr Reinhardt of the Northfield Military Hospital.'

'No. I've heard of Reinhardt's work, of course, but I had nothing to do with any reference for this man Rice.'

'So you didn't write the reference?'

'Certainly not. The man has obtained his post under false pretences. I cannot let my name, or the hospital's, be used in this fashion. I shall speak to Dr Reinhardt at once.'

'I'm afraid I can't allow you to do that, sir.'

'*Allow?* But—'

'This is a police investigation.' Stratton was aware that he'd raised his voice several decibels. 'I must insist that you don't do anything of the sort.'

'But—'

'I shall make it clear to Dr Reinhardt that you did not supply the reference.'

Haycraft mumbled something Stratton didn't catch, then—giant penny dropping with an almighty crash—he said, 'Is this to do with that man Dacre?'

'We are looking into it, sir—'

'And you'll let me know, won't you? This is a serious breach of—'

'I'm quite aware of how serious it is, sir.'

'Well, I...I shall...' More mumbling followed, as Haycraft, torn between the desire to revert to his usual vague pomposity and the consciousness of his negligence, tried to find the right tone.

'I'll say goodbye, then. *Sir.*' Stratton cut across him and put down the receiver.

He took a deep breath, trying to calm himself, then lit a cigarette and sat back in his chair, willing himself to relax as he waited for Ballard to return. He tilted his head back and, focusing on a particularly dark patch on the ceiling, which, after decades of smoking by the room's inhabitants, had an all-over greasy, ochre-coloured coating, he thought, we're finally getting some-where. As well as the prickings of hope, there were other things playing in his mind, faint but persistent, like a poorly tuned wire-less in the next room. But they could wait until the time came. First things first. He sat up straight and banged his fist down hard on the desk. 'The tables have bloody well turned,' he said to his invisible adversary. 'I'm in charge, now.' All things considered, he reflected, rubbing his smarting knuckles, it really was well overdue that life—or fate, or God, or possibly all three—stopped kicking him in the balls. It was time to go to work.

CHAPTER
73

Stratton sat with Dr Rice in the Smoking Room of the latter's London club, feeling completely out of place. They had ascended the enormous staircase, hung round with oils whose patina of age and grime made it almost impossible to make out their subjects, with a ceremonial chair, as big as a throne, on the corner of each landing. Everything was mahogany and leather, and either brown, holly green, or beef red. The ceiling was ornate, and there were framed 'Spy' cartoons on the walls, and bronzes of moustachioed men on polo ponies and busts of fierce-looking statesmen with chipped noses on the surfaces. The elderly servants wore black knee-breeches, and knew as well as Stratton did that he did not belong. Don't give yourself airs, said their eyes. We know you're one of us.

Dr Rice was, Stratton thought, in his middle fifties. He looked like a sportsman—lean and muscular, despite the thinning hair. He had a rather languid manner, which seemed unsuitable for children, and Stratton wondered if he altered it when he was at work. When Ballard had tracked him down, he'd turned out to be 'in town', and immediately agreed to meet Stratton. Now they were drinking muddy coffee, and Rice was staring intently at the photograph of Todd.

'Sorry,' he said. 'Don't recognise him. I might have seen him before, but...' He spread his hands.

'How about this?' Stratton passed over the photograph of Todd which Ballard, during his absence, had had doctored by a police artist to remove the moustache and darken the hair. It was pretty crude, but the likeness wasn't bad.

'Now, he does look familiar. I've certainly seen him before.'

'What's his name?'

'I have absolutely no idea.'

'But you're sure you've seen him?'

'Oh, yes. Before I explain, perhaps you could tell me *why* you require this information? Your sergeant was somewhat, shall we say, *vague*, on the telephone.'

'An enquiry into obtaining employment under false pretences, sir.'

The eyebrows rose gracefully. 'Then of course I shall co-operate. I first encountered this man when I was staying with my niece and her husband in Ferny Stratford, which is a few miles from Bletchley. My niece's husband is the local doctor. He was called to Bletchley railway station because there was a man there who'd been sitting on a bench all day and the porter couldn't get any sense out of him. When spoken to, he became distressed and appeared not to know who, or where, he was. When I questioned him several days later, I had the impression that he thought he'd blacked out—fainted, perhaps—but he hadn't been observed to fall down at any point. Dr Lonsdale—that's my niece's husband— brought him home and asked me to examine him. I couldn't get any sense out of him either, at first. He was dazed, bewildered, kept asking where he was. I thought he must be concussed. As I said, nobody had seen him fall, and there hadn't been any sort of altercation noticed on the platform, so I can only suppose that the trauma had occurred before he arrived there.'

'Do you know *how* he arrived there?'

'No. He'd been there quite a few hours, you see, so if he had got off a train the other passengers were long gone, and none of the staff could remember anything.'

'Was there nothing to identify him? Belongings? His ration book?'

'Not a thing. No identity card, nothing. He had a suitcase, but the only things in it were clothes, a razor...the usual sorts of things. We wondered if he might have been robbed, but he said he couldn't remember.'

'And no left-luggage ticket, or anything like that?'

'No.'

'His distress—could it have been put on?'

Dr Rice shook his head. 'He had several episodes of weeping, he was sweating profusely, trembling...I really don't think so. Most of my experience is with children, but I believe I can tell a man in the last stages of mental and physical exhaustion, Inspector.'

'I see. And what happened after that?'

'Well, he calmed down a for over the next few days, but he appeared to have no autobiographical memory—nothing before he arrived at my niece's house. He wasn't able to tell me his name or anything about himself—family, occupation, and so on. He didn't seem aware of external events, either. With concussion, these things generally go off, given time, but there seemed to be no change over the course of a week.' Rice shook his head. 'All very difficult. You see, Inspector, memory is—if you like—the bones of thought. Without it, there is nothing else—no past, and no future, either, because there's no anchor for it. There's no identity, and no real chance of building any sort of relationship with another person, so it's very isolating for the sufferer.

'He asked me a lot of questions—some of a personal nature, some about my work. At first, I was rather taken aback, but I think he was looking for something to build on. Something he could remember, so that it would be a place to start. I must say, I rather liked him. He certainly wasn't sub-normal in any way—quite the reverse, in fact. Intelligent. And a good sense of humour. My niece really took a shine to him.'

'Did you notice if he had any distinguishing marks?'

'A scar,' said Dr Rice, promptly. 'One of his hands. Can't remember which, but it was quite noticeable. At the base of his thumb.'

Up till then, Stratton had hoped, but hadn't allowed himself to feel certain. Now, the hairs on the back of his neck prickled. Piece by piece, it was falling into place...'Did you believe the memory loss?' he asked.

'That it was real, yes. As to the cause...There are many reasons for amnesia, Inspector. I'm sure it was absolutely genuine in the early stages, caused by some stress or pressure on him, or some external source. After that, who knows? Things usually do come back, but sometimes there are episodes that the person simply doesn't want to remember, so he blocks them out. The result, to the sufferer, can be just as real as a loss of memory.'

'And what happened after that?'

'He vanished. Quite suddenly. It was a couple of days before I was due to go back home. We had reported his appearance to the local police, with a description, in case anyone was looking for him, and naturally we told them he'd gone, but we never heard from them, so...' Rice shrugged.

'Did he take anything with him when he left?'

'Stealing, you mean? No, nothing from the house—no money or silver. My niece checked.'

'And from you?'

Dr Rice hesitated, looking less sure of himself than before. 'I don't know. You see, I'd taken some papers with me—things I needed to work on—and when I'd finished, I put them away, and had no reason to take them out again until a month or so after I returned home. It was only then that I noticed a few of the papers were missing—letters, and such. Nothing very important, except something relating to my new position at the Maudsley. I wrote to my niece asking her to look for them, but she couldn't find anything. It was easily remedied, and to be honest I didn't think any more of it.' He gave Stratton a shrewd look. 'You think he took them.'

'It's possible,' admitted Stratton.

'May I ask if you've found him?'

'Not yet, but we will.'

'Well, when you find him, I shall be interested to know his story. He sounds like a fascinating case.'

More than you know, chum, thought Stratton, as he descended the great staircase. Standing at the top of the steps, beneath the huge porch with its fluted pillars, he remembered Rice's words about memory being the bones of thought. *Without it, there is nothing else…*

Fancy names aside, he thought, it was Jenny who'd come closest to understanding what was wrong with Mrs Ingram when she said she didn't feel in her heart that Mr Ingram was her husband—or, to put it another way, she'd lost her emotional memory. And he'd thought she was being illogical. What an idiot.

He stood quite still, feeling the anger—against Dacre, against himself, against the world—boil up inside him. This time, he told himself, there would be no mistake. He'd get a warrant for obtaining employment under false pretences, and then he was going up to Northfield Military Hospital to nail the bastard. And, he decided, this time he was going alone. He had a score to settle, and—whatever the outcome—he'd fucking well settle it.

CHAPTER 74

The train was stuffy and crowded. Soldiers jammed the corridors, rifles and kitbags lay everywhere, and the air was blue with smoke and obscenities. Eventually, Stratton managed to find a free seat next to a rowdy group of sailors.

For some reason, most of the servicemen departed at Rugby, so he had the compartment to himself as he tried to collect his thoughts. He wondered if Chief Superintendent Dewhurst would have enough for a fingerprint match from the mortuary. He'd said there was a partial palm print and fingertips on the office bookshelf, but there might be more elsewhere. He'd just have to hope they didn't clean the place too thoroughly. Of course, that wouldn't prove that their man had killed Dr Byrne, and, if Ballard was right, Reynolds and Leadbetter—but it would prove that Todd, Dacre and Rice were the same person, which was certainly a start…'I'll have you for Byrne, mate, if it's the last thing I do,' he muttered. 'You are going to fucking swing.'

Northfield Hospital proved to be a five-mile journey from Birmingham on a rickety tram, followed by about a mile's walk uphill, and by the time Stratton reached the gatehouse he was tired, sweaty, and not best pleased to be told that it was another mile down the tree-lined drive to the building itself. As he walked closer, he suddenly stopped, turned to the side and retched. Head hanging down, hands on his knees, he told himself forcefully that there would be no Mrs Ingrams here: this place was not an institution for the criminally insane, like Broadmoor, but a place for shell-shocked soldiers, and therefore entirely different.

The main tower became visible before the rest of the institution, which turned out to be a vast and forbidding pile of Victorian red brick. As Stratton trudged towards it, working saliva into his mouth to try and remove the bitter taste of bile, he could hear intermittent bursts of machine-gun fire issuing from somewhere in the distance. He passed a group of men in PT singlets and shorts, who, apparently oblivious to the racket, were standing in the middle of a lawn, throwing a medicine ball around in an unenthusiastic manner, and several more, clad in bright blue serge suits and red ties, who were shuffling about aimlessly amongst the flowerbeds that bordered it. One of them, staring fixedly down at a row of petunias, was rubbing his groin vigorously enough to set his trousers on fire.

The florid orderly who opened the door to him explained that the gunfire was from the automatic weapon testing range at the Austin works across the valley. 'Very soothing,' muttered Stratton. The man led them through a maze of echoing stone corridors floored in cracked mosaic tiles, past enormous, barely furnished wards with rows of iron-framed beds.

'Here we are,' he said, halting in front of some imposing double doors. 'Harley Street. The psychiatrists' rooms, sir. Dr Reinhardt's at the end.'

When Dr Reinhardt, a mop of silver hair and a zealot's gleam behind glittering pince-nez, greeted him in a strong German accent, Stratton had to try very hard not to think of the mad scientists that he'd seen at the pictures. The iron bed covered by a grey blanket beside the desk—'Sometimes we hypnotise a patient'—did nothing to help this impression. Stratton deliberately hadn't informed him of his visit, and his manner was intensely suspicious—not that he could be blamed for that. The man had probably been interned for Christ knew how long in some hell-hole or other. Stratton had visited a few aliens' camps in the early years of the war, and they weren't exactly the Ritz, with draughty wooden huts, straw bedding, and no stoves in winter.

He did his best to calm the psychiatrist down, showing the warrant and explaining about the stolen documents and fraudulent references, but before he could get very far, Reinhardt intervened. 'There must be a mistake. Dr Rice impressed me greatly. We are developing a therapeutic community here, Inspector, and he has been helping to pioneer our group analysis, encouraging self-expression. It is at a critical stage and I cannot have it disturbed.'

Stratton didn't have the foggiest idea what he was talking about, although he didn't think that 'self-expression' sounded much like the army. 'We have very good reason to believe that Dr Rice may not be genuine,' he said.

'Nonsense, Inspector. I would know.'

'He's fooled people before, Dr Reinhardt. And,' Stratton placed both hands on the psychiatrist's desk and leant forward for emphasis, 'we have good reason to believe that he may have done worse.'

'Worse?'

'I'm not at liberty to say, sir. But it's serious.'

'His qualifications are impeccable.'

'They aren't his, and the reference—the one you have, that is—is false. I have spoken to the professor concerned, and I can assure you that there is no mistake about that. Apparently, it wasn't checked.' That, Stratton thought, is one in the eye for you, chum.

'I did not think it necessary.'

'That's a pity. Of course,' continued Stratton, blandly, 'we don't wish to cause embarrassment to you or your institution, but this does—potentially—put the army in rather a difficult position, and, as you say, you wouldn't wish to jeopardise your

operation...' He paused to make sure that Reinhardt had registered the threat.

'You are telling me that he is not qualified *at all*? That he
is an imposter?'

'That's right. Now, perhaps you could give me a physical
description of him.'

'But surely you know...'

'It's easy enough to alter one's appearance, Dr Reinhardt.'

'Well...he's of medium height...the physical build is
average...he's clean shaven, the hair is fair...I cannot say that
there's anything particular about him.'

'Any distinguishing marks? Scars?'

'I have not noticed...' Dr Reinhardt shook his head sadly.
'He is so good with the patients, Inspector.'

'I don't doubt it,' said Stratton, grimly. 'Where is he?'

Dr Sturgiss, a younger man with hair as untidy as Reinhardt's
who clearly had no idea of the seriousness of his errand, ushered
Stratton back down the corridor and into a dark quadrangle,
where a group of blue-suited men were tending to a stunted-
looking tree. 'Is that part of the group therapy?' he asked.

'Oh no,' said Sturgiss. 'Gardening, and carpentry and so
on, are occupational therapies. But we like to encourage groups,
because it gives them a common purpose.'

'I can see how it might,' said Stratton. 'How do the men
react to Dr Reinhardt?'

'To be honest, a lot of them aren't too keen. The foreign
accent, you know.'

'And Dr Rice?'

'Oh, they like him. Even the dullards. You might say he's the star
of the show. There's a much more lively atmosphere with him here.'
Sturgiss opened a door and took Stratton into a large room where
groups of men, this time in khaki, were sitting about playing cards and
smoking, watched by a couple of orderlies. Although the atmosphere

appeared, at first sight, to be fairly relaxed, when Stratton looked closer he could see that the faces were strained and the eyes apprehensive.

The ones nearest the door stopped talking when they entered, and a nervous silence spread through the room. When a man sitting alone in front of a jigsaw puzzle looked up, Stratton saw that he was missing an eye and half his face was covered in a graft, thick, shiny and yellowish, like the skin on custard. What had that poor fucker been through? Stratton wondered. Surely no psychiatrist, however learned, could hope to understand his state of mind unless he'd been through something similar. The man next to the jigsaw-puzzler, who had been frantically scribbling when they came in, stared at Stratton with intense hatred for a moment, then bent again to the inky hysteria of his paper. The rest remained as stiff and alert as dogs that sense a threat, and the silence seemed to crackle with hostile electricity.

'Dr Rice is in there,' said Sturgiss, indicating a door in the far wall, 'conducting a session.' They crossed the room, footsteps echoing on the parquet floor, and Stratton peered through the small glass window in the door. He saw eight men sitting in a circle, and, slightly apart, a man who looked—hair colour aside—remarkably like Dr Dacre. For the first time Dr Sturgiss, who had not asked any questions, looked apprehensive. 'Could you wait?' he asked. 'Dr Rice will be finished in…' he glanced at his wristwatch, 'five minutes.'

'That's all right,' said Stratton, who thought that, if the patients inside the room were anything like the ones surrounding him, bursting in there would probably be suicidal. 'I don't want to interrupt.'

The men continued to stare at them, and Stratton, feeling uncomfortable, gazed down at the floor. The electrical quiver in the room intensified, as if the air itself was unstable. He was, he told himself, in a confined space with around thirty potential murderers, all trained in the art of warfare, and, despite the group therapy and all the rest of it, any one of them might spark off at any moment. A corpulent orderly, sitting on the far side of the room, got heavily to his feet and came towards them. 'Is there a problem, Dr Sturgiss?'

'No, no...' Sturgiss's voice was hearty. 'This gentleman just needs a quick word with Dr Rice.'

The orderly nodded, then walked about amongst the groups of card-players, bending over tables, clapping a shoulder here, a back there. 'All right, lads, as you were. Nothing to worry about.'

This reduced the tension in the room somewhat, but the men, although they resumed their card games, remained watchful, glancing round at Stratton every few seconds.

Was Mrs Ingram in a room like this? wondered Stratton. Was she playing cards or doing a jigsaw? When he thought of her, he always imagined her howling in a padded cell, beating at the walls in a blind, insane fury, but perhaps that wasn't the case. And, separated from him only by a wall, was the man who'd killed Byrne, who'd wanted to kill him, who'd saved his life, and tried to save Jenny's, who'd encouraged Elsie Ingram in her delusional state by telling her that he was a policeman... He felt a black weight of confusion press in on him, as his resolve slipped its moorings and his brain began to spin. He clenched his fists hard, trying to steady himself. Why the hell hadn't he brought Ballard with him? He'd have given anything for some support, a friendly face...

He heard the sound of chairs being pushed back in the next room, and tried to collect himself. After a couple of seconds, the door opened and khaki-clad men began filing past them, casting curious looks in their direction before mingling with the card-players. This is it, thought Stratton. Just do your job, he told himself. Don't think of anything else.

Sturgiss waited until the last man had exited, then entered the room, Stratton at his heels. Dr Rice, still seated, was writing notes, but looked up as Sturgiss cleared his throat. 'Mr Stratton to see you,' he said, and withdrew, leaving Stratton and Rice staring at each other. There was a tiny, almost imperceptible flicker of recognition in Rice's eyes, and then, as if a shutter had closed behind them, a blandly polite gaze. 'Excuse me for a moment,' he said. In one swift movement he rose from his chair and went to the open door. For a split second, he stood ramrod straight in the manner of a sergeant-major, and then, before Stratton—who'd registered, too late, what was about to happen—could act, he bellowed, 'Attack!'

CHAPTER
75

The pandemonium was instantaneous. In a fury of shrieking whistles as the attendants tried to summon help, each man, recalled in a flash to the booby-trapped, mined nightmare of his memory, the private bombardment with the long-dead officer jumping like a jack-in-the-box inside his head to bellow commands, leapt into action. Some ran, in a crouch, across the room, zigzagging from side to side and looking wildly around them. Others screamed, and, goggle-eyed with fear and paranoia, began to barricade themselves behind the furniture. Others clambered onto tables and chairs, as if they had been ordered to advance, then stood, bewildered and blank-faced. One man, howling, banged his head repeatedly against the reinforced glass of a window pane and another, a giant, launched himself at Stratton, who collapsed flat on the floor under the weight, painfully winded and fearing that his back was broken. The man lay full length of top of him, scissoring his kicking legs and raining down blows on Stratton's face with his fists until the two orderlies, armed with leather cuffs, managed to haul him away.

As he staggered groggily to his feet and looked around at the mayhem Stratton spotted Rice running across the quadrangle. He sidestepped as a man fell in front of him, head hitting the wooden floor with a crack, back arched and eyes rolling up, juddering and twitching, and set off in pursuit.

Rice scattered the blue-suited gardeners, who broke up in confusion, allowing Stratton a clear path behind him, and disappeared through a side door. Following, Stratton found himself pounding down a passage, hearing shouts, banging doors and shrieking whistles behind him as the sound of running feet alerted inmates and staff. Skidding round a corner, he was just in time to see Rice yank open an outside door and take off again across the grass. Stratton could see, about half a mile away, the edge of a wood. Gunfire was issuing from somewhere behind it. Rice, he realised, was heading for the weapon-testing range.

'Oh no you fucking don't,' he muttered. The bastard wasn't going to cheat him that way—Rice was *his*. Stratton tried to increase his speed—the distance between them was lengthening—but he was panting now, fighting a stitch...Why the fuck wasn't Ballard there? He was younger, fitter, he'd be able to catch up with him, whereas he, Stratton, was going to lose him, chase him into the path of the guns, and then—

Rice fell, full length in the grass. So abruptly did it happen that, for a moment, Stratton thought that one of the shots must have gone wide. Then he saw that Rice was on his knees, clambering upright, and, in a final, agonising burst of speed, gasping, almost retching, with the effort, he forced himself forward, closing the gap until he was close—closer—close enough to launch himself into a rugby tackle and, catching Rice around the knees, bring him down.

'You killed her!' he grunted. One knee in the small of Rice's back, he grabbed a handful of the man's hair and slammed his face into the ground, over and over again, harder and harder. 'You killed her!' He wasn't even thinking of Rice as a person, just a punchbag of flesh. He lunged forward and held Rice round the neck in an armlock, yanking him upwards, taking out his anger at himself, at the world, in a serious of vicious jerks, unconsciously taking his rhythm from the stuttering rattle of the guns in the valley. 'You—killed—her!—I—will—fucking—murder—you!'

He felt Rice thrashing beneath him, heard him grunt as he tried to breathe, and then—and this took a moment to register— his body stilled and went limp. 'Oh, Jesus, no...' He'd broken his neck. He scrambled off and pushed Rice over, onto his back. The man's face was a bloody mess, a flattened nose, eyes swollen shut and burst lips. Stratton slapped it, hard, forehand and backhand. 'Don't you dare fucking die, you bastard.'

One eye opened a fraction, and the head came up an inch. 'You...' he croaked, 'want to...kill me.' The eye closed again.

'No...no.' Stratton, all rage dispelled, was aghast. He looked down at his hands, which were shaking from his exertions, blood smeared across the knuckles. 'I'm sorry.' Kneeling on the grass beside Rice's ruined head, he began to sob.

After a moment, he felt something touch his leg, and, looking down, saw Rice's muddy fingers. The single eye flickered again, and Rice murmured, 'Don't...don't...' before lapsing into unconsciousness.

Stratton wiped the tears and sweat from his face and looked around him. Standing at a distance, by the building, were a row of white-coated men—doctors, he supposed—all staring in his direction. His turn for the loony bin. For a moment, he wanted to laugh. Then he heard a deep gurgling sound that took him, instantly, back to Jenny in the Rest Centre kitchen, so that Rice's face and body became hers, and, raising the man up, he cradled him in his arms. 'It's all right,' he whispered. 'I've got you.'

How long they remained like that, Stratton didn't know. After a time, the guns stopped firing, and, sometime after that, he became aware of footsteps and voices, and, looking round, found himself staring at a pair of suit trousers and six blue serge legs. Looking up, he saw the worried faces of a detective and three policemen. Stratton fished in his pocket and handed the senior man his badge. Silently, the detective glanced at it, nodded briefly, and handed it back.

They stood round him in a ring, silent and keeping a wary distance as Stratton gave Rice a gentle shake. 'Can you hear me?'

Again, the flickering eye, accompanied by a slight inclination of the head.

'John Walter Strang, I am arresting you,' he produced the warrant and held it in front of Rice's nose, 'for obtaining your present position under false pretences.'

Rice shook his head in gentle reproach, and, for just a couple of seconds, Stratton really did believe that they had got it, or at least that part of it, wrong.

'You are John Walter Strang, aren't you?' Again, Rice shook his head. 'We know,' continued Stratton, 'that you have a scar at the base of your thumb. On your right hand.' One of the uniformed coppers peered at Rice's hand and nodded in confirmation. 'Your mother told us about it.'

Rice's slightly open eye widened in shock, but only for a split second.

'Is John Walter Strang your original name?' asked Stratton.

Rice's bloody face seemed to radiate contempt. 'He's... no-one,' he whispered. 'I know...who I am.'

'But you were born John Walter Strang?'

Rice nodded.

'And you have also used the name James Dacre?'

Another nod.

'And Sam Todd?'

Another nod.

'And John Watson?'

Another nod.

'And...' Stratton checked again. 'Norman Thomas?'

'Yes...' Rice parted his ruined lips in a crooked semblance of a smile. 'But...you've missed...some.'

'You can tell us later,' said Stratton. 'At the station. But first before we go—there's something I want to ask. Gentlemen,' he looked up at the circle of policemen, 'if you wouldn't mind...'

The detective rolled his eyes in a manner that said a strange day was getting even stranger, and jerked his thumb at the coppers, whereupon they all retreated some distance towards the wood.

'Why did you want to kill me?' asked Stratton, when he was sure they couldn't be overheard.

'Help...Fay.'

'You loved—love—her that much?'

'Makes...no sense.'

'Not even...*now?*'

'Nothing...makes sense.'

'You told Mrs Ingram that I was a police officer.'

'Thought...she...knew.'

'No. It made her worse, didn't it? Set her off. You wouldn't have mentioned it otherwise—in your letter.'

'She already...had the knife...I don't know. I'm sorry. You may not...believe...but it's the truth. Could have been...good doctor. Wanted to...save people. Not...an act.'

'I know that,' said Stratton. 'Thank you.'

CHAPTER

76

'So...' Some hours later, at a Birmingham police station, Stratton checked the names off the list he'd written. 'That's John Salter, Thomas Collis, Frank Patmore and Thomas Stanbridge. Besides the ones we already knew about. Are there any others?'

The man sitting on the other side of the table, battered, but speaking almost normally now, shook his head. 'That's the lot.'

'Humour me,' said Stratton. 'Who was your favourite?'

'Well...' The man paused, but not for long. 'I enjoyed Rice, but it was Dacre, I think. Yes. James Dacre.'

'Because of Fay Marchant?'

'Yes. But also because it was my first time. As a doctor, I mean. When I discovered I really could do it.'

That made sense, thought Stratton. Dacre, being a doctor, was the first identity with real status. And Dacre, of course, had had the admiration—and perhaps even the love—of Fay Marchant. It was a lot to lose—that was why Dacre had been prepared to kill in order to keep it. Stratton pushed his packet of cigarettes across the scarred wooden surface. 'Help yourself.'

'Thank you.'

They were sitting in the small interview room drinking tea. The prisoner, who had been fingerprinted, entered into the station log and seen by the doctor (with a lot of eyebrow raising at the cuts and bruises, but nothing actually said), had been subdued but calm throughout. Watching him smoke, Stratton decided it was time for that to change. Since their last exchange on the grass, the man had made no effort to ingratiate himself with Stratton in any way, which made things a lot easier. Banishing a lingering sense of gratitude for this, he prepared himself to go in for the kill.

'You know, Mr Strang...' A well-controlled flicker of irritation crossed the man's face. 'I think it's time you told us about that morphine.'

This was the first time since they'd sat down that Stratton had addressed him as anything—and reminding him of his true status was quite deliberate. If he addressed him as Rice, the man would, automatically, answer as a qualified person, a psychiatrist, and Stratton didn't want this because the persona of Rice, like that of Dacre, was more intelligent than he, as well as being a professional man and therefore several notches up on the social scale. He'd reached this decision during the car journey, in order to guard against any danger that *he* might become deferential, which, given what had just happened, was a definite risk. Also, he hoped that calling the man Strang—who, after all, was simply a criminal—would separate them both from the shared experience of Jenny's death.

'There's not really much I can add to what I've already told you,' said the man, easily.

'Yes there is, Mr Strang'—again, the slight tightening around the blackened eyes—'for instance, in your letter, you claimed to have stolen the morphine, but you didn't say *why* you took it.'

'Absent-mindedness, pure and simple,' said the man. Recognising the practised charm with which this was said, Stratton thought, I may have addressed him as Strang, but it's Dacre who's talking, and this is something he's rehearsed. Still, he told himself, it's Dacre who cares about Fay. 'As you suspected,' the man continued, 1 was rather distracted by Nurse Marchant— working myself up to asking her on a date, you know...' He gave a self-deprecating chuckle. 'And then of course there was that business with the torsion—I'd never seen one before, and when Mr Hambling tore a strip off me...not to mention the...well, what was involved...' Stratton, who remembered in vivid detail exactly what was involved, willed himself not to wince. 'It never occurred to me that Nurse Marchant could get into trouble until later, and by then I was feeling...well, rather a fool, to be honest. Besides, I'd used some of the stuff. That woman who walloped me.' He rubbed the side of his face and grimaced. 'Bloody painful, like this.'

'I'm sure,' said Stratton, whose own face, thanks to the fists of the giant who'd felled him in the hospital, was feeling extremely tender, 'but I'm afraid I don't believe you. You see, we happen to have very good reason for thinking that Nurse Marchant took that morphine.'

Alarm flickered in the man's eyes. 'No, Inspector. I took it. As I said, I'm the culprit.'

'Did you use it to kill Dr Byrne?'

The man shook his head.

'No,' agreed Stratton. 'You didn't. Nurse Marchant, on the other hand—'

'Nurse Marchant had nothing to do with that,' said the man flatly. 'You know she didn't.'

'Actually,' said Stratton, 'I don't know anything of the sort. And I suspect there's rather a lot that *you* don't know about Nurse Marchant.'

The man's face took on a worldly expression—time for the 'both-men-of-the-world' act, thought Stratton. The man opened his mouth as if to speak, but—perhaps clocking the look on Stratton's face, closed it again. Remembering the lengths that he'd been prepared to go to for Fay, Stratton felt a twinge of guilt. Stop it, he told himself. This is no place for emotions. Just get on with the fucking job.

'She was having an affair with Dr Reynolds,' said Stratton. The calmness with which the man received this told him that it wasn't news. However, he was willing to bet his month's salary that it was *all* he knew. 'Unfortunately,' he continued, keeping his eyes on the man's face, 'they were rather careless, and she managed to get herself pregnant.'

The man lowered his head and looked at the table. Didn't know about *that*, did you, thought Stratton. 'Reynolds, being a doctor,' he continued, 'was able to arrange a certain operation. Which he undertook himself, by the way.' Stratton leant forward. 'On his own child.' The man flinched as if he had been struck, but still did not meet Stratton's eyes. 'Soon after that, Reynolds met with an unfortunate accident. But you know all about that, don't you, because you were working in the Middlesex mortuary at the time as Sam Todd. We had one particular set of finger-prints that cropped up all over that mortuary, by the way—we haven't identified them, but now that we have yours I imagine it's only a matter of time, don't you? Because that's something you can't change about yourself, whether you're Strang, or Todd, or Dacre…or the man in the moon, come to that.'

Stratton paused to see if the man would challenge this, or make some remark, but he remained silent, staring down-wards. It was, as far as the murders were concerned, a fishing expedition, and he needed a hell of a lot more evidence. Well, he'd just have to stretch the truth a bit—a lot—and see if it had the desired effect. 'Now,' he said, 'you claim to have met Nurse Marchant for the first time when you bumped into her—the day the morphine disappeared—but I'm beginning to wonder if you didn't know her before that. I think you might have cooked all this up together.'

The man looked up, shaking his head. 'No. I told you. That was the first time I met her.'

'It's true,' said Stratton, thoughtfully, 'that if she could have a doctor—Reynolds, I mean—she'd hardly lower her sights to a mortuary attendant. Anyway…' he sighed deeply, 'the whole business with her and Reynolds was pretty sordid, as I'm sure you can imagine…' Stratton paused to allow the man to imagine it. 'I think that Dr Byrne got to know about what Reynolds did, and threatened to have him struck off and her dismissed in disgrace. You said yourself that you were prepared to kill to protect her, but of course if you didn't know her then…As you know,' he continued, 'some people have a very strong survival instinct. You do yourself. The odd thing is that it has nothing to do with physical strength—it's all in here.' Stratton tapped his forehead. 'Reynolds must have argued with Byrne—pleaded with him, begged him—not to report the pair of them. And I know that Fay, for her part, pleaded with Reynolds to run away with her, but,' here Stratton adopted a sarcastic tone, 'apparently for the first time, his conscience pricked him, and he refused. He was married, after all. The two of them had an argument on the night of Reynolds's death, and…' He let the implications of this hang in the air for a moment before resuming. 'If you remember—and of course you do remember, because you were on the spot, as Todd—it was Byrne who said that Reynolds's death was due to foul play and suggested we look into it. To be honest, we would probably have chalked it up as one of those unfortunate things that happened in the blackout, but of course…With Reynolds out of the way, Nurse Marchant had to deal with Byrne, didn't she? And before that, of course, there was Nurse Leadbetter… Nurse Marchant was upset—angry—Byrne was still threatening to report the matter, and perhaps he'd guessed about the nurse, too…She must have felt trapped, poor girl.

'Nurse Marchant was seen outside Byrne's office on the night of his death. By me.' Stratton paused and stared at the man, who blinked several times, but did not change his expression. 'She seemed…well, agitated. Which she would be if she'd just pumped poor Dr Byrne full of morphine. She must have caught him off guard, somehow, managed to knock him out. Strong girls, nurses.' Stratton paused, took a swig of his cooling tea, and lit another cigarette, deliberately not offering the packet. 'You are probably asking yourself why, having taken her in for questioning, we let her go, but that was for the other matter— the abortion. We suspected her of murder then, but now, with a witness who has just come forward, we have enough evidence to convict her. The only fly in the ointment has been you, Mr Strang. Naturally, we wanted to speak to you about the other matter—obtaining employment by fraudulent means is a serious business—but I wanted to be sure, in my own mind, that I could eliminate you from our enquiries. And now that I've got to know you better, Mr Strang, I can see that the explanation you provided for taking that morphine is, by your standards…well, not to put too fine a point on it, it's unsatisfactory. I'm sure you'll be very relieved to hear that I don't believe for a moment that you killed Dr Byrne, and I shall now instruct my colleagues in London to arrest Fay Marchant. That must be quite a weight off your mind, I should think.'

'I…' began the man. 'I…Yes. A weight off my mind,' he repeated, mechanically. Far from being relieved, he had the desperate, cornered look of a rat in a trap.

'Excellent,' said Stratton, cheerfully. 'I'll leave you to it. Apart from anything else, I need to check that they can put you up overnight. You can keep those.' He gestured to the packet of cigarettes. 'If you need a light, there's a policeman just outside the door. I'm sure he'll be happy to oblige.'

CHAPTER
77

Left alone, the man buried his face in his hands. Why the hell had he sent that letter? To try and help Fay, yes, but also to show off...And Stratton had seen through him. Understood. And the way he'd kept calling him Strang, trying to provoke him...

He'd wondered, occasionally, if it might be a relief to tell someone—a stranger—about his life, but when he had he'd imagined disbelief, then admiration for his daring. Nothing like this. Now he was right back where he started. Worse, in fact. Not only was John Strang a mere nobody, he was also a common criminal, a fraud. And as for Fay...It couldn't be true, could it? The affair with Dr Reynolds, yes, but the abortion...? And killing that nurse? It wasn't possible...Stratton had said something about a witness...Everything had spun horribly, hopelessly, out of his control. The moment he'd seen him at the hospital he'd known that he had lost, that was why he'd run towards the firing range. When Stratton had started bashing his head against the ground, the pain had scarcely registered, so divorced had he felt from even his physical self. Now, he ached all over...And then there was the question of his mother. Would she insist on seeing him? Could she insist? She was the cause of all this. He didn't want to see her, ever again.

His mind worked feverishly as he thought over the things Stratton had said. He was going to arrest Fay. Last time was bad enough, when he thought it was just for taking the morphine, but *this* time…And Stratton had seen Fay in the corridor, she'd told him that herself. But the business of the abortion…He felt sick. Reynolds must have made her, forced her. That was the only explanation. He'd tricked her into it, or…Bastard! He deserved to die. Stratton talking about her as if she were a common slut made him angry. He knew she wasn't. Dacre knew. Dacre could judge these things.

But he wasn't Dacre any more. He wasn't Rice. He was left alone with his old, useless self. He lifted his head and stared around him at the unpainted walls, the meagre, scarred furniture, the tin ashtray. This was all…Except: *he could still save Fay*. Fay loved Dacre, yes, not Strang, but Dacre couldn't help her now, and Strang could. It would be the one good thing that Strang had done—it would redeem him. Afterwards, what happened to Strang didn't matter…Suddenly, he laughed. How ironic, after all his hopes for Dacre, for Rice, that it would be Strang's name in the newspapers, that he would be—briefly, at least—famous for being his original self.

CHAPTER

78

Stratton took himself off to the Gents' where he saw, in the small mirror above the basin, that he, too, had the beginnings of a nice black eye, courtesy of the giant madman who'd attacked him. His nose looked a bit swollen, too, and he touched it gingerly, wondering if it was broken for the second time. It's not as if I've got looks to ruin, he thought—and in any case, there was no Jenny to cluck over his grotesque appearance when he finally got home…That thought reminded him that he ought to telephone to Doris and ask her to look after Monica and Peter overnight, as there was no way he'd be able to get back to London.

This done, he went outside for a think and a smoke. Leaning against the back wall of the station, the sensation he'd previously had of something faint and persistent in the back of his mind suddenly sharpened—the distant wireless, properly tuned, with the volume turned up loud. Of course! He threw down his cigarette and returned to the station, where he asked the duty sergeant to place a call to West End Central. It took Stratton almost twenty minutes to explain the position to DCI Lamb, who ummed and ahhed and asked irrelevant questions, while the duty sergeant looked askance at how long the conversation was taking. Finally,

Lamb agreed to do as Stratton asked. After that, he spoke to Ballard, who was quietly reproachful at not having been included, and issued some instructions. Then he asked the now pop-eyed duty sergeant to arrange him some accommodation for the night, thanked the man, and strolled back to the interview room.

'The good news is that we've found you a cell, Mr Strang,' he said, breezily. 'There's quite a crowd in here, but they're giving you a room of your own, so, if you'd like to come with us, we can get you settled.'

Strang stared at him but made no move to rise from his chair.

'Anything wrong?' said Stratton, very solicitous.

The expression of anguish on Strang's face was, he hoped, an accurate reflection of the turmoil in his mind.

'Wait,' he said. 'Please.'

'Very well.' Stratton remained standing, looking puzzled. Strang now looked agonised, as if some vital part were being pulled from him with instruments of torture—which, Stratton supposed, it was. As he waited, it occurred to him that the contract between the conman and the conned was now reversed, only Strang did not know it.

'You can't arrest Fay, Inspector Stratton. She's innocent.'

'Oh?' Stratton raised an incredulous eyebrow.

'Yes! Look, I know she was seeing Dr Reynolds, but that doesn't mean—well, any of what you said. She wouldn't do those things.'

'How do you know?'

'Because I killed Dr Byrne.'

'Oh, really?' Stratton laid on the disbelief.

'He recognised me. This...' The man held up his right hand, palm outwards. 'The scar.'

Stratton nodded, but still did not sit down. 'So? A lot of people have scars.'

'He'd spotted me that afternoon, in the Gents'. I was washing my hands, and that's when he noticed. I thought I'd got away with it—as you say, plenty of people have scars—but he came up later on, to Casualty. It was just after that business when the woman hit me. Byrne said he wanted to talk to me, and I knew he was going to confront me with what I'd done.'

'And then?'

'Well, I had the morphine and the syringe. One fell on the floor during the fracas in Casualty and I managed to pick it up without being spotted.'

'Why?'

'On impulse. I've found it's useful, taking things—you never know when they might come in.'

'And you thought it would "come in" to kill Dr Byrne?'

'Not at first. I went into the Gents' and filled it up. I'd thought of doing away with myself.'

'Why?'

'Because I was tired of being hounded, always having to look over my shoulder…It happens sometimes—I get a sense of depression, of not getting anywhere.' The man's tone switched suddenly from self-pitying to bitter, and he blurted out, 'Because I'd failed. Because I'm no bloody good, Inspector. I'm rotten.'

'No,' said Stratton, sincerely. 'You're not.'

Strang blinked in surprise.

'Everyone at the Middlesex thought you were a good doctor—until they found out you weren't a doctor at all, that is. Besides, if you really were rotten, you wouldn't be telling me all this, would you? You'd have let Nurse Marchant be tried, and perhaps hanged, for killing Dr Byrne. I'd have been none the wiser.'

'No, no…' Strang shook his head violently. '*I* killed him. Fay had nothing to do with it.'

'Do you want to make a confession?'

'Yes.'

'Very well.' Stratton went to the door and requested a policeman. When he'd arrived, and was ready with pen and paper, Stratton said, 'John Walter Strang, I am arresting you for the murder of Dr Arthur Mills Byrne, and I must warn you that anything you say will be taken down and may be used in evidence against you. Do you understand what I am saying?'

'I understand.'

'Good. Could you tell us about it from the beginning, please?'

It took two hours before the statement was completed and signed—laboriously, and after some hesitation—John Walter Strang.

Afterwards, Stratton despatched the policeman for cups of tea, and, when they were alone, asked, 'Is there anything else you'd like to tell me?'

Strang, slumped on his seat, his battered face slack with exhaustion, stared at him dully. 'Surely you haven't forgotten,' prompted Stratton. 'Dr Reynolds...Nurse Leadbetter...'

Strang nodded wearily, and sat up straight with a visible physical effort, but it was as if an inner electrical light had been switched off, and in his eyes Stratton saw only emptiness. He didn't think the man had enough mental energy, or heart, for his task, but—and you had to hand it to him—he was prepared to try.

'Well?'

'I hit Reynolds. I saw him on the bomb-site. I wanted to be a doctor, and I thought if he was out of the way, I could take his place. Now you can charge me.'

'Not just yet,' said Stratton. 'Why Reynolds?'

'Because of Fay.'

'So you *did* know her before you met in the corridor and took the morphine? You knew her when you were Todd.'

'No! I'd seen her, that's all. I...wanted her.'

'But how did you know she was involved with Reynolds?'

'I'd seen them together...outside.'

'When?'

'From time to time.'

'But why should you think that there was anything untoward in that?'

'The way he looked at her.'

'I see. Did you know Dr Reynolds?'

'Not personally. I knew he worked in the Casualty Department.'

'So,' said Stratton, sceptically, 'you killed a man you did not know because you thought that by doing so you could get both his position and his mistress?'

'Well, I did get them, didn't I?'

'Yes, but it was a pretty long shot that the one—or, rather, two—would follow.'

'Well,' said Strang, defiantly, 'it worked.'

'How did you kill him?'

'I crept up behind him and hit him. Simple as that.'

'What with?'

'A brick. I picked it up from the site.'

'What was Reynolds doing there?'

'I don't know. I saw him.'

'How? It was pitch dark.'

'That's not true. There was a moon.'

'But not enough light to spot Reynolds from the road, surely?'

'I recognised him.'

'You must been very close to him, then. Didn't he see you?'

'No.'

'But he must have heard you coming—scrambling over all that debris can be a noisy business. I must say, Mr Strang,' said Stratton, in the neutral tone of one making an observation about the weather, 'that the difference between the fluency with which you described the killing of Dr Byrne and this rigmarole is quite marked. You'll have to do better with the details...Did he hear you coming?'

'Well, if he did, he didn't turn round to see who it was.'

'Did you say anything to him before you hit him?'

'No.'

'How many times did you hit him?'

'Three, I think.'

'Are you sure?'

'Not positive, but I think that's right.'

'How did you know he would be there?'

'He...' Stratton could sense that, even with the information he'd picked up from the post-mortem, the man was flagging. 'He'd been in the pub. I followed him.'

'Which pub?'

'The Cambridge Arms, on Newman Street.'

'People from the Middlesex go in there, don't they?' Stratton decided to take a flyer. 'Strange that none of them remembered seeing him that night when we asked.'

'Perhaps they didn't notice him. He wasn't there for long.'

'How long? What time did he leave?'

'Just before closing time.'

'And you followed him, did you?'

'Yes.'

'You followed him to the bomb-site and killed him?'

'Yes.'

'Straight away? You said there was no conversation of any kind...Why do you think he chose to take that particular route? All that rubble...Pretty hazardous in the dark.'

'Short cut, I suppose. He'd had a few.'

'A few? You said he wasn't in the pub for long.'

'Well, something...'

'Did he appear drunk?'

'Not drunk, but—'

'That's hardly surprising, Mr Strang, because, according to the report, there was no alcohol in his bloodstream. I'm surprised you don't remember, but of course rather a lot's happened since then, hasn't it? Enough to make anyone slip up. Besides which, Dr Byrne told us that Reynolds died sometime between...' Stratton pulled out his notebook and flicked through it, 'two and six in the morning. And as I'm sure you know, the pubs on that side of Oxford Street close at half past ten, so unless the pair of you were wandering around in circles on that bomb-site for the best part of four hours, your story doesn't hold water. In fact, it's unworthy of you.' Stratton returned the notebook to his pocket. 'Nice try, Mr Strang.' He stood up to leave. 'Oh, by the way, I don't believe you killed Leadbetter either.'

'But...'

'All right. Why don't you tell me *where* she was killed?'

'The operating theatre. One of the unused ones.'

'Which one?'

'I...' Defeated, Strang shook his head. 'It's no use, Inspector. You didn't believe me from the first, did you? About Reynolds, I mean. Why? I don't understand.'

'I shouldn't tell you this,' said Stratton, 'but I shall because you and I have...well, we have some things between us, don't we? The reason I didn't believe you was that Fay Marchant as good as told me she'd killed Reynolds, only I was too stupid to realise it at the time. She knew, you see, that Reynolds had been hit with a brick—information that was kept confidential. Hospital gossip is one thing, and I don't doubt that everyone knew the man had been killed by blows to the head, but—although I suppose one could make a guess at the weapon—that wasn't on Dr Byrne's notes, because it wasn't known for certain at the time of the post-mortem, and all that the newspapers reported was that the death had taken place in suspicious circumstances. When I asked Nurse Marchant how she knew, she said, "Dr Dacre told me." Now, if Marchant had known that the man she knew as Dr Dacre was also Todd the mortuary attendant, that would make sense—Todd could have overheard something Byrne said—but she didn't know that. So, Mr Strang, I'm afraid it looks as though she was prepared to drop you right in it, doesn't it?'

Strang stared at him. The man's face, where it wasn't bruised, was chalk white.

'You look shocked,' Stratton continued. 'You know, it occurs to me that your whole career has been based on the fact that people believe what they see—the uniform, the authority, the myth, and so on. But you believed it, too, didn't you? You believed—just as I did, I have to admit—that, because Fay was a nurse, and, moreover, a beautiful, well-spoken girl with a gentle manner, she must be an angel. Caring, healing, selfless...she could do no wrong. You may have fooled her into believing you were a doctor, Mr Strang, but she fooled you, too.'

As he left the interview room and walked down the corridor, Stratton wondered about his exact reasons for telling the man about Fay. Although he told himself that it was six of one and half a dozen of the other, he knew that there was enough 'getting his own back' in there to dislike himself thoroughly for having done it, but without finding himself able to regret it.

CHAPTER 79

'Call from Chief Superintendent Dewhurst, sir.'

'Put him through.' Stratton, glad to be back in his office, settled into his chair.

'Stratton?'

'Yes, sir.'

'Good news at last. The unidentified prints from the mortuary are a match for this Strang chap. We couldn't do anything with the partials from the underside of the office desk, I'm afraid, but Strang's prints do match the ones found on the bookshelf. Not much to go on, but nevertheless—'

'I have a confession, sir...' Stratton was careful to keep any hint of triumph out of his voice. 'From Dr Dacre, formerly of the Middlesex Hospital, who turns out not to be Dr Dacre at all, but Strang. He killed Dr Byrne.'

'Have you indeed? That's wonderful news. Congratulations, Stratton. I look forward to hearing about it.'

At least, Stratton thought, as he replaced the receiver, Dewhurst's good wishes were genuine, whereas DCI Lamb's were, as usual, grudging. Frank Byrne had thanked him, too—relieved, Stratton thought, that his father's death would not be considered suicide, although having a parent murdered surely wasn't much of an alternative...On balance, Stratton thought he would have preferred the former, as at least one's father would have decided when to end his life and not had it snatched from him.

Fay Marchant, in custody in Cheltenham, charged—for the time being—with obstructing the police, would be fetched tomorrow. Meantime, Lamb, despite the news of Mussolini's death and the rest, was kicking up a fuss about how Piccadilly looked like a military slum and how half his men were deployed elsewhere while the cells were full to bursting. All of which was true—the cells were bunged up with drunk and disorderly soldiers of various nationalities who'd been celebrating prematurely, and whose inebriated roaring was issuing up the stairwell, as well as the usual complement of thugs, prostitutes of both sexes, burglars and the like, all of whom seemed intent on joining the fun. The thing was, according to Lamb, Stratton was the only person available to sort them all out, which, as well as being highly irregular, was a bloody awful prospect.

Stratton and Ballard descended the stairs together, accompanied by a rousing chorus, sung to the tune of 'What A Friend We Have In Jesus', of:

> *Life is full of disappointments,*
> *Dull and empty as a tomb,*
> *Father's got a strictured penis,*
> *Mother has a fallen womb...*

They found the custody sergeant, who, apparently able to ignore the racket, was silently mouthing the captions of a comic confiscated from one of the Yanks, lost in the vividly coloured world of simple violence. Arliss, sitting beside him, head tilted back to rest against the wall, had his eyes half closed. 'What the fuck are you doing?' yelled Stratton over the din. 'Waiting for someone to feed you grapes?'

> *Uncle Ted has been deported*
> *For a homosexual crime...*

'Sorry, sir.' Arliss's eyes opened wide at the sight of Stratton's battered face. 'Quite a shiner you got there, sir, if you don't mind my saying.'

'Thank you, Arliss. Come on, let's get this lot sorted out. Who's first?'

Sister Sue has just aborted,
For the forty-second time…

Despite Ballard's strenuous efforts, and Arliss's feeble ones, to get the occupants of the cells to shut up, the caterwauling broke out at intervals for the rest of the day and, by the time Stratton left for the evening, the stale air, smoke, din, general aggravation and crudity had given him a blinding headache.

He'd decided, by the time he got off the bus, that he might benefit from a half-pint at the Swan and a quiet chinwag with Donald, if he was there. Unfortunately, Reg was there, too, and after half an hour of bumptious, ill-informed speculation about (a) how Stratton came by his black eye, and (b) when we would get to Berlin and capture, or possibly kill, Hitler, he decided it was high time to collect the children from Doris's and go home.

He stood at the scullery window, watching Monica and Pete mucking about in the garden and wishing that Jenny were standing beside him. When the children had gone up to bed, he switched on the wireless and listened to the report of Mr Churchill's remarks to the House of Commons, wondering if there would be an official announcement of some sort about the end of the war. At some point, he must have dozed off, because he woke up to find that the wireless was still on and Monica was standing in front of him in her nightgown, looking concerned.

'Are you all right, Dad? You look awful.'

Stratton rubbed a hand over his face. 'I'm fine, love. What time is it?'

Monica glanced at the clock on the mantelpiece. 'Ten past midnight. Hitler's dead, Dad.'

'Is he?'

'It was on the wireless. Just now. Do you think it's true?'

'Well, if it was on the wireless...'

'But they might just *think* he's dead. What if he's pretending, and they've hidden him somewhere? He could wait for a few years and come back, and then there'll be another war.'

'I don't think so, love. Apart from anything else, he wouldn't have enough soldiers and tanks and things.'

'But how do they know it's really him? It might be just a man who looks like him.'

'I should think they made sure before they said anything.'

'They said another man was in charge of Germany now. Hitler chose him specially. He's an admiral, and he says they're going to go on fighting.'

Stratton looked at his daughter's worried face, and said, 'He might *say* that, but they're beaten. They can't go on fighting.'

'Can't they?' Monica sounded doubtful.

'No, love. They'll have to surrender.'

'But we're still fighting Japan, aren't we?'

'Yes, but that can't last much longer. Not now.'

'Really?'

'Really.' Stratton stood up, easing the crick in his neck. 'Come on,' he said. 'Bedtime. We'll find out all about it tomorrow.'

CHAPTER

80

In Pentonville, two days later, lying on his back in a cell, on a bed made from wooden boards, a thin coir mattress and pillow, canvas sheets and rough, stained blankets, Strang stared into the clanging, stinking darkness. This was worse than the police cells—it was like being locked in a safe. As if he was a thing and not a person at all. A number. He'd be a number for what remained of his life —he had no great hopes for the trial—with the prison smell of sweat and shit permeating his clothes and skin. They'd taken away his belt, his shoelaces and even the buttons off his coat. He supposed they must do that to everyone, just in case.

He'd failed. Of course he had. Strang would always fail... Of course Fay hadn't loved him, of course it was all pretence— she'd known, unconsciously, that he was not Dacre, not fit to be loved, and, ultimately, she had despised him. He was worthless. And he'd thought he was trying to protect her, when all the time the big policeman had known...He saw that, now. All along, Stratton had wanted his confession for Byrne, and he'd also wanted to make absolutely sure that Fay hadn't known him when he was Todd...And he'd fallen for it. He'd only stumbled across Reynolds's body because, unable to sleep and restless as hell, he'd decided there was enough light to take himself off for a walk. Talking to Stratton, he'd been so confused that he'd got the timing all wrong...

With Fay, it had been love at first sight. He had seen what he wanted to see. Even when she'd told him about Reynolds, even when Stratton had told him about the abortion...he'd made excuses for her: it couldn't have been her fault, she must have been driven to it, she was disturbed in her mind...But the fact remained that she'd tried to blame him. No matter how he tried to explain it away, that was the case. Perhaps his unconscious mind had known that Fay was a fraud all the time, and that was why he'd been so attracted to the bitch...

Aah, but she was so beautiful. If only she'd been *real*... There was nothing left. His mother...but he wasn't letting her come near him if he could help it.

Men were shouting from cell to cell now, something about Hitler and the end of the war. The warders seemed to be making only a half-hearted effort to quell the noise. He wished they'd all shut up. He didn't care about it. Why should he? He wasn't going to be around for the peace.

He wondered where Fay was. In a cell like this one? What would happen to her?

He couldn't think of Fay, of anything. I'm a blank, he said to himself. I'm nothing.

He turned onto his side, curled up, and closed his eyes. All I ever wanted, he thought, was to be part of the world.

The following morning, Stratton bought a copy of the *Daily Mail* before boarding the bus. The headline read: 'HITLER DEAD—DOENITZ APPOINTED FÜHRER'. That must be Monica's admiral, thought Stratton. *The German radio gave the news to the world at 10.25 last night in the following words: 'It is reported from the Führer's headquarters that our Führer, Adolf Hitler, has fallen this afternoon in his command post in the Reich Chancellery fighting to his last breath against Bolshevism.'*

Stratton scanned the rest of the column. It didn't say *how* Hitler had died, and Stratton wondered if he'd been killed by the Russians, or even by the Germans themselves. A shame, he thought, remembering the films he'd seen of the concentration camps, that he wasn't given a taste of his own medicine. Still, he was dead, and the world was a better place without him. The trouble was, they'd all spent so long learning not to believe things and preparing for the worst, that it was hard to adjust one's thinking or even take it in properly.

'Shame he won't be brought to trial,' he heard a woman say. 'I'd like to hear him try and defend himself after what he's done.'

Fay Marchant had lost some weight, Stratton noticed as he sat opposite her in the interview room. Compared to the robust

Policewoman Harris, who was standing beside her chair, she looked like a wraith. Her smart clothes—a blue costume, worn with high heels—seemed to hang on her, and she was hollow-cheeked. Her brown velvet eyes looked even bigger than before, with dark grooves beneath them that looked as if they might have been worn there by the passage of tears. She had a determined, almost iron-clad air about her, as if, come what may, she would remain calm. Stratton found himself taken aback by this—it was disconcerting, like putting a shell to one's ear and not hearing the sound of the sea. Offering her a cigarette, he said, 'You know why you're here, of course.'

'Yes, Inspector. But I don't understand why, with no evidence, you have suddenly decided to arrest me. It must be a mistake—that's why I haven't asked for a solicitor. I'm sure that between us we can sort out it.' She smiled at him.

'Let's start with the man you knew as Dr James Dacre, shall we?' said. Stratton. 'I'd like you to tell me, from the beginning, about your friendship with him.'

'I told you. I first met him when we bumped into each other in the corridor outside the Men's Surgical Ward and—'

'That was the first time you'd ever seen him, was it?'

'Yes.'

'So, as far as you know, you'd never seen him before in your life?'

'No.' Fay looked puzzled.

'Did you ever know a man called Todd? Sam Todd?'

Fay shook her head. 'I don't understand. Is that James's real name?'

Stratton ignored the question. 'So, you're telling me you're absolutely positive that you never met Dr Dacre before you bumped into him in that corridor?'

'Yes. But I don't understand what that has to do with…all this.'

'It was something you said to me, Miss Marchant.' Stratton kept his voice deliberately casual. 'On the telephone. About Dr Reynolds being hit over the head with a brick. That wasn't in the newspapers, or even in the medical reports—and it isn't customary, as you must know, for pathologists to broadcast such information to all and sundry. When I asked you how you'd come by this information, you said that Dr Dacre had told you. It didn't strike me until much later that you did not know—and our false Dr Dacre confirms this, as you have just done yourself—that he had been working in the mortuary, as an attendant. Sam Todd was his name then, by the way, one of many that he's used in a long career. So, as far as you were concerned, there was no reason for Dr Dacre to be in possession of that information. And no reason for you to have the information unless you knew a lot more about the events of the night of Dr Reynolds's death than you'd previously told me. A brick is an odd choice of weapon, Miss Marchant. There's not much leverage—unlike, say a club or a poker—and you'd have to bring it down several times with a lot of force in order to kill someone. However, the choice of a brick—plenty of those on a bomb-site—suggests that the killing was not premeditated, which, of course, is a point in your favour. Also, my sergeant has been hard at work looking into Dr Reynolds's bank account, and into yours, too, and there seem to be a number of identical sums of money that went out of his account and *into* yours very shortly afterwards, all of them last year, between Easter and the beginning of June. The final one was a fortnight before Reynolds's death. So, you see, we do have a lot to talk about. Perhaps you would start by explaining what actually happened. If you co-operate now, I may be persuaded to forget that you've lied to me on several occasions, but if you don't…Well, I'd like to help you, but it's not really up to me, I'm afraid. My hands are tied. My superior—well, you had the unfortunate experience of meeting him last time so you know he can be quite a martinet about these matters—he thinks I've been rather a soft touch where you're concerned…' Stratton let the rest of the sentence, with its implied threat, hang in the air between them.

Fay sat quite still for several minutes, her hands clasped in front of her on the table, then said, 'The night that Duncan—Dr Reynolds—died, I was there, but it was an accident.'

'I see.' Stratton took our his notebook.

'We'd been out together. Well, not exactly *out*, but to the flat I told you about, the one in Holborn.'

'The address?'

'Bedford Row. Number thirty-four.'

'You spent the entire evening there, did you?'

Fay shook her head. 'When I said I was in the nurses' quarters, I was telling the truth—well, partly. I went out at about half past nine—I made up my bed to look as if I was in it, with the covers pulled over my head. I'd often done it before, and nobody had ever spotted that I wasn't there. Nobody saw me—they were either asleep, or out, or working. Dr Reynolds was waiting for me at Bedford Row. We had an argument.'

'What about?'

'I was upset. Ever since the…what happened…he'd been ignoring me, going out of his way to avoid me, and I felt…I was unhappy, and there was no-one I could talk to. I said if he didn't meet me I'd write to his wife and tell her—and I did mean it, because I was desperate. I just wanted him to…to be like we were, I suppose, but he was so cold. When I arrived, he behaved as if I were just a nuisance, that I had no right to ask anything of him, or…I mean, I wasn't asking him to leave his wife or anything, I was just…just…'

'Blackmailing him,' said Stratton. 'It's perfectly true that the last thing you wanted was for Dr Reynolds to leave his wife. She's a very wealthy woman, and I don't believe he ever had any intention of leaving her. But *she* might have left *him* if she'd known about you. Oh, she might have forgiven an affair, but the pregnancy, *and then the deliberate and calculated murder of his own child*, when she herself had never conceived…But you know all this, don't you? That was why he was willing to pay up for so long. And then, that night at Bedford Row, he refused, didn't he? He called your bluff—challenged you to speak to his wife. I suppose you could have threatened to report him for an illegal operation, but that would have got you into trouble too, wouldn't it?' Stratton sat back and folded his arms.

Fay, whose expression had turned from puzzled amusement to outrage during the course of this speech, said, 'It isn't true!

None of it! I wanted reassurance from Duncan, I wanted him to tell me that he still loved me, and…It's so hard to explain. I'd gone through all that—a nightmare—and he'd just abandoned me. I tried to tell him how unhappy I was, but—'

'Stop wasting your breath, Fay, I don't believe a word of it.'

'You can't prove it.'

'Yes, we can. Banks keep records, you know.'

'He gave me the money. I didn't ask for it.'

'Why would he do that?'

'He felt sorry for me.'

'So, you're saying that he willingly gave you what amounted to a very large sum of money, and that he died by accident. Pull the other one, darling, it's got bells on.' Stratton regarded her, his head on one side, and decided it was time for the next broadside. 'You know, Fay, my sergeant's been a very busy man the past couple of days, but he managed to find the time to go to the Middlesex and talk to a couple of the younger doctors there about your friend Dr Dacre, and do you know what he learnt? Dr Dacre had told them he was married. We all know how fast news travels in a place like a hospital, especially if it's about an attractive young doctor. All the nurses would have been gasping to find out about him—of course, his being married would put most young women off, but not you… Or perhaps he told you himself. After all, you had him wrapped round your little finger from the first, didn't you? Perhaps you created a nice feeling of intimacy and trust by reciprocating with a few little confidences of your own…His being married was the attraction, wasn't it? You were planning to do the same to him. Not with a baby, perhaps, but…You might have made a bit out of it—not as much as you had from Dr Reynolds, but something. If, of course, he'd been genuine. I'll bet you thought you were pretty clever, lining up another mark so soon, but he fooled you, didn't he? Just like he fooled everyone else.'

Fay's eyes narrowed, and her mouth was set in a thin, mean line. She didn't look beautiful any more, just vindictive.

'I'll bet you played him—in fact, I know you did. You see, Dr Wemyss told my sergeant that he'd mislaid a key for the room kept by his family at the Clarendon Hotel. He'd sworn it was in his jacket pocket, but when he looked, it was gone. And then the next morning, by a miracle, as he thought, it was back. His friends, Dr Betterton and Dr Unwin, the only ones who knew about it, denied borrowing it without his permission—it was only in the course of the conversation with my sergeant that he recalled that Dacre knew of it, too. Can you guess when it went missing?'

Fay's expression told Stratton that she knew only too well, but she said nothing.

'I'll tell you, shall I? It was the evening our good doctor took you out for that first drink. My sergeant—what an efficient chap he is! —sent someone round to the hotel to make enquiries, and, sure enough, the two of you were seen. You'll be glad to hear they remembered you immediately. They don't often come across men being so importunate—or women defending their honour so vigor-ously—in the lobby. Because you did defend your honour, didn't you, Fay? You thought Dacre was rich, but you weren't going to give up the goods until you were sure of him, so you played coy... Clever girl. But you're wasted on nursing'—Stratton shook his head sadly—'you should have gone on the stage. Or,' he added thought-fully, 'on the streets. Whoring isn't respectable, but it's a damn sight more honest than what you did, or tried to do, to those men.'

Fay reared back, her cheeks flaming as red as if he'd slapped her. 'How dare you!'

'You're lower than a whore, Fay. You're a murderess.'

'No!' Fay screamed the word and burst into hysterical sobs. Policewoman Harris placed a hand on her shoulder.

Stratton folded his arms. 'Turning on the taps won't work,' he said. 'And you won't leave here until I get the truth.'

Harris proffered a handkerchief, and Fay, rocking back-wards and forwards, buried her face in it. After several minutes the weeping abated, and Fay, after a last few hiccups and sniffs, was silent.

Stratton sighed. 'Now,' he said, 'suppose we start again, from the beginning. You went with Dr Reynolds to Bedford Row. What happened after that?'

'It wasn't fair,' said Fay, in a hard voice. 'I deserved the money, after what I'd been through—what he put me through—but he wouldn't give me any more. He was horrible to me. I couldn't believe...I kept on arguing with him, but it was no good.

'Eventually, he said he'd walk me back. He kept saying that he had to get home, that his wife would be worried...'

'What time did you leave Bedford Row?'

'I don't know. Late. After midnight. The flat doesn't have a telephone, and he said he was going to call his wife from the hospital. We argued all the way back.'

'It must have been a tricky walk, in the dark.'

'We had our torches, but it took a long time.'

'Which route did you take?'

'We went down Theobald's Road, to Oxford Street, then up Tottenham Court Road and down Goodge Street, then we turned off.'

'Where?'

'Goodge Place, so we could use the back entrance. Duncan didn't want to go down Cleveland Street, next to the hospital, because he thought someone might see us. We were in the middle of Goodge Place, where the road sort of kinks round, when he said I should go back to the nurses' quarters and he would go round to the front of the hospital to telephone. We were still arguing, and he said...he said...'

'Yes?'

'He said I was no better than a tart,' said Fay, flatly. 'I lost my temper. I pushed him. It was just a little shove, to get him away from me—but the road's all broken up there, and he must have missed his footing, because he fell back, and I heard a noise. He'd hit his head on the corner of a building. He made a grunting sound—I couldn't see him for a moment, and then, when I shone my torch in the right place, there he was...I couldn't see any blood—he'd fallen backwards, you see, so if he'd cut himself it would have been in his hair...He wasn't wearing a hat. He called me a bitch—he said it was all my fault, that I'd led him on. He wasn't shouting or anything, just muttering...vile things. I was so upset, I didn't know what I was doing. I know that he staggered over towards where the bomb-site is, he was holding his head, and I followed him. I said something, that he couldn't treat me like that, and he kept telling me to get away from him and that he never wanted to see me again. I fell over on the rubble, and that's when I picked up the pieces of brick—I was throwing them. I couldn't really see what I was doing, and he was ahead of me, and then I saw him fall over. I was so angry...there was another piece of brick there, and I hit him, and then I just...just...I don't know. But I didn't mean...I never meant...I didn't...I was just so...empty, and I didn't know what I was doing, I...'

Stratton thought that Fay was going to cry again, but she didn't. Thumping both fists down hard on the table, she said, 'That *bastard*! I'm glad he's dead. And Dacre...' Her face tightened, so that, for a moment, she looked almost demonic. 'How could he do that to me? And he got me into trouble—that morphine...It wasn't fair.'

'What about Leadbetter?' asked Stratton.

'Her!' Fay's voice was full of contempt. 'Interfering, pious little...She saw me come back. She came into the bathroom as I was climbing through the window, she saw the dirt on my hands, and there was blood on them, and it was smeared on my clothes—I suppose I must have touched them. I told her I'd had an accident, fallen over in the blackout. She believed me, but when we heard about Duncan, bloody Maddox must have been gossiping...I didn't realise it was her until you more or less told me, Inspector, but she must have said something to Leadbetter, because Leadbetter told me I had to tell the police, or she would...She said a lot of things about how it was wrong—morals and religion—but I knew she was jealous because she couldn't get a man to look at her. I had to stop her. I had to.'

Stratton stared at her, seeing only self-pity and justification. Fay Marchant, he thought, saw other people merely as a means to an end, or—in the case of poor Nurse Leadbetter—as obstacles to be got out of the way. What a waste, he thought. A waste of a beautiful and intelligent girl. 'Let's stop for a minute,' he said, 'and I'll see if I can't rustle up a cup of tea.'

Policewoman Harris stepped forward, but Stratton held up his hand. 'I'll go.' Fay Marchant sickened him, and he wanted—if only for a couple of minutes—to get out of her presence.

Drawing the door of the interview room closed behind him, he went to ask Arliss to bring some cups of tea and fetch Sergeant Ballard to take a statement. He supposed he ought to have a sense of triumph—after all, he'd just solved three murders, hadn't he? But now that the blaze in his head as he'd forged connection after connection had died down, all he felt was weariness, disgust, and a sense of anticlimax. What did he have to look forward to now? Getting used to missing Jenny. He'd thought that collaring Dacre would lessen his guilt, if not his grief, but he saw now that it had made no difference. Looking back over the last few weeks, he realised that whole minutes had passed without him thinking of Jenny, and he knew that, as time went on, the minutes would turn into hours, and perhaps—although he could not imagine this—even days. He hated the idea, but common sense told him that it was inevitable. But she will be with me, he told himself. She will be in my heart. Whatever happens, I shall keep her there always.

CHAPTER

82

On VE day the station was, as Stratton had predicted, a madhouse. Thinking ahead, he'd warned Doris that he wasn't sure when he'd be home, and the events of the morning proved him right. There were already large crowds in Piccadilly, restless for information, when the radio announcement of Germany's unconditional surrender was made in the afternoon of the seventh, and many people didn't bother going home, but started to celebrate there and then. As more and more people poured in to join the revellers, the sirens and hooters of boats and tugs from the river could be heard above the cheers and singing.

In no time at all, the charge room was a maelstrom of roaring soldiers, hysterically tearful tarts, exhausted coppers who'd had their helmets pinched, lost children, stray dogs, and Freddie the flasher, who had been unable to restrain himself at the sight of such a large audience, and was, as usual, claiming that he had a weak bladder.

With hoards of people surging through Piccadilly, climbing up lamp-posts and jigging around the still boxed-up statue of Eros, DCI Lamb issued orders that everyone was to remain on duty until further notice.

'I doubt we'd be able to get home anyway, sir,' said Ballard philosophically. They'd taken five minutes off to go up to the fire-watchers' station on the roof of West End Central to survey the scene, and were staring out at a sea of waving Union Jacks and red, white and blue ribbons.

'It's quite a relief, isn't it, sir?'

'That's an understatement. I just wish my Jenny were here to see it.' Stratton hadn't meant to say this out loud, but it just seemed to come out of his mouth.

Ballard cleared his throat. 'I'm sorry, sir.'

Seeing that he'd embarrassed the younger man, Stratton gestured towards Piccadilly and said, 'Still, they seem to be having a good time, don't they?'

'Yes, sir. Looks quite a party.'

'When it's all over, I'm sure you'll be having a private celebration with Miss Gaines, won't you?'

Ballard grinned. 'I'm looking forward to it, sir. And, sir...'

'Ye-es?'

'Thank you. For not knowing, if you see what I mean.'

'I do indeed. It's been a while now, hasn't it? Are you planning to make an honest woman of her?'

'Yes, sir. In fact, I was thinking of asking her when we have that private celebration you mentioned.'

'Good idea. I'm sure you'll make a good husband. Just remember,' he added, thinking of Jenny, 'to come off duty when you get home.'

'I'll do my best, sir.'

'Good. Come on then, we'd better get back to the fray.'

For the next twenty-four hours, during which there had been a massive thunderstorm that sent all but the most hardened revellers scurrying for cover, Stratton barely had a moment to sit down, much less think, and by the time that Lamb—very much to his surprise—told him, at six p.m. the next day, that he was relieved, he felt that he barely had the energy to make his way through the packed crowds in Regent Street to catch the bus.

Despite the previous night's weather, the day was beautifully sunny, and with bright bunting and streamers that seemed to blur before his tired eyes, and roars of 'Knees up Mother Brown' and various less savoury ditties ringing in his ears, he jammed himself into a hot, packed bus and stood swaying in the press of bodies, many of whom were whooping and shouting at the tops of their voices. When he got out at the Swan at Tottenham, he felt bruised all over.

The pub's doors were open, and people were standing on the pavement, drinking beer. He went to the door and peered through the smoke for Donald, who spotted him from the middle of the crush and bellowed, 'Wait there, I'll bring you a drink!'

Stratton leant against the wall, tilted his face up to the sun, and closed his eyes. Images from the past week—the cheering crowds, Strang's despairing face, and Fay's venomous one—played across his mind like a film in slow motion. The—very difficult—interview he'd had with Strang's mother a couple of days earlier had revealed further information about how the family had lost all their money, so that it was never on the cards for Strang to go to university. It really was extraordinary, Stratton thought: Strang realised he couldn't change the world, so he'd simply changed himself. What a bloody waste...

Donald appeared, grinning and bearing two pints of beer, one of which he thrust into Stratton's hand. 'To victory!' he said, raising his glass.

'Victory!'

Donald took a swig of his beer, and said, 'And Reg's not here. Too busy supervising building the bonfire on the common. Happy as Larry, last time I saw him.'

'At least he's got something to do,' said Stratton. 'He's been like a lost lamb ever since the Home Guard was stood down.'

'Don't I know it,' said Donald. 'Christ knows what he'll do with himself now.'

'Probably hang around the allotment giving me instructions,' said Stratton. 'Oh, well...Cheers, then!'

Three pints later—the pubs had been sent extra supplies—Stratton and Donald wandered back home together, singing. *'I'm going back to Imazaz, Never again to roam, I'm jogging along, Singing a song, A day's march nearer home…'*

'I got some Union Jacks from the tobacconist,' said Donald. 'The kids helped me put them up. They were ever so excited. They've been collecting rags to stuff Hitler with, for the bonfire. Monica did his face. She's a good little artist, your daughter.'

'Yes, she is,' said Stratton, thinking that, while Doris and Donald's house would have bunting and all the rest of it, his own would be bare of decoration. Still, at least the kids were enjoying themselves…Pushing his thoughts aside, he began to sing again, and Donald joined in: *'There's a cottage so sweet, At the top of the street, And it's number ninety-four, So I'm going back to Imazaz, Imazaz the pub next door!'*

'You've been drinking, Daddy,' said Monica sternly as, arm in arm, Stratton and Donald stumbled through Doris's front door. 'With your black eye, it makes you look very disreputable.'

'Yes, love,' said Stratton, meekly. 'Sorry. I didn't think I'd be able to get home at all, and then I saw Donald in the Swan.'

'That's right, blame me,' said Donald.

He kissed Doris, who said, 'Whooh…' and laughed, fanning her face with her hand at his breath.

The bonfire was fun, and there were fireworks and lots of singing, and Reg had a wonderful time supervising the roasting of a whole pig on a spit. 'Where the hell did that come from?' Stratton asked Donald, who winked and said, 'Best not to ask.'

Later, when it got dark, someone brought out a gramophone, and he, Donald and Doris sat on the grass, sipping their drinks and watching Madeleine dancing with her new boyfriend, along with dozens of others, while the younger kids ran around and mucked about.

'We could have a holiday,' said Doris. 'All together, like the old days. Remember where we stayed at Eastbourne—Mrs Jenkins? We could go back.'

'If she's still there,' said Donald.

'Well, of course, silly. Be just like old times, wouldn't it?' Realising what she'd said, she looked at Stratton. 'I'm sorry, Ted. It won't be the same without Jenny, and of course you don't want to go back to the same place. It was a thoughtless thing to say.'

'No.' Stratton smiled at her. 'I know what you meant. And I'd like to go to Eastbourne again.'

'Oh, Ted...' Doris linked her arm through his, and Stratton patted her hand.

'It's all right, love. Let's just enjoy the evening, shall we?'

They sat in silence for a minute, then a boy put a new record on the gramophone, and Donald said, 'Come on, Doris, let's have a dance.'

'And get my feet trampled?'

'Come on.' Donald got up and pulled his wife with him. 'I can't remember the last time I trampled on your feet.'

Doris grimaced. 'Very romantic. And I don't know what this music is—it's all hooting and tooting.'

'We'll manage. Best foot forward.'

'You haven't got a best foot, Don,' grumbled Doris, but she let him pull her into the throng.

Monica must have caught sight of Stratton sitting alone, because she came and plumped herself down beside him.

'You're a bit of a ragamuffin yourself, now,' he said, noticing that she looked unusually tomboyish, with her face dged by soot from the bonfire and her legs stuck out in front of her.

'Who cares?' she said, happily. 'This is good, isn't it? Look at Auntie Doris and Uncle Donald.'

Doris and Donald were engaged in what looked more like a shin-kicking contest than a dance, with Doris hopping out of the way and protesting loudly. 'Oh, dear...' he said.

'You could have danced with Mum,' said Monica, sadly. 'She liked dancing.'

'Yes, she did,' said Stratton. 'I'm not sure she liked dancing with *me*, though. She always said I wasn't a whole lot better than your uncle.'

'She wouldn't have minded,' said Monica. 'Not this evening...Do you think about her a lot, Dad?'

'Yes,' said Stratton.

'I do, too.'

'Do you think Pete does?'

'Yes,' said Monica. 'But he doesn't like talking about her. I do, though. I didn't talk about her much to Mrs Chetwynd, because...' Monica paused, trying to find the right words to explain why not.

'Because...' prompted Stratton.

'Because...Well, because it didn't feel right, because Mrs Chetwynd didn't know Mum, not really, and I thought she might not like it because she was looking after us, so she... she...'

'She was like a foster-mother?'

'Well,' said Monica. 'She was really. Pam—from school— had a horrible time, but we were lucky. That was because of you and Mum arranging it. We are grateful, you know.'

Stratton smiled at her. 'We did our best. Did you think it might upset Mrs Chetwynd if you talked about Mum?'

'I thought it might not be fair,' said Monica.

'I'm sure she wouldn't have minded, love,' said Stratton, marvelling at his daughter's thoughtfulness in such circumstances, even though it was misplaced.

Stratton heard Monica's in-drawn breath and felt her sit up straight, as if she were priming herself to ask something.

'Can *we* talk about her sometimes, Dad?'

He had the feeling that she'd rehearsed this, just as he'd rehearsed his little speech, delivered when the children came home, about muddling along, and found himself more touched than he could have believed. Resisting the awful, and very strong, impulse to burst into tears, he said, 'Of course we can. I'd like that.'

'Good,' said Monica, calmly, and slipped her hand into his.

They sat on the grass for a while, hand in hand, until Stratton, seeing Monica catch the eye of a schoolfriend, said, 'Why don't you go and join your pals?'

'Do you mind?'

'Course not. You don't need to worry about me—I'll be fine.'

Left alone, Stratton surreptitiously wiped his eyes and blew his nose, then lit a cigarette, and leaning back and propping himself on one elbow, thought that, although the music seemed pleasantly familiar, he had no idea of its name. It was wild, parping and squealing and joyful, and, as he listened, he felt, despite the laughter and shouting from the people nearby, that he was alone, as if somehow sealed off from everything except the notes, which seemed to float towards him like squiggles on the air. They made him feel warm inside, comforted—although, he thought, that was probably the beer as well. He sat listening for a moment longer, then got up and made his way around the dancers to the boy with the gramophone.

'What is it?' he asked.

The kid, a lanky, redheaded boy, who was fussing with a box of needles, looked up. 'The music,' Stratton repeated. 'What

Waller,' said the boy.

the song called?'

'"Ain't Misbehavin'". Don't you like it?' the boy asked, his tone anxious. 'I can put something else on when it's finished, only I haven't got many.'

'I do like it,' said Stratton. 'It's good.'

The boy nodded, grinning. 'Wonderful, isn't it?'

'Yes.' Stratton grinned back, and they stood, side by side, listening, with happy, simple pleasure, until the record was finished.

A VERY BRIEF NOTE ON CAPGRAS SYNDROME

Capgras Syndrome is a disorder which is characterised by a delusional belief that a spouse or other close family member has been replaced by an identical-looking imposter. Also known as the Capgras delusion, it was named after the French psychiatrist, Jean Marie Joseph Capgras (1873-1950), who was the first person to describe it, in a paper published in 1923, co-authored by Jean Reboul-Lachaux.

Although Capgras Syndrome is most common in patients diagnosed with schizophrenia, it can also occur as a result of other conditions such as brain injury or dementia. Extremely unusual, it is more prevalent in women than in men, with some sufferers believing that their pets, or familiar household objects, have also been replaced by duplicates.

Nowadays, treatment tends to take the form of Cognitive-Behavioural therapy and/or antipsychotic drugs or Selective Serotonin Reuptake Inhibitors. However, in 1944, when this book is set, none of these things were available.